About the Authors

Michelle Smart is a *Publishers Weekly* bestselling author with a slight-to-severe coffee addiction. A book worm since birth, Michelle can usually be found hiding behind a paperback, or if it's an author she really loves, a hardback. Michelle lives in rural Northamptonshire in England with her husband and two young Smarties. When not reading or pretending to do the housework, she loves nothing more than creating worlds of her own. Preferably with lots of coffee on tap.

Sharon Kendrick started storytelling at the age of eleven and has never stopped. She likes to write fast-paced, feel-good romances with heroes who are so sexy they'll make your toes curl! She lives in the beautiful city of Winchester – where she can see the cathedral from her window (when standing on tip-toe!). She has two children, Celia and Patrick, and her passions include music, books, cooking and eating – and drifting into daydreams while working out new plots.

Lynne Graham lives in Northern Ireland and has been a keen romance reader since her teens. Happily married, Lynne has five children. Her eldest is her only natural child. Her other children, who are every bit as dear to her heart, are adopted. The family has a variety of pets, and Lynne loves gardening, cooking, collecting all sorts and is crazy about every aspect of Christmas.

Royal Temptation

Royal Temptation:

His Secret Heir

MICHELLE SMART

SHARON KENDRICK

LYNNE GRAHAM

MILLS & BOON

First Published in Great Britain 2023
by Mills & Boon, an imprint of HarperCollins*Publishers* Ltd,
1 London Bridge Street, London, SE1 9GF

www.harpercollins.co.uk

HarperCollins*Publishers*
Macken House, 39/40 Mayor Street Upper,
Dublin 1, D01 C9W8, Ireland

ISBN: 978-0-263-31930-9

MIX
Paper | Supporting
responsible forestry
FSC™ C007454

THESEUS DISCOVERS
HIS HEIR

MICHELLE SMART

This book is dedicated to Jo aka 'Cat', who has been there with me every step of the way.

CHAPTER ONE

JOANNE BROOKES COVERED her mouth to stifle a yawn and blinked rapidly to keep her eyes open. She was quite tempted to shove the thick pile of papers aside and have a nap at the small kitchen table, but she needed to read and digest as much as she could.

The floor creaked behind her and she turned to see Toby poke his head around the door of the tiny living space.

'What are you doing up, you little monkey?' she asked with a smile.

'I'm thirsty.'

'You've got water in your room.'

He gave an impish grin and padded over to her, his too-short pyjamas displaying his bare ankles. He hoisted himself up onto her lap and pressed his warm face into her neck.

'Do you *have* to go away?'

Wrapping her arms tightly around his skinny frame, Jo dropped a kiss in Toby's thick black hair. 'I wish I didn't.'

There was no point in explaining the finer details of why she had to leave for the island of Agon in the morning. Toby was four years old and any kind of rationalising normally went right over his head.

'Is ten days a long time?' he asked.

'It is to start with, but before you know it the time will have flown by and I'll be home.' She wouldn't lie to him, and could only dress her departure up into something bearable. Her stomach had been in knots all day, knitted so tightly she hadn't been able to eat a thing.

They'd only spent two nights apart since Toby's birth. Under normal circumstances she wouldn't even have considered going. It would have been a flat-out no.

'And just think what fun you'll have with Uncle Jonathan,' she added, injecting a huge dose of positivity into her voice.

'And Aunty Cathy?'

'Yes—and Aunty Cathy. And Lucy.'

Her brother and his wife lived in the local town with their year-old daughter. Toby adored them almost as much as they adored him. Even knowing that he would be in safe, loving hands, Jo hated the thought of being apart from him for such a long time.

But Giles, her boss, had been desperate. Fiona Samaras, their in-house biographer, who was working on the commemorative biography of the King of Agon, had been struck down with acute appendicitis. Jo was only a copywriter, but that didn't matter—she was the only other person who spoke Greek in the specialist publishing house she worked for. She wasn't completely fluent, but she knew enough to translate the research papers into English and make it readable.

If the biography wasn't complete by a week on Wednesday there wouldn't be time for it to be copy-edited and proofread and sent to the printers, who were waiting to print five thousand English language copies and courier them to the Agon palace in time for the gala.

The gala, exactly three weeks away, was to be a huge affair, celebrating fifty years of King Astraeus's reign. If they messed up the commemorative biography they would lose all the custom they'd gained from Agon's palace museum over the decades. Their reputation as a publisher of biographies and historical tomes would take a battering. Possibly a fatal one.

Jo loved her job—loved the work, loved the people. It might not be the exact career she'd dreamed of, but the support she'd received throughout the years had made up for it.

Giles had been so desperate for her to take on the job that he'd promised her a bonus and an extra fortnight's paid leave. How could she have said no? When everything was factored in, she hadn't been able to.

She'd been through the emotional mill enough to know she would survive this separation. It would rip her apart but she would get through it—and Toby would too. The past five years had taught her to be a survivor. And the money would be welcome. She would finally have enough to take Toby to Greece and begin the task of tracking down his father.

She wondered if she would have any time to begin her search whilst she was on Agon. Although Agon wasn't technically a Greek island, its closest neighbour was Crete and its people spoke Greek—which was why Jo had been the person her boss had turned to.

'We'll speak every day on the computer while I'm gone,' she said now, reiterating what she'd already told him a dozen times that day.

'And you'll get me a present?'

'I'll get you an *enormous* present,' she promised with a smile.

'The biggest present in the world?'

She tickled his sides. 'The biggest present I can stick in my suitcase.'

Toby giggled and tickled her neck. 'Can I see where you're going?'

'Sure.' She manoeuvred him around so that he faced her desk, pulled her laptop closer to them and clicked a button to bring it out of hibernation.

Having had only a day to prepare for the trip, she'd spent hours making arrangements for herself and Toby while trying to familiarise herself with the biography she needed to finish. She hadn't yet had the time to do any research on the island she was travelling to.

Keeping an arm around her son's waist to secure him on her lap, she typed *'Agon Royal Palace'* into the search bar and selected images.

Toby gasped when he saw what appeared and pressed a finger to the screen. 'You're going *there*?'

Jo was just as taken with the images, which showed an enormous sprawling palace that evoked romantic thoughts of hot Arabian nights.

'Yes, I am.'

'Will you have your own room?'

'I'll get an apartment in the palace.'

Until that moment she hadn't had time to consider the fact that she would be staying in a royal palace for ten nights. She moved her cursor down the screen slowly, looking for a better picture.

'Will you meet the King?'

She smiled at the eagerness in Toby's voice. She wondered how he would react if she were to tell him that she and Toby were distantly—*very* distantly—related to the British royal family. He'd probably spring to the ceiling with excitement.

'I'll be working for the King's grandson, who's a prince, but I might meet the King too. Shall I find a picture of him?'

She typed in *'King of Agon'* and hit the search button.

She supposed she should send Toby back to bed, but she really didn't want to—not when he was so warm and snuggly on her lap, and especially not when she knew he wouldn't be warm and snuggly on her lap again for another ten days.

The search revealed hundreds, if not thousands of pictures of the King. Scrolling through them, she thought how distinguished he looked. There were pictures of him with his late wife, Queen Rhea, who had died five years ago, others with his eldest grandson and heir, Helios, and one of King Astraeus standing with all three of his grandsons— one of whom must be Theseus, the Prince she would be directly reporting to…

She stared hard at the picture of the King and his grandsons and felt the hairs on her arms lifting. With a hand that suddenly seemed to be filled with lead, she enlarged the photo to fill the screen.

It couldn't be.

Making sure not to squash her son, she leaned forward and adjusted the screen so she could peer at it more closely. The picture was too grainy for her to see with any certainty.

It couldn't be…

'Are those men kings too?' Toby asked.

She couldn't speak, could only manage a quick shake of her head before she clicked on to another picture of the King with his grandsons.

This photo was of a much higher quality and had been taken from less distance.

Her head buzzed and burned, every pulse in her body hammering.

Working frantically, she clicked through dozens of pictures until she found one that showed him alone. She enlarged it.

It was him.

For an age she did nothing but hold her son so tightly she could feel the thrum of his little heart vibrating through his back.

How was it possible?

Two hours later she was still there on her laptop, searching through everything the internet had to offer about Prince Theseus Kalliakis. Somehow she'd managed to pull

herself out of the cold stupor she'd slipped into at seeing
Theo's face on the screen for long enough to tuck Toby
back into bed and kiss him goodnight.

All that ran through her head now was crystal clarity.

No wonder her years of searching for Theo had been
fruitless. She'd assumed that living in the age of social
media would have made it an easy task, but she had been
foiled at every turn. It hadn't stopped her looking. She'd
never given up hope of finding him.

But she might have searched for a thousand years and
would still never have found him. Because the man she'd
been seeking didn't exist.

It had all been a big lie.

Toby's father wasn't Theo Patakis, an engineer from
Athens. He was Theseus Kalliakis. A prince.

Prince Theseus Kalliakis stepped out of his office and
into his private apartment just as his phone vibrated in his
pocket. He dug it out and put it to his ear.

'She's on her way,' said Dimitris, his private secretary,
without any preamble.

Theseus killed the call, strode into his bedroom and put
the phone on his bureau.

He'd spent most of the day sleeping off the after-effects
of the Royal Ball his older brother, Helios had hosted the
night before, and catching up on reports relating to the various businesses he and his two brothers invested in under
the Kalliakis Investment Company name. Now it was time
to change out of his jeans and T-shirt.

He would greet Miss Brookes, then spend some time
with his grandfather while she settled in. His grandfather's
nurse had messaged him to say the King was having a good
spell and Theseus was loath to miss spending private time
with him when he was lucid.

Nikos, his right-hand man, had laid out a freshly pressed

suit for him. Theseus had heard tales of royalty from other nations actually being dressed by their personal staff, something that had always struck him as slightly ludicrous. He was a man. He dressed himself. His lips curved in amusement as he imagined Nikos's reaction should he request that the man do his shirt buttons up for him. All Nikos's respect would be gone in an instant. He would think Theseus had lost his testosterone.

Once dressed, he rubbed a little wax between his hands and worked it quickly into his hair, then added a splash of cologne. He was done.

Exiting his apartment, he headed down a flight of stairs and walked briskly along a long, narrow corridor lit up by tiny ceiling lights. After walking through three more corridors he cut through the palace kitchens, then through four more corridors, until he arrived at the stateroom where he would meet Fiona Samaras's replacement.

Murmured voices sounded from behind the open door. The replacement had clearly arrived—something that relieved him greatly.

His grandfather's illness had forced the brothers to bring the Jubilee Gala forward by three months. That had meant that the deadline for completing a biography of his grandfather—which Theseus had tasked himself with producing—had been brought forward too.

His relationship with his grandfather had never been easy. Theseus freely admitted he'd been a nightmare to raise. He'd thoroughly enjoyed the outdoor pursuits which had come with being a young Agon prince, but had openly despised the rest of it—the boundaries, the stuffy protocol and all the other constraints that came with his title.

His demand for a sabbatical and the consequences of his absence had caused a further rift between him and his grandfather that had never fully healed. He hoped the biography would go some way to mending that rift before his grandfather's frail body succumbed to the cancer eating at it.

Five years of exemplary behaviour did not make up for almost three decades of errant behaviour. This was his last chance to prove to his grandfather that the Kalliakis name *did* mean something to him.

But first the damn thing needed to be completed. The deadline was tight enough without Fiona's appendicitis derailing the project further.

Her replacement had better be up for the task. Giles had sworn she was perfect for it... Theseus had no choice but to trust his judgement.

Dimitris stood with his back to the door, talking to the woman Theseus assumed to be Despinis Brookes.

'You got back from the airport quickly,' he said as he stepped into the stateroom.

Dimitris turned around and straightened. 'Traffic was light, Your Highness.'

The woman behind him stepped forward. He moved towards her, his hand outstretched. 'It is a pleasure to meet you, Miss Brookes,' he said in English. 'Thank you for coming at such short notice.'

He would keep his doubts to himself. She would be under enough pressure to deliver without him adding to it. His job, from this point onwards, was as support vehicle. He would treat her as if she were one of the young men and women whose start-up businesses he and his brothers invested in.

His role in their company was officially finance director. Unofficially he saw himself as chief cheerleader—good cop to his younger brother Talos's bad cop—there to give encouragement and help those people realise their dreams in a way he could never realise his own. But woe betide them if they should lie to him or cheat him. The few who'd been foolish enough to do that had been taught a lesson they would never forget.

He wasn't a Kalliakis for nothing.

He waited for Miss Brookes to take his hand. Possibly she would curtsey. Many non-islanders did, although protocol did not insist on it unless it was an official function.

She didn't take his offered hand. Just stared at him with an expression he didn't quite understand but which made the hairs on his nape shoot up.

'Despinis?'

Possibly she was overwhelmed at meeting a prince? It happened...

In the hanging silence he looked at her properly, seeing things that he'd failed to notice in his hurry to be introduced and get down to business. The colour of her hair was familiar, a deep russet-red, like the colour of the autumn leaves he'd used to crunch through when he'd been at boarding school in England. It fell like an undulating wave over her shoulders and down her back, framing a pretty face with an English rose complexion, high cheekbones and generous bee-stung lips. Blue-grey eyes pierced him with a look of intense concentration...

He *knew* those eyes. He *knew* that hair. It wasn't a common colour, more like something from the artistic imagination of the old masters of the Renaissance than anything real. But it was those eyes that really cut him short. They too were an unusual shade—impossible to define, but evocative of early-morning skies before the sun had fully risen.

And as all these thoughts rushed through his mind she finally advanced her hand into his and spoke two words. The final two little syllables were delivered with a compacted tightness that sliced through him upon impact.

'Hello, *Theo*.'

He didn't recognise her.

Jo didn't know what she'd expected. A hundred scenarios had played out in her mind over the past twenty hours.

Not one of those scenarios had involved him not remembering her.

It was like rubbing salt in an open, festering wound.

Something flickered in his dark eyes, and then she caught the flare of recognition.

'Jo?'

As he spoke her name, the question strongly inflected in a rich, accented voice that sounded just as she imagined a creamy chocolate mousse would sound if it could talk, his long fingers wrapped around hers.

She nodded and bit into her bottom lip, which had gone decidedly wobbly. Her whole body suddenly felt very wobbly, as if her bones had turned into overcooked noodles.

His hand felt so *warm*.

It shouldn't feel warm. It should feel as cold as his lying heart.

And she shouldn't feel an overwhelming urge to burst into tears.

She wouldn't give him the satisfaction.

Straightening her spine, Jo tugged her hand out of his warm hold and resisted the impulse to wipe it on her skirt, to rid herself of a touch she had once yearned for.

'It's been a long time,' she said, deliberately keeping her tone cool, trying to turn her lips upwards into the semblance of a smile.

But how could you smile when your one and only lover, the man you'd spent five years searching for, the father of your child, didn't remember your face?

How could you force a smile when you'd spent five years searching for a lie?

Dimitris, the man who'd collected her from the airport and introduced himself as His Highness's private secretary, was watching their interaction with interest.

'Do you two know each other?'

'Despinis Brookes is an old acquaintance of mine,' said

Theo—or Theseus—or whatever his name was. 'We met when I was on my sabbatical.'

Oh, was *that* what he'd been doing on Illya? He'd been on a *sabbatical*?

And she was an *acquaintance*?

She supposed it was better than being described as one of his one-night stands.

And at least he hadn't had the temerity to call her an old friend.

'I saw a picture of you on the internet last night when I was researching your island,' she said, injecting brightness into her tone, giving no hint that she'd even *thought* of him during the intervening years. 'I thought it looked like you.'

She might not have much pride left after spending the last four years as a single mother, but she still had enough to be wounded and not to want to show it, especially as they had an audience. One thing motherhood had taught her was resilience. In fact it had taught her a lot of things, all of which had made her infinitely stronger than she'd been before.

Theseus appraised her openly, his dark brown eyes sweeping over her body. 'You look different to how I remember you.'

She knew she was physically memorable—it had been the bane of her childhood. Red hair and a weight problem had made her an easy target for bullies. Having Toby had been the kick she'd needed to shift the weight and keep it off. She would never be a stick-thin model but she'd grown to accept her curves.

She might be a few stone lighter, and her hair a few inches longer, but there was nothing else different about her.

'Your hair's shorter than I remember,' she said in return.

Five years ago Theseus's hair—so dark it appeared black—had been long, skimming his shoulders. Now it was short at the back, with the front sweeping across his forehead. On Illya she'd only ever seen him in shorts and the occasional T-shirt. Half the time he hadn't bothered with footwear. Now he wore a blue suit that looked as if it had cost more than her annual food bill, and shoes that shone so brightly he could probably see his reflection in them.

'You're looking good, though,' she added, nodding her head to add extra sincerity to her words.

What a shame that it was the truth.

Theo—or Theseus—or His Highness—wasn't the most handsome man she'd ever met, but there was something about him that captured the eye and kept you looking. A magnetism. He had a nose too bumpy to be considered ideal, deep-set dark brown eyes, a wide mouth that smiled easily and a strong jawline. This combined with his olive colouring, his height—which had to be a good foot over her own five foot four inches—and the wiry athleticism of his physique, gave the immediate impression of an un-reconstructed 'man's man'.

Her awareness of him had been instant, from the second he'd stepped into Marin's Bar on Illya with a crowd of Scandinavian travellers hanging onto his every word. She'd taken one look at him and her heart had flipped over.

It had been a mad infatuation. Totally crazy. Irrational. All the things she'd reached the age of twenty-one without having once experienced had hit her with the force of a tsunami.

But now she was five years older, five years wiser, and she had a child to protect. Any infatuation had long gone.

Or so she'd thought.

But when he'd strode through the door of the stateroom the effect had been the same; as if the past five years had been erased.

'Different to all those years ago,' Theseus agreed, looking at his watch. 'I appreciate you've had a long day, but time is against us to get the biography complete. Let's take a walk to your apartment so you can freshen up and settle in. We can talk en route.'

He set off with Dimitris at his side.

Staring at his retreating back, it took Jo a few beats before she pulled herself together and scrambled after them.

Dull thuds pounded in her brain, bruising it, as the magnitude of her situation hit her.

For all these years she'd sworn to herself that she would find Toby's father and tell Theo about their son. She'd had no expectations of what would happen afterwards, but had known that at the very least she owed it to Toby to find him. She'd also thought she owed it to Theo to tell him he had a child.

But Theo didn't exist.

Whoever this man was, he was not the Theo Patakis she had once fallen in love with.

Theseus wasn't the father of her son; he was a stranger dressed in his skin.

CHAPTER TWO

'VISITORS TO THE palace often get lost, so I've arranged for a map to be left in your apartment,' Theseus said as they climbed a narrow set of stairs.

'A map? Seriously?' She would remain civil if it killed her. Which it probably would.

So many emotions were running through her she didn't know where one began and another ended.

He nodded, still steaming ahead. Her legs were working at a quick march to keep up with him as he turned into a dark corridor lit by tiny round ceiling lights.

'The palace has five hundred and seventy-three rooms.'

'Then I guess a map could come in handy,' she conceded, for want of anything else to say.

'There will not be time for you to explore the palace as you might like,' he said. 'However, we will do everything in our power to make your stay here as comfortable as it can be.'

'That's very kind of you,' she said, trying not to choke on her words.

'Are you up to speed with the project?'

'I read a good chunk of it on the plane,' she confirmed tightly.

As the deadline for the biography's completion was so tight, Fiona had been emailing each chapter as she'd finished it so they could be immediately edited. The editor working on it had spent the past six weeks or so with a distinctly frazzled look about her.

'Fiona has completed the bulk of the biography, but there is still another twenty-five years of my grandfather's life to be written about. I appreciate this must sound daunting, but you will find when you read through the research papers that there is much less complexity there than in his early years. Are you confident you can do this within the time constraints?'

'I wouldn't have accepted the job if I wasn't.' Fiona's editor, who Jo was now working with, had assured her that the last three decades of King Astraeus's life had been comparatively quiet after his early years.

But Jo had accepted the job before discovering who she would be working for and exactly who he was.

As she clung to the gold banister that lined the wall above a wide, cantilevered staircase that plunged them into another warren of passageways and corridors Jo remembered a trip to Buckingham Palace a few years back, and recalled how bright and airy it had seemed. The Agon Royal Palace matched Buckingham Palace for size, but it had a much darker, far greater gothic quality to it. It was a palace of secrets and intrigue.

Or was that just her rioting emotions making her read more into things? Her body had never felt so tight with nerves, while her brain had become a fog of hurt, anger, bewilderment and confusion.

'I don't remember you speaking Greek when we were on Illya,' he said, casting her a curious, almost suspicious glance that made her heart shudder.

'Everyone spoke English there,' she replied in faultless Greek, staring pointedly ahead and praying the dim light bouncing off the dark hardwood flooring would hide the burn suddenly ravaging her skin.

'That is true.' He came to a halt by a door at the beginning of another wide corridor. He turned the handle and pushed it open. 'This is your apartment for the duration of your stay. I'm going to visit my grandfather while you settle in—a maid will be with you shortly to unpack. Dimitris will come for you in an hour, and then we can sit down and discuss the project properly.'

And just like that he walked back down the corridor, leaving Jo staring at his retreating figure with a mixture of fury and incredibly lancing pain raging through her.

Was that *it*?

Was that all she was worth?

A woman he's once been intimate with suddenly reappears in his life and he doesn't even ask how she's been? Not the slightest hint of curiosity?

The only real reference to their past had been a comment about her speaking his language.

He'd sought *her* out back then. It had been *her* comfort he'd needed that night. And now she wasn't worth even a simple, *How are you?* or *How have you been?*

But then, she thought bitterly, it had all been a lie.

This man *wasn't* Theo.

A soft cough behind her reminded her that Dimitris was still there. He handed her a set of keys, wished her a pleasant stay and left her alone to explore her apartment.

Theseus blew air out of his mouth, nodding an automatic greeting to a passing servant.

Joanne Brookes.

Or, as he'd known her five years ago, Jo.

Now, *this* was a complication he hadn't anticipated. A most unwelcome complication.

Hers was a face from his past he'd never expected to see again, and certainly not in the palace, where a twist of fate had decreed she would spend ten days working closely with him.

She'd been there for him during the second worst night of his life, when he'd been forced to wait until the morning before he could leave the island of Illya and be taken to his seriously ill grandmother.

Jo had taken care of him. In more ways than one.

He remembered his surprise when he'd learned her age—twenty-one and fresh out of university. She'd looked much younger. She'd seemed younger than her years too.

He supposed that would now make her twenty-six. Strangely, she now seemed *older* than her years—not in her appearance, but in the way she held herself.

He experienced an awful sinking feeling as he remembered taking her number and making promises to call.

That sinking feeling deepened as he recalled his certainty after they'd had sex that she'd been a virgin.

She couldn't have been. She would have told you. Who would give her virginity to a man who was effectively a stranger?

Irrelevant, he told himself sharply.

Illya and his entire sabbatical had been a different life, and it was one he could never return to.

He was Prince Theseus Kalliakis, second in line to the Agon throne. *This* was his life. The fact that the new biographer was a face from the best time of his life meant nothing.

Theo Patakis was dead and all his memories had gone with him.

'*This* is where I'll be working?' Jo asked, hoping against hope that she was wrong.

She'd spent the past hour giving herself a good talking-to, reminding herself that anger didn't achieve anything. Whatever the next ten days had in store, holding on to her fury would do nothing but give her an ulcer. But then Dimitris had collected her from the small but well-appointed apartment she'd been given and taken her to Theseus's private offices, just across the corridor, and the fury had surged anew.

Her office was inside his private apartment and connected to his own office without so much as a doorway to separate them.

'This is the office Fiona used.' Theseus waved a hand at the sprawling fitted desks set against two walls to make an L shape. 'Nobody has touched it since she was admitted into hospital.'

'There's a spare room in my apartment that will make a perfectly functional office.'

'Fiona used that room when she first came here, but it proved problematic. The research papers I collated and my own notes only give the facts about my grandfather's life. I want this biography to show the man behind the throne. As I know you're aware, this project is going to be a surprise for my grandfather so any questions need to be directed to me. With the time constraints we're working under it is better for me to be on hand for whatever you need.'

'Whatever you feel is for the best.'

A black eyebrow rose at her tone but he nodded. 'Are you happy with your apartment?'

'It's perfectly adequate.'

Apart from being in the same wing as his.

How was she going to be able to concentrate on anything whilst being in such close proximity to him? Her stomach was a tangle of knots, her heart was all twisted and aching…and her head burned as her son's gorgeous little face swam before her eyes.

Toby deserved better than to have been conceived from a lie.

She knew nothing of this man other than the fact that he was a prince in a nation that revered its monarchy.

He was descended from warriors. He and his brothers had forged a reputation for being savvy businessmen. They'd also forged a reputation as ruthless. It didn't pay to cross any of them.

Theseus was powerful.

Until she got to know this man she couldn't even consider telling him about Toby. Not until she knew in her heart that he posed no threat to either of them.

'Only "adequate"?' he asked. 'If there is anything you feel is lacking, or anything you want, you need only say. I want your head free of trivia so you can concentrate on getting the biography completed on time.'

'I'll be sure to remember that.'

'Make sure you do. I have lived and breathed this project for many months. I will not have it derailed at the last hurdle.'

The threat in his voice was implicit.

Now she believed what Giles had told her when he'd begged her to take the job—if she failed Hamlin & Associates would lose their best client and likely their reputation in the process.

'I have ten days to complete it,' she replied tightly. 'I will make the deadline.'

'So long as we have an understanding, I suggest we don't waste another minute.'

Where was the charmer she remembered from Illya? The man who had made every woman's IQ plummet by just being in his presence?

She'd spent five years thinking about this man, four years living with a miniature version of him, and his presence in her life had been so great she'd been incapable of meeting anyone else. Once Toby had been born the secret dream she'd held of Theo—*Theseus*—calling her out of the blue with apologies that he'd lost his phone had died. As had the fantasy that she would tell him of their son and he would want to be involved in their lives.

Motherhood had brought out a pragmatism she hadn't known existed inside her. Until precisely one day ago she hadn't given up on her dream of finding him, but that wish had been purely for Toby's sake. All she'd wanted for herself was to find the courage to move on. She'd accepted she'd been nothing but a one-night stand for him and had found peace with that idea. Or so she'd thought.

Because somehow that was the worst part of it. Her body still reacted to him in exactly the way it had on Illya, with a sick, almost helpless longing. If he looked closely enough he'd be able to see her heart beating beneath the smart black top she wore.

His indifference towards her cut like a scalpel slicing through flesh.

He couldn't give a damn about her.

A swell of nausea rose in her and she knew she had to say something.

She couldn't spend the next ten days with such an enormous elephant in the room, even if she was the only one who could see it.

Heart hammering, she plunged in. 'Before I start work there's something we need to talk about.'

He contemplated her with narrowed eyes that showed nothing but indifference.

'I'm sorry,' she continued, swallowing back the fear, 'but if you want me focused I need to know why you let me and everyone else on Illya believe you were an engineer from Athens, travelling the world on the fruits of an inheritance, when you were really a prince from Agon.'

'It hardly matters—it was five years ago,' he said sardonically.

'You lied to me and every person you met on Illya.'

You lied to him too, her conscience reminded her, and she felt her cheeks flame as she recalled how her one lie had been the most grievous of all, a remembrance that knocked back a little of her fury and allowed her to gain a touch of perspective.

Her lie had been the catalyst for everything.

He contemplated her a little longer before leaning back against the wall and folding his arms across his chest.

'Let me tell you about life here on Agon,' he said thoughtfully. 'Outsiders struggle to understand but Agonites revere my family and have done so for over eight hundred years, ever since my ancestor Ares Patakis led a successful rebellion against the Venetian invaders.'

'Patakis?' she repeated. 'Is that where you got your assumed surname from?'

He nodded. 'My family have held the throne since then by overwhelming popular consent. With my family at the helm we've repelled any other nation foolish enough to think it can invade us. To prevent any despotic behaviour down the years my ancestors introduced a senate, for the people to have a voice, but still they look to us—their royal family—for leadership.'

Theseus's mind filtered to his father; the man who would have been king if a tragic car crash hadn't killed him prematurely along with his wife, Theseus's mother. Lelantos Kalliakis had been exactly the kind of man his ancestors had feared taking the throne and having absolute power. Yet, regardless of how debauched and narcissistic the man had been, the Agonites had mourned him as if a member of their own family had been killed. His sons, however, had only truly mourned their mother.

'We live in a goldfish bowl. The people here look up to my family. They revere us. Children on this island learn to read with picture books depicting tales of my ancestors. I wanted to meet *real* people and explore the world as a normal person would. I was curious as to how people would react to *me*—the man, not the Prince. So, yes, I lied to you about my true identity, just as I lied to everyone else. And if I had my time again I would tell the same lies, because they gave me a freedom I hadn't experienced before and will never experience again.'

The majority of this speech was one he had spouted numerous times, first to his grandfather, when he'd announced his intention to see the world, and then to his brothers, who'd seen his actions as a snub to the family name. After a lifetime of bad behaviour, when he'd effectively turned his back on protocol, taking off and renouncing the family name had been his most heinous crime of all. Even now he was still trying to make amends.

'If I hurt your feelings I apologise,' he added when she gave no response.

He didn't owe Jo anything, but neither did he want working with her to be a trial. There wasn't time to bring in anyone else to complete the biography and they'd already lost three precious days.

If getting her to soften towards him meant he had to eat a little humble pie, then so be it. He would accept it as penance for the greater good.

And, if he was being honest with himself, apologising went a little way towards easing the guilt that had been nibbling at his guts.

The only change in her demeanour was a deep breath and the clenching of her jaw. When she did speak it was through gritted teeth. 'I don't even know what to call you. Are you Theo or Theseus? Do I address you as Your Highness or Your Grace? Am I expected to curtsey to you?'

In the hazy realms of his memory lay the whisper of her shy smile and the memory of how her cheeks would turn as red as her hair whenever he spoke to her.

It was on the tip of his tongue to tell her to call him Theo. Being Theo had been the best time of his life…

No. He would not let those memories spring free. He'd locked them away for a reason and they could damn well stay there.

'You can call me Theseus. And no curtseying.'

Having people bow and scrape to him turned his stomach. All his life people had treated him with a reverence he'd done nothing to earn other than be born.

She nodded, biting her bottom lip. And what a gorgeous lip it was, he thought. How eminently kissable. He'd kissed that delectable mouth once…

'I ask you to put your bad feelings towards me to one side so we can work together effectively. Can you do that?'

After a long pause she inclined her head and her long red hair fell forward. She brushed it back and tucked it behind her ears.

'Do you remember the night those American travellers came into Marin's Bar?' she asked, in a voice that was definitely milder than the tone she'd used so far. 'You were with the Scandinavians on the big round table…'

He raised a shoulder in a shrug, unsure of what day she was speaking of. He'd hit it off with a group of Scandinavian travellers on the ferry from Split to Illya and had spent the majority of his fortnight on the unspoilt island in their company. Marin's Bar, which was two steps from the beach, had been the only place to go, but with its excellent beer, good food and a juke box that had pumped out classic tracks, it had engendered an easy, relaxed atmosphere.

Jo and her friends, whose names he didn't think he'd ever known, had always been on the periphery—there but in the background, rather like wallpaper.

'They were touching us up,' she reminded him.

'Ah.'

Now he remembered. The Americans—college graduates taking time out before joining the corporate world—had drunk far too much of the local liquor and had started harassing Jo and her friends. He remembered there had been something nasty about it, well beyond the usual banter one might expect in such an environment. He'd taken exception to it and had personally thrown the men out, then he had insisted Jo and her friends join him and his friends at their table.

And now her face did soften. Not completely—her cheeks were still clenched—but enough that her lips regained their plumpness. They almost curled into a smile.

'You stepped in to help us,' she said. 'Whether you were there as a lie or not, in that one aspect it doesn't matter. You did a good thing. I'll try to hold on to that whenever I feel like stabbing you. How does that sound?'

A bubble of laughter was propelled up his throat, startling him. He quickly recovered.

'I think that sounds like an excellent start.'

She rocked her head forward. 'Good.'

'But just in case you ever do feel like stabbing me I'll be sure to hide all the sharp objects.'

The plump lips finally formed into a smile and something dark flickered in her eyes, but was gone before he could analyse it.

'It's a deal. Now, if you'll excuse me, I believe this is the perfect cue for me to go back to my apartment and carry on reading Fiona's work.'

'Will you be ready to start writing in the morning?'

'That's very unlikely—I'm only two-thirds through and I still need to familiarise myself with the research papers. What I *can* promise is that I will have this biography completed by the deadline even if I have to kill myself doing it.'

She stepped out of the door, giving him a full view of her round bottom, perfectly displayed in the smart navy blue skirt she wore. What kind of underwear lay beneath…?

He blinked away the inappropriate thought.

Her underwear was none of his business.

But there was no denying the gauche young girl he'd known before had gone; in her place was a confident and, yes, a sexy woman.

It had been a long time since he'd considered a woman sexy or pondered over her underwear.

There was nothing wrong with admitting she had an allure about her. Thoughts and actions were different things. The days when he would already have been plotting her seduction were long gone. The Theseus who had put pleasure above duty had been banished.

The next woman he shared a bed with would be his wife.

CHAPTER THREE

Jo GAZED AT the picture Toby proudly held up. Apparently it was a drawing of the two of them. It resembled a pair of colourful ants, one of which had been given long purple hair as his red felt-tip pen had run out.

'That's amazing,' she said, trying not to laugh, and inordinately proud of his attempt at a family portrait.

'Uncle Jon says he'll scab it for you.'

She stifled another giggle at his word for scan. At some point she knew she would have to tell him when he mangled words and mixed them up—like using alligator for escalator and Camilla for vanilla—but for the moment it was too cute. She'd start correcting him properly when he started school in five months' time.

She was dreading it—her baby growing up. They'd only been apart for one night so far, and this was already the second time they'd spoken via video-link. Thank God for technology.

She wondered how parents had handled time away from their children before video conferencing had been invented. A voice on the end of a phone was no substitute to seeing their faces as they spoke. Not that she would count her own parents in that equation.

She remembered going on a week-long school trip when she'd been eleven and calling home after three days only to have her mother say, 'Is there an emergency?'

'No, I—'

'Then I don't have the time to talk. It's feeding time.'

And that had been the end of *that* conversation. In the Brookes household the animals came first, Jonathan came second, with Jo and her father vying for last place.

'Sorry, sweet pea, but I have to go to work now,' Jo said, infusing her words with all the love her own mother had denied her.

He pulled a face. 'Already?'

'We'll talk again later.' Theseus would be expecting her at any minute.

'After lunch?'

'Tell Aunty Cathy we'll speak before you go to bed,' she promised, knowing full well that Cathy would be listening to their conversation and would make sure Toby was ready for her.

'Have you brought me a present yet, Mummy?' Toby asked, clearly doing everything he could to keep her talking for a little longer.

'I haven't been anywhere to get you one yet, you little monkey. Now, blow me a kiss and shoo before you're late for preschool.'

Toby did better than blow her a kiss. He put his face to the screen, puckered his lips and kissed it.

With her heart feeling as if it were about to expand out of her body, she pressed her fingers to her lips and then extended them to touch her screen. 'Love you.'

Before he could respond the connection was lost. No doubt he'd leaned on something he shouldn't have pressed when he'd leaned forward to kiss her.

Laughing whilst simultaneously wiping away a tear, Jo turned off her laptop.

She took three deep breaths to compose herself, then left her apartment, took four paces to the door opposite and entered her office, yawning widely.

'Late night?'

Theseus's voice startled her.

He stood in the archway that separated their offices, dressed in a navy suit and white shirt, without a tie.

She would never have imagined Theo in a suit, much less that he would look so unutterably gorgeous in it. On Illya he had lived in shorts, his golden chest with those defined muscles and that fine hair dusting over his pecs unashamedly on display.

But this man wasn't Theo, she reminded herself sharply. He was *nothing* like him. *This* man's lips seemed not to know how to smile. *This* man carried none of the warmth Theo had had in spades.

The only thing the two had in common was that same vivid masculinity. That vital presence. Her eyes would have been drawn to him even if she'd never known him as Theo.

'I stayed up to finish reading what Fiona had written,' she answered.

'Was that necessary?'

'I needed to find the rhythm of her work,' she explained evenly. 'I'll need to replicate it if I'm to make the transition seamless for the reader.'

'And are you ready to start writing now?'

'Not yet. I need to read through the research papers for the period of your grandfather's life I'm covering.'

He inclined his head and straightened. 'I shall leave you to it. I'll be back later if you find you have any questions for me.'

She forced a smile in acknowledgement, but the second she was alone she dropped her head onto the desk and closed her eyes.

Barely five minutes in his company and now not a single part of her felt right, as if being with him had caused her entire body to turn itself inside out.

She would have to find a way to manage it.

With grim determination she forced her attention to the piles of research papers before her.

The work Fiona had done on the biography had made for compelling reading.

King Astraeus had led a fascinating life, one filled with glory and honour. While many men of his nation had fought for the allies in the war—his brother among them—the then Prince Astraeus had led the defence of his own island. When a battalion of naval ships had approached the island with the intention to occupy it, Astraeus had led the counterattack. The fleet had been obliterated before it had reached the shore.

No other enemy ship had attempted to land on Agon since.

That would have been impressive on its own, but only the day before Astraeus had been given the news that his only brother had been killed in action.

This was Jo's son's heritage—a family that led from the front and who were all prepared to put their lives on the line to defend their home and their people.

A powerful family. And in it fitted Theseus—the father of her son.

The chapter Fiona had finished just before being taken ill detailed the death of Astraeus's only son and daughter-in-law in a tragic car crash twenty-six years ago. Theseus's parents. He'd been nine years old. So very young.

Her heart cracked a little to imagine what he must have gone through.

But that had been a long time ago, she reminded herself. Theseus the child had no bearing on Theseus the adult. She could not allow sympathy to lower her guard. Until she knew the real Theseus she couldn't afford to lower it for one second.

Theseus put his phone down. He could hear the soft rustle of papers being turned in the adjoining office.

When Fiona had worked on the biography he'd hardly

been aware of her. Other than the times when she would ask him questions, she might not have existed. Fiona using that office hadn't interrupted the flow of his own work.

As the financial figurehead of the Kalliakis Investment Company, and with his newer role of overseeing the palace accounts, which his grandfather had finally agreed to a year ago, he had plenty to keep his brain occupied.

In his childhood he'd dreamed of being an astronaut, of flying through the universe exploring new planets and solar systems. Astronauts had to be good with numbers, and he'd practised his arithmetic with a zeal that had astounded his tutor.

He could still remember one of the rare occasions when his father had come into Theseus's bedroom, mere months before he'd died. He'd looked at the star charts and pictures of rockets that had filled the walls and told him to rid his mind of such nonsense. A Kalliakis prince could *never* be an astronaut.

Even now Theseus would stare up at the night sky and be filled with longing.

He could have done it. He had the talent and the enthusiasm. He was fit, healthy and active.

But it could never be.

Now he used his talents, if not his enthusiasm, for financial reports. At least when he was going through the accounts he didn't have to put on a face and make small talk; didn't have to remember he was an ambassador for his family and his island.

So he kept himself busy. Too much time on his hands left his mind free to wander, to dream, to imagine *what if...?*

Today, though, the woman next door with hair like autumn leaves kept intruding. And she hadn't made so much as a peep of noise.

He couldn't get over how damned sexy she'd become. Even now, wearing nothing but charcoal three-quarter-length leggings, and a plain long-sleeved tunic-style black top that made her hair appear even more vibrant, she exuded a beguiling allure.

It had been a long time since he'd experienced such a primitive reaction to a woman.

Five years, to be exact.

His return to Agon from his sabbatical had been a turning point for him. Battling grief for his grandmother and ugly home truths from his grandfather, he'd known it was time to stop fighting. He would never be free. Sitting on the summit of Aconcagua in Argentina, the highest point in the Southern Hemisphere, was the closest he would ever get to the stars.

It had been time to accept his destiny.

He had decided he would curb his pleasure-seeking and throw himself into palace life. His grandfather had already been an old man. Helios had taken on many of his duties. It had been time for Theseus to take his share of them and relieve the burden.

He had been determined to prove to his grandfather that the Kalliakis name *did* mean something to him and had spent the years since his sabbatical doing exactly that— throwing himself into palace life and royal duties. In that time his appetite for sex had diminished to nothing, which suited him perfectly. Women who would usually turn his head had elicited minimal reaction. Neither his heart not his libido had been in it.

Now, for the first time in years, he felt the thrill of the chase coiling in his veins and cursed that such feelings should be unleashed.

Jo might be walking temptation, but there was no place in his life for desire. His next relationship would be with the woman he made his wife, even if he did intend on putting off the moment for as long as he could.

He stepped away from his desk and crossed the threshold into the adjoining office.

'How are you getting on?'

She didn't respond.

He was about to repeat his question but then saw she had earphones in.

She must have sensed his presence, for she turned her head and pulled them out.

'I will be leaving the palace shortly. Is there anything you need to talk to me about?'

'Not yet. I'm still going through the research papers and making notes on anything I feel could be relevant. As so many aspects are connected I think it will be best if we sit down and discuss it all when I'm done.'

'Will that not eat into your writing time?'

'It will make it easier—it means it will be solid in my head and I'll be in a position to work through it all without having to stop and interrupt you every five minutes. I'll probably still have further questions, but they will be far fewer this way.'

'I'm hosting a function for a delegation of French businessmen today, and I have a dinner at the US Embassy to attend this evening, but I can clear most of my diary for the next few days so I'll be available when you're ready.'

'That would be good, thank you,' she answered with a brief smile, her brilliant blue-grey eyes meeting his. She looked away, casting her gaze to her desk, then back up to him. 'Can I ask you something?'

'Of course.' So long as it wasn't about Illya. He refused to give headspace to memories from that time.

'Your grandfather's ill, isn't he?'

'How do you know that?' he asked, taken aback.

No one outside of the family circle and some select palace staff were supposed to know of his grandfather's cancer—which naturally meant the whole palace knew. However,

Theseus knew none of them would discuss it with anyone on the outside. Working in the Agon Royal Palace was considered an honour. To share confidential matters would be deemed treasonous.

'The publishing deadline was brought forward by three months and it was a tight enough deadline to begin with.' She shrugged, as if ashamed of her conclusion.

But it *was* the right conclusion.

It had occurred to Theseus, when the Jubilee Gala plans were first being discussed, that his grandfather had never seen his legacy in print. Usually Agon biographies were written after the reigning monarch had abdicated, then another would be written upon their death. As his grandfather had never abdicated that first book had never been written. He'd spent fifty years on the throne—the longest reign in three hundred years.

Suddenly he'd stumbled upon a tangible way to prove to his grandfather that he was proud of his heritage, proud to be a Kalliakis and, more than any of that, proud to call Astraeus his grandfather.

The more he'd immersed himself in his grandfather's life, the greater his pride had become. Astraeus Kalliakis was a true king. A man of honour. A man Theseus knew he should have emulated, not turned his back on for all those years.

This biography would be his personal tribute to him.

But then fate had stepped in. No sooner had he finished his research, and Fiona had flown over to the island to start writing it, than his grandfather had been given his diagnosis and everything had been brought forward by three months.

The Gala, the biography…everything was being rushed. Because now there lay the real danger that his grandfather wouldn't live long enough to see any of it.

The day drew nearer when he would have to say goodbye for the last time to the man who had raised him from the age of nine.

Theos, he would give his soul for a miracle.

Jo watched Theseus carefully. For a man usually so full of vitality he had a sudden stillness about him that she found unnerving.

Then his lips curved into a pensive smile and he nodded. 'Your intuition is right. My grandfather has cancer.'

'I'm sorry.'

'He's eighty-seven,' he said philosophically, but his eyes had dimmed.

'That doesn't make it any easier.' Jo had only known one of her grandparents: her paternal grandfather. She'd never seen much of him when she'd been growing up but she remembered how she'd always looked forward to his visits. When Granddad Bill came over her mother would bake even more cakes than usual and her father would drag himself out of the study where he spent his days drinking cheap whisky.

His death had saddened her but the distance between their lives had meant it had caused a dull ache rather than an acute pain.

It would be a thousand times harder for Theseus. The King was like a father to him.

He must be going through hell.

She remembered his despondency five years ago, when he'd learned his grandmother was dying. Whatever regrets Jo might have over that night, she would never regret being there for him.

Who amongst this palace of courtiers did he turn to for solace now? Who wrapped their arms around his neck and stroked his hair? Who tried to absorb his pain and give him comfort?

Because surely—*surely*—his pain that night had been real. Even if everything else had been a lie, that had been true.

Somewhere beneath the brooding façade Theseus was in agony. She would bet every penny she owned on it.

He tugged at his shirt collar as if it constricted him. 'The hardest thing to understand is why he didn't say anything sooner. He's known for a number of years that something was wrong but didn't say a word until the pain became intolerable. If he'd spoken sooner they might have been able to cure him, but...' He shrugged and closed his eyes. 'He left it too late. He's riddled with it.'

'Is he having any treatment?'

'Against the doctor's advice, yes.'

'They don't think it's a good idea?'

'His age and frailty are factors against it, but my grandfather is a stubborn old man who has never had to bow to the opinions of those he disagrees with—he is a king. He wants to live long enough to celebrate his jubilee and see Helios married. He has tasked the doctors with making that happen.'

Silence hung, forming a strangely intimate atmosphere that was broken by a knock on the door.

Theseus's eyes held hers for a beat longer before he called out, 'Come,' and a courtier entered with news that the delegation he was expecting had arrived.

Excusing himself, he disappeared, leaving Jo with nothing but her own confused thoughts for company.

She doubled over and laid her cheek on the desk, gazing at the closed door with unfocused eyes, trying to control the savage beat of her heart.

The King—her son's great-grandfather—was dying.

It brought it home as nothing else had that this family, however great and powerful they might be, were Toby's kin.

She gripped her head, felt a cramping pain catching in her belly. Her emotions were riding an unpredictable roller coaster. She might as well be blindfolded for all she knew of what the immediate future would bring.

But her conscience spoke loud and clear. Toby would start school in five months and the innocence with which he looked at the world would change. He knew he had a daddy who lived in Greece, but so far that was the extent of his knowledge and his curiosity. Soon the notion of a father wouldn't be some abstract thing but something concrete that all the other kids had and he would want too.

And didn't Theseus deserve to know that he was a father and be given the choice to be in Toby's life?

If only she had a crystal ball.

But no matter how much guilt she carried she could not forget that her overriding priority was her son. She would do *anything* to keep him safe, and if that meant keeping Theseus in the dark until she was certain his knowing could bring no harm to Toby, then that was what she must do.

Dictaphone and notepad in hand, Jo slipped through the archway into Theseus's office. After almost two days of going through the research papers she was ready for him.

He was on the phone. His desk—which, like her own, curved to cover two walls but was twice the size—was heaped with neat piles of files and folders. His three desktop computers were all switched on.

He nodded briefly in acknowledgement and raised a hand to indicate that he wouldn't be long.

While he continued his conversation she felt his eyes follow her as she stepped over to the window.

She loved gazing out over the palace grounds. No matter which window she looked out from the vista was always spectacular, with sprawling gardens that ran as far as the eye could see, lush with colourful spring flowers and verdant lawn, and the palace maze rising high in the distance.

When she looked back he was unabashedly studying her.

Prickles of self-consciousness swept through her. Flustered, she smoothed her sweater down over her stomach and forced her gaze back outside, scolding herself for reading anything into his contemplative study of her. Her thin cream sweater and faded blue jeans were hardly the height of fashion.

'What can I help you with?' he asked once he'd finished his call.

'I'm ready with my questions for you.'

'Ask away.'

'It'll probably take a couple of hours to go through them all,' she warned him, conscious of how busy he must be.

'My diary is clear. I'm at your disposal. Please, take a seat.' He pointed to the armchair in the corner of his office and put his computers into sleep mode.

Sinking into the armchair's cosy softness, she resisted the urge to tuck her feet under her bottom.

'Before we discuss anything, I want to say how sorry I was to read about your parents' accident.'

Their tragic car crash had changed the course of Agon's history. It was something Jo knew would reverberate through the rest of her work, and as much as she would have liked to steer away from it, knowing that to talk about it would bring back painful memories for him, it wasn't something she could avoid.

His gaze held hers before he brushed away a lock of hair that had fallen into his eyes.

'See,' he said quietly, emotion swirling in his brown eyes, 'I didn't lie to you about everything.'

She didn't answer, keeping her gaze on his and then wrenching her eyes away to look at her notebook, trying to keep her thoughts coherent.

When they'd sat in his cabin on Illya he'd swigged at his bottle of gin and told her how much his grandmother meant to him, that she'd been the one to whom he'd turned after the death of his parents. Jo's heart had broken when she'd known he would be returning home to say his final goodbye.

'Did you know when you left Illya that that would be it for Theo Patakis?' she asked.

'Yes.'

'And are you happy with your real life or were you happier as Theo?'

His demeanour didn't change but his eyes became steely. 'I don't think these questions have any relevance to my grandfather's biography.'

'I know.'

'I am a prince of Agon. My duty is to my family and my island.'

'But does it make you *happy*?' she persisted.

'Happiness is not quantifiable,' he answered shortly, looking away to press a button on one of the four landline telephones on his desk. 'I'll order refreshments.'

With the thread of their conversation dismissed, Jo pulled out a small table tucked next to her so it sat between them, and put her Dictaphone on it.

'Do you mind if I record our conversation rather than take notes?' she asked once he'd ordered coffee and cake.

'If that's what works for you, then by all means.'

She pressed 'record' and glanced again at her notes.

'Am I right in thinking your grandfather would have abdicated when your father reached the age of forty?'

'That is correct. Agon monarchs traditionally step down when their heir turns forty. When my parents died Helios became heir.'

'And Helios was ten at the time?'

'Yes.'

'So any thoughts of abdication and retirement had to be put to one side?'

'My father was an only child. My grandfather's only sibling died fighting in the war, so there was no one suitable to act as regent until Helios came of age.'

'What plans did your grandfather have for his retirement?'

A shadow crossed his face, lines forming on his forehead. 'He was going to take a back seat for my grandmother.'

'She was a violinist?'

'Yes. When they married she was already world-famous. My grandfather's coronation limited the scope of when and where she could perform, so she concentrated on composing music rather than performing, which was her first love.'

'So that was their plan? For her to start performing again?'

'She still performed, but only a couple of times a year at carefully arranged events. His abdication would have freed her and enabled her to tour the world—something my grandfather was fully behind. He was looking forward to travelling with her.'

'He'd travelled much of the world as a monarch,' she pointed out.

'Travelling as monarch is different. He was an ambassador for our island.' He smiled grimly. 'When a member of my family travels on royal business he has a retinue of staff and an itinerary that leaves no room for spontaneity. Every minute is accounted for.'

Jo tried to imagine the Theo she'd met five years ago, the carefree adrenaline addict with the infectious smile and an impulsive zest for life, living under such restrictions.

An image flashed into her mind of a fully mature lion trapped in a small cage.

'Is that why your grandfather agreed you could take a sabbatical from your duties at the palace and travel the world?'

'It wasn't a question of agreement,' he replied shortly.

When Theseus had decided to leave he'd discussed it with his grandfather as a matter of courtesy. He'd wanted his blessing but it hadn't been imperative. He would have gone anyway. He'd graduated from Sandhurst and, loving military life, had stayed on in the army for a few more years. But then he'd turned twenty-eight and his family's eyes had turned to him. He'd been expected to take his place in the palace, as a good prince was supposed to do...

It had felt as if a hook had been placed around his neck, tightening as the day had loomed ever closer.

He'd known that once he was in the palace permanently, any hope of freedom would be gone for ever. His childhood dream of becoming an astronaut had long been buried, but that yearning for freedom, the wish to see new horizons and control his own destiny without thinking of the impact on the palace, had still been so vivid he'd been able to taste it on his tongue.

He'd thought of his parents, dead at an age not much older than he was now, their lives snuffed out in the blink of an eye. Would they have lived that final day in the same way if they'd known it would be their last?

And so he'd made up his mind to leave before protocol engulfed him and to live his life as if each day really was his last.

He'd become Theo Patakis: the man he might have been if fate hadn't made him a prince.

CHAPTER FOUR

A STRANGE DISQUIET slipped through him. Theseus shrugged it off, and was thankful when a maid came into the office with their refreshments, placing a tray down on the table where Jo had put her Dictaphone.

He saw her gaze flitter to the *karidopita*, a walnut and spice cake.

'Have a slice.' He lifted the plate for her.

'No, thank you.' While she poured the coffee her gaze lingered on the cake.

'Are you sure?'

She pulled a face. 'I put on weight just looking at it.'

'One slice won't hurt.'

'If I have one slice I'll want the rest of it, and before we know it I'll be running to the kitchen and holding the chef to ransom until he's made me a fresh one.' She said it with laughter in her voice, but there was no disguising the longing on her face.

He was about to encourage her again—to his mind a little bit of everything never hurt anyone—when he remembered her as she'd been on Illya. She still had her luscious curves now, but there was no denying that she'd lost weight—perhaps a couple of stone if he were any judge. It seemed her weight loss was an ongoing battle.

Moving the plate to his desk and out of her eyeline, he settled back in his chair, cradling his coffee cup in his hands.

He didn't miss the quick smile of gratitude she threw his

way. It was a smile that made his stomach pull and a wave of something he couldn't distinguish race through him.

'We were discussing my grandfather's plans for abdication,' he prompted her, keen to steer them back to their conversation and focus his mind on the job at hand rather than on *her*.

She threw him another grateful smile and leaned forward to press 'record' on her Dictaphone again. The movement pulled her sweater down enough to give him the tiniest glimpse of her milky cleavage.

A stab of lust pierced him. Thoughts he'd done his damnedest to keep at bay pushed through.

She had skin like satin. Breasts that...

With resolve like steel he pushed the unbidden memory away.

He was not that man who put his own pleasure above everything else any more.

Holding on to his steely resolve and keeping his head together, he answered her many questions, one leading directly to another, all the while stopping his thoughts from straying any further into forbidden territory.

It was a hard thing to do when the mouth posing the questions was so sinfully kissable.

By the time she'd asked her last question Jo's lower back ached from sitting in the same position for so long—three hours, according to her watch. She got up to stretch her legs and went to stand at the window.

Discussing his grandfather's life had felt strangely intimate and she was relieved that it was over. The way Theseus had stared at her throughout...

His dark eyes had never left her face. And she hadn't been able to wrench her gaze from his.

'There's a load of schoolchildren in your garden,' she said, saying the first thing that popped into her mind as she tried desperately to break through the weird atmosphere that had shrunk the spacious office into a tight, claustrophobic room.

'They'll be here for the tour,' he murmured, coming to stand by her side. 'The palace museum and grounds only open at weekends in the off season, but we arrange private midweek tours for schools and other groups. From the first of May until the first of September the grounds, museum and some parts of the palace are open every day. You can't walk anywhere without tripping over a tourist.'

'Is it hard, opening your home to strangers?'

He gave a tight smile. 'This is a palace—not a home.'

'It's *your* home.'

'Our private quarters are off-limits to visitors, but look around you. Where can I go if I want to enjoy the sun in privacy? As soon as I step out of my apartment there are courtiers by my side—' He broke off and muttered what sounded like an oath.

Jo would have pressed him further, but her throat had closed up. Theseus's nearness, his heat and the warm, oaky scent she remembered so well were all there, igniting her senses… She clenched her fists, fighting her body and its yearning to press closer, to actually touch him.

A heavily fortified black four-by-four pulled to a stop below them.

A tall man, very similar in looks to Theseus, stepped out of the back, followed by a rake-thin woman with raven-black hair and enormous sunglasses.

'Is that Helios?' she asked, grabbing at the distraction.

'Yes. And that's Princess Catalina from the principality of Monte Cleure.' Theseus placed his enormous hands on the windowsill. 'Between you and me, he'll be announcing their engagement at the Gala.'

'That's quick. Didn't they only meet at the ball last Saturday?'

'Our families have been friends for decades. Catalina's brother went to boarding school with us.'

'They don't look like a couple in love.'

Jo wasn't an expert in body language, but the way they walked together—past the schoolchildren who had all stopped what they were doing to gape at them—reminded her of her parents, who walked as if even brushing against each other might give them a disease.

And as she thought this, Theseus's arm brushed lightly against hers.

Her lungs tightened.

She could *feel* him.

'Heirs to the Agon throne marry for duty, not love,' he said, his voice unusually hard.

She looked at him. He was gazing intently out of the window, his jaw set.

'It's the twenty-first century.'

'And protocol has been adapted. Helios is the first Agon heir free to choose his own bride.'

'Can he choose anyone?'

'Anyone of royal blood.'

'Freedom with caveats? How sad.'

'It is the way things work here. Change takes time.'

'I hope they at least like and respect each other.'

She wondered if her parents' marriage would have been different if her mother had ever respected her father. Would her father have resorted to the demon drink if her mother hadn't been so disparaging towards him?

'My brother would never have married someone he didn't respect.' A marriage without respect had to be just as bad as a marriage without love, if not worse.

'When will they marry?'

'As soon as it can be arranged. Hopefully before...'

He didn't need to finish his sentence. Jo knew what he meant.

Before his grandfather died.

The mood shifted, the atmosphere becoming even heavier.

'It will be a full state wedding,' he explained curtly. 'That usually takes a good six months to organise. Helios wants this one to be arranged in a maximum of two months.'

'That's asking a lot.'

He shrugged. 'Our staff are the best. It will be done.'

'Are you expected to marry too?'

'The spare to the heir must produce more spares,' he said scathingly. 'Once Helios is married I will have to find a suitable royal bride of my own.'

'And what do you consider "suitable"?' she asked.

Of course it was only the fact that Theseus marrying meant Toby would have a stepmother, and eventually half-siblings to contend with, that made it feel as if a knife had been plunged into her heart.

Theseus was a prince. Princes needed their princesses.

'Someone who understands that it will be a union within which to make children.'

She strove to keep her voice casual. 'Don't you want love?'

The look he cast her could have curdled milk. 'Absolutely not. Only fools marry for love.'

'That's very cynical.'

'You think? Well, my mother loved my father, and all she got for her trouble was endless infidelity. My grandparents loved each other, but when my grandmother died my grandfather aged a decade overnight. It's not the cancer that's killing him; it's his broken heart. Love causes misery and I want no part of it. I want a bride who understands what palace life entails and who I can respect. Nothing more.'

Jo swallowed the bile rising in her throat.

Her memories of this man were filled with such warmth that this coldness chilled her.

Where had that man gone?

She wanted to argue with him, to tell him that surely the sweetness of love overrode anything else, but what would she know about it? The only person who'd ever truly loved her was her son, and in all honesty he had no choice in the matter, just as she had no choice but to love her own cold mother. In Jo's experience filial love was as automatic as breathing. Parental love was not.

What if Theseus's disdain for love extended to his children? There was a cynicism to him that scared her.

She couldn't bring herself to ask. Instead she took a quick breath and said, 'Will Helios's children be sent to boarding school, like you and your brothers were?'

This was a question that had played on her mind since she'd realised all the Princes had been packed off to boarding school. If she told Theseus about Toby, and if he recognised him as his son, would he expect him to be sent away too?

That was *if* he recognised him as his son.

What if he demanded a DNA test? The thought made her shudder.

So many 'what ifs'.

If only she could see what the future held.

'Of course. It is the Kalliakis tradition.'

'Is it traditional to be sent away at *eight*?'

'Yes.'

'That's such a young age.' She thought again of Toby, who still struggled to put his own socks on. To imagine being separated from him for months on end... No, she couldn't do it. Being apart from him while she was here on Agon was hard enough.

'I agree. Too young.'

She swallowed back her relief. 'Did you find it hard, leaving your home and family?'

'You have no idea,' he said, his tone harsher than she'd ever heard it.

'Was it easier for you, having Helios there already when you went?'

He looked at her and paused for a moment. 'Harder. I was always being compared to him. I wanted to be judged in my own right.'

'So were you always rivals?'

'What makes you ask that?' The intensity of his stare grew.

She pulled a rueful face, knowing she was reaching dangerous territory. 'I've been putting two and two together again. I saw a press cutting about your grandparents' wedding anniversary party, where you punched him in the face.'

To her amazement he shook his head and burst into laughter.

The transformation took her breath away.

It was the first time she'd heard him laugh since she'd arrived at the palace, and the sound dived straight through her skin.

Almost lazily he reached out and pressed a finger to her lips. 'You are a very astute woman.'

It was the lightest of touches, but enough for all the breath in her lungs to rush out in a whoosh and for her heart, which was already hammering, to accelerate.

'Yes, we were rivals,' he murmured. 'Helios was always destined to be King. My destiny was to be the perfect Prince, tucked in his shadow. It was a destiny I fought against. I didn't want to be in his shadow. I wanted to be in the sun.'

His finger drifted away from her mouth and slid across her cheek, leaving flickers of heat following his trail. If he moved any closer he'd be able to feel the thundering of her heart...

He stepped closer. 'My childhood was a battle for attention and freedom.'

He was going to kiss her.

Her senses were filled with him; his scent, his heat, the masculine essence he carried so effortlessly and that every part of her sang to.

She mustn't give in to it. She mustn't.

She cleared her throat. 'Is that why you're the perfect Prince now? Are you making up for your behaviour then?' Judging by the press cuttings, his behaviour over these past few years had been exemplary.

He stiffened. The hazy mist that had appeared in his eyes cleared. He pulled his hand away from her face and stepped back, his regal skin slipping into place effortlessly.

Breathing heavily, Jo tried to collect her scattered thoughts, tried dispelling the tingles racing through her.

He'd been about to kiss her.

And she'd been about to kiss him right back.

She still wanted to. Her mouth *ached* to feel his warm, firm lips upon hers again.

She could feel the invisible mark his finger had left on her lips, had to clench her hands into fists to stop them tracing it.

'Yes, you *are* an astute woman.' Theseus had regained his composure. 'Now, unless you have further questions about my grandfather, I have work to do.'

'I'm done,' she said quietly, edging away from him, side-stepping into her own office, glad of the dismissal.

Only when she was completely alone did she place her fingers to her lips and trace the mark he'd made on her mouth.

Theseus stood in the adjoining archway and looked into Joanne's office, as he'd done numerous times since she'd arrived on his island.

There she sat, hunched over her computer, earphones in, seemingly oblivious to his pursuing eyes.

Any doubts he'd had about Hamlin & Associates sending a relative novice to take Fiona's place had gone. Unashamed of asking for help with translation when needed, Jo had finished four chapters in three days, passing them to him for approval before sending them to the Oxford office for editing. At the rate she was going she would beat the Wednesday deadline by a comfortable margin.

It wasn't only her speed and work ethic that impressed him, but also the quality of the chapters she'd produced. He was certain the reader wouldn't be able to spot the transition between the two biographers.

His grandfather was coming to life on the page in a way he'd never anticipated. He'd enjoyed Fiona's chapters, and had read them almost like a history lesson. But Jo had taken up the story from Theseus's own childhood. Reading her chapters was like seeing his own life through his grandfather's eyes, with events he'd lived through taking on greater significance.

His grandparents' fortieth wedding anniversary celebrations were vivid on the page. He could taste the food that had been served, hear the music of the Agon orchestra, see the dancing couples on the ballroom floor... And, although she'd wisely left it unwritten, he could see his fourteen-year-old self launching at fifteen-year-old Helios in full view of all the distinguished guests, breaking his nose.

He could see his brother's blood soaking into the royal purple sash, see his grandmother's horror and his grandfather's fury. He could still taste his own blood as Helios—never one to shy away from a fight like any good Agonite—had launched himself right back at him.

What he couldn't remember was *why* he'd done it.

He remembered hating the stupid penguin suits he and his brothers had been forced to wear, hating the forced small talk with boring old people, hating it that a president's daughter he'd taken a liking to had made a beeline for his older brother.

Everyone had made a beeline for Helios.

Helios lived under even greater restrictions than he did, but his brother had always taken it in his stride, acting as if going on a date with three burly men with guns accompanying him was natural and not something to resent.

Their rivalry had been immense.

He smiled as he recalled their younger brother, Talos, then only twelve, pulling them apart.

Theseus had been in disgrace for months and confined to the five-hundred-and-seventy-three-roomed palace over the long hot summer.

And then his smile dropped.

He'd ruined his grandparents' special day. He'd shamed them.

He had shamed them many times with his selfish behaviour. Royal military parades, state banquets—all the events the three young Princes had attended Theseus had treated with an indifference bordering on disdain. He'd wanted to be somewhere, *anywhere* else, and he hadn't cared who'd known it.

Reading about these events in the book, even with his churlish behaviour omitted, had brought it all back to him—everything he was fighting to atone for. It was the humanity Jo brought to both his grandparents on the page that made it all seem so vivid again.

Yes. His doubts about her ability had truly been expelled. He enjoyed working with her, their back and forth conversations, the flashes of shared humour. He especially liked the way she blushed when she caught him looking at her. She made his veins bubble and his skin tingle, long-dead sensations blazing back to life.

He found it fascinating to watch her work; her face scrunched with intensity, her fingers flying over the keys of her computer, completely in the zone. Sometimes she sensed his presence and would turn her head, colour creeping over her cheeks when she saw him…

She drove him crazy. It had become a constant battle to keep his hands to himself. He'd been so close to kissing her. *So close.* He'd breathed in her scent and every part of him had reacted.

And that was dangerous.

He was about to turn away and return to the safety of his own desk when her phone vibrated loudly next to her.

With her earphones still in, she grabbed it with her right hand and swiped the screen in an absent manner. Whoever had messaged her must have been deemed worthy, for she straightened, brought the phone close to her face and pressed the screen.

She gazed at whatever she'd received, brushing her fingers gently over it, before lifting the phone to her mouth and kissing it gently.

His stomach roiled.

He'd assumed she didn't have a lover. It was easy to tell if a woman was in love—there was a certain glow she carried. Jo didn't have that glow. But the way she'd pressed her lips to that phone…as if she'd been trying to breathe in the essence of whoever had sent that message to her…

It was a gesture that made his skin feel as if needles were being pricked into it.

He remembered the way those lips had once felt under his own mouth, the clumsy eagerness he'd found there. The innocence.

'Who was that?' he asked loudly, stepping into the room, his curiosity burning.

But of course she didn't hear him. By the time he'd tapped on her shoulder, making her almost jump out of her seat, the screen on her phone had gone black.

'Who was that?' he repeated, when she'd tugged the earphones out with trembling hands.

Dark colour stained her cheeks, her teeth bit into her full lips and her eyes were wide...*fearful*?

What on earth did she have to be frightened of?

Her throat moved before she answered. 'It's private.'

'Private?'

'Private,' she repeated more decisively. 'Did you want me for anything?'

'Yes.' He folded his arms across his chest and without even considering his words said, 'I'm taking you out for dinner tonight.'

If there had been fear in her eyes before, all that rang out of them now was confusion. 'Why?'

'You need a break. You haven't seen anything of my island.'

'I'm here to work—not sightsee.'

'You'll burn out if you don't take a break.' He needed a break too, time away from the palace and the reams of courtiers if only for a few hours.

He knew next to nothing of this woman who had once been a beacon of light for him on a long, cold night.

An evening out would do them both good.

Her brows furrowed. 'I thought Agon was closed on Sundays.'

He fixed her with the stare his brother Talos used to such great effect. 'Let me worry about finding somewhere to go. You need a break from this office. I want you ready for a night out by seven o'clock—and no arguments or I'll have you taken to the dungeons.'

Her eyes widened in surprise before she let out a bark of laughter.

He felt his own bubble of mirth rise up too, but smothered it. 'Seven o'clock,' he said, his voice brooking no argument.

'I haven't got anything to wear,' she said matter-of-factly, as if that clinched it. As if that would let her off the hook.

On impulse, he leaned down to place his face before hers, taking in the ringing blue-grey eyes. He caught a hint of a light, feminine scent and inhaled.

'Dress casually. And if suitable clothing is an issue I would suggest not wearing anything at all.'

Her cheeks turned so red they nearly matched the colour of her hair.

Pulling back, feeling lighter than he'd felt in years, he sauntered through to his office, pausing at the threshold to add, 'If you're not finished by five o'clock Nikos will escort you out of here. The office door will be locked until the morning. See you at seven.'

He walked into his apartment, his pulse thundering in his ears, and closed the door behind him.

What the *hell* was he playing at? A night out was one thing—but suggesting she go *naked*? That was inviting trouble. It was the kind of comment Theo would have made.

For five years his physical desires had been dormant. Being around beautiful women was a regular occurrence in his life, but not one of them had tempted him. None of them made him feel as if his veins had been injected with red-hot treacle the way being with Jo did.

None of them had propelled him to make an impulsive offer of a date. Well, give an *order* for a date.

No, *not* a date. Merely an evening away from the confines of the palace for them both.

Now his senses were straining to remember what she had looked like naked, but their night together was still a blur; a ghost that couldn't be seen.

Something told him it would be best for that memory to remain a ghost.

CHAPTER FIVE

A LOUD KNOCK on her apartment door announced Theseus's arrival.

Jo took a deep breath through her nose and pulled open the door, her heart thundering erratically.

And there he stood.

Tonight he'd forsaken the business attire he usually wore and donned a pair of slim-fitting dark blue jeans that hugged his long, muscular thighs, a light grey shirt unbuttoned at the neck and a fitted brown leather jacket that showed off the breadth of his chest to perfection.

All of that, coupled with his deep olive features and thick dark hair... He looked sexy. And dangerous. So dangerous she should close the door in his face and plead a headache.

He looked...

He looked like *Theo*.

He stepped over the threshold and stood before her, gazing down with a slow shake of his head. The look in his eyes threatened to send her pulses racing out of her skin.

She tried to swallow but her throat had dried up. Only once had she seen that look. Five years ago.

She'd thought he was beautiful. She hadn't been stupid; had known she'd had no chance with him. He'd been as unobtainable as the film stars she'd loved to watch so much. Even then he'd been a man surrounded by a legion of admirers, men and women who all hung on to his every word and laughed at his every joke. Men like him didn't notice girls like her apart from to make fun of them.

The last thing she'd expected—the very last thing—was for him to stand up for her. To protect her. That one action had turned her crush into something more, making her heart swell and attach itself to him.

Even then she hadn't been naïve enough to think her adoration would be reciprocated. The world didn't work like that. Gorgeous, fit Greeks didn't fall for plump, shy English girls. He could befriend her, but desire her? Impossible.

And then he'd turned up at the chalet she'd shared with her friends, bottle of gin in hand, hair in disarray and wildness in his eyes...

That look in his eyes when he'd first kissed her... That same look was in his eyes now. It was a look that pierced her skin and made her recall for the thousandth time their one night together.

That night...

Losing her virginity to a drunk, melancholic man had been something she could never have expected, but it was something she would never regret, and not just because that one time had created Toby.

Theseus had needed her that night. That hadn't been a lie. He'd lain on the bed with the back of his head resting against her breasts, swigging from the bottle of gin. She'd run her fingers through his hair and listened to him talk.

He'd told her about his brothers and their fierce competitiveness, the penknives they'd each been given at the age of ten by their grandfather and how they would spend hours finding inanimate objects to throw them at as target practice, how the loser would be subjected to knuckle-rubs.

And then—she had never figured out how or why—the atmosphere had changed and he'd stopped talking. His eyes had gazed into hers with an expression she had never seen before but which had acted like a magnet, pulling her to him.

The stars might not have shone and fireworks might

not have exploded but she hadn't needed them to. For a few precious moments she had belonged to him and he had belonged to her.

For one solitary night she had been needed and loved and wanted, and it had filled her romantic heart with hope and tenderness.

She couldn't bear to think it had *all* been a lie.

She'd stood in the shower an hour ago with anticipation thrumming through her and had known she had to tell him about Toby. She could not in all good conscience keep it from him any longer.

Theseus was arrogant, and often curt, but he was also generous and thoughtful. He was a powerful man, but she'd seen no sign of him abusing that power. He wasn't Theo, but there had been a couple of times when she'd sworn she'd glimpsed the man she'd fallen in love with five years before.

She would wait until the biography was complete. It meant everything to him. For all his talk about disavowing love, she knew he loved his grandfather just as he'd loved his grandmother.

A few more days—that was all it would take. Two days at the most. Then her job would be done and she could turn his life upside down with the truth.

All she had to do was smother the awful feeling of deception she carried everywhere.

She felt such guilt. Every minute with him was clouded by her total awareness of him and the knowledge that she was hiding something so monumental. She'd thought her heart might jump out of her ribcage earlier, when he had almost caught her looking at another picture Toby had drawn which Jonathan had scanned and emailed over to her.

And now her heart was beating just as frantically, but with a hugely different rhythm. Flames licked through her veins at the look in Theseus's eyes. It was as if he wanted nothing more than to eat her whole. As if her knee-length mint crêpe dress with its flared sleeves and her flat black sandals made up the sexiest outfit he'd ever seen on a woman.

The nervous excitement that had built in her stomach almost skipped up and out of her throat when he dived a hand around her neck and gathered her hair in a bunch.

Without breaking stride, he kicked the door shut behind him, moved his other hand to her cheek and brought his mouth down on hers.

If a body could spontaneously combust, then Jo's did. The lit flames became a blaze—a dark, fiery ache which deepened in her pelvis as his lips moved over hers, firm but gentle, seductive but checked. Firmly controlled. His tongue darted out, prising her lips apart so it could slide slowly inside and dance against her own. His fingers were making gentle kneading motions against her cheek.

Everything was pushed out of her mind, clearing it to only him; his hot, lightly coffee-scented breath, his warm strong fingers, the heat unfurling from him and moving through her aching body. Sensation threaded everywhere… right through to the soles of her feet and the delicate skin of her eyelids.

She gripped his jacket, then reached up to wind her arms around his neck, the tips of her fingers skimming the smooth skin and rubbing against the soft bristles running up from his nape.

Deepening the kiss, he dropped his hand from her cheek to snake it around her waist, breaching that final physical distance between them so she stood flush against him, lost to everything but the rush of his deeply sensuous assault.

And then he jerked away and the kiss was broken.

Ramming his hands into his jeans pockets, he closed his eyes and swore. 'I apologise,' he said, his jaw clenched, his breathing heavy. 'I never meant for that to happen.'

'Neither did I,' she said quietly. She looked away, not wanting him to see the enormous dollop of guilt she knew must be reflected in her eyes.

'You're driving me crazy,' he said, with such starkness her gaze flew back to him.

Hunger. That was what she saw. His hunger for her.

She was slipping into dangerous waters and had no idea how to navigate her way out, a task made harder by the fact that her body throbbed from head to toe. She knew if he were to touch her again she would respond with the same wantonness.

How could she have allowed him to kiss her when she was keeping such a huge secret from him? Even if he knew about Toby it would be madness to think anything could happen between them. In a few months he would be searching for a bride. A *royal* bride.

She was as far removed from his ideal of the perfect royal bride as possible.

He held her gaze a beat longer before striding to the door and yanking it open.

His eyes flashed as he said, 'I suggest we leave now, because if you keep looking at me like that, I will not be responsible for the consequences.'

Jo paused for far too long, desire waging war with common sense.

Common sense clinched the victory.

She held her breath as she slipped past him, then followed him in silence out into the clear spring evening.

Her lips still burned from his kiss.

When he'd made love to her on Illya he'd been drunk.

This time he'd kissed her when he was sober. He desired her.

It shouldn't have made a difference.

It made all the difference in the world.

* * *

That had been the journey from hell, Theseus thought as Nikos brought the car to a stop.

What had he been *thinking*, kissing her like that?

He *hadn't* been thinking. At least not with his brain.

It had been that expression in her eyes that had done it for him, that open, wide-eyed desire.

Theos, how could *any* man look into those eyes and not want to drown in them?

Sitting in the back of the car for twenty minutes with her so close had been tantamount to torture. They hadn't exchanged a word.

He ran through all the reasons why he couldn't allow anything to happen between them. Or he tried to.

He couldn't think of one good reason why he shouldn't make love to her when every ounce of his being burned for her touch...

Because Jo wants more than you can ever give.

His spine stiffened as he recalled the promise he'd made to her on Illya. The promise he'd broken. Try as he might to ignore it, the guilt ate at him.

Jo wasn't the type of woman to go in for casual flings. She just wasn't. He'd known that five years ago but had allowed his desire and the emotions that had racked him that dark night to take over.

He would not do it again, would not take advantage of a woman who needed more from a lover than a solitary night. He could never offer her anything more, especially not now, when marriage loomed ever closer.

He might desire her, but he would control it.

Whatever the night might bring.

Club Giroud was one of the best kept secrets on Agon, open twenty-four-seven and located in a deceptively shabby secluded stone building near the top of Agon's highest mountain. No casual passer-by would guess that inside, at any one time, were dozens of the world's richest people and a fleet of parked cars collectively worth millions of dollars.

The interior was an entirely different matter.

They were met at the door by the concierge, who'd been watching out for them. Puffed up with importance at one of the royal Princes paying the establishment a visit, the man led them through a cavernous golden-hued dining hall, filled with beautiful, thin, chic women and men of varying shapes and sizes, all of whom turned their heads to stare at them. The concierge took them past the sweeping staircase that led up to the club itself, and outside to the sprawling terrace.

'I am totally underdressed,' Jo hissed the moment the fawning concierge had left them alone. 'All those women look as if they've just come off a catwalk.'

'You look beautiful,' he said simply, his eyes taking in every inch of her. Again.

There was nothing wrong with looking. Nothing at all.

'And don't forget I'm a prince of this island. I could wear a sack and my guest a binliner and I'd still be treated like royalty.'

'You *are* royalty,' she said with a mock scowl, although her cheeks heightened with colour at his compliment.

'Exactly. My presence gives the place a certain cache. It's a secret club for the filthy rich—playboys and billionaires who moor their yachts in our harbour and like to dine and play somewhere elusive and exclusive.'

'You like to come here?' she asked doubtfully, as if she knew of his disdain for these people whose lives were consumed with money: how to make it and how to spend it.

'If I were to take you anywhere else our picture would be all over the press by morning.' He gave a rueful shrug.

'I can always take you to Talos's boxing gym, if you would prefer?'

She raised her pretty red-brown eyebrows.

'And here you get to see my island.'

'Do I?'

'If you look, you'll see this is the best view in the whole of Agon.'

He'd ensured she had the best seat at the table—one that looked out from the mountain over the villages and towns dotted in the distance, towards the palace in the thickets of trees on the adjacent mountain and the dark blue of the Mediterranean, where the sun blinked its last goodnight. In a couple of hours the moon would be high enough to illuminate the whole island. It was a sight he wanted her to see.

It gave him enormous satisfaction to see she hadn't paid the blindest bit of attention to the view. Since they'd been seated she'd only had eyes for *him*.

He pointed. 'Do you see that high, rocky mountain in the distance?'

She nodded.

'When we were teenagers, my brothers and I would have races to the top.'

'You were allowed?'

'Of course. Within the palace walls we were expected to behave like princes, but outside we were expected to be fighting fit.'

'And who would win?'

'Normally Talos. Helios and I were so intent on beating each other we always forgot what a mountain Talos was himself. We'd get to the top and find him already there.' He smiled at the memories.

Jo squinted as she took it all in, her features softening. She nodded in the direction of the palace. 'Is that the maze all lit up?'

'It is,' he confirmed. 'There must be a group doing

an evening tour—there are night lights embedded in the hedges to light the way for them.'

She gave a sigh of wonder. 'I bet that's a fabulous experience. Your maze is huge—much bigger than the one at Hampton Court Palace. I got lost in that on a school trip when I was twelve.'

Her delight at the recollection of being lost in a maze made her whole face light up, whilst the mention of the British palace sparked a memory of his own. 'Aren't you distantly related to *your* royal family?'

Surprise ringed her blue-grey eyes. 'How can you remember that?'

'I have an excellent memory.'

The truth was his memories of those last few days on Illya were becoming clearer. The hazy details were crystallising.

The night after he'd evicted those Americans from Marin's Bar for their ill-treatment of her, he'd gone back there with his Scandinavian friends and invited Jo and her friends to join them again. Conversation had turned to everyone having to say one interesting fact about themselves. Jo's had been that she was distantly related to the British royal family. She'd found it so amusing that she'd burst into laughter.

It had been the first time he'd heard or seen her laugh— usually she was so shy. Her whole face had lit up, just as it was doing now. It had been the first time he'd noticed what a pretty face she had. It had been such a transformation that his interest had been well and truly piqued. He'd spent the rest of the evening talking to her, enchanted by this shy young woman who, once she got going, became witty and talkative.

Talking to her had been like bathing in a clear, sun-drenched lake after months of soaking in the salty sea. He remembered how torn she'd looked when her friends had said they wanted to return to their chalet. How disappointed he'd been when she'd got up from the table and wished him goodnight.

The next day he'd tried to convince her to go surfing on the north side of the island with them all. Her friends had jumped at the chance but Jo had politely refused. She'd happily tagged along to watch, however, sitting on the beach and refusing to acknowledge his cajoling to come into the water.

Shortly after that he'd gone with his Scandinavian friends to a nearby uninhabited island for a couple of days of mountain climbing.

When they'd returned, the first thing he'd heard when he'd charged his phone had been Helios's message telling him to come home. Their grandmother had been taken seriously ill and wasn't expected to survive.

For the second time in his life he'd been lost. The first time had been the night their grandfather had flown to their English boarding school to tell him and Helios that their parents had been killed. Nothing could ever touch that night for pain, but he'd had his brother there, and for that one night his grandfather—who in that moment had been a true grandfather to them—had held his two grandsons close.

On Illya he'd been alone, and far from his family. He'd been on an island in the middle of the Adriatic Sea where the only means of transport had been the daily ferry.

He'd finished half a bottle of gin in his chalet alone, waiting until he'd figured everyone would be in bed before staggering outside, intending to sit on the beach.

There had been a light on in Jo's chalet.

Thinking back, he was surprised he'd known which chalet had been hers.

'According to my mother, her side of the family has a direct link to Queen Victoria via many marriages,' she said now, in that same amused tone he remembered from five years ago. 'I think I'm something like six-hundred-and-thirty-ninth in line to the throne.'

'Being that far up the chain you must have grown up in your own palace,' he teased, playing along with her irreverence.

'I grew up in an Oxfordshire manor house so old and draughty it would have been warmer sleeping in an igloo.'

'Rather like sleeping in a palace, then,' he observed with a grin.

She laughed, her eyes meeting his. 'Your palace is wonderful and has hot running water. My parents' house has a boiler so old my mother passes it off as an original feature. Saying that, the kennels and the stables always have decent heating.'

'Did you have a lot of pets?' He could just see her fussing over a small army of dogs.

She pulled a face. 'Not quite. My mother turned the old outhouses into an animal sanctuary. She'll take any animal in: cats, dogs, hedgehogs, horses—donkeys, even. Those she can't rehome, she keeps.'

'How many animals does she have?'

Her lips pursed as she thought. 'Anything up to fifty of them. If she runs out of space she brings them into the house.'

'That must have been magical for you as a child.'

She gave a shrug, her answer delayed by the waiter coming over with a jug of water and taking their order.

'So your mother runs an animal sanctuary—what does your father do?' he asked once they were alone again.

'He drinks.'

His hand paused on his glass.

'He's an alcoholic.'

'I'm sorry. Is he violent?' He thought again of the drunken American college students who'd been so abusive to Jo and her friends. Drink had a habit of making some people cruel.

'God, no. He's actually very placid. He just sits in his study all day, working his way through his whisky.'

'How does your mother cope?'

'By ignoring him.'

'Really?'

'She despises him,' Jo said flatly. 'As far as she's concerned, Dad spending his days pickling his liver is the best thing for him.'

His brow furrowed. 'That's harsh.'

'It's the truth. She thinks he's weak and foolish. Maybe she's right. He was a stockbroker, but he lost his job to the drink when I was a baby.'

'So how do they survive?' He couldn't imagine an animal sanctuary made much money.

'Mum's got a tiny trust fund, and she makes a little from donations to the sanctuary. She bakes a lot of cakes and sells them for high prices which our rich neighbours are happy to pay because they are utterly gorgeous.'

Not as gorgeous as the mouth doing the talking now, Theseus thought, noticing the faraway look in her eyes as she spoke of the cakes and remembering the longing she'd shown towards the *karidopita*.

'She sounds like a formidable woman,' he observed. His own mother had been the opposite of formidable.

Jo met his eyes. 'That's one way of describing her. She's very blunt with her opinions, and has no time for people she considers to be fools. Most people are scared of her and she knows it—she leaves the cakes in the front room with price tags on and no one has ever tried to short-change her or steal the money box.' She sighed. 'I'll say this much for her, though—she's dotty about the animals. It's only creatures who *don't* walk on four legs she has no interest in.'

The waiter returned with their wine and poured them each a glass.

'Do you still live with your parents?' Theseus asked after taking a sip of the mellow red liquid.

'I'm in Oxford itself now. It's easier to commute to work.'

That reminded him of something else she'd once told him. 'I thought you were moving to London?'

Her eyes widened. 'Gosh, your memory is on fire to-night.'

He flashed her a grin, wondering if he'd imagined the flicker of fright that had crossed over her face.

'So what happened to London?' he asked, watching as she reached for her glass of wine and noting the tremor in her hands. She reminded him of a jumpy cat walking on freshly tossed hot coals.

She looked out over the mountains. 'Life. But never mind about me—tell me about the business you run with your brothers. You invest in young start-up companies?'

He eyed her contemplatively. Yes. The jumpy cat anal-ogy perfectly described her at this moment. Her discomfort had come on so suddenly it made him suspicious—until he reminded himself that he had no right to her secrets.

Jo was in his employ. The fact that they had once made love half a decade ago didn't mean he had the right to know everything about her.

Yet the more he was with her, the more he wanted to peel back every secret until she was stripped bare before him.

Did she have a lover? Instinct told him no—she wasn't the kind of woman to kiss a man if she was involved with someone else—but there was something going on with her...something she had no intention of sharing with him.

He took another sip of wine and pulled his errant thoughts back under control.

No more intimacies. This was *not* a seduction.

There would be no peeling back of anything; not secrets nor clothes.

So he told her about the business, keeping the conversation throughout their meal light and easy. By the time they'd finished their starters and main course—the pair of them having shared a generous *souvlaki* platter filled with marinated pork and chicken skewers, roasted vegetables, hot pitta, salads and tzatziki—and ordered coffee, she was as relaxed as he'd seen her on his island. So relaxed that when she declined dessert he held himself back from asking if her refusal of sweet foods was related to her mother's cakes.

And he'd relaxed too. With each sip of wine and every bite of food he'd felt the weight he lived with lift until it was just them. Two people who couldn't keep their eyes off each other.

Jo truly was glorious, with her autumn leaf hair thick around her shoulders, a lock falling around her cleavage. It would take no effort to lean across the table and slowly sweep it away, to trace his fingers over her satin skin...

'What?' she asked, one brow raised.

She must have read something in his expression, for her eyes suddenly widened and she grabbed her glass, holding it up like a shield.

Another memory flashed through his mind, of lying on his bed with her, his head cushioned on those wonderful breasts...

She'd been awake, book in hand, when he'd knocked on her chalet door. Her friends had been fast asleep.

When he'd swigged from his bottle of gin, shrugged his shoulders helplessly and said, 'I think I need a friend,' she'd stared at him, taking in his disarrayed state, then giving the most loving, sympathetic smile he'd ever been on the receiving end of.

'Come on,' she'd said, putting her book down and taking his hand to lead him back to his own chalet.

The bed being the only place to sit, she'd climbed on and sat against the headboard. He'd leaned into her. She'd laced her fingers through his hair and let him talk.

He still couldn't pinpoint when the mood had changed. He'd been drunk, but there had come a moment when he'd suddenly become aware of the erratic thud of her heart. He'd tilted his head to look at her and realised that while he'd been talking so self-indulgently his head had been resting on her comforting breasts. Breasts separated from him by nothing but a thin white T-shirt.

She'd worn no bra.

She'd smiled with those stunning blue-grey eyes and suddenly he'd known he could lose himself in them.

And just like that he'd been in a full state of arousal.

Forget comforting. She wasn't *comforting*. She was the sexiest creature on the planet and his desire for her in that moment had been the most concentrated, intense desire he'd ever experienced.

By the time he'd pulled her T-shirt off and wriggled out of his shorts he'd been ready to devour her. And he had done just that.

He'd fallen asleep as soon as it was over and had slept until she'd gently woken him to say that the ferry was approaching the island.

'That night in Illya,' he asked quietly, 'was I your first?'

'My first?'

'Lover.'

Understanding flashed over her and she covered her mouth with her hand.

'I was, wasn't I?'

She gave the barest of nods. 'I'm surprised you remember anything.'

Her face was suffused with colour. Abruptly she got to her feet, knocking into the table as she did so, spilling water from her glass.

'I need to use the ladies',' she said starkly.

He captured her wrist and stared at her, concerned. 'Are you okay?'

She nodded, but her eyes were wild. She tugged her hand free. 'I won't be long.'

Puzzled, he watched her flee inside.

No sooner had the door shut behind her than her phone began to vibrate and dance on the table.

CHAPTER SIX

JOANNE STARED AT her reflection in the lavish ladies' rest-room—which was mercifully empty—and prayed for cour-age. Her hands were clammy, her skin burned and a heavy beat played in her head.

She had to tell him. Tonight. Forget waiting until the biography was finished. Things had gone too far to keep it hidden from him any longer. He was seducing her with his every word and every look.

She hadn't tasted a morsel of her food; could hardly re-member what she'd had. Her senses had been too busy rel-ishing the taste of his earlier kisses, the whispers of which still lay on her tongue and lips. She could still feel his huge hand warm on her wrist.

She inhaled deeply a couple of times before smoothing her hair and straightening her dress. She would drink her coffee, Nikos would drive them back to the palace and then, as soon as they were alone, she would tell Theseus the truth.

She slipped back into the club's restaurant and weaved her way through the tables of beautiful people, all looking at her with unabashed curiosity. She heard their whispers as she passed: this stranger in their midst was the guest of one of Agon's most eligible bachelors.

Avoiding Theseus's eyes, she took her seat and reached for her coffee, which had been brought in her absence.

Before she could plead a headache and ask if they could return to the palace, Theseus said, 'Jonathan called.'

Startled, she looked at him.

Impassively he handed over her phone. 'He called when you were in the bathroom.'

In her rush to escape from him and in the haze she'd fallen into she'd left her phone exposed on the table.

She swallowed, her heart immediately starting to hammer. 'Did you answer it?'

'Yes. I thought it might be important.' Curiosity rang from his dark eyes. And something else…something darker.

'What did he say?' she croaked, fighting the cold paralysis sweeping through her.

'Only that he was calling for a chat and that his scanner's broken, so he'll give you Toby's pictures when you get home.'

Jo felt the colour drain from her face at hearing him vocalise their son's name, the blood abandoning her head and leaving a cold fog in its place.

She hadn't told Jonathan or Cathy about finding Toby's father. She hadn't told anyone.

This was it. This was where the truth came out.

A pulse flickered in Theseus's jaw. 'So who are they?'

'Jonathan's my brother.'

'And Toby? Is he your nephew?'

It was a struggle to breathe. Her body didn't know what it was doing. She was hot and cold, thrumming and paralysed all at once.

Hot. Cold. Hot. Cold.

Fat tears welled in her eyes and spilled over before she had the chance to feel them form.

She took the biggest, most painful breath of her life.

'Toby is my son.'

The shock on his face was so stark it was clear that hadn't been the answer he'd expected. 'You have a *child*?'

She nodded and swiped the tears away, only to find them replaced with more.

He rubbed a hand through his hair and shook his head

in disbelief. 'I had no idea. You have a child...? How old is he?'

She wrapped her arms around herself and whispered, 'Four.'

His hand froze on his head. Slowly his gaze drifted to fix on her, then stilled, his expression like those on the statues of the fierce Minoan gods that lined the palace corridors.

Her stomach churned as she watched him make the connection.

An age passed before he showed any sign of movement other than the narrowing of his unblinking eyes. Slowly he brought his hand down from his head to grip his glass, which still had a little red wine in it. Without taking his eyes from her face he knocked it back, emptied the remnants of the bottle into the glass and knocked that back too.

He wiped his mouth with the back of his hand and got to his feet.

When he spoke, his words were laced with a snarl. 'Get up. We leave *now*.'

He was a father.

Those four words were all Theseus could focus on.

He'd known there was something in her life that was putting her on edge, but the truth was nothing like he'd imagined.

Jo had a child.

And *he* was the father.

He'd been on the brink of tossing away his vow of celibacy for a lying, deceptive...

Theos. He had a four-year-old boy out there—a child of his blood.

He hadn't needed to do more than rudimentary maths to know the child was his. One look at Jo's terrified, tearful face had confirmed the truth.

She'd denied him their son's existence.

She was sitting in the back of the stretch Mercedes alone while he rode in front with Nikos, who wisely hadn't uttered a word since they'd come out of Club Giroud. The partition was up. He couldn't bring himself to look at her.

His control hung by the tiniest of threads. There were so many emotions playing through him it was as if a tsunami had been set loose in his chest.

When they arrived back at the palace he got straight out of the car and yanked open the back door. 'Get out.'

Not looking at her, or waiting to see if she obeyed, Theseus unlocked the door to his private apartment and held it open for her.

As she walked past him he caught a whiff of that feminine scent that had been driving him crazy all week and his loathing ratcheted up another notch.

When they were alone in his apartment he slammed the door shut behind him and faced her.

'I was going to tell you,' she said, jumping in before he could say anything. She stood in the middle of the living area, her arms folded across her chest, her face as white as a freshly laundered sheet. 'I swear.'

'I'm sure you were,' he said with deliberate silkiness. 'Tell me, when *were* you planning on telling me? When my son was ten? When I was on my deathbed?'

'When the biography was finished.'

'You should have told me the minute you landed on Agon.' He gritted his teeth. 'You've had a whole week to tell me the truth. A whole week during which you have lied to me—so *many* lies. You sicken me.'

She blanched under the assault of his words, but straightened and kept her composure. 'I didn't know who you were until a week ago. I spent *five years* searching for an engineer called Theo, not a prince called Theseus. I thought *Theo* was Toby's father. When I realised, I had to do what was right for Toby. I had to protect him.'

He stopped his voice turning into a roar by the skin of his teeth. 'Protect him from me? His own father?'

'*Yes!* Look at you! You're a prince from a hugely powerful family with a reputation for ferocity. I didn't know *you*—I still don't. When I arrived here you were a stranger in Theo's skin. I had to be sure you posed no risk. To be honest, I'm still not sure. But I knew today that I had to tell you.'

'You *would* say that,' he said, fighting to hold on to his temper before it exploded out of him.

'It's the truth!' she cried. 'I know how much the biography means to you and I knew that to tell you before we'd finished it would derail you. I swear I was going to tell you as soon as it was done. I *swear.*'

'Stop with the swearing. Right now I don't know if I even care to believe your lies.' Something else occurred to him—something so profound he couldn't believe it had taken him so long to consider it. 'You said you were on the pill.'

She winced and gazed down at the floor. 'I lied,' she whispered. 'I'm so very sorry.'

'What?' He grabbed at his hair, then grazed his fingers down his face. 'How could you lie about such a thing?'

'I didn't mean to. I'm sorry. I wasn't thinking of the consequences,' she said, her voice muffled by her hair. 'I…'

But he didn't want to hear her excuses. There was only one thing he wanted from her, and that—*he*—was thousands of miles away.

'Where is my son?'

'At my brother's house.'

'*Where?*'

'In Oxford.'

'Where in Oxford?'

'At…' She stopped talking and raised her head to look at him. 'Why?'

'I'm going to send Nikos to collect him.'

She shook her head. 'He hasn't got a passport.'

'That is not a problem. The address?'

'You can't conjure a passport out of thin air,' she said with an air of desperation. 'There's a form that needs to be filled in, photos to be taken—it doesn't happen overnight.'

'I can make it happen overnight.'

'He's a British citizen. Only *I* can complete those forms because only *my* name is on his birth certificate.'

That cut him short.

Jo gave a hollow laugh. 'Yes, Theseus, your son has *my* name. Because his father promised he would be in touch, then probably deleted my number before the ferry had lost sight of Illya. You can condemn me for lying about being on the pill, but if you'd kept your promise I would have told you the minute the pregnancy test came back positive. You could have had your name put on that birth certificate alongside mine. If you'd told me the truth about who you were you would already *know* your son.'

That her words were mostly true did nothing to placate him. Did she really expect him to believe she would have told him? He didn't believe a word that came out of her pretty, lying mouth.

All he could think was that his son and heir had some sort of version of *'father unknown'* on his birth certificate. It was like another iced dagger being pushed through his frozen heart.

'Trust me,' he said coldly, 'I have ways of getting things done. My son will have my name and an Agon passport by morning.'

'You can't bring him here yet. He doesn't know you…'

'And it's past time that he did. Now, for the last time, give me the address.'

'I won't.' Jo refused to back down. However guilty she felt, and however understandably furious Theseus was, her first priority was her son. She would not have him frightened.

The pulse in his jaw throbbed. Her heart was beating to match it. He stalked over, crouched before her on his haunches and cupped her cheek.

'I want to see my son and you *will* facilitate this.'

He spoke the words with such quiet menace that acrid bile surged up her throat. She had never seen such naked rage before.

'Toby is not a toy,' she said, with as much steely control as she could muster, refusing to quail under the weight of his power and loathing. Strangely, his hold on her cheek, although firm, was surprisingly soothing. 'Your wish to see him does not trump his need to be and feel safe. I am not having a complete stranger whisk him away from everything he knows and loves. He's a *little boy.*'

His thumb brushed her cheekbone. 'A little boy who is my son. He belongs here in Agon.'

'Right now he belongs in England. You're a stranger to him—he needs time to get to know you before we even *think* about bringing him here.'

Was this really happening? Were they really having this discussion? She'd prepared herself for anger, or rejection, or if she was lucky faint promises of future contact—but not *this*.

'I have a four-year-old son I have never met. He *will* be brought here.'

She clamped her jaw together and forced air into her lungs. All she succeeded in doing was filling herself with his scent. She almost wished he would shout or throw something. Anything had to be better than this cool yet venomous reasoning.

'*I'm* his legal parent. I *want* you to be a part of his life, for Toby's sake, but I will not allow you to rush things.'

'How little you understand the workings of my country,'

he said, with what almost sounded like a purr—although there was nothing kitten-like about his tone. Its timbre and his stance were reminiscent of an alpha lion, getting ready to pounce. He stood up to his full height and headed to the apartment's front door. 'I have the means to bring him here and I *will* use them.'

Fresh panic clawed at her.

Where was he going?

'You *will* meet Toby, I promise. I know learning about him has come as a complete shock to you. You need time to process it—'

'Save me the psychobabble,' he cut in icily. 'All you need to think about is this: you will not be allowed to leave Agon until my son is brought here.'

Something cold and sharp pierced her chest.

'What are you talking about?' she whispered.

'I will put out an order that you're not to leave the palace without my express permission.' His lips curved but his brown eyes fired bullets at her. 'Even if you manage to escape you'll find yourself unable to leave the island. The minute you turn up at the airport or the harbour you'll be arrested.'

'You can't do that.' But the needles crawling over her skin reminded her that he could.

'You know the history of Agon as well as I do. My family may not rule the island alone any more but we do hold power. A lot of it. One phone call is all it will take.'

'Please, Theseus, think about what you're saying. I promise you will meet your son—but not like *this*.'

He turned the handle of the door. 'Do you think I will trust a single word you say when you have proved yourself to be a remorseless liar? I want my son here in his rightful home and I don't trust you to bring this about. If that means keeping you locked up until you come round to my way of thinking, then so be it.'

* * *

The clock's hands had barely turned to one a.m. when the apartment door was thrown open. Theseus strode in, a sheaf of papers in his hand.

After his threat to keep her locked up he'd left, disappearing into the maze that was the Agon Royal Palace.

She'd felt it best to let him go, hoping a little distance would give him time to calm down and see reason. She'd stayed where she was on his sofa, clutching at her hair, alternating between feeling frozen to her core one minute and burning hot the next.

And now, judging by the grim, dishevelled look on his handsome face and the wild, dangerous glint in his eye, she saw the past hour hadn't calmed him down at all.

Their time apart hadn't worked to restore her own equilibrium either, leaving her stuck in a strange form of paralysed limbo. It was almost a relief to have him charge back in.

'Fill this out and sign where the cross is,' he said without preamble, placing the papers on the bureau in the corner and stabbing the one on top with a finger.

'What is it?'

'A form acknowledging me as Toby's natural father. I need the relevant birth details from you. From this I will produce an Agon birth certificate. When you've completed this form I need you to sign this one for his passport.' He held up a pink sheet of paper. 'Nikos will fly to England and meet up with Agon's Ambassador. They will collect Toby, take his photo and produce the passport, then fly him here. Tell your brother to have Toby ready for midday.'

'Be reasonable,' she pleaded, knowing she was being backed into a corner she couldn't fight her way out of, but knowing that she *had* to fight—for Toby's sake if not her own. 'Toby will be *terrified* when two strangers turn up to spirit him away.'

'Not if he's properly prepared. You can call him first thing and tell him that two nice men are coming to bring him to you. Tell him to think of it as a great adventure.'

'If having Toby here means so much to you, then why aren't you going to get him yourself?' she asked, a sudden burst of bitterness running through her.

'Because my absence will be noted. I can't afford for anyone to know about him yet.'

'So you're going to bring him here and hide him away— is that what you're saying?'

'Only until after the Gala. That will give me almost a fortnight to get things organised and time to prepare my family—especially my grandfather—for the shock Toby's appearance will bring.'

'What are you going to do?' she demanded, spreading out her hands. 'Hide him in the dungeons? He looks *exactly* like you. Anyone will take one look at him and know he's of Kalliakis blood.'

Theseus felt his heart jolt at that information. He'd been so full of fire and fury that he hadn't yet considered what his son looked like. Or what his personality was like. *Theos*, did four-year-old boys even *have* personalities?

'I have a private villa on the outskirts of Resina,' he said, referring to Agon's capital. 'Toby will be taken there until after the Gala.'

'And what about me?' Her voice was high with anxiety. 'You can't keep him away from me. That would be beyond cruel.'

His lips curved into a sneer but he shook his head. 'Do not hold me to your own low standards. You will be taken there in the morning to wait for him.'

Not even in the darkest recess of his mind had he entertained the thought of keeping them apart—not even before he'd spoken to Dimitris and been given the hard facts about what having a child here would mean…not just for him but for Jo too.

For a moment his throat thickened as he saw the despair in her eyes.

She'd lied to him about being on the pill, he reminded himself angrily, whilst images of leaving Illya rained down in his mind.

He'd stood at the back of the ferry, staring at the woman who had helped him through one of the worst nights of his life. Jo had sat on the beach, hugging her legs and watching him leave. He'd kissed her goodbye before boarding, had tasted her sweetness for what he had thought would be the last time.

Why had he strung her along as he had? He'd never made false promises to a woman before. He'd known even as he'd stored her number in his phone that he would never call her. He'd never done that to a woman before. If he had no intention of calling, he never pretended that he would.

But she had *really* lied to him. He might have broken a minor promise to call but she had lied about being on the pill. If she hadn't told such a wicked lie…

He wouldn't have a son.

She'd hit a nerve when she'd asked why he wasn't going to collect him personally. *Theos*, he wanted to. If he had superhuman powers he would have already flown to him. And yet…

Trepidation had taken root.

He wasn't ready for this—wasn't ready to be an instant father. These few hours while his son was being brought to him would allow him to prepare himself and get his villa made suitable for a small boy.

'I'll give you twenty minutes to get the paperwork complete,' he said.

He'd left Dimitris in the palace library, researching constitutional matters, and he needed to check in with him. He could also do without Jo's accusatory stare following his every move. She had no right to look at him as if *he* were the bad guy.

If she thought things were bad for her now, she was in for a nasty shock when he told her the rest of it.

CHAPTER SEVEN

Jo HAD LONG given up trying to sleep.

It had been three hours since she'd completed those forms. She'd left them on Theseus's bureau and returned to her own apartment, locking the door behind her.

She wanted to be alone, was too mentally exhausted to cope with anything else.

Padding over to the kitchen, she poured herself a glass of water and then rummaged in her handbag for some headache tablets. Just as she popped them into her mouth there was a soft rap on the door, followed by the sound of the handle being turned.

She swallowed the tablets down, more pathetic tears swimming in her eyes. It could only be Theseus.

She didn't want to see him. Not right now, when she was so angry and heartsick that she could punch him in the face. She ignored the knock.

Her numb shock had gone…had been replaced with a burning anger that he could be so cruel. Whatever wrong she'd done—and she'd always known what a terrible wrong it was—this was infinitely worse.

All those years of searching, all those years of raising her child as a single parent, and he thought he could sweep in and turn it all upside down with no consideration for Toby's emotional state.

And there was nothing she could do about it.

Every scratch of the pen on those forms had felt like a scratch on her heart.

But what choice had she had but to sign them? Theseus was fully prepared to keep her a prisoner until Toby was brought to him. She'd seen the threat in his eyes.

What this meant for her future she didn't know. His power was too much for her to fight—more than she could ever have appreciated. She was fighting from a power base of zero.

Her head pounded. And her eyes... They'd never felt so gritty—not even when she'd spent a whole day sobbing in fear over how her mother would react to her unexpected pregnancy. The fact that her mother's only comment had been, 'For God's sake, girl, I thought you had more sense than that,' had been rather anticlimactic after all the angst she'd put herself through.

She should have known her mother wouldn't be angry. For her to be angry would mean she cared, and if there was one thing Joanne had grown up knowing it was that her mother didn't care. Harriet Brookes had done her duty. She had fed her and clothed her. But that was the extent of any mothering she'd extended towards her daughter.

Even when Jo had spent a month in hospital whilst pregnant her mother had paid only one visit, and that had been to drive her back to the frigid shell she called a home.

At least her father had shown some kindness—but she'd had to catch him at the right time if she'd wanted any coherence from him, considering he started drinking in the morning and was generally comatose in the chair in his study by mid-afternoon.

Her poor father... That weak-willed, spineless man, who'd realised too late that the pretty young woman he'd impregnated and been forced to marry was far too strong for him. He'd once said, intoxicated over Sunday dinner, that she'd emasculated him. Her mother had replied in her usual no-nonsense manner that one needed balls to begin with in order to be emasculated.

Jo had not understood why they stayed together—and had *never* understood how they'd come to make *her*.

She knew she must get some sleep. Even if she only managed a couple of hours that would be better than nothing at all.

As she was about to climb back into the huge four-poster bed she froze when she heard the click of a door being unlocked, followed by a creak.

Slowly she turned her head to look at the door adjacent to her dressing room. She'd never been able to open it and had wondered a couple of times what lay on the other side. Now she stared as it opened, too frozen with fear to move.

Fight or flight? At that moment she wasn't capable of either option.

And then Theseus stepped over the threshold, allowing her to expel the breath she'd been holding.

He looked haggard, as if the events of the night had caused him to unravel.

'You scared the life out of me!' she said, on the verge of tears with shock. Her heart had been kick-started and was now pumping at the rate of knots. 'Where did you come from?'

'You didn't answer my knock so I came through the hidden passageway connecting your apartment with mine.' He pushed the door shut with his back and folded his arms. 'We need to talk.'

'It's four o'clock in the morning.' And she was wearing nothing but an old T-shirt that only just skimmed her fortunately covered bottom.

'And you're managing to sleep as well as I am.' His eyes flickered over her, taking in her attire. 'Nikos is on his way to England. There's a helicopter on standby to fly him and the ambassador to Oxford,' he added.

Jo gnawed at her lip and tried to fight the fresh tide of panic she felt as she did the maths. With the time difference between Agon and the UK, Nikos and the ambassador would easily make it to Toby by midday—just as Theseus had promised.

'I think it would be best if I meet him at the airport.' She mentally prepared herself for another fight she knew she was in no position to win.

To her surprise he gave a sharp nod of agreement. 'I'll get that arranged.'

'And we'll go straight to your villa?' she clarified.

'Yes.'

She chose her next words with care. Theseus might have calmed down, but she was aware that his temper was currently as flammable as dry kindling. 'I know you want us to stay until the Gala, and then introduce Toby to your family, but I need to know how long you'll want us to stay afterwards so I can make arrangements with work.'

At that moment she couldn't think about the biography and the work that still needed to be done to finish it.

When Theseus didn't answer, and simply stared at her with an unfathomable expression on his handsome face, alarm bells began to chime softly, reverberating through her stomach.

'How long do you envisage us staying on Agon for?' she asked again, more forcefully.

He rubbed the back of his neck. 'Dimitris and I have been refreshing our memories of Agon laws...'

'What's that got to do with how long Toby and I stay?'

'Everything.'

The alarm bells in her stomach upped their tempo, clanging loudly enough that they seemed to echo through her skin.

The silence thickened, closing in.

'You'll be staying on Agon indefinitely.'

'What are you talking about?'

'The only way Toby can be my heir is if we marry.'

Jo felt her jaw go slack. 'You have *got* to be joking.'

'I wish I was.' Theseus closed his eyes, then snapped them open to focus on her. 'Agon law states clearly that only legitimate heirs of the royal family can be recognised and allowed to inherit.'

'I don't understand...' she whispered, although the implications were already rushing through her.

'The law was created two hundred years ago, when the eldest of King Helios the Second's illegitimate children fought with his lawful heir for the right to take the throne. To prevent such a situation happening again it was explicitly spelt out in the constitution that only legitimate heirs can be recognised.'

'But Toby wasn't born in wedlock, so he'll be illegitimate regardless.'

'Our marriage will legitimise him. There is nothing in the constitution that states that the child must have been conceived or born in wedlock—only that they must be a child of a lawful marriage.'

Her hands fluttered to her throat. Her head shook slowly from left to right as she tried to take in exactly what he was saying. 'We can't marry. The idea is just...stupid.'

'Do you think I *want* to marry you?' he said harshly. 'It's the only way I can claim Toby as my own and give him the protection of the Kalliakis name.'

'He doesn't need protection. We live in Middle England—not a war zone.'

'The minute it's made public that I have a son he'll be a target for kidnappers the world over. But that's missing the point, which is that Toby is my son and deserves to be recognised as such. He deserves to be allowed to inherit my personal wealth.'

'What would you do if you were already married?' she challenged. 'Because you surely couldn't marry me then? Unless bigamy is legal on Agon?'

'We are not in that situation, so that's irrelevant. Let me put this in simple terms for you. You and I will marry as soon as we can. If you refuse you will be escorted— alone—off Agon and never allowed to return.'

'You wouldn't…' She shook her head, swallowing back her fury and distress as the full weight of his threat hit her like a brick.

His nostrils flared and he eased himself away from the door. 'Try me. If you refuse to marry me Toby will be raised on Agon without you. He will know the reason he's not recognised as a member of his own family and is unable to be my heir is because of his mother's selfishness.'

The room swam. 'Would you really stoop so low as to keep us apart and twist his mind against me?'

He raised a strong shoulder and sauntered to stand before her, where she still stood rooted to the spot beside the bed. 'Whatever I tell him would be nothing compared to the conclusions he would draw on his own. Now, do I have your agreement?'

She backed away lest she give in to her fingers' need to slap him. She wasn't being selfish. *She wasn't*. What Theseus demanded of her was unconscionable.

A thought raced through her, which she grasped and clung on to. 'You *can't* marry me—you have to marry a princess. Remember? You told me that yourself.'

'No, I have to marry someone with royal blood—which you have.'

'But my blood is so diluted it's weaker than supermarket own-brand blackcurrant squash!' She clung on to the thought desperately, too scared to let go of this last glimmer of hope. 'My family don't have titles or acres of land. There's not a lord or a viscount in sight!'

'It's enough to satisfy the constitution. It would be different if Helios was in my position—*he* is expected to marry a princess, or someone of equal heritage. Now, for the last time, do I have your agreement?'

With her stomach curdling and her skin feeling so tight she could feel her bones pushing through the flesh, Jo blinked frantically to keep her focus, to maintain some measure of control.

There was no way out. No other avenue to take. Theseus had thought of everything and had an answer to everything.

But she wouldn't let him have it all his own way.

'Seeing as I have no choice, I'll marry you. But only for long enough to satisfy whatever draconian law your ridiculous island insists on before we can divorce.'

He shook his head, his mouth twisting into a rueful grimace. 'It is illegal for members of the Agon royal family to divorce.'

'That's not possible.' Coldness like nothing she'd experienced before crept through her bones.

'The constitution—'

But she cut him off before he could say another word. All the fear and anger that had been brewing within her converged to the point of explosion and she launched herself at him, pushing him onto the bed, her fists striking his chest.

'Your constitution can take a running jump, for all I care, and so can you,' she raged. 'I'm *not* giving up my entire life for you.'

Theseus had her hands pinned and her body trapped beneath him before she could take another breath.

'You're not sacrificing your life for me but for Toby,' he snarled, his breath hot on her face.

She could sense his fury, matching hers in its strength. Her blood was pumping so fast it heated her veins to boiling point.

She bucked beneath him, kicking her legs out wildly. 'Toby is the happiest child in the world! I've sacrificed *everything* to love and care for him and now you want me to throw our lives away just so you can lay claim to him, as if he's some possession and not a flesh and blood boy.'

'He's a prince of Agon and he deserves the protection and everything else that comes with the title.'

Theseus trapped her kicking legs with a thigh. *Theos*, the shy wallflower he'd met in Illya had more fight in her than he'd ever imagined. Even though his emotions were as intense as he'd ever known them, his body could not help but react to her.

'If *you're* a reflection of the way a prince of Agon turns out then I'd much rather he stays a commoner,' she spat back.

He gazed down at her, fully pinned beneath him, and took in the fire shooting at him from her beautiful eyes, the heightened colour of her cheeks.

'No amount of insults will change anything,' he said roughly. 'Accept it, *agapi mou*. You and I are going to marry.'

After all the lies she'd told, she should repulse him. Yet he was far from being repelled.

He'd spent a whole week with this woman's scent playing to his senses like an orchestra. A whole week fighting his fantasies, fighting his baser instincts.

Now, with her hair fanned out on the sheets like an autumnal cloud, it was like gazing down at the *Venus de Milo*. And as he stared the fire blazing from her eyes suddenly burned in a wholly different manner, her look turning from hate to confusion to desire.

She stilled, her body's only movement her heaving chest.

He *ached* for her.

They were going to marry. There was nothing to stop them acting on their desires. There was no need to fight any longer.

He brought his mouth down at the same moment she

raised her face to his, bringing them together in a mesh of lips and tongues and merging breath.

Their kisses were hard, almost cruel, all pleasure and pain at once. Everything rushed out of him, leaving behind only the desire that had held him in its tightening grip since she'd walked into the palace.

He had no recollection of releasing her hands, but a groan ripped through him when her fingers found his scalp and dug into it, her nails grazing through his hair and scratching down his neck.

There was no slow burn. Every inch of flesh she touched became scorched, and his hunger for her accelerated in a rush of blood that burned. *Everything* burned.

He pulled away to stare at her, taking in the dilation of her pupils and the heightened colour of her cheeks.

He wanted to drown in her.

Touching her, holding her… Whatever deceptions there had been between them, this hunger couldn't be faked.

He straddled her thighs and pulled his shirt over his head, too impatient to bother with the buttons. No sooner had he thrown it to the floor than her hands were flat on his chest, spreading all over him, her touch penetrating through to his veins.

It had been like this on Illya; his desire for her so instantaneous and combustible that one touch had blinded him to everything else. It had turned from nothing to the deepest desire he had ever known.

And that had been nothing compared to the way he felt at this moment.

Had he been naked he would already be buried deep inside her.

From the darkness in Jo's eyes, her short ragged breaths, the way her hands roamed his chest as if she *needed* to touch him, he could tell this desire was just as flammable for her too.

Wordlessly she lifted herself, enough for him to bunch her T-shirt up to her waist and slide it off, just as he'd done once before. As he pulled it free her russet hair fell down with the motion, sprawling over her naked shoulders and spilling out over the breasts he'd spent the past week wishing he could remember with the same clarity he remembered everything else. They were better than anything his imagination could have conjured, the nipples a dark, tempting pink.

She lay down, her smouldering eyes never leaving his face. He swooped in to kiss her again, needing to feel the sweetness of her lips merging with his own. Her arms wrapped tightly around him and her legs bucked, this time not to throw him off but in an attempt to part and wrap around him.

He shifted so the weight of his thighs was no longer trapping her and propped himself up on an elbow to gaze at her.

He couldn't stop himself from staring at her.

He'd never known his heart to beat so hard or so fast.

He ran a hand over the buttery skin of her thigh, which had risen to jut against him, and traced his fingers up over her soft stomach. He spread his hands to cover her breasts, a huge jolt of need coursing through him as he felt the joyous weight of them.

Save for her knickers, she was naked. Her curvaceous figure was every bit as enticing and womanly as the last time he'd lain with her, exuding a soft ripeness begging to be touched and tasted.

Bending his head, he caught a taut nipple in his mouth, felt more jolts bursting through him when he tasted her for himself.

Massaging her with his mouth and fingers, he used his free hand to unbuckle his belt and work off his trousers and underwear. The relief at being released from the confines of their material was immense. All that lay between them now was the cotton of her underwear.

She might not be clad in expensive silky lingerie, but he had never seen a more tempting, beautiful sight.

Joanne...a glorious *Venus de Milo* that only he knew about...

'Have there been many others?' He hauled himself up, the words falling from his tongue too quickly for him to stop them.

Her throat moved, hate suddenly flashing in her eyes. 'You have no right to ask.'

'You're going to be my wife. I have every right.' The thought of another man's eyes seeing her like this, another man's hands touching her...

'And I have every right not to answer.'

Her hand brushed down his stomach to his freed erection, encircling it. Her breaths deepened.

Theseus closed his eyes and counted to three. All thoughts of her with other men disappeared as he gritted his teeth at the delight of her gentle touch. The pressure was light—too light. Torturously light.

He swooped down to claim her mouth for his own. Whatever men there might have been in the intervening years, he would drive them from her mind. He would mark her. He would make her understand with more than words that from this moment on she would be his and only his.

For the rest of her life.

In a swarm of kisses and touches he explored her, trailing his lips over her breasts and stomach, finding a strawberry birthmark as he tugged her underwear down and threw it onto the heap of clothes piled on the floor beside them, discovering a small mole at the top of her thigh... It was all for him. All for his eyes only.

Jo thrashed beneath him, her own hands reaching out and grasping, her nails digging into his back, her hips bucking upwards, inviting his possession. She gasped and cried out when he dipped his head between her legs.

He shuddered with need.

Five years without a woman...

Was it any wonder he felt so desperately on the edge?

But he had felt like this before. Once. With Jo...

He drove the thought from his mind.

He pressed his tongue against her.

Theos, she tasted divine.

She pushed her pelvis into him, her back arching. Her little moans of pleasure were like music to his ears and he increased the friction just a little, enough so that when she grabbed at his head she caught his hair in her hands and clasped it tightly. She was on the brink.

But he didn't want her to come yet. Not this time. He wanted to read her eyes as she cried out with the pleasure of him being inside her. Selfishly, he wanted it all, and he wanted it now, before the craven need in him burst.

Trailing his tongue all the way back up her body, helpless to resist nuzzling into her gorgeous breasts once more, he lay between her parted legs and kissed her, possessing her with his mouth before guiding his erection to the heart of her and sliding into the tight, welcoming heat.

She cried out and stiffened.

'Okay?' he asked, only just able to get the word out.

Her answer was to nip at his cheek with her teeth and wrap her legs around him.

He thrust as deep as he could go, the sensations spreading through him at being fully sheathed inside her making him groan out loud.

Forget savouring the moment—he was long past that point. If he'd ever been there. All he wanted was to lose himself in the incredible feelings rushing through him, to listen to the wanton moans escaping her delicious mouth, and to find the release clamouring inside him.

As he pushed feverishly into her all he knew was that she must have some magical quality he reacted to. That she cast a spell that turned his body into a slave for pleasure.

Her response was as fevered as his own, her arms clasping him so tightly that he lay fully locked inside her, on her, fused with her into one being. Nothing mattered but this heady hunger that had to be satisfied or else they would both fall off the precipice.

Then she broke away from his kisses, pressing her cheek tightly to his own, and her moans deepened as her nails dug painfully—but oh, so pleasurably—into his back. He felt her climax swell within her, thickening around him and then pulling him into the headiness of release. Of surrender.

CHAPTER EIGHT

JO'S EYES FLEW OPEN. Instant wakefulness.

The room was dusky, the early-morning sun making its first peeks through the heavy drapes. The only sound to be heard was the deep, heavy breathing of Theseus in sleep.

She'd awoken to the same sounds on Illya. To the same weight of his arm slung around her waist, the same body pressed into her back, encircling her almost protectively.

It had been nothing but an illusion. However protectively he'd behaved in his sleep he'd sailed away the next morning and never given her another thought...

Everything came back in a flood.

Theseus learning about Toby. His demands of marriage. Making love.

Oh, Lord, what had possessed her?

Where was her pride? Her self-control?

The only crumb of comfort she could take was that whatever mad fever she'd fallen into, Theseus had fallen into it as well.

Flames licked her cheeks as she remembered how willingly she had given herself to him. His caresses and kisses had lit the touch-paper to her desperate, emotion-ridden body.

A tear trickled down her cheek and landed on her pillow. Blinking furiously, she tried her hardest to stop any more from forming but they fell through her lashes, soaking the fabric.

Helpless to stop them, she let the tears fall, wishing with

all her heart that she could turn the clock back a week and tell him about Toby the minute they'd been alone in his office for the first time. The outcome wouldn't be any different—Theseus would still be insisting on marriage, of that she was certain—but *they* would be different. This loathing wouldn't be there.

Making love wouldn't have felt like waging war with their bodies.

She'd never imagined sex could be like that—angry, yet tender, with shining highlights of bliss that had taken her to a place she'd never known existed.

It had been beautiful.

But how could she do it? How could she spend her life with a man who despised her?

Lust was transient. When desire was spent, and without a deeper bond to glue them together, hate and resentment would fill the space, and there was already enough loathing between them to fill a room.

Her parents had once lusted after each other. Her brother Jonathan had been the result of their passion and the reason they had been forced to marry. A decade later, when Jo had been born, their marriage had deteriorated into a union as cold and barren as Siberia. It was a surprise they'd thawed enough to make *her*.

For Jo, having a father who spent his days in an alcoholic stupor and a mother who treated flea-ridden hedgehogs with more compassion than she extended to her husband or daughter had been normal.

As she'd grown up and seen how other families interacted she'd slowly realised it *wasn't* normal.

And so she'd vowed never to be like them, to never treat her husband or any children she might have that way.

Her very worst nightmare was being trapped in a cold, loveless marriage like her parents.

She choked in a breath.

All her dreams were over. The nightmare had come to life.

She would never find love. And love would never find her.

Theseus would never love her. All he wanted was their son. She was the unwanted appendage that came with Toby.

She was trapped.

With fresh tears falling, she shuffled out from under Theseus's arm and rooted around until she found her T-shirt, slipped it back on and stole into the bathroom. She blew her nose, trying desperately to get a grip on herself.

She couldn't fall to pieces. All she could do was try and salvage something from this mess. If she could survive pregnancy and motherhood alone, she could survive anything.

When she stepped back into the bedroom her eyes were drawn straight to him. The dusky light solidified his sleeping form. A lock of black hair had fallen over his cheek. The lines that had etched his face since their return from the club had been smoothed away.

Her heart stuck in her throat. He looked so peaceful.

Hate was an alien emotion to her. Even throughout all the years of her mother's cold indifference she'd never hated her. Neither had she hated her father for his weakness and failure to stand up for her, nor hated her brother for being treated as if he mattered.

She didn't want to hate Theseus. He was the father of her son.

She'd loved him once. To hate him would be to turn all those memories into dust.

As she climbed back into bed, trying hard to keep her movements smooth so as not to wake him, she realised his breathing had quietened.

Pinching the bridge of her nose to stop another batch of tears from falling, she slid under the covers and held herself tightly.

After long minutes of silence, during which she became certain that he was as awake as she was, the words playing in her head finally came out. 'I want to tell you the story of a young woman who graduated from university with her virginity intact.'

She spoke quietly, keeping her eyes trained on the ceiling. She could feel his gaze upon her. If she said it as if she were talking about someone else, maybe she could tell it all without any more tears.

'That young woman had spent her life as the butt of her schoolmates' jokes—mostly on account of the size of her actual butt.'

She laughed quietly, but there was nothing funny about the memory. Jo's only truly happy memories were of that magical time on Illya and the birth of her son.

'She thought university would be different but it wasn't. She made a couple of good friends, but socially she was never accepted. She graduated with her virginity because the only men who had wanted to sleep with her had only tried it on for a bet.'

Theseus jerked, as if recoiling, but she didn't look at him. She had to stay dispassionate or she would fall to pieces, and that was the last thing she wanted. Theseus had enough power over her as it was.

'She had her life mapped out. She was finally leaving the home she'd never felt wanted in and moving to London with her friends. She even had a job lined up. And before she moved into her new life she took her first trip abroad, as a goodbye to her old life. There she met a man—a Greek engineer.'

She laughed again at her naivety.

'One night some men came into the bar and started harassing her. Her Greek crush stepped in and... Well, you know the rest.'

She swallowed and finally turned onto her side to face him. His expression in the half-light was unreadable.

'You were good to me like no one had ever been before. You *included* me. You were *nice* to me. And do you remember when you turned up at my chalet? You were a mess.'

She caught the briefest of flickers in his eyes.

'I'd never been in love before,' she whispered, staring intently at him.

His face was inches from her own, close enough for her to feel the warmth of his breath.

'I hero-worshipped you like you were a sun-kissed idol. And you needed me that night. You made me feel…*necessary*. When you kissed me…it was like a dream. You *wanted* me. That was the best moment of my life. So my lie about being on the pill came out without any thought or regard for the consequences. I didn't want that moment to end so I was stupid and reckless, and I deserve your contempt. I hate that I lied to you, and I will live with it on my conscience for the rest of my life. But even if you never believe anything else, please believe that I was going to tell you about our son and that I'm more sorry than I can ever say.'

He was silent for a long time before he hoisted himself onto an elbow to stare down at her. His eyes were penetrating, as if he were trying to read her.

Jo held her breath as she waited for him to speak.

Instead of saying anything, he turned away and threw off the covers, then swung his legs over to sit on the edge of the bed.

'That night on Illya, I behaved very badly towards you,' he said, his back to her.

'No…'

'I knew you had feelings for me. I took advantage of that.' Now he turned his head. His jaw clenched and he looked at her with hard eyes. 'But those feelings you once had for me…keep them locked away. Never let them return. You know what I expect from a marriage and there will be no place in ours for love. You need to get that in your head *now*.'

He rubbed his palm over his face, then slid his underwear on.

'Any romantic notions you may have—kill them. I will try to be a good husband to you but I will never love you. Protect your heart. Because if you don't it will not only be you who suffers for it but our son.'

She stared at him, the heart he wanted her to protect against him beating so hard that pain shuddered against her ribcage.

He pulled his trousers on, slung his shirt over his shoulder and faced her.

'My parents' marriage was a disaster. If they hadn't died so young they would have likely killed each other anyway. She loved him too much to share him; he loved himself too much and was too spoiled and pampered to deny himself anything he wanted—and that included other women. He would hit my mother for questioning his infidelities and yet, still she loved him. It was a lethal combination and not the kind of marriage I would wish on anyone. I will not have our son exposed to the horrors I witnessed. I will not have him used as a pawn in a game between two adults who should know better.'

He reached the door to the secret passage which led to his apartment and looked at her one last time.

'Just think—you will be a princess, *agapi mou*. That must go some way to mitigating the restrictions you will now face.'

'Like being a prince has in any way mitigated the restrictions *you* live with?' she countered pointedly, a tremor in her voice.

Eyes narrowed, he slowly inclined his head. 'I learned,

and you will learn too—fighting destiny is pointless. Embrace your new life. It's the only way to survive it.'

Knowing there was no chance of falling back to sleep, Theseus took a long shower, hoping the steaming water would do something to soothe the darkness that had dragged him under after his dawn-lit talk with Jo.

He hoped she'd take his warnings to heart.

She was a dreamer like his mother. He'd seen it in her eyes when he'd told her not to fall in love with him and bluntly spelt out that he would never love her.

He had done it the way a cruel child might pick the wings off an injured fly. Except he'd taken no enjoyment in destroying her dreams.

Yes, she'd told him a lie, but listening to her explain how it had been for her had released more memories and he'd found himself feeling sickened. At himself.

He'd *known* she'd had feelings for him and had taken advantage of that because he hadn't been able to cope with his grief alone. He had turned to the one person on the island he'd instinctively known would be able to give him comfort.

But he couldn't forgive her for not telling him of his son sooner. They'd spent a week working closely together and all that time she'd been keeping something life-changing from him. No, that was a deception he would struggle ever to forgive.

Yet he would try. The only way they were going to endure spending the rest of their lives together would be through mutual respect. He needed to find a way to let the anger go, otherwise his bitterness towards her would nullify any respect.

At least making love to her and those few hours of snatched sleep had driven out much of the anger, allowing him to look at the situation with a fresh perspective.

He laughed bitterly. A fresh perspective? In less than

twelve hours his whole life had changed. He'd learned he was a father. And soon—very soon—he would be a husband: a role he'd known was looming but which he had hoped to avoid a little longer...at least until after Helios had married Princess Catalina.

After years of silent dread at the thought of marrying and starting a family it turned out he had a ready-made one. He would laugh at the irony, but his humour had dried up over the past twenty-four hours.

After drying himself and dressing, he splashed cologne on his face and caught sight of his reflection in the mirror. He looked exactly like a man who had managed only two hours' sleep.

He was surprised he'd managed even those. So many thoughts in his head had clamoured for attention, the loudest of which was trying to ensure the news of his son was kept secret for another two weeks. He had a good body of personal staff in his employ, whom he trusted implicitly, but, short of keeping Jo and Toby locked up there was nothing he could do to remove the danger that someone would see them and put two and two together.

God alone knew how his grandfather would react. Would the fact that his most wayward grandson had fathered a child out of wedlock and intended to marry a woman with minimal royal blood be another disappointment to add to the long list?

He closed his eyes, his brain burning as he recalled his grandfather's words when Theseus had finally arrived back on Agon.

He'd gone straight to his grandmother's room, knowing this would be his last goodbye. His grandfather had been alone with her, holding her hand.

He'd looked at him with eyes swimming with tears. 'You're too late.'

Too late?

He'd inched closer to the bed and, his heart in his mouth, had seen the essence which made life had gone.

He'd staggered back, reeling, while his grandfather had pulled himself to his feet and faced him. The King had aged a decade since he'd last seen him.

'How could you not be here for her? She asked for you—many times—but you let her down again. And this time right at the moment she needed you the most. You disappointed her. I'm ashamed to call you my blood.'

It had been five years and still the words were as fresh to Theseus's ears as they'd been back then.

He *wanted* them fresh.

He *needed* to remember how low he'd felt and how sickened he'd been with himself. It was what kept him focused when the walls of the palace threatened to close in on him and the urge in his heart for freedom beat too hard.

A quiet knock on the door that connected his apartment with Jo's brought him out of his painful reverie.

Opening it, he found her standing there, shielding her stomach with her laptop, her eyes wary.

She'd donned a pair of black jeans and a pale blue sweater that hugged her generous curves. Her hair was damp.

'I thought you'd like to be there when I call Toby,' she said, making no move to enter the room.

His pulse raced and a lump formed in his throat.

'I've spoken to my brother and told him what's going on,' she added, pulling a wry face. 'They're expecting me to connect in the next five minutes so I can prepare Toby.'

A blast of dread shot through him.

Theseus had no experience whatsoever with children. How was he supposed to talk to his son? He didn't know the language of four-year-olds.

'I think it's best if you stay off-camera.' She looked unashamedly around his bedroom. 'Let me talk to him.'

He gave a curt nod and led her through to the living area. 'How did your brother take the news?' he asked.

'He was shocked. I don't think any of my family ever expected me to find you.' She shook her head, then flashed him a sly grin. 'I should warn you he's liable to punch you in the face for lying about your identity.'

'He's protective of you?'

'He discovered his protective gene when I had Toby.'

So at least there was one member of her family who acted as they should towards her. In Theseus's world blood looked out for blood, even if someone was in the process of spilling another's blood. That had been what had made his desertion and subsequent failure to be there during his grandmother's final hours so unforgivable.

'What about when you were growing up?' he asked, determined to keep his mind focused and far away from his own past.

'I was the nuisance kid sister, ten years younger than him. He had zero interest in me.'

'There's *ten years* between you?' Theseus thought of the tiny age gaps between him and his brothers, who had all been born in quick succession. It had led to much fighting and sibling rivalry, but it had also given them ready-made playmates—something he felt was an important aspect of a child's life, especially for children unable to form other friendships in their homeland.

'I was an accident,' she said matter-of-factly.

'Talos was a happy accident too,' he mused. 'My parents bred their heir and their spare and then two years later he came along.'

Her eyes flashed with something dark, but her lips moved into a smile. 'I don't think my mother has ever regarded me as a happy accident.'

'Surely you don't mean that?' But then he recalled how

she'd described her parents' marriage and her mother's coldness and knew that she did mean it.

'She never wanted more children. She especially didn't want a girl.'

She must have felt his shock, for she raised a shoulder in a half-shrug.

'My mother is one of four girls. Her sisters are all very girly, which she's very contemptuous of. She has no time for what she considers "frills and fancy". I don't think she actually sees herself as a woman.'

'How does she treat you?'

'My mother is difficult—my relationship with her even more so. Maybe she would have treated me differently if I'd been a boy. Who knows? Still, that's all ancient history. Let's concentrate on Toby and not on my mother.'

Jo took a long, steadying breath and brought her son's face to the front of her mind as a reminder to stay calm. Talking of her mother's contempt towards her did nothing to induce serenity.

Now that she had semi-recovered from the distress she'd felt at Theseus's reaction last night she could appreciate the charms of his apartment, which was a shop of wonders.

While his offices were functional spaces, created for maximum efficiency, his private rooms were a masculine yet homely delight. The huge living space with its high ceilings had dark wood flooring and enormous arched windows, the walls filled with vibrant paintings, ceramics and wooden carvings that had a strong South American vibe—no doubt objects collected on his travels. She remembered him telling her he'd scaled the highest peaks of the Andes and remembered how impressed she'd been. *She* had trouble scaling an anthill.

She placed her laptop on the bureau where only hours before she had been forced into signing the forms which recognised Toby as Theseus's son.

For all his fury towards her, not once had he questioned Toby's paternity. He hadn't even asked to see a photograph as evidence. But then, he'd been too busy laying down the law over his rights as a father to bother with anything so trivial as what his son actually looked like.

Stop it, she chided herself. *You can't judge him for his reaction. You don't walk in his shoes. You knew it wouldn't be easy.*

Whatever Theseus might think of her—and she knew it would be a long time before he forgave her—it seemed not to have crossed his mind that someone else might be the father, and from that she took comfort.

It was the only comfort she *could* take.

She had no idea what the future held, and that terrified her.

How could she keep her heart away from him when they would be sharing a bed and a life together? Making love…

His words of warning against loving him had come at the right time. She'd loved him once. Desperately. She couldn't take that pain again. Especially not now, when he'd categorically told her he would never love her.

She would build on the strength she had gathered over these past few years and make her heart as impenetrable to love as his.

Even if it *did* mean saying goodbye to all her dreams.

Most little girls dreamed of being princesses, but for her it had never been about that. All she'd wanted was someone to love her for who she was.

Had that really been such a big thing to want?

Shaking off the melancholy, she opened her laptop and turned it on. She took a seat and adjusted the screen.

'Do you know what you're going to say?' he asked, standing behind her, close enough for her to smell his freshly showered scent and that gorgeous cologne she could never get enough of.

She jerked her head in a nod and did a test run of the camera. 'You need to stand to my left a bit more to keep out of shot.'

His heart thumping erratically, the palms of his hands damp, Theseus watched as the call rang out from the computer.

It connected almost immediately. The screen went blue, and then suddenly a little face appeared.

'I'm eating my breakfast!' the face said, in a high, chirpy voice.

'Good morning to you too!' Jo laughed.

The face grinned and laughed as a pudgy hand pushed away a lock of black hair that had fallen over his eyes.

Theseus couldn't move. His body was frozen as he gazed at the happy little boy dressed in cartoon pyjamas.

Jo had been right.

No one looking at this child could ever doubt he was a Kalliakis. It was like looking at a living version of his own childhood photographs.

CHAPTER NINE

'I'VE DRAWN YOU another picture,' the boy—Toby—his son—was saying. 'I'll go and get it.'

The screen emptied, then seconds later he reappeared, waving a piece of paper.

'Keep still so I can see it,' Jo chided lightly.

Toby pressed the paper right to the screen.

'Wow, that's an *amazing* dinosaur,' she said.

The picture was dropped and Toby was back. 'Silly Mummy—is not a 'saur,' he said crossly. 'Is a *plane*.'

Theseus covered his mouth to stop the sudden burst of laughter that wanted to escape.

'It's good that you've drawn an aeroplane,' Jo said, clearly holding back her own amusement, 'because guess what?'

'What?'

'*You're* going on an aeroplane.'

'Wow! Am I? When?'

'Today! Two nice men are coming to collect you and you're going to get on an aeroplane with them and come and see Mummy on Agon.'

'What—now? Right now?'

'Lunchtime.'

Toby's eyebrows drew in. Theseus almost laughed again. It was the same face Talos pulled when he was unamused about something.

'Aunty Cathy is making meatballs for lunch,' he said,

as if missing that would be the biggest disappointment of his short life.

'I'm sure they'll let you eat the meatballs before you leave.'

That cheered him up. 'Can I bring my cars?'

'Of course you can.'

'And can I meet the King?'

Finally her voice faltered. 'Let's get you here first, and then we can see about meeting the King.'

'Can I meet your Prince?'

The knuckles of her fists whitened. 'Yes, sweet pea, you can definitely meet the Prince.'

'Have you got me a present yet?'

'Enough with the questions! Finish your breakfast and then go and help Aunty Cathy pack.'

The cute, mischievous face pressed right against the screen, a pair of lips kissed the monitor with a slapping noise and then the screen went blank.

Jo's shoulders rose in a laugh, then she fell quiet.

'*Have* you got him a present?' Theseus asked, breaking the heavy silence that had come over the room.

She shook her head, keeping her gaze fixed on the computer screen. 'I was going to get him something from the museum gift shop when I'd finished the biography.'

Suddenly she seemed to crumple before him, her head sinking into her hands.

'God, what are we going to do about the biography?'

With all that had been going on the biography had completely slipped from his mind.

Theos. Right then all he could see was that little face, so like his own—the child he had helped create.

So many emotions were driving through him, filling him so completely that he felt as if his heart might explode out of his chest.

She staggered to her feet. 'I need to get back to work.'

Her face was white. He could see how much keeping her composure in front of their son had cost her.

'Now?'

'Yes. Now. I need to do something.' Her hands had balled back into fists. 'We're turning his life upside down, ripping him away from everything and everyone he knows—'

'No,' he cut in. 'You can't think of it like that. We're building him a new, *better* life.'

'I *am* trying to think of it like that. I'm trying not to be selfish and not to think of the personal cost. I'm trying not to think that I'm throwing away my future happiness just so you can secure your heir when your heir is happy exactly as he is!'

The colour on her face had risen to match the raising of her voice.

'He will be happy *here*,' he said with authority. He would ensure it. Whatever it took.

But would she…?

'We will work together to make him happy,' he added in a softer tone.

She breathed heavily, then unfurled her fists and gave a long sigh. She nodded almost absently.

He watched her closely to see if she had herself under control.

'The book needs to be finished. Are you sure you can carry on with it?'

Her face twitched and she looked away, biting into her lip. Then she seemed to shake herself and met his gaze. 'Your grandfather is our son's great-grandfather. He is a remarkable man and deserves to have his story told. I will do it for him.'

Those blue-grey eyes held his, and understanding flew between them.

Jo understood.

'But *you'll* need to do the bulk of the childcare when

Toby gets here,' she added, after a beat in which the tension between them had grown thick enough to swim through.

'I know nothing about childcare.'

She laughed, but there was no humour in the sound. 'You're the one insisting on being an instant father. I'll work until he arrives—the distraction will be good for me—but when he gets here… Trust me, there is nothing like an energetic four-year-old to put the brakes on whatever you're supposed to be doing.'

'How much longer do you think you'll need to get it finished?'

'I can make the deadline, but I will need help with Toby for the next few days.'

'I have excellent staff at my home who will happily entertain a child.' He began to think who amongst them would be best placed for the job.

Jo's eyes hardened, then sent him a look he was already starting to recognise—it was the mother tiger preparing to appear.

'You are not turning his life upside down only to palm him off on *staff*,' she said steadily. 'Being a father requires a lot more than marrying the child's mother, giving him a title and writing him into your will.'

His temperature rose at her implied rebuke, but he spoke coolly. 'I know exactly what being a father entails, but it is impossible for me to put all my work and duties to one side without prior planning.'

'Don't lie to me.' Her eyes flashed a warning. 'There have been enough lies between us. Now we draw a line in the sand and tell no more. From now on we speak only the truth. You want Toby here and in your life, so it's up to you to forge a relationship with him. You're the adult, so it must come from you. He's a sociable, gregarious boy and I know that the second he learns you're his father he'll be stuck to your side like glue.'

That was what scared him.

Theseus remembered being a small boy and wanting nothing more than his father's attention. But his father's attention had been wrapped up entirely in his eldest son and heir, Helios. As the spare, Theseus had never been deemed worthy of his father's time, had always been left trailing in Helios's wake.

The favouritism had been blatant, and with only a year between them Theseus had felt the rift deeply. His mother had tried to make up for it, lavishing him with love, but it hadn't been enough. It had been his father's respect and love he had so desired.

What if Toby found him lacking? What if he was as great a disappointment as a father as he had been as a son and a grandson?

He needed time.

His overriding priority was to get his son safely to the island and under his protection. Anything after that…

'I will make the necessary arrangements after I have spoken to Helios,' he said, ignoring her swift intake of breath. 'There is much to arrange, *agapi mou*,' he continued smoothly. 'A prince's wedding on this island is usually a state affair, but I am not prepared to wait for the months of planning that will take. I am going to tell Helios of our plans—I want my ring on your finger as soon as it can be arranged.'

'I thought you were going to keep things a secret until after the Gala?' This time there was no hiding her bitterness. He knew he was railroading her into this marriage, but he also knew it was the best course of action for all of them—especially for Toby.

'Only from my grandfather. Since we've known of his illness Helios has been running things in preparation for when…' He shook his head. She knew when. 'Helios's staff can work with mine to get the preparations up and running.'

'You don't hang around, do you?'

'Not when it comes to important matters, no.'

She rubbed her eyes, then sighed. 'Will Helios want to meet me?'

'For sure. But don't worry about it—he's a good guy.'

'And what about Talos? Will you tell him too?'

'If I can get him to myself for more than a minute. He's working closely with the Gala's solo violinist, and if the rumours are to be believed—which they probably are, as palace gossip here is generally reliable—she's playing more than just her violin for him.'

Jo gave a bark of surprised laughter at his innuendo.

He grinned as the sound lightened his heart. That was better. Seeing Jo laugh was a whole lot better than seeing her cry.

He might not be anywhere near a place of forgiveness, but he was no sadist.

He swallowed down the notion that seeing Jo cry felt like a knife being stabbed in his heart.

The sun had long gone down over Theseus's Mediterranean beachside villa when the driver pulled to a stop outside. Toby had fallen asleep in the car, curled up in her arms. According to Nikos he'd spent the entire flight talking. No wonder he was so exhausted.

But, other than being worn out with all the travel and excitement of the day, Toby had been his usual happy self and overjoyed to be with his mummy.

The butler, a man who looked as if he should be surfing in Hawaii rather than running a prince's household, was there to greet them. Nikos took Toby's suitcase inside, leaving Jo, at her insistence, to carry Toby inside.

She'd packed her clothes and then worked on the biography until the call had come through that the plane was circling above the island. Dimitris had accompanied her to the airport. She'd had no idea where Theseus was; she hadn't seen him since the morning.

Her blood had boiled. She had been totally unable to believe that the man who was turning three lives inside out was failing to meet his own son.

Now, as she followed the butler inside, treading over the cool marble tiles, she wondered if all her work stuff had been brought over as Dimitris had promised. She hoped they'd remembered to bring her suitcase. There were so many things to think of her head was full enough to overspill.

Although not as grand as the palace—how could *any* dwelling possibly compare with that?—Theseus's villa had an eclectic majesty all of its own. The façade a dusky yellow, the interiors were wide and spacious; filled with more of the South American vibe she'd felt in his palace apartment. Bold colours, stunning canvases and statuettes— homely, yet rich. A place she felt immediately at ease in.

It was the kind of vibe she'd always imagined Theo's home would have.

Shivers coiled up her spine.

For all of Theseus's talk that Theo didn't exist, this house proved that he did.

She and Toby had been given rooms opposite each other on the second floor. Toby's was large and airy, with a double bed. His sleepy eyes widened to see it.

'Is that mine?' he asked, yawning.

'While we're here, yes.' Placing him on the bed, she rooted through his suitcase until she found a pair of pyjamas.

'How long are we staying for, Mummy?'

What could she say? He'd only just arrived. Did she have to tell him so soon that their stay here would be for ever and that the life he knew and loved was gone?

She was saved from having to answer by a soft tap on the door. A young woman, no older than twenty, stood at the doorway almost bouncing with excitement. She introduced herself as her maid, Elektra.

'My maid?' Jo asked, puzzled.

'Yes, *despinis*. I am excited to meet you and your son.'

Elektra stepped into the room. When she looked at Toby her eyes widened. 'He has—'

'I need to get Toby settled down for the night,' Jo interrupted, certain the maid was about to make a reference to Toby's likeness to Theseus. 'If you give me ten minutes, then you can show me what's what.'

Understanding flashed in Elektra's eyes. 'I'll unpack your cases. Nice to meet you, Toby.'

When she was alone with her son, Jo got him washed, teeth brushed and into his pyjamas. He was already falling asleep when she kissed him goodnight and slipped from his room, going across the corridor into her own.

She stepped inside on weary feet, but still had enough energy to sigh with pleasure at the room's graceful simplicity and creamy palette. Looking at the four-poster bed, with its inviting plump pillows, she knew she at least had a sanctuary that was all her own. This room was entirely feminine.

Her chest squeezed and she shut her eyes tight, fighting back a sudden batch of tears.

Shouldn't she be happy? She was going to be a princess! Her son would never want for anything ever again. There would be no more juggling money or eking out her salary, no more shame at sending Toby to preschool with trousers an inch too short. As Theseus's son he would have the best of everything, from clothing to education. And so would she, as his wife.

She would never have to struggle again.

She should be as happy as one of her mother's pampered animals.

So why did she feel so heartsick?

* * *

The villa sat in silence when Nikos dropped Theseus off outside the main door.

Philippe, his young, energetic butler, greeted him. After exchanging a few words about the two new members of the household, Theseus dismissed him for the night.

At the palace there were always staff members on shift. If he wanted a three-course meal at three o'clock in the morning, a three-course meal would appear. Always somewhere there would be activity.

Here, in his personal domain, away from stuffy protocol, he liked a more relaxed, informal atmosphere. If he wanted a three-course meal at three o'clock in the morning he would damn well make it himself. Not that he could cook anything other than cheese on toast—a hangover from his English boarding school days and still his favourite evening snack.

Tonight he was too tired to eat.

Dragging himself up the stairs on legs that felt as if they had weights in them, he reached the room his son slept in. He stood at the partly open door for an age before stepping inside.

A night light in the shape of a train had been placed by the bed, giving the room a soft, warm glow. On the bed itself he could see nothing but a tiny bundle, swamped by the outsized proportions of the sheets, fast asleep.

He trod forward silently and reached Toby's side. All that was visible of him in the pile of sheets was a shock of black hair. He stood there for a long time, doing nothing but watching the little bundle's frame rise and fall.

He waited for a feeling of triumph to hit him.

His son was here, sleeping in his home, safe under his protection. But there was no triumph he could discern in the assortment of emotions raging through him, just a swelling of his chest and a tightness in his gut.

He went to lean over and kiss him but stopped. If he woke him it would scare him. In his son's eyes Theseus was a stranger.

Jo's bedroom door opposite was also ajar. A light, fruity scent pervaded the air. He went in and stuck his head around the open en-suite bathroom door.

Jo lay in the sunken bath, her russet hair piled on top of her head, her eyes shut.

She must have sensed his presence for she turned her head, jolted, and sat up quickly, sloshing water everywhere. She folded her arms to cover her breasts and glared at him.

'Sorry—I didn't mean to scare you,' he said, his mood lifting. After feeling as if he could fall asleep standing up, he now felt a burst of energy zing through him at seeing her in all her delicious nakedness. Not that he could see much of her; the bath was filled with so many bubbles he suspected she'd poured in half the bottle of bubble bath.

'Have you never heard of knocking?' she asked crossly.

'The door was open,' he said with a shrug.

She lay down again, still keeping her arms across her breasts. She raised her left thigh and twisted slightly away from him, to keep her modesty. 'I kept the door open so I could hear if Toby woke up.'

He perched on the edge of the bath. 'Does he normally wake?'

'No, but he's been flown here from England to this strange place with hardly any warning—that's got to be un-settling.' Her accusatory glare dared him to contradict her.

'He's fast asleep now,' he pointed out reasonably. He studied her face, taking in the dark shadows under her eyes. 'You look as if you'll be fast asleep soon too.'

'I'm shattered.' Thus saying, she smothered a yawn, al-though still taking care to cover as much of her breasts as she could.

'It's been a long day,' he agreed, unable to tear his eyes

away from her. Every inch of her was perfect, from the autumn-leaf-coloured hair to the softly curved stomach and shapely legs. She was a treasure trove of womanly delights he was certain had not been shared by many others.

Her cheeks coloured under the weight of his stare. 'Did you speak to Helios?'

'Yes.'

'How did he react?' She looked as if she hoped his brother had put the brakes on their marriage.

'He was shocked.'

An understatement. Helios had looked as if he'd walked into a door. But after he'd got over the shock he'd given his full, enthusiastic backing. Thinking back, there had been something in his brother's manner which had made Theseus think Helios was relieved, but he couldn't for the life of him fathom why.

'He was also in agreement that we should keep it from our grandfather until after the Gala.'

Her eyes narrowed. '*It*? Do you mean *Toby*?'

'I mean the whole situation—Toby and our forthcoming marriage.'

He leaned forward and traced a thumb over her cheekbone. 'The date has been set for a fortnight after the Gala. We marry in four weeks.'

CHAPTER TEN

WITH TINGLES CREEPING along her skin at his touch, Jo swallowed. 'Four weeks? That soon?'

'Yes, *agapi mou*. Helios agrees the sooner the better.'

'But he has his own wedding to arrange. Shouldn't his take precedence?'

His thumb brushed over to dance around her ear. 'His will be a large state affair and will take months to arrange.' His voice thickened. 'Ours will be more intimate. There will have to be some pomp to it, as that is expected, but nothing like his.'

Jo closed her eyes, thinking her head might just spin off. Four weeks… *Four weeks?*

Who the hell could organise a royal wedding in four weeks? She knew he wanted to get his ring on her finger quickly, but this…

Her eyes flew open as she felt his fingertips trail down her neck to her chest, then dip lower to run gently along the top of her cleavage. He took hold of her arms, still stubbornly covering her breasts, and gently prised them apart, exposing her to him.

'You're beautiful,' he murmured. 'Don't hide yourself from me.'

She sucked in air, willing herself not to respond.

'You're going to be my wife,' he continued, a finger now encircling a nipple. 'And you might already have the cells of a new life growing within you,' he added, reminding her of their failure to use contraception the night before, something that hadn't yet been spoken of.

His hand flattened over her stomach and continued to move lower.

'Think of how much fun we can have while we make another spare for the throne.'

'What a crass thing to… *Ohhh*…' Her head fell back as he reached under the bubbles to rub a finger against her, the pleasure like salve on a wound.

She should tell him to stop. She should be outraged that he would behave so proprietorially, as if her body were his to do with as he liked…

But his touch felt so good, somehow driving out all the angst she'd been carrying. The gentle friction increased and sensation built inside her.

'You're getting wet,' she whispered, struggling to find her voice under this assault on her senses.

His eyes gleamed and dilated, and he increased the pressure a touch. 'So are you.'

His free hand cradled her head, pulling her up to meet his mouth and begin a fresh assault with his lips.

'You are remarkably responsive,' he murmured, moving his mouth across her cheek and burying his face in her neck, then moving down to taste her breast, all the while keeping the pressure of his hand firm.

It was as if he knew her body better than she did—as if he knew exactly what she needed—bringing her to a peak until the pleasure exploded out of her, making her clamp her thighs around his hand and cry out as she gripped his scalp and clung to him.

He kissed her again, riding the shudders rippling through her body, murmuring words that deepened the sensations, until she felt weak and depleted and utterly dazed.

Where had *that* come from?

How was it possible to go from nothing to total bliss in seconds?

Theseus brought her to life, made all the atoms that created her fuse together into a bright ball of ecstasy that stopped her thinking and left her only feeling.

He kissed her one more time. 'On your feet.'

Beyond caring that she was naked, Jo held his hand for support and stood, water and foamy bubbles dripping off her. Immediately she was enveloped in his arms and pressed against his hard chest, his fresh, deeply passionate kisses preventing her legs from falling from under her.

She knew Theseus was strong, but his lifting her out of the bath took away what little was left of her breath. When he stood her on her feet she gazed up at him in wonderment, her heart swelling as she took in the defined angles of his face and the dark, dizzying desire ringing from his eyes.

One touch and she melted like butter for him.

Was it possible that one touch and he melted for her too...?

His white shirt had become transparent with the soaking her wet body had just given it, leaving the dark hairs of his chest vivid, emphasising his deep, potent masculinity.

Theseus caught her look. 'Do you want to take it off?'

She didn't answer, simply flattened her hands over his pecs, delighting in the feel of him.

She worked on his buttons, tugging the shirt open and sliding the sleeves off his muscular arms, gazing greedily at his magnificent torso, the smooth olive skin, the dark hair...

'Damn, you are so sexy,' he muttered, breathing into her hair and pulling her close. His hands raced up and down her back, then moved lower to cup her bottom.

She believed him. She could sense it in the urgency of his words and the rapid beat of his heart reverberating in her ear.

And then she was back in his arms, with his hot mouth

devouring hers, pressing her backwards to the chair in the corner of the room.

Holding her tight, he sat her down, then sank to his knees before her, unfastening the buttons and zipper of his trousers.

'You have no idea what you do to me,' he growled, biting gently into her neck.

Emboldened, she cupped his chin and stared into his liquid eyes. 'It's nothing that you don't do to me.'

Their mouths connected again in a kiss that blew away the last of her coherence. All she could do was feel…and it all felt incredible, every touch scalding her, every kiss marking her. She was losing herself in him.

His arms tightened and pulled her to the edge of the chair, then he guided himself to her and pushed inside her with one long thrust.

She stilled in his arms, closing her eyes as she savoured the feel of him inside her, filling her. When she opened them again he was staring right at her, as if trying to peer into the innermost reaches of her mind.

Their lips came together in the lightest of touches. With his arm still around her, Theseus began to move. Hesitantly at first she moved with him, but soon the last of her inhibitions vanished and she found his rhythm, holding on to him as tightly as she could.

As the speed of his thrusts increased she clung to him, her lips still pressed to his, their breaths merging into one. Dark heat swirled and built between them, until the sensations he'd released in her such a short time ago spilled over again—yet somehow deeper and *fuller*—and she was crying out his name.

She managed to hold on to it, riding the climax until his hands gripped her and he thrust into her one final time.

When the shudders coursing through his great body finally subsided he enveloped her in his arms. With her face buried in his neck, his hands stroking her hair, the strong thud of his heart reverberating through him to her, the moment was as close to bliss as Jo had ever known.

She wanted to cry when he finally disentangled himself. She couldn't speak. She could hardly think.

What was he *doing* to her?

'You're cold,' he chided, his voice hoarse.

So she was. After the warmth of the bath and the heat of Theseus's body the chill felt particularly acute.

He pulled a large fluffy white towel from the heated towel rack and gently wrapped it around her.

It was such a touching gesture that her heart doubled over, aching with a need she knew could never be fulfilled no matter what beautiful things he did to her body.

'I need to get some sleep,' she muttered, no longer able to look at him.

'We both do,' he agreed. 'But first I need a shower. I'll join you in a few minutes.'

Anxiety fluttered through her. 'You can't sleep *here*,' she said, ignoring the fact that this was Theseus's home and he could sleep wherever he liked.

His eyes narrowed.

'If Toby wakes up and sees you in my bed it will confuse him.'

'He's not used to seeing you with men?' Theseus's question was delivered evenly, but with an undertone she couldn't distinguish.

'No. Never.'

His lips clamped into a tight line before he nodded. 'We're going to spend the rest of our lives together. He will have to get used to us sleeping together.'

'You mean we'll share a bed?'

'It's the only upside of marriage,' he said sardonically, pulling his trousers up. 'We'll have our own separate rooms, but I have no intention of sleeping in a cold bed alone when we can keep each other warm.'

'It's too soon. Toby will need time.'

I'll need time, she almost added. Night after night of being held in his arms, made love to... Where would that leave her already frazzled emotions?

Theseus slipped his shirt back on and fixed her with a hard stare.

'I will allow you to sleep alone for the next couple of nights, so Toby isn't upset in the morning, but from then on we will sleep together. For the avoidance of any doubt: our marriage might not be a love match but it *will* be a real marriage.'

She nodded, her chin jutting up. 'Fine. But just so you know, I snore.'

He shook his head and laughed, killing the dark atmosphere that had been brewing between them. 'I thought you said you didn't want there to be any more lies between us?'

Theseus slept long and deep, but when he awoke he didn't feel refreshed. On the contrary—he felt as if he'd slept through a battle.

Apprehension lay heavily on him. He debated with himself whether to have his breakfast brought to his room but then dismissed the idea. He'd never been scared of anything in his life. Why should he be frightened of a four-year-old boy?

Making his way downstairs, he headed towards the dining room, where voices could be heard.

Swallowing to try and rid himself of the lump in his throat, he entered to find Jo and Toby seated at the table.

They fell silent. Toby's spoon hovered between his cereal bowl and his mouth, his dark brown eyes widening.

Jo placed a hand on his back and shuffled her chair closer to him. 'Toby, this is Theseus.'

'Are you the Prince?' Toby asked, his eyes still as wide as an owl's.

Theseus nodded. That damn lump in his throat was still there.

One of the maids came into the dining room to take his breakfast order. He used the time to collect his thoughts and sit opposite his family.

After his coffee was poured for him the maid bustled off, leaving the three of them alone in the most awkward silence he had ever experienced.

Toby gawped at him as if he'd been taking lessons from a goldfish. 'Do you have a crown?'

'No.' Theseus could not take his eyes off him. He hadn't known children could be so perfectly formed and so damnably cute. 'My grandfather does, though.'

'Is he the King?'

'He is.'

Toby's face screwed up. 'Does he have a flying carpet?'

'I'm sure he would like one,' he said, and laughed, feeling the tension slowly lessen.

'Do *you* have a flying carpet?'

'No, but I *do* have some really fast sports cars I can take you for a drive in.'

Toby pulled a face Theseus recognised as the one which Jo made when she was unimpressed about something.

'If I ever get a flying carpet you'll be the first person I take on it,' Theseus said, ignoring Jo's raised eyebrows.

Now Toby beamed. *'Yes!'*

And just like that his son came to life, peppering him with questions about being a prince, demanding to know if they still kept 'naughty men' in the dungeons and asking if there were any dinosaurs at the palace.

This was *much* easier than Theseus had envisaged.

The knots in his stomach loosened and he relaxed, enjoying the moment for what it was: the first of many meals he would share with his son over the course of the rest of his life.

'Has your mother told you who I am?' he asked when they'd all finished eating and Toby had finally paused for breath.

Jo's eyebrows rose again and she straightened.

'You're a prince!'

'Would *you* like to be a prince?'

Toby contemplated the question, twiddling with the buttons of his pyjamas. 'Would I have to kiss girls?'

Theseus's eyes flickered to Jo. 'Not if you didn't want to.'

'Would I have a flying carpet?'

'No, but you could have horses, and when you're old enough sports cars like mine.'

'I *would* like to be a prince,' Toby said, as if confiding something important. 'But when I'm growed up I want to clean windows on a ladder.'

'You could do both,' Theseus said gravely, fighting to stop his lips from twitching in laughter. 'You see, Toby, you *are* a prince.'

'Mummy says I'm a cheeky monkey.'

'My mummy used to say the same thing to my brother Talos. He was a cheeky monkey when he was a little boy—just like you.'

'I'm not little,' Toby said indignantly, lifting his arm and flexing it to show off his non-existent muscles. 'I'm a big boy. I'm going to big school in September.'

As she relaxed from her previously ramrod-straight position it was obvious Jo was fighting her own laughter. Finally she took pity and stepped in to save him.

'Remember what Mummy told you about having a Greek daddy who was lost?'

Toby nodded.

'Well, Mummy's found him. Theseus is your daddy.'

A look of utmost suspicion crossed his tiny face. 'My daddy's name is Theo—not Theseus.'

'Theo's his nickname,' she said smoothly, although her eyes darted to Theseus with an expression that sliced through his guts.

She really *had* spoken of him to their son...

'Theseus is his real name.'

Toby contemplated him some more. 'You're my daddy?'

'Yes. And because I'm a prince, that means you're a prince too.'

The suspicion vanished, a beaming smile replacing it. 'Does that mean Mummy is a princess?'

'Kind of,' Jo said, taking control again. 'How would you like to spend the day with Theseus? He can tell you all about being a prince. Ask him anything you like—he just *loves* answering questions. And you can explore this brilliant house with him.'

Toby nodded really hard, his eyes like an owl's again.

Theseus felt his own eyes widen too, at the underhand stunt Jo had just pulled, but knew he couldn't say anything to the contrary—not unless he wanted to disappoint his son on their first meeting.

She kissed Toby's cheek and threw Theseus a beatific smile. 'He's not a fussy eater, so ignore him if he tells you he doesn't like carrots. Have fun!'

And with that she left the dining room, leaving Theseus with the miniature version of himself.

Jo turned her head in time to see Theseus step into the room that had been converted into an office for her. He closed the door behind him and folded his arms.

'What?' she asked innocently.

'You are a cruel woman.'

'It was for the greater good. Have you had a good day?'

A half-smile played on his lips. 'It's been something. I've

left Toby in the kitchen with Elektra and the kitchen staff—
he's already got them eating out of his hands. They're baking flapjacks for him.'

'Flapjacks are his favourite.'

'He made a point of telling all of us that.'

She sniggered. 'You must be exhausted.'

He nodded. 'Does he ever stop?'

'Stop what? Talking? Or wanting to do things?'

'Both.'

'Nope. I swear he's got rocket fuel in his veins. Still,
he sleeps really well—that must be when he recharges his
batteries.'

'And he eats so *much*!' He shook his head with incredulity.

'Tell me about it,' she said drily. 'He costs a fortune to
feed.' She stretched her back, which had gone stiff after
hours hunched over the laptop. 'Other than being worn out,
how did you get on?'

'I think he had a nice time.'

'Sorry for coercing you into it,' she said, without an
ounce of penitence in her tone.

Theseus brushed a stray lock of hair from his eyes. 'I'm
glad you did. I admit I was a little nervous. All I know of
children is what I remember from my own childhood, and
that was hardly normal.'

'No, I suppose it wasn't,' she said softly, wondering how
anyone could have a normal childhood after losing both
parents at the age of nine as well as being something akin
to a deity in his own country. 'I know being an instant father is going to be hard, but this is what you wanted. All
you can do is try your hardest and make the best of it.'

'Is that what you're doing?' he asked, a strange expression on his face.

'That's all I've done since I found out I was pregnant.
I will try my hardest to make our marriage work but only

because it's best for Toby, and not because you've black-mailed me into it.'

He winced, then nodded sharply. 'That's all I can ask from you.'

'But first we need to get this biography finished. Right now I can't think of anything else.' Well, she could. She just didn't want to...

The words she'd spouted about parenthood had come from the same store of pragmatism that had driven her to move out of her family home when Toby had been three months old and she'd realised that her mother's indifference to her only daughter had extended to her only grandson.

It had been a particularly chilly day, and the manor had been even more draughty than usual. She'd put the heating on. Her mother had promptly turned it off, overriding Jo's protests with a sharp, 'If the child's cold, put another blanket on him.'

In the snap of two fingers Jo had known she had to leave. She'd gone straight into action, borrowing money from her brother to rent a tiny flat from a sympathetic landlady.

She'd refused to dwell on it. Whatever the future held for them, she'd reasoned at the time, it would be better for Toby than living with her parents.

She didn't want her son running up to his grandmother and being met with cold indifference, or thinking that drinking a bottle of whisky a day was normal.

Jo had spent her childhood devouring her mother's cakes, getting fatter and fatter in the process, all in the vain hope of gaining attention—even if only a reprimand for eating too much. She hadn't been worth even that...not even when the school nurse had sent a letter home warning that Jo was dangerously overweight. Her mother had carried on letting her eat as much as she liked. She simply hadn't cared.

Jo would rather have put her head in a vice than put Toby through that.

Much like the time she'd left home, to think of her future now was to feel a weight sink in her stomach and drag her to the floor. Finishing the biography had turned into a godsend. If she kept her mind active and distracted she would survive.

'How have you done today?'

'I'm nearly there. I emailed you an hour ago with the latest chapters.'

'I'll read them after dinner,' he promised. 'We'll be eating at six—does that suit you?'

'That's early for you.'

'I didn't think Toby would last much longer than that. He's been saying he's starving since half an hour after lunch.'

She smiled, unable to believe how deeply that touched her. 'I'll stop now and do some more tonight. If I fuel myself with caffeine there's a good chance I'll get it finished before the sun comes up.'

'Don't kill yourself.'

'It's what I signed up for.'

He inclined his head, his chest rising. 'I'm going to catch up on some work. I'll see you at dinner.'

Dinner itself was a relaxed affair. Toby happily wolfed down the spaghetti bolognaise the chef had made especially for him, but with the threat that tomorrow he would have to learn to eat 'proper' Agon fare.

'Are chicken nuggets from Agon?' he'd asked with total solemnity, to many smothered smiles.

All things considered, however, his son's first day on the island had gone much better than Theseus could have hoped. He'd enjoyed being with him, which he hadn't expected.

Maybe he *could* do this fatherhood thing.

'I have to go to the palace in the morning. I thought I'd borrow my brother's dog and bring him back. We could take him for a walk on the beach,' he said to Toby, who had insisted on sitting next to him, which had filled him with pride.

'Can I go to the palace with you?' he asked hopefully. His face and T-shirt were covered in tomato sauce.

'Not yet. It's too busy there at the moment. I'll take you in a week or two.'

Toby thought about this answer, then darted panicked eyes to his mother. 'Am I still going to Ellie's party on Saturday?'

Now Jo was the one to look panic-stricken. 'I'm sorry, but we're going to have to miss that.'

'But Aunty Cathy's got me a Waspman outfit.'

'I know… I know.'

She inhaled deeply through her nose and smiled at their son, a smile that looked forced to Theseus's eyes.

'We'll do something fun on Saturday to make up for missing it.'

'But I want to go to Ellie's party. You *promised*.'

To Theseus's distress, huge tears pooled in Toby's eyes and rolled down his cheeks, landing on his plate.

He placed a tentative hand on his son's thin shoulder, wanting to give comfort, but Toby shrugged it away and slipped off his chair to run around the table to Jo and throw himself into her arms.

She shoved her chair back and scooped him up, sitting him on her lap so he could bury himself in her softness.

'I want to go home!' Toby sobbed, his tiny frame shaking.

'I know… I know,' she soothed again, stroking his hair.

She met Theseus's gaze. He'd expected to see recrimination in her stare, but all he could see was anguish. She dropped a kiss on Toby's head, saying nothing more, just letting him cry it out.

Only when he'd stopped sobbing and blown his nose did she say, 'How about we ask the chef for some ice cream?'

Toby nodded bravely, but still clung to her.

Theseus remembered the cold days that had followed his return to the palace from his sabbatical. Night after night he'd lain in his bed, in the moonless dark, and had found his thoughts returning over and over to the woman he'd met on Illya. To Jo.

He would have given anything—all his wealth, his royal title, everything he had—to be enfolded in her arms once again and to feel her gentle hands stroke his pain away... just as they were doing now to their son.

The image of her sitting on the beach watching him sail away had haunted him until he'd blotted her from his mind.

'I'll see to it,' he said, getting to his feet and making no mention of the bell that he could ring if he required service. Suddenly he was desperate to get out of the dining room.

He did not want the look of gratitude Jo threw at him. He didn't deserve it. Toby's distress was *his* fault.

As soon as he was out of the room and out of their sight he rubbed at his temples and blew out a breath of air.

He couldn't explain even to himself how agonising he'd found that scene.

CHAPTER ELEVEN

Jo HIT 'SEND' and threw her head back to gaze at the ceiling.

She'd done it. She'd finished the biography.

Theseus had given her the green light on the chapters she'd completed earlier and she'd forwarded them to her editor in Oxford. All that was left was for Theseus to approve the last two.

Once she'd imagined that she would want to celebrate. Now she felt that any celebration would be more like a wake.

Her work hadn't just opened up the King's life for her, but the lives of his family too. *Theseus's* life. This was a family bound by blood and duty.

When she'd arrived on Agon she'd been too angry at Theseus's deception to understand why he'd lied about his identity. Now she understood.

He'd spent his entire life being scrutinised, having his every waking hour planned for him—whether at home in the palace, at boarding school, or in the armed forces. His life had never been his own to do as he wanted. He really *had* been like a trapped grown lion in a tiny cage.

No wonder he had kicked back. Who could blame him for wanting to experience what most people took for granted?

But now he was a model prince—a model Kalliakis.

She admired him for the way he handled his role, but wondered what it had cost him.

He'd been happy on Illya. Here, it was clear he did his duty but she saw no joy in it for him.

Stretching her back, she listened carefully. Unlike in the palace, where there was always the undercurrent of movement even if it couldn't be heard, the villa lay in silence. If she strained her ears she could hear Toby snoring lightly in his bedroom next door to her makeshift office. After his earlier meltdown she'd worried he would struggle to sleep, but he'd been out for the count within minutes of his head hitting the pillow.

She'd felt so bad for Theseus, who had watched the unfolding scene with something akin to horror. She wished she could ask him what he'd been thinking, but no sooner had their dessert been cleared away than he'd excused himself. Other than his email confirming approval for the earlier chapters she hadn't heard from him.

She'd bathed Toby and put him to bed alone. Theseus hadn't even come to give him a goodnight kiss.

Had that been the moment when the reality of parenthood had hit home and he'd decided that keeping his distance was the way forward? Not having to deal with any of the literal or figurative messy stuff?

Inexplicably, hot tears welled up, gushing out of her in a torrent. She didn't try to hold them back.

She didn't have a clue what she was crying about.

When Theseus returned to the villa from the palace the next day, the beaming smile Toby gave him lightened the weight bearing down on his shoulders.

Toby even jumped down from his seat at the garden table where he and Jo were sitting and ran to him.

It was only when he got close that Theseus realised all of Toby's joy was bound up in Theseus's companion—Helios's black Labrador. It didn't matter. It was good to see him smile after his misery the night before.

'What's his name?' Toby asked, flinging his arms around the dog's neck.

'Benedict.'

Luckily Benedict was the softest dog in the world, and happy to have a four-year-old hurtle into him. His only response was to give Toby a great big lick on the cheek. If Benedict had been a human he would have been a slur on the Kalliakis name, but because he was a dog everyone could love him and fuss over him unimpeded.

'That's a silly name for a dog.'

'I'll be sure to tell my brother that,' he answered drily, not adding that his brother was in fact Toby's uncle. He didn't want to upset him any more, and had no idea what the triggers might be.

'Can we take him for a walk on the beach?'

'Sure. Give me five minutes to change and we can go.'

Throughout this exchange Jo didn't say a word as she leaned over the table, putting in the pieces of what he saw to be a jigsaw.

'Are you going to join us?' he called, certain that she'd been listening.

'I would love to.'

'Five minutes.'

He strolled inside and headed up to his room, changing out of his trousers and shirt into a pair of his favourite cargo shorts and a white T-shirt. When he got back Jo and Toby were waiting for him, bottles of water in hand.

Jo looked pointedly at his feet. 'No shoes?'

'I like to feel the sand on my feet.'

The strangest expression crossed her face. But if she meant to say anything the moment was lost when Toby tugged at her hand.

'Come *on*,' he urged impatiently.

Together they walked out of the garden and down a

rocky trail, with Jo holding Toby's hand tightly until they reached Theseus's private beach.

As soon as his feet hit the sand Toby pulled his socks and trainers off and went chasing after Benedict.

'He seems happier now,' Theseus observed nonchalantly.

His attempt at indifference was met with a wry smile. 'Don't beat yourself up about last night. He was tired.'

'He was also very upset.'

'Tiredness always affects his mood. Don't forget he's in a strange place, with strange people, and a man claiming to be his father...'

'I *am* his father.'

She looked at him. 'He's only ever had a mother. Stories of his father have been, in his head, the same as stories about the tooth fairy. He'll be okay. Children accept change and adapt to it far more easily than we do, but it's unrealistic to expect that to happen immediately. He needs time, that's all. Be patient. He'll come to accept you *and* our new life.'

He wasn't convinced. Did he really want his son to be just *okay*? Childhood was a time of innocence and magic. Break the innocence and the magic evaporated.

Even before his parents' deaths he'd had little innocence left. Having a father who'd made no attempt to disguise his irritation with his second son had had an insidious effect on him. His mother had tried her hardest to make up for it and he'd worshipped her in return. When she'd died it had been as if his whole world had ended. Yet he'd mourned his father too. Loving him and hating him had lived side by side within him. For his mother, though, he had felt only love, and it had been the hole left in his heart by her loss that had cut the most. If not for his grandparents he would have been completely lost. They'd always been there for him.

As he'd read through the final chapters of his grandfather's biography that morning, before heading to the palace, it had played on his mind how much his grandparents had given up for him and his brothers to ensure they had stability. It wasn't just that his grandfather had kept the monarch's crown, but the way his grandparents had enfolded their grandsons in their care.

Given that Helios was heir, it was hardly surprising that Astraeus had taken him under his wing more than he had Theseus or Talos. But Theseus had never felt excluded by it, in the way his father had made him feel excluded. His grandfather was often remote—he was the King after all—and he'd been strict with them all, but growing up Theseus had never doubted his love. And his remoteness had been countered by their grandmother; a loving, generous woman with all the time in the world for him.

Theos, he missed her as much as he missed his mother.

After reading the biography in its entirety, with all the pieces of his research stitched together to create the final picture, he'd understood just how much they'd given up for their grandchildren and for duty. The death of their son and heir had meant the death of their dreams, but they'd risen to the challenge with a grace that left him humbled and aching with regret. It was too late to tell his grandmother how much he loved her and to thank her for all she'd done and all she'd given up.

Toby bounded back to them, waving an enormous stick in his hand. Theseus marvelled at the freedom that came with simply being a child.

Did he really want to take that freedom away from him?

And could he do it to Jo too?

'I've found a stick,' Toby said, coming right up to him and holding it out like an offering.

'Throw it to Benedict and see if he'll catch it.'

''Kay. How will he know what to do?'

'He'll know,' he said, smiling down at him. 'You can always yell *ferto* to him when you throw it—that's the Greek word for fetch.'

'*Ferto,*' Toby repeated, then ran off, shouting, '*Sas efcharisto,*' over his shoulder.

'Did he just say thank you to me?' he asked, staring at Jo in astonishment, certain that his ears must be blocked with water from his morning swim.

'I've taught him a few words and phrases in Greek,' she conceded.

The admission caught him right in the throat.

He'd become so accustomed to speaking to her in both their languages that he'd taken her fluency in his language for granted. It was a joke amongst Greeks, Cretans and Agonites alike how dismally the British spoke their tongue.

Fate did indeed work in strange ways.

If Jo hadn't been fluent in his language and the only credible person to take over the workings of the biography—

Suddenly he was certain that she hadn't spoken Greek when he'd known her on Illya. Her speech now was practised, but not flawless. She could read the language well, but struggled with the more obscure words. He'd never seen her attempt to write it, but he was sure it would be an area she would have trouble with.

This wasn't a woman who'd been taught his language from a young age.

'When did you learn Greek?'

'When I couldn't find you.' She looked briefly at him, then shifted her focus back to the light pink sand before them, following in Toby's little footsteps. 'I bought some of those audio lessons and spent every night listening to them, and I got Fiona to give me lessons too. She helped me with context and pronunciation.'

'You did all that in five years?'

'Four,' she corrected. 'And now I'm trying to teach Toby too.'

'But why?' His head spun to think of all the hours she must have spent studying, the determination it must have taken...

'I told you before—I wanted to find you. I even started a savings account to pay for me and Toby to go to Athens.'

'How did you think you would find me?' he asked, more harshly than he'd intended. 'Athens is a huge city. It would have been like looking for a specific tile in a mosaic.'

She shrugged. 'I knew it was a long shot, but I'd have tried for Toby's sake.'

'And what did you think would happen if you'd found me?'

'I stopped thinking about that. All the potential consequences were too scary.'

'But you were still going to try?'

Her smile was wan. 'It was the right thing to do. If I hadn't have found you I still could have shown Toby your culture. Or what I *thought* was your culture.'

She cast her eyes a few metres into the distance, to where Toby was splashing at the shoreline.

'No further!' she called to him, before adding to Theseus, 'He can't swim.'

As she joined their son Theseus hung back, watching them.

They were the tightest of units. Seeing them together, he could appreciate how hard it must have been for her to leave Toby behind and come to Agon.

It seemed she'd accepted the job because of the large bonus she'd been offered, which would have meant she'd have been able to take Toby to Greece to find *him*.

If he hadn't believed her before, he did now. With all his heart.

She really had searched for him.

She really had wanted him to be a part of Toby's life.

If fate hadn't brought her to the palace she would never have found him. He would have spent the rest of his life unaware of the miracle that had occurred and he would have had no one to blame but himself.

Jo followed the squeals of delight echoing from the swimming pool with a smile playing on her face.

The sun was bright, the sky was blue—in all it was a glorious day. She'd caught a snippet of the English weather forecast and had given a sly snigger to see her country was expecting torrential downpours and heavy gales.

There could certainly be worse places to be a forced wife than on Agon, she thought wryly.

Toby spotted her first, and waved cheerfully from Theseus's arms.

For his part, Theseus's eyes gleamed to see her, and a knowing look spread over his face when she removed her sarong to reveal the modest bikini she'd bought the day before on a shopping trip with Elektra.

'Sexy,' he growled, for her ears only, when she slipped tentatively down the steps and into the cool water.

She stopped with the water at mid-thigh. 'Inappropriate,' she whispered.

'He's not listening.'

That was true enough. Toby had paddled off in his armbands to the shallow end, to play with the array of water guns, lilos and balls Theseus had bought for him.

'I've never seen you in a bikini before.' Theseus grinned, sitting on the step beside her.

'I was so fat I never dared wear one,' she admitted wistfully. 'Everyone else on Illya had such fabulous figures.'

She still wasn't fully confident displaying her body, but after spending her nights sharing a bed with Theseus and having him revel in her curves, her confidence was increasing by the day.

He tilted his head and stared at her, then reached out a hand to tuck a lock of her hair behind her ear. 'Never feel you aren't good enough, *agapi mou*. Those women on Illya couldn't hold a light to you, whatever size you were. You're beautiful.'

Everything in her contracted—from her toes to her pelvis to the hairs on her head. She couldn't think of a reply; was too stunned that this glorious, gorgeous man could call her beautiful. If she could float she would be sky-high by now...

Theseus didn't care how thin she was. No matter what, he would still desire her.

She giggled.

'What?' he asked, his eyes puzzled.

She clamped a hand over her mouth.

'What?' he demanded to know, playfully pulling her hand away. 'Why are you laughing? Share the joke. I command it!'

But she couldn't. How could she say that his compliment was the most wonderful she'd ever heard?

'Tell me or I'll get you wet,' he threatened, clearly remembering her aversion to water from their time on Illya.

But she could no more stop the laughter that erupted than she could have grown wings.

Theseus was as good as his word.

He got to his feet, scooped her up in his arms, then threw her into the middle of the pool.

She was still laughing when she came up for air.

Preparations for the Gala meant Theseus was caught up at the palace more than he would have liked over the next few days. He made sure always to eat breakfast with his new family, and spent snatches of time with them, but he knew it wasn't enough. Not for him. He wanted them...*close*.

He brushed away the strange word.

Things would change after the Gala, when he would be able to announce their existence to his grandfather and the rest of the world. Jo and Toby would move into the palace then.

Living in his villa was like a holiday for them. The sun shone whilst they played in the pool and built sandcastles on the beach. The magic of it all had caught him too. The memory of last night lay fresh in his mind; taking a moonlit walk with Jo down to the cove, making love to her on the sand and then, when they were replete and naked in each other's arms, gazing up at the stars in peaceable silence.

For the first time he'd stared up at the night sky and not felt the pull to be up there in space. The only pull he'd felt was to the woman in his arms, and he'd rolled her onto her back and made love to her again.

More and more it played on his mind... How was she going to cope with palace life? She'd lived there briefly, but that had been there for a specific purpose, not as a member of the household. She would need time to settle in and then, once they were married in a few weeks, her royal duties would begin.

His good memories from the beach evaporated as he recalled her startled face that morning, when they'd lingered over breakfast. Toby had disappeared into the kitchen to badger the chef into making more flapjacks for him and he'd given her the résumés of the staff he was recommending she interview after the Gala.

She'd looked at him blankly.

'Your private staff,' he'd explained. 'You'll need staff to manage your diary, to do research for you for when we meet with ambassadors and business people. You'll need someone to help with your wardrobe—my grandmother and my mother both had a personal seamstress to make their clothes—and you'll need a private secretary to manage all of them...'

By the time he'd stopped talking she'd looked quite faint. The reality of palace life was clearly not something she was prepared for.

He threw his pen at the wall and swore.

How much guilt could one man carry?

It was late when he returned to the villa. A few members of staff were still up, but Jo and Toby had both gone to bed.

He found Toby fast asleep, lying spread out like a starfish. Theseus padded quietly to him and pulled the covers which had been thrown off back over him, before placing a kiss on his forehead.

With his guts playing havoc inside him, he went into Jo's room, closing the door behind him.

She was sitting up in bed, reading.

'I thought you'd be asleep,' he said.

'So did I.'

He sat on the edge of the bed and reached out to bury a hand in her hair. She shuffled closer and wrapped her arms around him.

'How are things going with the Gala?' she asked softly.

'Like a well-oiled machine. Apart from the soloist Talos found to play our grandmother's final composition...'

'What's wrong with her?'

'Turns out she suffers from severe stage fright.'

'Ah—is *that* why they've been spending so much time together?'

The suggestive tone in her voice made him laugh. He raised one eyebrow. 'Talos says he's *helping* her...'

With that, they both rolled back onto the bed, smothering their sniggers so as not to wake Toby across the hall. Their laughter quickly turned into passion as Jo's hungry lips found his and her robe fell open to showcase her unashamed nakedness…

Time sped away in whirl of sunshine until suddenly it was the eve of the Gala.

Where had the time gone? Jo wondered in amazement.

Theseus had spent the day at the palace and arrived back so late she was dozing off when he slipped into the dark bedroom.

'All done?' she asked, raising her head.

He turned the light on at a low setting. 'All done. The books are en route as we speak.'

A problem with the printers had kept him at the palace long into the night. All week he'd had to work late. The pace had been relentless. She'd found herself missing him, constantly checking her watch and waiting for the time when he would come back to the villa.

'Have you slept?' he asked, unbuttoning his shirt.

'A little.' She sat up, hugging the sheets to her. 'I think there's too much going on in my brain for me to switch off properly.'

'Nervous?'

'Terrified.'

Tomorrow she would meet the King. When the Gala was all over he would be informed about Toby. Their lives would change irrevocably.

'Don't be.'

She sighed. That was easy for *him* to say.

'I spoke to Giles earlier.'

'How was he?'

'Busy.' He slid his trousers off. 'He said to pass on his congratulations for your part in the book.'

She smiled wistfully.

'You never told me you got the job with him by working for free.'

She shrugged. 'I was desperate. I'd had to give up the job I'd originally had lined up in London...'

'Why?'

'I suffered from a condition commonly known as acute morning sickness. I was sick pretty much all the time. I could hardly get out of bed, never mind move to London and start a new job. I ended up being hospitalised for a month. By the time I'd recovered, when I was just over four months pregnant, the job had been given to someone else.'

Stark, stunned silence greeted her news.

'It wasn't all bad,' she said, trying to reassure him. 'I lost a load of weight, and Toby didn't suffer for it.'

'It must have been hell,' he refuted flatly.

'At the time, yes—but Toby was worth it. And I turned into slimline Jo, so that was a bonus.'

'With the way you always refuse cake I assumed you'd dieted.'

'Not initially. Once I got better the temptation was still there, but I stopped myself. I knew things had to change—for my health *and* my emotional wellbeing.' She shook her head and sighed. 'I fell in love with Toby long before he was born, and that was what made me see that I could eat as many of my mother's cakes as possible and she'd *still* never love me. Not as a mother should.'

At his shocked stare, she went on.

'When I was little I was allowed to eat as much cake as I liked. I thought that was how mums showed their love. Looking back, I can see that it was just her way of keeping me quiet. Carrying Toby, feeling him grow inside me... it changed me. I knew I couldn't let her have that kind of power over me any more.'

'And what's your relationship with her like now?'

'Challenging... I pop in every month or so, to make sure Dad's okay. If he's not comatose he's happy to see me.'

'How does Toby get on with them?'

'I never take him. Maybe when he's older...' Her voice trailed off.

'So what *were* you going to do in London?' he asked quietly.

Theseus hadn't intended to open a Pandora's box with his innocuous comment about Giles, but now it was open he needed to know it all.

'I was going to work at a children's book publishing company.' She pushed a lock of hair from her face. 'I loved reading as a child. Anything was possible in the books I read. Good overcame evil. The ugly ducklings became beautiful swans. Anyone could find love. I wanted to work with those books and be a part of the magic.'

And instead she'd ended up working on historical tomes and museum pieces. He could just see her, sitting in her bedroom, forgetting her mother's cruel indifference and her father's love affair with the bottle by burying her head in dreams.

'When I recovered from the morning sickness I went to every publisher I could find in Oxford and offered my services for free until the baby was born—the deal being that if I proved myself they had to consider me when a suitable job came up. Giles took me up on it.'

Theseus shook his head to imagine that he'd once dismissed this woman as 'wallpaper'. She had more tenacity than anyone he'd ever met.

'They say fortune favours the brave,' she continued, 'and it really does. A week after I'd decided I couldn't raise Toby in the toxic atmosphere of Brookes Manor and we'd moved into our own flat, Giles called with the offer of a job as copywriter. It came at just the right time too—I was hours away from starting my first shift as a waitress.'

He smiled, although he felt anything but amused. 'And you were happy there?'

'Gosh, yes. Very happy. The staff are wonderful. I grew to love it.'

Of course she had. She could have wallowed in self-pity at the destruction of her dreams, but instead she had embraced the cards she'd been dealt, just as she would put on a brave smile when she married into his family and became royalty.

He thought of his grandmother, who'd curtailed her performing career when she'd married his grandfather. The difference was his grandmother had been born a princess and been promised to his grandfather from birth. She'd always known that marriage would mean a limit to what she could do with her career.

He thought of his mother. Had *she* ever dreamed of being anything other than Lelantos Kalliakis's wife?

Yes, he thought, remembering the wistful look that had used to come into her eyes when he'd spoken of his naïve childhood plan to become an astronaut. She'd had dreams of something different too. It was the greatest tragedy of his life that he would never know what they had been.

CHAPTER TWELVE

'Do I LOOK all right?' Jo asked, the second Theseus stepped into the room.

The appreciative gleam that came into his eyes gave her the answer.

When he pulled her into his arms and made to kiss her, she turned her cheek. 'You'll smudge my lipstick!' she chided.

'I don't care.'

'Well, *I* do. I've spent over two hours getting ready.'

'And you look spectacular.'

She felt her cheeks flame at his heartfelt compliment and couldn't resist one more glance in the mirror.

Another shopping trip with Elektra had resulted in Jo picking an ivory crêpe dress that dipped in a V at the front and fell to mid-calf. She'd finished the outfit with a wide tan leather belt across her middle and pair of high, braided white leather sandals.

A fortnight ago she wouldn't have dreamed of wearing something that put so much emphasis on her buxom figure—although the height of the sandals elongated her nicely—but Theseus's genuine delight in her curves had given her real confidence. She'd never shown so much cleavage in her life!

Elektra had twisted her hair into an elegant knot and gone to work on her face. The result was a dream. Her eyes had never looked so blue, her lips so…kissable. Yes, the lips she'd always hated for being as plump as her bottom looked *kissable*. She even had defined cheekbones!

Today she was going to meet the King and dozens of other dignitaries as Theseus's guest at a select pre-Gala lunch.

Boxes of the biography had arrived in the early hours, and a dozen members of the palace staff were already organising them for distribution amongst the five thousand Gala attendees.

But first Theseus wanted to present his grandfather with his own copy.

He hadn't said anything but she knew he was apprehensive about his grandfather's reaction, so she was trying hard to smother her terror at the thought of all the important people she would be forced to converse with as an equal and to be bright and cheerful for Theseus, in the hope that it might settle his own silent nerves.

Once the lunch was over they would go to the amphitheatre. Theseus would sit with his family in the royal box and Jo would sit with Toby and Elektra, who was caring for him in the meantime.

After kissing Toby goodbye—and his, 'Wow, Mummy, you look like a princess!' had made her feel ten feet tall— she and Theseus got into the car and were driven to the palace.

It felt strange, coming back to it.

Barely a fortnight had passed since she'd moved into Theseus's villa but it felt like so much longer. It felt as if she was looking at the palace with fresh eyes.

The sun shone high above, its rays beaming down and soaking the palace in glorious sunlight, making the different coloured roofs brighter and all the ornate gothic and mythological statues and frescoes come to life.

When they arrived, entering through Theseus's private entrance, they passed the door of her old apartment. She looked at it with a touch of wistfulness, wondering who the next person to inhabit it would be.

Climbing the stairs, she watched as the carefree man who had slowly re-emerged during her time in his villa put his princely skin back on. She wished with all her heart that she could pull it off him.

Theseus felt no joy as a prince, spending his days at official functions with stuffy dignitaries and being sent abroad to protect and advance his island's interests. There was no time to climb the peaks or stare at the stars.

He needed to be out in the air. He needed to be free.

The man she'd met five years ago had been free and happy. Joy had radiated from him.

Courtiers appeared at their side and Dimitris was with them. In his hand was a hardback book, with a portrait of the King on the cover... It was the biography...

'He's ready for you,' Dimitris murmured.

He had to mean King Astraeus.

This was the moment when he would learn what his grandson had done in his honour. She hoped he'd recognise the incredible effort Theseus had put into it. She hoped the King would be proud.

Theseus turned to Jo. 'A courtier will take you to the stateroom where the guests are meeting for lunch. Wait for me there.'

The strain was huge in his eyes.

'Are you okay?' she asked softly.

He met her gaze. Understanding passed between them.

Theseus brushed a thumb along her cheekbone, resisting the urge to kiss her. Instead he gave a curt nod and left for his grandfather's quarters.

He found him sat in his wheelchair, looking out of a high window, dressed in full regalia, with his dark purple sash tied from shoulder to hip in the same way as Theseus's own. Only his nurse was in attendance.

'You wanted to see me?' his grandfather said, interest on his wizened face.

Taking a deep breath, Theseus crossed the threshold.

He'd prepared a speech for this moment; words which might explain the regret he carried for all the shame and worry he'd put on this great man's shoulders and how this book had been created to honour him.

But the words stuck.

He held the book out to him.

With curiosity on his face, his grandfather took it from him. Wordlessly he placed it on his lap, and with hands that shook he opened it.

After several long minutes during which the only sound in the room was the King's wheezy breathing, his grandfather raised misty eyes to him.

'You did this?'

Theseus bowed his head.

'It is incredible.' His grandfather shook his head, turning the pages slowly. 'When did you do this…? How…? I knew nothing of it.'

'I wanted it to be a surprise.'

'It's not often a secret is kept in this palace,' his grandfather observed, a tremble in his aged voice.

'Loss of limbs may have been threatened…'

Astraeus's laugh turned into a cough, and then the amusement faded. 'This is a wonderful thing you have done for me, and I thank you with all my heart.'

Theseus took a breath. 'I wanted to create something that would show how much you mean to me. I used to be disrespectful, and I brought much dishonour upon you, but I truly am proud to be your grandson.'

His words were met with a shake of the old King's head. 'Theseus, you weren't a bad boy. Rhea always said you were a lost soul.'

At the mention of his grandmother's name Theseus felt his throat close.

'She adored you.'

'I know. I will never forgive myself for not being there—' His voice cracked, guilt filling him all over again.

Astraeus gripped his wrist and tugged him down so they were at eye level. 'The past is over. What you have created here for me...' A tear ran down his cheek. 'Your grandmother would be very proud of you—for this and for how you've turned your life around. You are a credit to the Kalliakis name and I'm proud to call you my grandson.'

The backs of his retinas burning, Theseus closed his eyes, then leaned forward to place a kiss on his grandfather's cheek. But before he could absorb the moment, and his grandfather's words, a knock on the door preceded his brothers strolling into the room.

'Is there a lovefest going on that we weren't invited to?' Helios asked.

Talos snatched the book out of their grandfather's hands and soon all four of them were going through the pictures within, reminiscing with sad amusement, until the King's private secretary announced that it was time for them to greet their guests.

An army of staff bustled around, handing out champagne and fresh juices as the stateroom filled. On an antique table to the left of the door sat a pile of hardback copies of the biography.

'May I?' Jo asked, dazzled.

'Of course.' A courtier handed one to her.

She studied the cover and the back, then flipped through the pages, inhaling the lovely papery scent only a new book emitted.

At the bottom of the front cover were the words *Fiona Samaras & Joanne Brookes*.

She traced her finger over her name, then carefully turned some pages. Pride filled her to know that this was something *she'd* helped create, but with it came a tinge of sadness that Fiona couldn't be there to revel in their accomplishment too. After four years of working together, and all Fiona's Greek tuition, they'd become good friends. Jo knew how much she would have loved to be there today.

While she waited for Theseus to join her she studied the photographs in the biography, which dated back a century, to the King's own parents' marriage. What a family she was moving into...

Where before she'd felt terror at the mere thought of becoming a Kalliakis, she now felt an immense pride and a determination to play her part. She'd grown to love the island, and the fierce but passionate people who inhabited it.

And what a man she was pledging the rest of her life to...

An image floated in her mind of when she had watched him teach Toby to swim in the villa's outdoor pool the day before. She could still hear their laughter. He'd come back from the palace especially. She'd watched them with a heart so full she had wanted to burst. All her fears for Toby had gone. Seeing them together had been like watching two peas in a pod.

Toby loved his father. And Theseus loved him. She could see it in his tenderness towards him. And sometimes when he looked at her she thought she saw the same tenderness directed at *her*.

It gave her hope. Maybe love really *could* grow between them...

Activity at the entrance of the stateroom caught her attention.

An old wizened man in a wheelchair, who nonetheless had the most incredible aura about him, had entered the room. Theseus was at his side, Helios and another man who had to be Talos were with them.

The four of them together looked majestic. But it was only Theseus she had eyes for.

It came to her then in a burst of crystal clear clarity.

She was head over heels in love with him.

She had belonged to him since he'd stood up for her on Illya, and no matter how hard she'd tried to dislodge him from her heart—had convinced herself for years that she'd succeeded—he was nestled in too deep.

She stared at him as if she'd never seen him before, her heart as swollen as the highest river.

She *loved* him.

He came straight to her and took her hand. 'My grandfather wishes to meet you before we go in to lunch.'

There was a lightness to him and his eyes were brighter than she had seen them since her arrival on Agon.

She cleared her throat, almost dumbstruck at what she had finally admitted to herself. 'Do I curtsey?'

'As it's an official function, yes—but only to my grandfather.'

And then she was there before him, this wonderful man who'd sacrificed so much for his glorious island and his magnificent grandsons.

It was with enormous pride that Theseus made the introductions. Jo, pale and shaking, was obviously overcome by the occasion, but she curtseyed gracefully.

His grandfather reached for her hand. 'Thank you,' he rasped, clasping her hand in both his own. 'My book… I will treasure it.'

'It was an honour to be involved,' she said with feeling. 'But Fiona wrote most of it.'

'My grandson tells me you came at short notice and have barely slept?'

'It was all down to Theseus.' She stepped closer to meet his grandfather's gaze properly. 'However many hours

Fiona and I have put into this book, it's nothing compared to the time Theseus spent on the research.'

His grandfather turned his face to him, his eyes brimming. 'Yes. I am a lucky man. I have three fine grandsons—my island is in safe hands.'

Theseus's chest had grown so tight during this exchange it felt bruised. *She was championing him.*

A footman came into the room to announce that lunch was ready to be served. Before they could file out Astraeus caught hold of Theseus's wrist and beckoned him down.

'I am guessing she is the mother of your son?'

His mouth dropped open.

His grandfather gave a laugh. 'Did you think you could keep such a secret from me? A biography is one thing but a child…? I might be on my way to my deathbed, but I am still King.'

'I was going to tell you…'

'I know—after the Gala.' There was no sign of irritation. 'I am disappointed to have heard the news from a third party, but I do understand your reasons. How *is* the boy?'

'Settling in well.'

'I am very much looking forward to meeting him.'

'He is looking forward to meeting you too.'

'Have him brought to me when lunch is finished.'

'He would like that,' Theseus said, imagining Toby's delight at meeting a real-life king. 'Be warned: he's hoping you have a flying carpet.'

Astraeus gave a laugh, which quickly turned into a cough that made Theseus flinch, although he took pains not to show it. His grandfather despised pity.

'I hear he looks like you?' he said, when he'd recovered from his coughing fit.

'Your spies are very reliable,' Theseus said drily.

'That is why they're my spies. You can inherit them when I'm dead.'

Theseus wasn't quick enough to hide his wince. Here was his grandfather, welcoming death with open arms and a smile, and here was Theseus, who would give the flesh from his bones to keep him alive for ever.

'You are planning to marry the mother in a few weeks, I believe?'

'Yes. I apologise for not asking your permission.'

Astraeus waved a frail dismissive hand. 'You have never asked for my permission for anything—why should this be any different?'

'I've *always* asked your blessing.'

'Having already made up your mind,' his grandfather countered, with a twinkle in his eye that made them both laugh. 'Does the mother *want* to marry you?'

'She knows it's the best thing for our son.'

'Don't evade the question, Theseus. Does she want to marry you or not?'

There was a moment when his vocal cords stuck together.

'Do I take your silence as a negative?'

'What alternative do we have? The law forbids Toby from being a part of our family or inheriting my wealth unless we marry.'

The dismissive hand rose again. 'Do you think you are the first member of our family to impregnate a woman out of wedlock? You're wealthy in your own right. There are means, if the will is strong enough.'

'Are you suggesting that I *shouldn't* marry her?' Now he really *was* shocked. He knew how much importance his grandfather placed on matrimony, and how important it was to him to see the family line secured.

'I am suggesting you think in more depth about it before you tie yourself into a marriage neither of you can back away from.' His lined face softened. 'Whatever you choose…know that I will support you. Now, let us meet our guests and enjoy the day.'

Theseus dragged himself off the sofa in his palace apartment, clutching his head with one hand. From the look of the sunlight filtering through the shutters he hadn't closed properly it seemed that the sun had long beaten him awake.

He hadn't intended to stay the night. His plan had been to return to the villa once the official after-Gala party in the palace had finished. But with Talos long gone—chasing after the fabulous violinist who'd brought the entire audience to tears—and their grandfather having already retired, it had been left to him and Helios to play hosts to their distinguished guests.

When the last of the crowds had gone, all abuzz with the news of Helios's engagement to Princess Catalina, which had been announced during the gala, the Princess had flown home with her father and Helios had muttered that he needed a 'proper' drink.

Armed with a bottle of gin and two glasses, they'd hidden away in Helios's apartment and drunk until the small hours. He didn't know which of them had needed it the most. It was the first time Theseus had drunk so much in years.

They should have been celebrating.

Theseus had achieved the one thing he'd set out to do all those years ago, when he'd turned his back on being Theo and embraced who he truly was: he'd made his grandfather proud. The biography had been completed on time and it was a true celebration of the King's life—exactly as Theseus had wanted it to be.

And Helios had just got engaged to be married, so he should have been celebrating too.

Instead, the pair of them had drowned their sorrows.

All Theseus had been able to think about was Jo, and

how animated her face had been when she'd championed him to his grandfather.

No one had ever done that before—spoken so passionately on his behalf. Not since his mother, who would implore his father to treat him as an equal to Helios only to be slapped or, if she was lucky, just ignored for her efforts.

His mother had loved all her children fiercely. He could never have disappointed her, because in her eyes her boys had been perfect and incapable of doing wrong.

Jo loved Toby just as fiercely. Like his mother, she was a good, pure person. She deserved everything that was good in life. She deserved better than him.

He might not have disappointed his mother, but at some time or another he'd let the rest of his family down. When he'd selfishly left the palace to see the world he'd left the fledging business he and his brothers had just formed in their hands.

What a monstrously selfish person he had been.

Even his years of doing his princely duty had been done with the ulterior motive of gaining his family's forgiveness. His heart had never been in it. Indeed, he'd had to shut off his heart to get through it, to be Prince Theseus.

He knew that to make it through the rest of his life he would have to keep it closed. His dreams had to be stuffed away with the memories of his travels before they crowded his head with taunts of what could never be.

'Those people watching the Gala. They have no idea of our sacrifices,' Helios had said, finishing another glass.

It was the first time Theseus had ever heard his brother say something disparaging about being a member of the Kalliakis family, and with hindsight he should have probed his brother about his comment, but his mind had immediately flown to Jo and the sacrifices *she'd* made. The sacrifices she would continue to make for the rest of her life...

She'd been so pale during lunch, and when Toby had

been introduced to his grandfather she'd hung back, her eyes fluttering from Theseus to Toby and back to his grandfather.

Toby hadn't been even slightly overawed, and had happily chattered away as if the King had been a fixture in his life from birth.

But Jo…

His heart lurched.

He knew what he must do.

CHAPTER THIRTEEN

HE FOUND HER in the pool with Toby.

Her lips widened into a huge smile when she saw him. Then a quizzical expression formed as she noticed his set face and the smile dropped. She had learned to read him very well.

Toby had no such intuition. 'Daddy!' he cried. 'Look! Mummy's helping me swim. Come in with us!'

Theseus stiffened.

Daddy?

His son had called him Daddy.

It was the one word he'd been waiting to hear. He'd been content for Toby to call him Theseus, hadn't wanted to upset the apple cart by demanding a title he'd done nothing to earn. Rather like his title of Prince, he mused darkly.

He hadn't been at Toby's birth, and neither had he been there for the first four years of his life. And it was all his own fault for not seeing what his heart had known from the start—that Joanne Brookes was the best person he'd ever met.

And for that reason he had to let her go.

For her, he would cast aside his selfishness and actually do something for the benefit of someone else. To hell with the consequences.

He stepped to the pool's edge and smiled at his son. *I love you, Toby Kalliakis. I will never abandon you. I will always be there for you. Always.*

The words went unsaid.

'Chef is making cookies,' he said to Toby. 'If you get changed, they'll be ready for you to eat.'

'Can I, Mummy?' he asked eagerly, wriggling in Jo's arms.

Her eyes were fixed on Theseus, but she nodded, wading to the edge of the pool and lifting Toby onto it.

Elektra wrapped a towel around him and scooped him up.

Jo's heart shuddered and juddered. Something was badly wrong. She could feel it in her bones.

Please, not his grandfather...

Climbing out of the pool, she reached for her own towel, her heart juddering even more when Theseus made no move to hand it to her.

She wrapped the towel around herself and followed him to the poolside table. A jug of fruit juice and two glasses had been placed on it. He poured them both a glass and pushed Jo's towards her.

'Have you packed your bags yet?' he asked heavily, looking at the jug rather than at her.

'Yes. We're ready to go. Is there a problem with the apartment? It won't be a problem staying here longer. To be honest, Toby and I both love it—'

'There won't be an apartment,' he interrupted. 'Jo, you're going home.'

His words made no sense. 'What are you talking about?'

'Our wedding is off. You and Toby are going back England.'

No. They still made no sense.

'What are you talking about?' she repeated.

He lifted his gaze to meet hers. Unlike the stunned incomprehension that must be clear in her eyes, in his there was nothing. Nothing at all.

'I was wrong to insist on marriage. You conceived a child with Theo the engineer, not Theseus the Prince. None of this was your doing. I'm the one who lied about my identity and made it impossible for you to find me. For me to ask you to give up the rest of your life after all the sacrifices you've already made... I can't do it.' He kneaded his forehead with his knuckles. 'I've caused enough damage. I won't be a party to any more. You deserve the freedom to live your life as you want, not in a way that's dictated and forced on you.'

'Where has *this* come from?' she asked hoarsely. 'I don't understand. Have I done something wrong?'

'No.' He laughed without humour. 'You've done everything right. It's me who's done everything wrong, and now I'm putting it right.'

'But what about Toby?'

'Toby needs to be with *you*. I will recognise him as my son. He can come here for holidays. I'll visit whenever I can. We can video call.'

'You wanted to be a *real* father to him. You can't have a hug with a computer. It isn't the same—it just isn't.' She knew she was gabbling but she couldn't control it. 'Toby needs *you*. Wherever you are is where he'll be happy— whether it's here or in England.

'My wealth is mine to do with as I like while I'm alive.' He dug a hand into his pocket and pulled out a folded envelope. 'Here. It's a cheque. Maintenance for the past five years...for when you had to struggle alone.'

She took it automatically, having hardly heard him. Her head was cold and reeling. She thought she might be sick.

This had to be a joke. It couldn't be anything else.

'I'll buy you a house,' he continued. 'Choose whatever you like, wherever you like. There will be further maintenance too, and I'll make investments and open accounts in Toby's name...'

On and on he went, but his words were just noise.

Panic, the like of which she'd never known—not even

during the night when he'd learned about Toby—clawed at her with talons so deep they cut through to the bone.

'But you wanted Toby to be your heir...' She was clutching at straws, her pride very much smothered in her stark shock. 'If you want to get rid of me we can marry and *then* Toby and I can move back to England. We don't have to live under the same roof unless your constitution demands it.'

He shook his head. 'What if you meet another man and want to marry him?'

'Meet another man?' Now her voice rose to a high pitch. 'How can I *ever* do that? You're the only man—don't you see that? It's only ever been you. I *love* you.'

His face paled and a pulse throbbed at his temple. 'I never asked for your love. I told you to keep your heart closed.'

'Do you think I had a *choice*?' Her whole body shook, fury and anguish and terror all circling inside her, smashing her heart. She wanted to lash out at him so badly, to inflict on him the pain he was wreaking on her.

Theseus jumped to his feet, gripping on to the edge of the table as he leaned over. 'Love does not equate to happiness. My mother loved my father and all he gave her was misery. I can't make you happy. Maybe for a few weeks or a few months—but what then? What happens when you wake one day with a hole of discontent in your stomach so wide that nothing can ever fill it? When the reality of your life hits you and you understand that this is all there is and all there will *ever* be?'

'But *why* is that all there will be?'

And as she shouted the words understanding hit her.

'Haven't you punished yourself enough?' she demanded, lowering her voice. 'You've spent years making amends for the times when you were less than dutiful—do you really have to sacrifice the rest of your life too?'

With lightning-quick reflexes Theseus grabbed the jug

of juice and hurled it. It flew through the air and landed with an enormous splash in the middle of the swimming pool.

She had never seen him so full of fury, not even when he'd learned about Toby.

'Do not speak as if you know anything. My grandparents made more sacrifices than I could make if I lived to be a thousand years old. My grandmother loved me, but I was such a selfish bastard I wasn't even there to say goodbye.'

'What...?'

'I was too late. By the time I got home she'd already died.'

Her hands flew to her cheeks, wretchedness for him—for her—raging through her. He'd been so desperate to get back to her. 'Please...you can't blame yourself for that. You tried...'

'Yes, I can—and I do. If I'd taken my phone with me when I went climbing, Helios would have reached me sooner and I would have had three extra days to get home. Dammit, she was *asking* for me.'

'It wasn't your fault.'

'Wherever the fault lies, the result is the same—I failed her when she needed me. I made a vow that as I failed to honour her in life I would honour her in death, and honour my grandfather in the manner I should have done from when I was old enough to know better. *This* is who I am. It's who I was born to be and who I will be for the rest of my life. I am a prince of Agon, and if we marry you'll be my wife—a princess. All the freedoms you take for granted will be gone. I will not do that to you. I know the cost, and I will not allow you to pay it.'

Loud silence rang out. Even the birds had stopped chirping.

On jelly-like legs, Jo rose. 'There's nothing wrong with wanting your freedom. You can have it still. It doesn't have

to be all or nothing. The happiness you had when you travelled the world and the happiness we've shared here, in
this villa—'

He cut her off. 'Your time here hasn't been real, you
know that. I saw your reaction to the number of staff you'd
need to employ, the schedule you'd have to follow. And
that's only the beginning. It will swallow you up and spit
you out.'

Despite the harshness of his tone, there was something
in his eyes that gave her the courage to fight on.

'My feelings for you are real. I'm not a precious flower,
ready to wilt at the first sign of pressure. Don't you see?
You've made me strong enough to bloom. Meeting you all
those years ago... Theo, you made me feel as if I was actually *worth* something. Even here, even during the days
when you hated me, you still made me feel like a woman
deserving of desire and affection in her own right.'

It was the wrong thing to say. His eyes turned into two
black blocks of ice.

His voice was every bit as cold. 'When are you going
to understand? I am not Theo. The man you love is dead.'

'No.' She shook her head desperately and gave a last
roll of the dice. 'No. Theo's still there. He's a part of you.'

But she might as well have been talking to the leaves
on the trees.

'Nikos will be here in a couple of hours to take you to
the airport,' he said, turning away from her and heading
back to the villa.

No, no, no, no, no. It *couldn't* be over.

But the stiffness in his frame told her that it was.

He stepped through the patio doors without looking
back.

Was it possible to hear someone's heart breaking?

Theseus sat with Talos, discussing a new company he'd

discovered that had the potential to be a good investment, but all he could think about was Jo.

He had the impression Talos was only half paying attention too. He'd announced his engagement to his beautiful violinist and it was clear his mind was on how quickly he could get back to her. And Helios had stayed at their meeting for all of five minutes before staggering out, saying he had stuff to do.

Even in the depths of his own misery Theseus could see something was badly wrong with his elder brother. Usually it was Helios who was the sunniest of the three Kalliakis brothers, while Talos normally walked around with a demeanour akin to that of a bear with a sore head. The switch between them would have been startling if Theseus had been able to summon the energy to care.

He'd assumed Jo would be happy to leave, that once it sank in that she had her freedom back she would grab Toby and speed away to the airport, singing, 'Freedom!' at the top of her voice.

She'd been like a wounded animal.

There he'd been, giving her a way out, handing it to her on a plate, and she'd refused to take it. He'd had to force it.

She'd said she *loved* him.

How could she love him? It wasn't possible. He'd done nothing to earn it, nothing to deserve it. He'd lied to her, impregnated her... Yes, she'd lied about being on the pill, but if he'd had his wits about him he would have seen her inexperience and not used her for his own selfish needs. He'd forced her to give up the job she loved, to give up *everything*, and she said she *loved* him?

Theos, he missed her. He missed her sunny smile at breakfast. He missed resting his head on her breasts while she stroked his hair.

'What is wrong with you?' Talos demanded, breaking through his thoughts.

'Nothing.'

'Well, your "nothing" is getting on my nerves.'

'Sorry.'

Talos shook his head with incredulity. 'Get up.'

'What?'

'Get up. You're coming to my gym. You need to work your "nothing" out. You're no good for anything with your head in Oxford.'

Theseus jumped to his feet. 'What would *you* know about it?' he snarled.

Talos folded his arms and fixed him with his stare. 'More than you think.'

Her coffee had gone cold.

Oh, well, it was disgusting anyway.

The coffee Theseus's staff served had ruined her palate for anything else.

At least it was only her taste buds. It wasn't as if the coffee had ruined everything else. No, Theseus had done that all on his own.

She'd been back in England for a week. A whole week. One hundred and sixty-eight interminably long hours, spent doing little other than trying not to wallow in front of Toby.

His preschool had taken him back with open arms so she had a few hours each day in which to bawl and rant and punch pillows. He was a resilient little thing, and his resilience had been helped when her landlady had let them move straight back in as she'd not yet relet their flat.

It was as if they'd never left England in the first place.

Their whole time on Agon might as well have been a dream.

Except no dream would have had her waking with cramping in her chest and awful flu-like symptoms.

She was thankful she'd never told Toby they were moving permanently to Agon. She'd figured it was best to just take things one day at a time. Having achieved his dream of meeting the King—his great-grandfather—and with the promise that he could go back and visit his daddy soon, he'd been happy to return to England and see his friends and his aunt, uncle and cousin.

At a loss for what to do, she stood at the window and looked out over the bustling street below. All those people going somewhere in the miserable spring drizzle.

Pressing her cheek against the cold glass, she closed her eyes.

What was he doing right now? Who was he with?

Did he miss Toby?

Did he miss *her*?

Did he even think about her?

She brushed away another tear, wondering when they would dry up. So many pathetic tears…

She had battled too hard in her life to be a victim.

If Theo didn't love her, then there was nothing she could do about it. All she could do was pull herself up and carry on.

But she felt so cold.

She would give anything to feel some warmth.

Theseus sat in his grandfather's study, ostensibly studying the chessboard while waiting for his grandfather to make his move. Yet his mind was far from the intricately carved black and white pieces before him. It was thousands of miles away. In Oxford. Where it had been for well over a week now.

'Are you going to make your move?'

He blinked rapidly, snapping himself out of the trance he'd fallen into.

His grandfather was staring at him, concern on his aged face.

It was the first game of chess they'd played since the

Gala. Since he'd sent Jo away. He'd made a brief visit to his grandfather to inform him that the engagement was off and that Jo and Toby would be returning to England. He'd braced himself for a barrage of questions but none had come forth. His announcement had been met with a slow nod and the words, 'You're a grown man. You know what's best for you and your family.'

Theseus moved his Bishop, realising too late he'd left his Queen exposed.

'It will get better,' his grandfather said.

Instead of denying that there was anything to improve, Theseus shook his head. 'Will it?'

His grandfather's eyes drilled into him. 'Can it get any worse?'

'No.'

But of course it could get worse. One day Toby—who now had his own phone, on which he could have face-to-face conversations with him at any time he liked—would casually mention a new uncle.

It wouldn't happen soon. Jo wasn't the kind of woman to jump out of one man's bed and straight into another...

He closed his eyes, waiting for the lance of pain imagining her with another man would bring. It didn't come. The picture wouldn't form. His brain simply could not conjure up an image of Jo with someone else.

She'd said there had been no other. She'd been a virgin when she had met him. He remained her only lover.

It suddenly occurred to him that she'd been his last lover too.

There had been no one but her since Illya.

'Do I understand that you finally gave her the choice of whether or not to marry you and she chose the latter?' his grandfather asked, studying the board before them.

Theseus swallowed. 'No. I set her free.'

'Did she want to be set free?'

He paused before answering truthfully, 'No.'

His grandfather's finger rested on his castle. 'You took away her choice in the matter?'

'For her own good.'

The watery eyes sharpened. 'People should make their own choices.'

'Even if they're the wrong ones?'

'I thought your grandmother was the wrong choice for me,' his grandfather said lightly, after a small pause. 'She was born a princess, but I thought her too independent-minded to cope with being a queen. If I'd been given the choice I would have chosen someone else—and that would have been the wrong choice. We complemented each other, despite our differences. She gave me a fresh perspective on life.'

A twinkle came into his grandfather's eyes.

'She understood *your* struggles and helped me to understand them too. She was a queen in every way, and I thanked God every day of our life together that the choice had been taken out of my hands, because I would never have found the love we shared with anyone else.'

Theseus rubbed the nape of his neck, breathing heavily.

There was that word again. *Love.*

He'd loved his parents, but they'd died before he'd had the chance to know them properly. Losing them, especially losing his mother, had smashed his heart into pieces.

He'd loved his grandmother. Her death had smashed the pieces that had been left of his heart.

He looked at his grandfather, spears of pain lancing him at the knowledge that soon he would be gone too.

He thought of Jo—her sweet smiling face, her soft skin, her gentle touch. Her sharp tongue when it came to protecting their son.

Theos, if anything were to happen to her...

It would kill him.

And as this realisation hit him his grandfather slid his Castle to Theseus's Queen and knocked it over.

'Your Queen is the heart of your game both in chess and in life,' his grandfather said quietly. 'Without her by your side your game will be poorer. Without her by your side...' His eyes glistened with a sudden burst of ferocity as he growled, 'Checkmate.'

There was a light knock on the door and then Nikos entered.

'You said to tell you if anything significant occurred.' He handed Theseus a piece of paper and left.

Theseus read it quickly. Then he read it again.

A ray of warmth broke through the chill that had lived in his veins for these past ten days. It trickled through him, lightly at first, then expanded until every single part of him was suffused with it.

CHAPTER FOURTEEN

JO SLIPPED HER brown leather flip-flops off and dangled them from a finger, letting her toes sink into the warm Illyan sand.

She tilted her head back and breathed in the salty scent, feeling the light breeze play on her skin.

She stood there for ages, soaking it all in. There was no rush. No need to be anywhere or do anything.

There was only one place she wanted to visit.

She walked along the shore, the cool lapping waves bouncing over her feet and sinking between her toes, the May sun bright and inviting and heating her skin, driving out the coldness that had been in her bones since she'd left Agon a fortnight ago.

Her time on this island five years ago had been the happiest of her life. On this island she had lost her inhibitions, her virginity and her heart. And, for all the heartache, she wouldn't trade a second of it.

Nothing much had changed in Illya. It was part of a cluster of rocky islands in the Adriatic, and the daily ferry was still the only means of getting to or from the mainland without a yacht, or a canoe and very strong arms. And Marin's Bar was still the only bar on the south of the island.

Really, 'bar' was a loose term for what it was—a large wooden shack with a thatched roof and a kitchen stuck on at the back, surrounded by tiny chalets. Most people who found the island were real travellers, not university graduates like Jo, Jenna and Imogen, who had been there for a cheap couple of weeks in the sunshine.

She supposed one day it would change. Developers would get their tentacles on it. Maybe it would lose its charm. Maybe it wouldn't. Change was often scary, but it didn't have to be bad. She'd gone through a lot of change recently and it had made her stronger.

Soon she was standing at the front of the shack with her heart in her mouth, taking deep, steadying breaths.

No more tears. That was what she'd promised herself. No more. Even if today *was* the day she had been supposed to marry Theseus...

What was she even doing here?

Three days ago she'd dropped Toby off at preschool, then walked back along a busy shopping street. A travel agent's window had been advertising trips to Korcula; another Croatian island.

Three days later and here she was. Back on Illya. Back in the same spot where she'd once watched Theseus play football on the beach with his Scandinavian friends.

The bar was empty, save for a blonde barmaid who greeted her with a friendly smile.

'Is Marin here?' Jo asked. She'd always liked the owner; an aging hippy with a pet Dalmatian that had a habit of falling asleep by customers' feet. She'd lost count of the number of people she'd seen trip over him.

'He's gone out, but he'll be back soon. Can I get you a drink?'

'A lemonade, please.'

While the barmaid poured her drink Jo cast her eyes around. It was pretty much as she remembered it. The walls were covered with photos of the travellers who had passed through—hundreds and hundreds of pictures, crammed in every available bit of space. And the large noticeboard where people could leave messages for friends still hung above the jukebox.

Sipping at her lemonade, she gazed at the pictures, wondering if she would see any familiar faces…

There was one image that rooted her to the spot.

It was a picture of her and Theo, the night after he'd come to her rescue. Their glasses were raised, their cheeks pressed together and they were both poking their tongues out at the camera.

When had that been put up?

She reached out a shaking finger and traced their image. Together their faces formed a heart shape.

A roll of pain gushed through her, so powerful that she had to grip a table for support.

Taking deep breaths, she waited for it to pass. The waves of pain always did, leaving nothing but a constant heavy ache that balled in her chest and pumped around her blood.

'I thought I'd find you here.'

Sending lemonade flying everywhere, Jo spun around to find Theseus standing in the doorway.

She blinked. And blinked again. And again.

He was still there, dressed in a pair of familiar cargo pants and nothing else. His hair was tousled; dark stubble covered his jaw. Wry amusement played on his face, but his eyes…his brown eyes were full of apprehension.

She opened her mouth but nothing came out.

She blinked again, totally uncomprehending.

'What are you doing here?' she croaked eventually.

'Waiting for you.'

'But how…?'

He smiled ruefully. 'You're the mother of my child. You and Toby have had bodyguards watching you since you left Agon. As soon as they told me you'd booked a holiday to Korcula I knew you'd come here.'

He came over to stand beside her.

'I put this up,' he said, putting his finger on their picture and brushing it lightly, just as she'd done minutes before.

'You did?' Her words sounded distant to her ears.

Any second now and she would wake up and still be on the ferry from Korcula, the large Adriatic island an hour's sail away, where she'd left Toby in a family hotel with her brother and sister-in-law.

'I found it last week in a box in my dressing room. When I returned from Illya I put everything to do with my travels in boxes and tried to forget about them. In one of the boxes was my old phone. I got Stieg—do you remember him?—to take that picture of us.' He finally looked at her, a crooked smile on his handsome face. 'There were a lot of pictures of you on that phone. More pictures of you than anyone else. Let me show you.'

He reached into the back pocket of his cargo shorts and pulled out his old phone. He went to his photo gallery and offered it to her. 'See?'

But her hands were shaking too much to take it.

With his warm body pressed against her, Theseus scrolled through the photos of his time on Illya—dozens and dozens and dozens of them. Most of them were of the surf on the north side of the island, or the mountains of the neighbouring islands. Only a few had people in them. Of those she was in over half. Only in two of them was she posing—in the rest he'd captured her unawares.

There was even a picture of her sitting alone on the beach in her swimsuit. She remembered that day. She'd been too embarrassed at the thought of what she'd look like in a wetsuit to surf with him and the others. She'd been scared someone would call her a hippo, and even more scared that Theo would laugh at it.

But now she knew differently. If anyone had insulted her he would have probably flushed their heads down a toilet.

How she wished she'd had the confidence to say to hell with them all and go surfing.

'There's more,' he said quietly, opening his phone's contacts box. 'There. Do you see?'

She nodded. It was all she was capable of.

There was her name. *Jo.* And beneath it was her old mobile number.

'Come,' he said, tugging at her frozen hand. 'Let's go and sit on the beach together.'

In a daze, Jo let him guide her out into the sun.

They sat on the deserted beach and Theseus leaned back on his elbows. Jo sat forward, hugging her knees and watching the sailing boats in the distance.

Had she fallen into a dream?

'Why do you think I remembered you had royal blood in your veins?' he asked quietly.

'Because you remember everything,' she whispered.

From out of the corner of her eye she saw him shake his head.

'I have a good memory, but when it comes to *you* I remember everything. I remember standing on the ferry and pressing "delete" on your number. But when I got the message asking if I wanted to carry on with the action I cancelled it. I couldn't do it. When I got home…'

He sat up and grabbed her hand, pulling it to his mouth. It wasn't a kiss. It was a brush of his lips and a warm breath of his air that sent tingles of sensation scurrying through her.

Dear God, he really was here. Theseus was *here.*

And just like that the stupor left her and her heart kick-started in thunderous jolts.

His eyes were dark and intense. 'Helios has always known he will one day be king. His destiny is carved in stone. My own destiny was to be nothing more than his shadow—his spare—but I wanted something so much more. I craved freedom. I wanted to play with other children and run free.' He pointed to the cobalt sky. 'I wanted to be up there in the stars. But I was born to be a prince. After my parents died I kept thinking, *Is this it?*, and I struggled endlessly to reconcile myself with my destiny, never realising that to my family it was like I was spitting on the Kalliakis name.

'When I was too late to say goodbye to my grandmother, and I saw the depth of my grandfather's pain, I knew I had a choice to either be a real part of my family or leave it for ever. So I put everything about my time exploring the world into boxes, taped them up and put them away. All my memories. I packed Theo into that box. I couldn't be that man *and* be the Prince I had to be.'

He swallowed.

'I wanted to make amends to my grandmother's memory and prove to my grandfather that I *am* proud to be a Kalliakis. I'd spent thirty years pursuing my own pleasure and it was time to grow up and be the man he'd raised me to be. I threw myself into palace life and the Kalliakis business with my brothers. I was determined to prove myself. But inside I was empty. And then you walked back into my life.'

He reached to brush a thumb down her cheek, a wan smile playing on his lips.

'If you'd told me a month ago that I'd fallen in love with a woman I slept with once five years ago I would have said you were mad. But that's the truth. You were there to catch me when I was at my lowest point and you caught my heart. It's been yours ever since that night. There hasn't been another, and only now do I know why—it's because I've belonged to you heart, body and soul since the night we conceived Toby. You came back into my life and the emptiness disappeared. But I didn't see it until I sent you away and the hole was ripped open again. Don't speak,' he urged when she parted her lips. 'I *know* you love me. I've always known. Just answer me this. When I sent you back to England it was so you could have your freedom. I was so high and mighty, thinking that I was doing the right thing, that I took away your freedom to make a choice.'

'My choice would be you,' she said immediately, before he could ask.

'But—'

This time Jo placed her finger to his lips. 'Your turn to keep quiet. I've never craved to see the stars. All I've ever wanted was to find a place where I belong, and I've found that with you. You make me whole. You make me proud to live in my skin. And that's the greatest gift you could ever have given me.'

She traced her fingers across his jaw, finally able to believe that this was real—that he had come to her, had met her back in the place where it had all started between them.

'Palace life doesn't frighten me the way you think it should, and as long as you're by my side I will adapt. I will be proud to be your princess and to represent the greatest family on this planet.'

He sighed and pressed a light kiss to her mouth. 'After the way I treated you I didn't dare to presume...'

'Freedom comes in many forms,' she said gently. 'You don't have to hide the essence of yourself away for ever.'

'I know that now. My grandmother was a strong, warm-hearted woman—she would have forgiven me. Now it's time to forgive myself.'

The look he gave her warmed her right down to the marrow of her bones.

'It's strange, but when I'm with you all my craving for freedom disappears. *You* make me feel free. You bring sunshine into my life and I swear I will never let you or Toby go again.'

She cupped his cheeks in her hands. His skin felt so warm. 'I will love you for ever.'

'And I will love *you* for ever.'

His hands dived into her hair and then his mouth came crashing onto hers.

It hadn't been a kiss, Jo thought a few hours later, when they were entangled in the sheets of the bed in the cabin where they'd first made love five years before. It had been more like the breath of life. It had been filled with promises for the future, something that bound them together for ever.

'Where are you going?' she asked when he slid off the bed.

He grinned and dug his hands into his shorts pocket. He pulled out the penknife he carried everywhere.

He climbed back onto the bed and placed the blade on the wooden wall. He etched the letters 'TK' and 'JB' into the wood.

'There,' he decreed in his most regal voice, snapping the blade shut and dropping it onto the floor. 'It's official. You and me—together for ever.'

EPILOGUE

'GOOD MORNING, PRINCESS.'

Jo opened a bleary eye and found her husband sitting on the edge of the bed beside her.

She smiled and yawned. 'What time is it?'

'Six o'clock.'

'It's the middle of the night.' And, considering they'd spent most of the night making love, she was shattered.

He laughed and ruffled her hair.

'The surf's up.'

That woke her up.

Theseus had insisted on giving her surfing lessons, and she'd been thrilled to discover that she wasn't completely awful at it. Now, three months after their wedding, they loved nothing more than leaving their villa early, when surf conditions were right, and spending the morning with Toby in the sea and on the beach before heading off to the palace to undertake their royal engagements. As per their instructions to their respective private secretaries, their mornings were always kept clear.

Yes, it had all worked out beautifully. With the family's blessing they had decided to make the villa their main dwelling. They used their apartment in the palace when it was convenient, but to all intents and purposes the villa was their home.

Theseus was staring at her expectantly.

'I think it might be a good idea for me to give it a miss today,' she said, her heart thumping at the thought of the news she was about to share with him; a secret she'd been hugging to herself for almost a week.

'Oh?' He cocked an eyebrow. 'Are you not feeling well?'

'I'm feeling fine. Fantastic. I just think it would be wise to get a doctor's advice before I go surfing over the next seven or eight months.'

She giggled when his mouth dropped open.

It was good few moments before comprehension spread over his features. 'You're not...?'

She couldn't stop the beam widening over her face. 'I'm over a week late...' She'd noticed her breasts growing tender, but it had been her stomach turning over at the scent of the barbecued spare ribs they'd had for dinner two nights before that had decided it for her.

'I'm going to be a father again?'

'There's only one way to find out.'

Jumping out of bed, she hurried into her dressing room and pulled a pregnancy test out of the chest of drawers. She'd got Elektra, whom she trusted implicitly, to buy it for her the day before. With Theseus hovering outside the bathroom, she did the necessary.

Three minutes later, buzzing with excitement, she poked her head out of the door.

'What do you want? A boy or a girl?'

The dazed look on his face evaporated. With a whoop, Theseus lifted her into his arms and carried her back to bed.

* * * * *

THE SHEIKH'S
SECRET BABY

SHARON KENDRICK

This book is for Elaine 'Lainey' Glasspool,who not only has the sunniest smile, the most Rapunzel-like hair and a spirit of joie-de-vivre which is positively inspirational, she also knows a wagonload of facts about horses.

So thanks for all the equine help, Lainey!

CHAPTER ONE

IT WAS THE LAST place he'd imagined her living.

Zuhal frowned. Jasmine? *Here?* In a tiny cottage in the middle of the English countryside, down a lane so narrow it had challenged the progress of his wide limousine? The woman who had loved the sparkle and buzz of the city, hiding herself away in some remote spot. There had to be some kind of mistake.

His frown became a flickering smile of anticipation. Not that he had given a lot of thought to her accommodation. If ever he'd stopped to think about his lusciously proportioned ex-lover—something he tried not to do, for obvious reasons—then it had usually been a predictable flashback to her soft skin. Or the tempting pertness of her breasts. Or the way she used to rain kisses all over his face so that his heart used to punch with pleasure. His groin, too.

He swallowed.

And that, of course, was the reason for his unexpected appearance today. The reason he'd decided to drop in and surprise her.

His throat dried. Why not? He liked sex and so did

Jasmine. Of all his lovers, she had been the one who
had really lit his fire. Sparks had flown between them
from the start and it seemed a pity not to capitalise on
that explosive chemistry with a little trip down memory lane. After all, it wasn't as if either of them had
entertained any unrealistic expectations. There had
been no dreams to be shattered. They hadn't asked
for the impossible and had known exactly where the
boundaries lay. They had conducted their affair like
adults. What possible harm could it do to revisit the
past and revel in a little uncomplicated bliss at a time
in his life when he needed some light relief like never
before?

He felt the smile die on his lips as part of him questioned the sanity of revisiting the past—and a woman—
like this. Because he never went back. If you reignited
an old relationship, then a woman could almost be excused for thinking it meant more to you than it really
did...and no relationship ever meant more than sex to
Zuhal Al Haidar.

And since Jazz was realistic enough to accept that,
maybe this one time he could be excused for breaking one of his own rules, because destiny was leading him down an unwanted path—a path which had
altered his whole future. Silently, he simultaneously
cursed and mourned his foolish brother, but all the
wishing in the world wasn't going to bring him back,
or rewrite the pages of history which had changed
his own destiny. He wasn't going to think about that.
He was going to concentrate on Jasmine Jones and
her soft body. To have her obliterate everything ex-

cept desire and fulfilment. He was growing hard just thinking about it, because she was the sweetest lover he had ever known.

He stepped over a cracked flagstone, through which a healthy-looking weed was pushing through. It had crossed his mind that she might have replaced him in her affections during the eighteen months they'd been apart, but deep down Zuhal refused to countenance such a scenario—mainly because his ego would not allow him to.

And if she had?

If that were the case, then he would graciously bow out. He was, after all, a desert king, not a savage—even if at times Jazz Jones had possessed the ability to make him feel as primitive as it was possible for a man to feel. He would wish her well and take his pleasure elsewhere, although he couldn't deny he would be disappointed not to revisit her enchanting curves and seeking mouth.

He pushed open the little gate, which even his untrained eye could tell needed a coat of paint, and made a mental note as he walked up the narrow path. Perhaps he would send someone out here to do just that. He lifted the loose door-knocker, which clearly had a screw missing, and frowned. Maybe even get someone to fix that for her, too.

Afterwards.

After he had enjoyed some badly needed solace.

He lifted the knocker, and as it fell heavily against the peeling paintwork he could hear the sound echoing through the tiny house.

* * *

Bringing the whirring drone of the sewing machine to a halt, Jasmine lifted her head to hear the sound of loud knocking, and she narrowed her eyes. Eyes which were tired and gritty from sewing until late last night. She rubbed them with the back of her fist, and yawned. Who was disturbing her during this quiet time when she'd got a rare opportunity to do some work? For a moment she was tempted to ignore it and stay there, neatly hemming the velvet curtains which needed to be delivered to her demanding client by next Wednesday, at the latest.

But she chided herself as she got up from her work spot in the corner of the sitting room and went to answer the unexpected summons. Surely she wasn't being suspicious just because someone was knocking at the door? If she wasn't careful she would become one of those sad people who became nervous at the thought of an unplanned caller. Who twitched whenever they heard a loud noise and were too scared to face the world outside. Just because she'd recently completed a radical lifestyle change and moved out of the city lock, stock and barrel didn't mean she had to start acting like some kind of hermit! Especially since she had discovered nothing but friendliness from the locals since arriving in this quiet hamlet—a factor which had helped cushion her sudden and dramatic change in circumstances. It was probably somebody selling raffle tickets for the local spring fayre.

She pulled open the door.

It wasn't.

It most definitely wasn't.

Shock coursed through her like a tidal wave. She could feel the physical effects of it and fleetingly thought how much they resembled desire. The rapid increase in her pulse and the rush of blood to her face. The wobbly knees, which made her glad she was gripping the door handle for support. And most of all, that slightly out-of-body sensation, which made her think this couldn't be happening.

It couldn't.

Heart still pounding, she studied the man who was standing on her doorstep—as if he might disappear in a puff of smoke if she stared at him long enough. But he stayed exactly where he was, as solid as dark marble and as vital as the mighty oak tree which towered over the nearby village green. She wanted to somehow be immune to him but how could she, when just seeing him again made her heart clench with longing and her body quiver with long-suppressed lust?

His face was angled—slashed with hard planes and contours which spoke of an aristocratic lineage, even if his proud bearing hadn't confirmed it. With hair as black as coal and eyes a gleaming shade almost as dark, his rich gold complexion was dominated by a hawk-like nose and the most sensual lips she'd ever seen. Yet the suit he wore contradicted his identity for it was urbane and modern, as was the crisp white shirt and silken tie. But Jasmine had seen photos of him in flowing robes, which made him look as if he'd stepped straight from the pages of a fairy tale. Pale robes which had emphasised his burnished skin and hinted at a hard body which had been honed on the saddle of a horse, in one of the world's most unforgiving desert landscapes.

Zuhal Al Haidar—sheikh and royal prince. Second son of an ancient dynasty which ruled the oil-rich country of Razrastan, where diamonds had been discovered close to its immense mountains and world-class racing horses were bred. The man to whom she had given her body and heart—although he had wanted only her body and she had pretended to be okay with that because there hadn't been an alternative. Well, the alternative would have been to have spurned his unexpected advances and that had been something she'd found herself unable to do. There hadn't been a day since they'd parted that she hadn't thought about him but she'd never thought she'd see him again because he had cut her out of his life completely.

And that was the thing she needed to remember. That he hadn't wanted her. He'd cast her aside like yesterday's newspaper. She bit her lip as questions flooded through her mind.

Why was he here?

And then, much more crucial…

She mustn't let him stay here.

But Jasmine wasn't stupid. At least, not any more. She might once have acted like a complete idiot where Zuhal was concerned, but not now. She had grown up since splitting with him. She'd had to. She'd learned that you sometimes had to stop and think about what was the best thing to do in the long term, rather than what you really wanted to do. So she resisted the urge to close the door firmly in his face and instead forced a polite smile to her lips.

'Good heavens, Zuhal,' she said, in a voice which sounded strangely calm. 'This is a…surprise.'

Zuhal frowned, irritation dwarfing the anticipation which was shafting through him. It wasn't the greeting he had been expecting. Surely she should have been rapturously hurling herself into his arms by now? Even if she had decided to act out a little game-playing resistance for the sake of her pride, he still would have expected to see her eyes darkening with desire, or the parting of those rosy lips in unconscious invitation.

But no. Instead of desire he saw wariness and something else. Something he didn't recognise. Just as he didn't recognise the woman who stood before him. He remembered Jazz Jones as being a bit of a fashion queen. Someone who was always beautifully turned out—even if she'd made most of her clothes herself because her budget had been tight. But she had always had a definite *style* about her—it had been one of the things which had first drawn him to her, and presumably why the Granchester Hotel had employed her as manager in its sleek London boutique.

He remembered her honey-coloured hair swinging to her chin, not grown out and tied back into a functional plait, which hung down the back of a plain jumper, which inexplicably had some unidentifiable stain on the shoulder. Her legs weren't on show either; their shapely curves were covered by a pair of very ugly jeans—a garment she'd never worn in his company after he'd explained his intense dislike of them.

But he told himself that her clothes didn't matter, because he didn't intend her to be wearing them for much longer. Nothing mattered—other than the yearning which was already heating his blood like a fever. And wasn't it ironic that Zuhal found himself resenting this sensual power she'd always had over him, even while his body hungrily responded to it? He let his voice dip into a velvety caress as it had done so often in the past, adopting the intimate tone of two people who had once been lovers. *And who would soon be lovers again.* 'Hello, Jazz.'

But there was no lessening of her wary expression. No answering smile or impulsive opening of the door to admit him to her home and her arms. No ecstatic acknowledgement that he was here, after nearly two years of not seeing each other. Instead, she nodded in recognition and once again there was a flash of something he didn't recognise in her eyes.

'How did you find me?'

He raised his eyebrows, because her unwelcoming attitude was something he wasn't familiar with—and neither was her bald question, which was bordering on the insolent. Was she really planning to interrogate him as if he were a passing salesman? Did she think it acceptable to leave the future King of Razrastan standing on her doorstep?

His words became tinged with a distinct note of reprimand, which had been known to make grown men shudder. 'Isn't this a conversation we should be having in the comfort of your home, Jazz, even if it doesn't strike me as very *comfortable*?'

She flinched. She actually flinched—before seeming to pull herself together. She was smiling now, but he could sense it was forced, as if she were pushing her mouth against the soft resistance of slowly setting concrete. He was confused. Hadn't they parted on good terms—or as good as they could be when a man was terminating what had been a very satisfying relationship? Although Jazz had been that little bit different from his other lovers, he recalled. She alone had refused to accept the keepsake piece of jewellery he always offered his ex-lovers as a memento. To his surprise—and, yes, his annoyance too—she had carefully repackaged the emerald and diamond pendant, along with a polite note telling him she couldn't possibly accept such a generous gift.

His mouth hardened as he looked at the peeling paint on the front door. She above all people could have done with an injection of cash.

'I'm afraid you can't come in,' she was saying. 'I'm sorry, Zuhal. It isn't…well, it isn't really convenient right now. Perhaps if you'd given me some warning.'

And then he understood. Of course. It was exactly as he had anticipated. Outwardly, she had accepted their break-up with dignity and a remarkable absence of begging, or tantrums. As he recalled, she hadn't even shed a single tear when he'd ended their affair—at least, not in his presence. But Jasmine Jones wasn't made of stone. She was the sexiest woman he'd ever met and had thrived under his expert tuition. Having awoken her body, surely he wouldn't have expected her to return to her celibate lifestyle after he'd introduced her to the joys of sex?

He felt the slow and heavy beat of a pulse to his temple. It was hard to believe—but why wouldn't she have replaced him in her bed with someone more suitable? Someone of her own class who might be willing or able to marry her. Perhaps he should have rung first. Or written. Given her time to prepare herself—to rid herself of her current squeeze and pretty herself up for his arrival. But since when did Zuhal Al Haidar ever have to ring ahead to make some sort of appointment?

He attempted to sound reasonable but could do nothing about the sudden dark clench of jealousy in his gut. 'You have another man in your life, Jazz?'

She looked genuinely taken aback—as if he had said something shocking and contemptible. 'Of course not!'

Zuhal expelled a breath he hadn't even realised he was holding. And wasn't it crazy how swiftly jealousy could become an overwhelming sense of triumph and then hot anticipation? 'Well, then. I have come a long way to see you.' He smiled. 'As I recall, when we went our separate ways we did it in the most civilised way possible. Which makes me wonder why you are so reluctant to let me in. Isn't that the modern way, for lovers to remain friends? To sit and talk of old times, with affection.'

Jasmine felt her body stiffen, grateful her left hand was still hidden behind the partially open door. Glancing over the Sheikh's burly shoulder, she could see the black gleam of his limousine sitting in the narrow lane, easily visible through the still-bare bushes. She supposed his driver was sitting there waiting, as people always waited for Zuhal. His bodyguards would be there, too, and there would probably be another carload of security people a little further along the lane, hidden from sight.

Hidden from sight.

Her heart contracted painfully but she tried to keep her face serene, even though the fear inside her was growing. She'd been so certain that the course she had taken had been the right one but now, as she looked into the carved perfection of Zuhal's dark features, she felt the disconcerting flurry of doubt—along with the far more worrying pang of recognition. What should she do?

If she refused to let him in it would arouse his suspicions—she knew it would. It would arouse his interest too, because he was alpha enough to always want what was denied him. And she still had at least an hour of freedom before the matter became more urgent than academic. So why not ask him inside? Find out what he had come for and politely listen before sending him on his way, no harm done. She felt the prick of conscience as she opened the door wider and saw him register the gold ring she wore on her wedding finger, and she saw his face darken as he bent his head to accommodate the low ceiling.

'I thought you said there wasn't a man in your life,' he accused as the door swung squeakily shut behind him.

'There isn't.'

'So why the wedding ring?' he demanded. 'Are you back with your husband?'

She flushed. 'Of course I'm not. That was never going to happen. We're divorced, Zuhal. You knew that. I was divorced when I met you.'

'So why the ring?' he demanded again.

Jasmine told herself he had no right to ask her questions about her personal life and maybe she should tell him so—but that would be pointless because Zuhal had never been brought up to conform to the rules of normal behaviour. And wasn't the truth that he *did* have the right to ask, even if he was unaware of it? She felt another painful twist of conscience before realising he was appraising her with a look she recognised only too well. The look which said he was hungry for her body. And that was all he ever wanted you for, she reminded herself bitterly. When the chips were down he wasn't offering you any kind of future. He took without giving anything back and she needed to protect herself to make sure that never happened again.

He was probably married by now—married to the suitable royal bride he had always told her he would one day marry.

She needed to get rid of him.

'I wear the ring as a deterrent,' she said.

He raised his dark eyebrows. 'Because men are regularly beating down your door with lustful intention?'

Ignoring the sardonic tone of his query, she shook her head. 'Hardly.'

'It's true that your appearance is a little drab,' he

conceded. 'But we both know how magnificent you can look when you try.'

Jasmine gritted her teeth, telling herself not to rise to the backhanded compliment. 'I realised I hadn't made the best relationship choices in the past and that I needed some time on my own,' she explained. 'Time to get my career up and running.'

'And what career might that be, Jazz?' he questioned softly. 'What made you stop working at the hotel boutique—I thought it paid reasonably well?'

Jasmine shrugged. She wasn't going to tell him about her soft furnishings business, which was still in an embryo stage but gaining in popularity all the time. Or her plans for designing baby clothes, which she hoped would one day provide her with a modest living. Because none of that was any of his business. 'London was getting too expensive and I wanted a change,' she said. 'And you still haven't told me why you're here.'

With genuine surprise, Zuhal realised that maybe he had misjudged his impact on her. Was it possible she hadn't been as besotted by him as he'd thought—and that she wouldn't take him into her bed without forethought or ceremony, as she'd done so often in the past? He remembered how her soft and undemanding nature had always acted like a balm on his troubled senses. How she had always been eager and hungry to see him. But now her distinct lack of interest punctured his erotic thoughts and instead he was filled with the unusual urge to confide in her. He sighed as he walked to the window and looked out at the yellow flash of the few straggly daffodils which were poking out from the overgrown grass in the tiny garden.

'You know my brother is missing?' he questioned, without preamble. 'Presumed dead.'

She gasped and when he turned round her fingers were lying against her throat, as if she were starved of air. '*Dead?*' she managed eventually. 'No, I didn't know that. Oh, Zuhal, I'm so sorry. I mean, I never met him—obviously—but I remember he was your only sibling.'

He narrowed his eyes. 'We kept it quiet for as long as possible, but now it's out there in the public domain. You hadn't heard?'

She shook her head. 'I don't… I don't get much chance to read the papers these days. World news is so depressing—and my TV isn't actually working at the moment,' she added, before biting down on the lushness of her lower lip and fixing him with a wary look. 'What happened, or would you rather not talk about it?'

He'd thought she might take him in her arms and comfort him and wasn't that what he wanted more than anything else? To feel the warmth of another body—the soft squeeze of flesh reminding him that he was very much alive instead of lying prone and cold somewhere in a merciless desert, while vultures hovered overhead. But she didn't. She just stood on the other side of the small room, her green-gold eyes dark with distress, though her body language remained stiff and awkward—as if she didn't know how to be around him.

But still he found himself talking about it, in a way he might not have done so freely with anyone else. Almost imperceptibly, his voice grew harsh. 'Although

Kamal was King of Razrastan, with all the responsibilities which came with that exalted role, my brother
never lost his love of recklessness.'

'I do remember you saying he was a bit of a dare-
devil,' she offered cautiously.

He gave another heavy sigh as he nodded. 'He was.
All through his youth he embraced the most dangerous of sports and nobody could do a thing to stop him.
Our father tried often enough, but our mother actively
encouraged his daring behaviour. Which was why he
piloted his own plane and heli-skied whenever possible. Why he deep-sea-dived and climbed the world's
most challenging mountains—and nobody could deny
that he excelled at everything he put his mind to.' He
paused. 'His coronation as King inevitably curtailed
most of these activities, but he was still prone to taking
off on his horse, often alone. He said it gave him time
to think. To be away from the hurly-burly of palace life.
And that's what happened last year...'

'What did?' she prompted uneasily as his words
tailed off.

Zuhal felt the inevitable sense of sorrow mounting
inside him but there was bitterness, too. Because hadn't
Kamal's actions impacted on so many people—and on
him more than anyone? 'One morning he mounted his
beloved Akhal-Teke horse and rode off into the desert
as the sun was rising, or so one of the stable boys told
us later. By the time we realised he had ridden off unac-
companied, a fierce storm was blasting its way through
the desert. Even from within the protection of the palace

walls we could see the sky growing as red as blood and the wind whipping itself up into a wild frenzy.'

His voice grew unsteady for a moment before he continued. 'They say there is no escape from the blanket of sand which results from those storms, that it infiltrates everything. You can't see, or hear, or breathe. For a while it feels as if hell has unleashed all its demons and set them free upon the world.' He swallowed. 'We never found either of them—neither man nor horse—during one of the biggest search operations our country has ever mounted. Not a trace. It is inconceivable that he could have survived such an onslaught.' There was a pause as his mouth twisted. 'And the desert is very efficient at disposing of bodies.'

'Oh, Zuhal,' she whispered. 'That's awful. I'm so sorry for your loss.'

He gave a brief nod of his head, dismissing her soft words of sympathy because he hadn't come here for *words*. 'We're all sorry,' he said matter-of-factly.

'So what will happen?'

'Kamal cannot be officially pronounced dead for seven years, but the law states that the country cannot be without a king during that time.' Like a boxer in the ring, Zuhal clenched his fists so that the knuckles cracked and turned deathly white beneath the olive skin. 'And so, I have agreed to rule in his absence.'

She blinked at him as if the significance of what he had told her had only just sunk in. 'What exactly does that…mean?'

'It means that in seven years' time, if Kamal has still not returned, then I will be crowned, since I am the sole surviving heir. Until that time I will be King in everything but name, and I will be known as the Sheikh Regent.'

It was the mention of the word *heir* which set Jasmine's senses jangling with renewed fear. A trickle of sweat whispered down her back and settled at the base of her spine, soaking into the waistband of her jeans. Did he *know*? Was that why he was here today?

But no, of course he didn't know. He wouldn't be standing there with that bleak look on his face talking about his powerful new role if he had any inkling of the momentous thing which had happened in *her* life. And there were reasons he didn't know, she reminded herself painfully. Reasons which had helped spur her desire to stop reading the papers and listening to the news.

'And is your *wife...*' Somehow her voice didn't tremble on the word. 'Is she happy about her position as the new ruler's consort?'

'My wife?' he echoed, frowning at her uncomprehendingly. 'I don't have a wife, Jazz.'

'But I thought...' Jasmine swallowed as her perceived view of the world did a dramatic shift. 'I thought you were seeing a princess from a neighbouring desert region, soon after we split. Zara, I think her name was.'

Zuhal nodded. 'I was.' His eyes narrowed as they swept over her. 'Yes, Zara was the latest in a long line of mooted royal brides, with a pedigree almost equal to my own.' He shrugged. 'But she had a laugh which used to set my teeth on edge and I could not contemplate a life-long partnership with her. And back then, there was no sense of urgency. Now it is different, of course. Now I must rule my country and for that I will need a wife by my side.'

Jasmine's heart flooded with heat and began to pound loudly with something which felt like hope, even though afterwards she would ask herself how she could have been so stupid. But for a few seconds she actually allowed herself to believe in the fantasy which still haunted her some nights when sleep stubbornly refused to come—of her desert prince returning to sweep her off her feet. 'I still don't understand,' she said cautiously, 'why you're here.'

He lifted up the palms of his hands like a man on the point of surrender. 'I'll tell you exactly why I'm here, Jazz,' he said, a hard smile flattening the edges of his sensual lips. 'Next month my life will change beyond recognition, when I sign the papers which are currently being drawn up to officially recognise me as the Sheikh Regent. But beneath all the inevitable celebrations that the line will continue my people are grieving and uncertain, for my brother's disappearance has unsettled them. The country needs stability and they are looking to me to provide it, for while Kamal had many commendable character traits, steadfastness was not one of them. I need a bride,' he said, not seeming to notice that she had gasped again, or that her hands had started trembling. 'But this time I cannot afford to be picky. I must marry someone suitable—and quickly.'

She gulped the words out breathlessly. She just couldn't help herself. 'Someone l-like?'

'Someone of royal blood. Obviously.' His black eyes crinkled with that rare flash of mischief which used to tie her up in knots. 'Not a divorced girl from England, I'm afraid, Jazz—just in case you were getting your hopes up.'

'I wasn't,' she said, furious with him, but even more furious with herself—for allowing herself that stupid little daydream which had made her heart begin to race. Hadn't she learnt *anything* during the time she'd been his secret mistress? That she was as disposable as an empty baked-beans can? 'Is that why you're here, Zuhal?' she demanded. 'To talk about your marriage prospects? What were you hoping for—my advice? Perhaps you'd like me to help you vet your future bride for you?'

'No, that's not why I'm here. Do you want me to show you why I'm here, my beautiful Jazz?' He had started moving across the small room until he was standing right in front of her. Until he had pulled her without warning into his powerful arms, his black eyes glittering with pain and desire and something else, as he stared down into her face. 'I'm here because I'm empty and aching and because I know you can take that ache away.'

She should have given him a piece of her mind. Should have told him she wasn't just something he could put down and then pick up again, as the whim took him. So why didn't she? Was it his touch which made common sense fly out of the window, or just the yearning inside her which had never gone away? She should have realised that by *aching* he meant sex, but for one crazy moment Jasmine thought he was talking about his heart. So she let him tilt her chin with those strong, olive-dark fingers, just as she let his mouth travel towards hers in what felt like a slow extension of time. She had to urge herself not to rise up on tiptoe to make the kiss come sooner, but somehow she retained enough restraint to hold back. But perhaps that wasn't such a good idea because by the time their lips touched, she felt a flash of connection so intense that she gave a little moan of joy.

And Jazz forgot everything. Forgot why he shouldn't be there and why she shouldn't be reacting to him like this. Why it was wrong to allow his strong hands to burrow beneath the thick-knit sweater she was wearing and to cup her breasts with luxuriant familiarity. It felt like the best place she'd been for a very long time as his mouth explored hers with a thoroughness which left her reeling, his tongue licking at her with intimate familiarity. The blood pumped through her veins like honey as she felt the drift of his fingers over her nipples—briefly flicking over the engorged buds before creeping down to her torso.

And this was heaven. Jasmine's throat dried as he reacquainted himself with the curve of her belly and she wriggled accommodatingly as he slipped his thumb beneath the waistband of her jeans and began to tease the warm, bare skin. Did she suck her stomach in, hoping that he would move his hands further inside the thick denim to caress her where she was hot and wet and longing to be caressed, and didn't she want that more than anything else? She could feel the hard press of his erection and instinctively her thighs parted by a fraction and she could hear his low murmur of appreciation.

He drew his lips away. 'You've changed shape,' he observed unevenly.

'Y-yes.' She nearly asked him whether or not he liked it—and how crazy was *that*?—when a sudden thought hit her like a squirt of icy water and fear began to whisper over her. Drawing in a deep breath, she looked directly into his eyes as comprehension began to dawn on her. 'Are you here just because…because you want to have sex with me, Zuhal?'

He seemed momentarily taken aback by her question but she knew the moment she saw him shrug that her worst fear was true. Well, maybe not her *worst* fear…

'You…you want some kind of physical release, is that it?' she continued unsteadily. 'Some easy, uncomplicated sex, before you return home in search of your suitable royal bride?'

At least he had the grace to look abashed but the look was quickly replaced by one of defiance. 'What did you expect, Jazz?' he murmured. 'That I would present to my very conservative people a foreign divorcee as the woman I had chosen?' His black gaze burned into her. 'We both know that was always going to be a nonstarter. Just as we both know that the chemistry which has always sparked between us is still there. Nothing about that has changed. I still want you so much that I could explode with it—and so do you. You come alive whenever I touch you, don't you? Your body cries out for mine, the same way it always did. So why waste it?' His voice dipped into a sensual caress. 'Why not give into what we both want—and make love one last and beautiful time?'

Dazedly, Jasmine listened to his arrogant statement—and didn't his attitude justify some of the tough decisions she'd been forced to make? She was about to tell him that it was a mistake to call what he had in mind *making love* and wondering if he would attempt to persuade her otherwise, when a distant sound changed everything. She moved away from him—not so quickly as to arouse suspicion—praying that Darius was only whimpering in some kind of happy little infant dream and would shortly go back to sleep.

But her prayers went unanswered. The whimper became louder. It morphed into a cry and then a protesting yell and she saw Zuhal's face change. Watched the black eyes narrow as his gaze swept questioningly over her and she quickly stared down at the threadbare rug for fear that he might see the sudden tears welling up in her eyes. She thought about all the things she *could* say.

She could pretend that it was a peacock, because weren't they supposed to sound like young babies? Or maybe that was babies younger than Darius which sounded like those squawking birds. And anyway, peacocks lived in the grounds of stately homes, didn't they? They promenaded elegantly over manicured lawns—their magnificent blue-green plumage wouldn't dream of gracing the scruffy little garden of a rented cottage just outside Oxford.

'What was that, Jazz?' Zuhal questioned ominously.

She knew then that the game was up. That she could attempt evasion to try to deflect his attention and send him on his way by pretending that the baby belonged to someone else and she was just childminding. But she couldn't. Not really—and not just because the time frame would prove her a liar. No. No matter what had happened in the past or how little Zuhal thought of her now, she was going to have to come clean. And hadn't she always wanted that anyway, on some subliminal level?

'What was that, Jazz?' he repeated, only now a note of something dangerous had been added into the mix to make his voice grow even darker.

Slowly she lifted her gaze to meet the accusation in his eyes and prepared for her whole world to change in the telling of a single sentence. 'It's my child. Or rather, our child,' she said, sucking in a breath of air. 'You have a son, Zuhal, and his name is Darius.'

CHAPTER TWO

AND THEN, AS IF by magic, Darius went back to sleep. Jasmine could hear it quite plainly in the sounds which were issuing from his baby monitor. The lessening of his cry into a gulping sob which gradually became a little coo, which was so much a feature of his daily nap. She knew he would now be peacefully asleep again and that if only her son's timing had been a little better, Zuhal would have been none the wiser.

But Jasmine knew there was no point wishing that Darius had delayed his cry until the Sheikh had been hurried away from the premises. If Zuhal hadn't been kissing her, then he would already have left. If she hadn't been stupidly *letting* him kiss her and wanting the kind of things she should be ashamed of wanting…

And anyway—wasn't this what she had always wanted to happen? Had tried to make happen, if she hadn't been blocked along the way by his position and power. *So don't let guilt beat you up*, she told herself fiercely, even though it was difficult not to flinch as she met the naked accusation in his black eyes. You've tried to do your best.

'My son?' he repeated incredulously.

She nodded. 'Yes, he—'

'Don't you dare say another word. Just take me to see him,' he cut over her words, his voice laced with a layer of ice she'd heard him use before—though never with her.

'You will see him. I promise—just not yet. Let him sleep, Zuhal. Please,' she said, with the confidence of someone who'd been bringing up a baby on her own for the last nine months and knew how cranky they could get if they were woken prematurely.

'I won't waken him but I want to see him.' His autocratic command hissed through the air. 'Take me to him, Jazz. Now.'

Her lips dry, Jasmine nodded. How had she ever thought she could oppose his wishes? She'd never managed it in the past—so why should now be any different? He had dumped her without warning—and, even though he had told her from the start that she could never have any future with him, it had still seemed to come out of the blue. But she had held it together then, just as she must hold it together now. 'Come with me,' she said in a low voice, the hairs on the back of her neck prickling with unease as she led the way from the room.

Feeling like a participant in some bizarre dream, Zuhal followed Jazz up the narrow staircase, his mind spinning with disbelief as she reached the top and gestured towards the open door of a nursery painted in sunny shades of yellow. He wanted to convince himself that she'd been lying and that it was no child of his who lay sleeping in a cot beneath the window. But as he silently crossed the room to gaze down at the infant, he knew there was absolutely no question that this was his baby. It was more than the shock of ebony hair so like his own. More than the olive skin, which was a paler version of his. It was something fundamental and almost *primitive* which activated a powerful surge of recognition deep within him as he gazed down at the gently parted lips of the baby boy. He saw Jazz tense as he reached down and briefly laid his forefinger against the baby's soft cheek, before withdrawing it and turning abruptly on his heel, to walk out the way he had come. He didn't say a word until they were back downstairs—he didn't trust himself to speak—and even though he wanted to rage and rail at her, he kept his voice low.

'Do you realise the constitutional significance of what you've done?' he hissed.

Jasmine flinched and a part of her wished she could have given into the luxury of tears if she hadn't recognised the need to stay strong. *Constitutional significance?* Was that the only thing he cared about in the light of his discovery? Of course it was. It was why he'd ended their relationship and why he had turned up here today, to use her body as he might use a stone vessel filled with water to quench his thirst. For him nothing mattered other than the needs and demands of his beloved country and everything else came second to that.

'Did you not think to tell me, Jazz?' he continued, still in that icy undertone of suppressed fury. 'That the seed of my loins had borne fruit?'

Jasmine shivered as his words created a powerful image in her mind which made her heart clench with impotent longing until she forced herself to push it away and focus on what was important. 'I did try to tell you.'

His cold expression suggested he didn't believe her. 'When?'

'After we…split up.' *When he'd sweetly informed her that she was the kind of woman who made a perfect mistress, but not the kind of woman he could ever marry.* 'Not for many weeks, it's true. I… I didn't realise I was pregnant. At least, not straight away.'

'Why not?' he bit out witheringly. 'You may have been a virgin when we met but please don't make out you were born yesterday, Jazz. What do you mean, you *didn't realise* you were pregnant? What, were you waiting for the stork to fly in through the window and surprise you?'

His words were cruel. Sarcastic. Deliberately so, it seemed. Jasmine tried to convince herself that his anger was understandable. Wouldn't she have felt just as angry if the situation were reversed—to have discovered that she'd become a parent and have been kept in the dark about it? 'I was all over the place,' she admitted. 'I was operating in a bit of a fog—on autopilot, if you like. Just getting through the day took all my energy and I felt disorientated because…well, it was *weird* getting used to life without you.'

Zuhal's lips tightened but to his surprise he found he couldn't disagree with her because he too had been disconcerted by the discovery that Jazz had left a peculiar hole in his life. He had explained it away by reminding himself that it had all been about sex—the best sex he'd ever had. Against all the odds she had captivated him—

for he had never been with someone as low-born as her before. She'd been working in the boutique attached to London's famous Granchester Hotel where he'd been staying, and on a primitive level he had initially been drawn to her pert breasts and curvy hips. By the buttery swing of her blonde hair and the way her lips curved into a sweet smile whenever she was serving customers. But although many women caught his eye and made it clear they were his for the taking, Zuhal rarely gave into his most base desires. Sometimes he took pleasure in denying himself sexual gratification because deprivation was good for the spirit and what was easily gained was easily discarded. Plus, he liked a challenge—and a challenge had certainly been presented to him when the humble shop girl had blushed as he'd spoken to her and had had difficulty meeting his gaze.

His hunger ignited, he had been pleased to discover she was divorced because divorced women were often cynical about marriage, with few of the marital ambitions of single women, which bored the hell out of him. They also possessed an earthy expertise which made them the best lovers.

But Jazz hadn't been experienced.

He remembered his shock—and then his pleasure— when he had discovered her innocence. When she had opened those soft thighs and he had broken through the tight hymen, which had flagged up the gratifying knowledge that he was her first ever lover. He remembered the orgasm which had followed. Which had rocked him to the core of his being. And the one after, and the one after that…

With an effort he dragged his mind back to the present because none of that was relevant now. Not in the light of his discovery that she was a secretive little manipulator.

'Talk me through what happened, Jazz,' he bit out and could see her trying to compose herself, rubbing her hands up and down over the arms of her sweater, as if she were cold.

She swallowed. 'When you went back to Razrastan I just carried on as normal, terrified someone at the hotel was going to discover I'd been having intimate relations with a guest.'

'But nobody did?' he probed.

Jasmine shook her head. 'No. Not a soul. But then, we were very discreet, weren't we, Zuhal? You made sure of that. I was never even permitted to stay with you in your fancy penthouse suite and we only ever went to the borrowed house of one of your rich friends, under cover of darkness.'

'I have always tried to be discreet about my relationships—and the newspapers would have had a field day if they'd discovered I was sleeping with someone like you,' he said coldly.

'Someone like me?' she echoed.

'You know what I'm talking about. It was almost a cliché—the prince and the shop girl. In a way, I was protecting you.'

Jasmine bit her lip, because it had been much more likely he had been protecting his own precious reputation. Should she tell him how difficult it had felt to carry on serving behind the till with that bright smile pinned to her lips, when she had been missing him so much? Maybe it was the effort of that—of trying to appear normal—which had meant her first missed period had passed by without her noticing. And then when she *had* noticed something was amiss, she'd been unable to confide in anyone. Her parents were dead and she hadn't dared place her trust in friends and colleagues, terrified someone might run to the press with the story. She had a cousin she was close to, but Emily lived miles away and Jasmine had never felt quite so lonely.

Even now, as she looked up into Zuhal's flinty features, she could still remember the scary sense of isolation she'd felt as she'd realised she was pretty much on her own, with a tiny life to support. Factor in the fact that she'd been missing him so badly and you ended up with someone who had found herself in a precarious situation. 'I tried to ring you but your number came up as unobtainable.'

He met the question in her eyes. 'I make a point of regularly changing my phone number,' he informed her coolly. 'My security people tell me it's safer that way.'

'And, of course, it keeps troublesome ex-girlfriends at bay?' she guessed, forcing herself to confront the bitter truth.

He shrugged. 'Something like that,' he conceded. 'When did you try to contact me?'

Accurately, she was able to relay the exact month—because at that stage her pregnancy had been well established. She'd been determined to show Zuhal that she intended going ahead with the birth, with or without his approval. That she didn't need a man—or a husband—

in order to survive, because experience had taught her that marriage was by no means the magic bullet which so many women imagined it was.

Feeling on firmer footing now, she sucked in a steadying breath. 'Eventually, I managed to get through to one of your aides. Adham, I think his name was. I told him I needed to speak to you urgently and he promised he would pass on the message to you.'

'But I never got it,' he said, his voice hardening.

'So blame him.'

'Adham is a loyal servant who would have been acting in my best interests. The palace was in uproar because of my brother's disappearance and, of course, that impacted profoundly on my future. And not just that.' His black eyes bored into her. 'Do you have any idea of the amount of women who are eager to speak to me, who try to phone the palace switchboard?'

'Strangely enough no, I don't,' she answered, colour rising in her cheeks so that suddenly she felt hot and uncomfortable. 'Tallying up the numbers of your ex-lovers isn't a pastime which has ever appealed to me.'

'You could have told him you were pregnant!' he accused. 'You knew that would have ensured you got through to me straight away. Why didn't you do that, Jazz?'

Jasmine licked her lips. Because she'd been scared. Scared of Zuhal's influence and of the reality of confronting it for the first time. He'd always left his sheikh status at the door of the bedroom, but during that brief and fruitless phone call, she'd got an inkling of the real man behind the very sexy facade. It had taken her ages to get through to his office and during the long wait she'd realised just how powerful her former lover really was. She remembered the way his aide had spoken to her—as if she were a piece of dirt he'd found on the bottom of his shoe. And she'd been fearful that, although Zuhal obviously didn't want her any more, he might want to claim sole custody of their baby—and he'd have the wherewithal to make it happen.

And that was something she could never allow.

'You told me you were planning to marry a royal princess,' she reminded him. 'I thought that was another reason why your aide was so *off* with me. There were reports about your burgeoning romance in all the papers. About how two desert kingdoms were going to be united and it was going to be the greatest thing to happen in the region for decades. The Dream Desert ticket, I think the tabloids called it.' Which had been another reason why she'd stopped reading them. 'Wouldn't it have completely ruined everything if some casual lover had come forward with the news that you were to become a father?'

Zuhal's eyes narrowed as he forced himself to dismiss her persuasive words. Because weren't these accusations and counter-accusations diverting his attention from the monumental discovery he had just made?

He had a son.

A ready-made heir.

Perhaps fate was showing him a little benevolence for once.

He looked at the woman standing in front of him. A few minutes ago he'd been kissing her and her response had indicated that if it hadn't been for the baby's cry, she would have allowed him to be deep inside her by now. *Would* she, he found himself wondering, with a brand-new disdain which had blossomed as a result of his unbelievable discovery? Had she become one of those women who would cast aside the needs of her baby in pursuit of her own carnal pleasures? And if that were the case, then wouldn't that be easy to prove in a court of law—thereby putting him in a morally superior position and demonstrating his own suitability to bring up the child, instead of her? Surely that would be simpler all round.

He noted the trepidation flickering in the depths of her green-gold eyes as she returned his gaze, just as he noted the sudden tension which was stiffening her narrow shoulders. The silence between them was growing into something immense and uncomfortable but, unlike most people would be, Zuhal was unperturbed by it. Indeed, he often *orchestrated* silence when necessary, for it was a powerful tool in negotiation and never had negotiation been more vital than now.

'How are you managing for money?' he questioned casually.

He could see a look of faint confusion criss-cross her brow and wondered if she was disorientated by his sudden change of subject.

'I manage,' she said defensively.

'I said "how", Jazz?'

She shrugged. 'I sew.'

He frowned. 'You sew?'

'Yes. You remember. I always liked sewing. I was

planning to go to fashion college when my mother got sick and I had to defer my place to look after her.'

He thought back. Had she told him that? Even if she *had*, he suspected it would have gone in one ear and straight out of the other. He hadn't really been interested in her past, just as he hadn't been interested in her future, because he'd known there could never be one—not for them. The only thing which had interested him, and for a time had obsessed him, had been the magnificence of her body and the sheer sexual dynamite of their coming together.

'That's right,' he prevaricated as some long-buried fact swam up from the depths of his subconscious. 'You wanted to be a fashion designer. Is that what you're doing now?'

She gave him the kind of look which suggested he had no idea how normal mortals lived. 'I wish,' she said. 'You can't just set yourself up as a fashion designer, Zuhal, especially when you've got no real qualifications. For one thing, the overheads would be prohibitive, and for another, there's a whole heap of competition out there. You see that sewing machine over there?' Her finger trembled a little as she pointed to it. 'That's what I was doing when you arrived. Mostly, I specialise in soft furnishings—cushions and curtains, that sort of thing. People always need those and Oxford isn't far away. There are plenty of folk with deep pockets who change their decor all the time, even if there's nothing wrong with it. Probably because they're rich and bored and can't think of anything better to do,' she added.

She seemed eager to deflect his attention from

the life-changing news with her mundane chatter, he thought grimly. And she would be, wouldn't she? But her words made him consider both her income and her environment and for the first time Zuhal took proper notice of his surroundings, his lips curving with ill-concealed contempt. The furniture was of the cheapest variety, the rug threadbare and the paint on the window frames peeling. Only the curtains and cushions redeemed the place, their brightness adding an unexpected touch of jollity to the small room. Presumably her own handiwork.

His disdain turned into anger. And she was bringing up his son in a place like this! The heir to the Al Haidar dynasty was growing up in some scruffy little house on the outskirts of Oxford, with no security at the door and barely enough warmth inside. He wanted to berate her. To tell her she was unfit to care for his child, but something made him bite back his words as he sensed that hostility would be counterproductive to his cause. He looked at her faded jeans and the sweater with that ugly stain on the shoulder. Wouldn't it be sensible to offer her an easy way out? To leave her free to live the kind of life she had been destined to live before their paths had unpredictably crossed in an upmarket London hotel.

'We need to discuss the future,' he said.

She looked at him warily. 'What do you mean?'

He took a step closer and then wished he hadn't because her unsophisticated soapy scent suddenly made his senses become keen and raw. And wasn't it crazy that, despite his anger, he could still feel the powerful jerk of his erection pressing uncomfortably hard against the zipper of his trousers? Hadn't she always had that power over him—and hadn't it been that power which had made him terminate their relationship sooner than he'd intended?

'What do you think I mean, Jazz?' he demanded. 'Did you think I would be content to be granted a brief look at my son before shrugging my shoulders and walking away? That I would be prepared to say good-bye to a child who has been kept a stranger to me until now?'

She swallowed. 'Of course I didn't.'

'You say that with remarkably little conviction!' he accused.

'Because it's all happened so quickly! I wasn't expecting you to just turn up like this, Zuhal. It's difficult to know what to think.'

'At least we are agreed on something,' he said. 'Though I think that, of the two of us, I have received by far the greater surprise today. I need a little time to assess the situation properly and work out where we must go from here. Decisions made in the heat of the moment will benefit no one, least of all my son.'

'You mean...' Her green-gold eyes looked hopeful. 'You mean you'll go back to Razrastan and contact me when you've had a chance to mull it over?'

He gave a short laugh. 'Go back to Razrastan? Are you really that naïve, Jazz? Do you think that, having found my child, I will now exit myself from his life?' Ruthlessly, he found himself taking pleasure from her lip-biting response to his words. And why *shouldn't* he enjoy her distress? She hadn't given *his* feelings a second thought when she'd kept his progeny hidden from him, had she? 'I will return later to take you to dinner. Somewhere neutral away from here, where we can consider our options. I will have one of my people book somewhere suitable.'

'No. I can't. That isn't going to work,' she protested. 'I'm not leaving Darius while I go out for dinner with you!'

'Why not?' he demanded. 'Do you think I'm going to have him spirited away while you're out?'

She met his gaze with a fierce challenge on her face—a look he had never seen her use before. 'I wouldn't put it past you.'

He inclined his head in unwilling admiration. 'You are wise indeed not to underestimate my determination,' he conceded. 'But you still haven't explained your refusal to dine with me.'

'Because I don't have a local babysitter, not yet,' she babbled. 'And I'm not leaving Darius with a stranger!'

His lips twisted. 'You think I would compromise childcare, Jazz? He is a royal Prince of Razrastan—and he will be cared for by the finest professional money can buy.'

'No.'

'*No?*' he verified incredulously.

'I'm not leaving him with a stranger,' she repeated stubbornly.

A pulse flickered at his temple as he trained his gaze on the minuscule kitchen which could just be glimpsed over her shoulder. 'You expect me to eat dinner here?'

'I don't particularly care whether you eat or not, since food is the last thing on my mind,' she returned. 'But since you are determined to have this meeting, I dare say I can rustle up something for supper.'

There was a moment of tense silence before, slowly, he nodded his head. 'Very well. I will return at eight.' He paused. 'In the meantime, my bodyguards will be stationed around the property, so if you're contemplating making some dramatic break for freedom, I urge you think again.'

Jasmine stared at him, feeling as if she was being backed into a corner. Was that how he intended her to feel? As if he had all the power and she had none? *Because that was true, wasn't it?* She looked at him. 'Bodyguards?' she echoed. 'Are you out of your mind? We've been living here perfectly safely for the last six months. This is rural Oxfordshire. We don't need bodyguards.'

'On the contrary, you most certainly do. You may have lived that way in the past, Jazz, but those days are over. This child has pure Al Haidar blood pulsing through his veins and will be treated accordingly.' He slanted her a warning look. 'I will see you later. Just make sure you are ready to receive me.'

His final request was like a throwback to the past and she wondered how she was supposed to do that. Was he hinting that he'd like her to be waiting for him wearing some tiny scrap of silk-satin lingerie the way she'd done in the past—showing as much flesh as possible without actually being naked? She studied his hard face. Unlikely. At this precise moment, his expression betrayed nothing but contempt. His bearing was both regal and imperious as he turned and walked out of the front door, closing it softly behind him. Jasmine could hear the purr of a powerful car engine as it started to move and now that the shock of seeing him again had begun to wear off, she began to tremble.

Unwanted tears stung her eyes, but she brushed them away as she tried to centre herself and make sense of what had just happened and to wonder how it had all come to this.

She heard Darius beginning to wake again and determination flooded through her in a hot rush as she recognised that she needed to have her wits about her when dealing with a man as powerful as Zuhal.

But most of all she needed to be strong.

CHAPTER THREE

SHE SHOULD NEVER have fallen for the royal Sheikh—
that was the thought which plagued Jasmine for the rest
of the afternoon, even while she was playing peep-oh
with Darius then splashing him in the bath and making
him giggle in that heartbreakingly innocent way of his.

But Zuhal had been determined to seduce her, despite the fact that she had been a shop girl and he a
royal prince of noble descent. Her marriage had ended
and she'd been feeling a failure when the Sheikh had
waltzed into the Granchester boutique and subjected
her to a highly effective charm offensive. She remembered his dark gaze licking over her skin and it had felt
like being bathed in sweet black molasses. Sensing an
unknown danger, she had let the other, rather pushy
assistant deal with him, but her reluctance to engage
had only seemed to increase his desire. Had she been
surprised when he had turned up the following day to
subject her to some more of that lazy charm? Not really. And she would have challenged any woman with
a pulse to have resisted him for long. The strict rules of
the hotel concerning relationships between guests and

staff meant their resulting flirtation had been conducted amid great secrecy, and afterwards she'd realised that had probably added an extra layer of piquancy.

But the tumultuous ending of her marriage had left her feeling undesirable and Zuhal had changed all that so, of course, she'd agreed to have dinner with him. The restaurant had been small and badly lit—chosen mainly for discretion, she'd suspected—and even though the implied secrecy of that had been a little disappointing, already she'd been in too deep to care. To her astonishment—but not his—she had ended up in bed with him.

It had been…bliss. No other word for it. The soft plunder of his lips. His slow undressing as he had peeled off her cheap clothes. Her first sight of him naked—all that honed and burnished flesh and the unmistakable evidence of just how much he'd wanted her. She should have been shy, or even daunted—but she had been neither. In fact, she had been wet and ready, uttering nameless pleas as he'd stroked erotic pathways over her heated skin. Even the brief pain of losing her virginity hadn't marred her mounting enjoyment and Zuhal had confessed afterwards that it had added an extra layer of excitement to his. Orgasm had followed orgasm and he hadn't said anything until afterwards, when she'd been lying gazing up at the ceiling in dazed disbelief as he'd circled a puckered nipple with one careless finger. Turning her flushed face towards his, he had drawled out a single word.

'Why?'

And then she'd told him about Richard and her non-consummated marriage. About how he'd insisted on waiting until their wedding night and how flattered she had been by that seemingly old-fashioned restraint. Because she'd thought it was an essential ingredient for a happy marriage—though she had been basing her opinion on guesswork rather than experience, because she had no idea what a happy marriage was like. Because she'd blocked her eyes and ears to the reality of her own parents' marriage for so long, hadn't she? She'd learnt to ignore dark undercurrents and pretend they simply weren't happening. She'd become an expert in normalising dysfunctional relationships. As if by normalising them it would make everything all right...but of course, it never did. She had been the lonely child, caught in the crossfire of two warring parents. And it had been hell. Perhaps that had been another reason why she'd agreed to become Richard's wife. He had felt *safe*—a bit like a small boat discovering a calm harbour after a rocky and unpredictable voyage.

Yet when her own wedding night had come—sex just hadn't happened. It had been embarrassing and disappointing and as time had gone on and still she'd remained a virgin, Jasmine had asked Richard whether it was something to do with her. It was then that he had broken down in tears to tell her he actually preferred men. To be honest, it had come as something of a relief to know the simple cause of their incompatibility and Jasmine had wished him well before they had separated. But it had left her wondering whether she was a bad judge of character not to have picked up on it before.

She had also wondered if Zuhal would think her less of a woman because of her unusual past. Or if her lack of experience would turn him off, but, to her pleasure and surprise, it had seemed to do the exact opposite.

'Perfect,' he'd murmured, while fingering her quivering flesh. 'Just perfect.'

'Wh-what is?' she remembered asking dazedly.

And that was when he'd explained that being a divorcee automatically precluded her from any kind of future with him, just in case she'd been getting any ideas—something she'd denied vehemently.

But afterwards she'd wondered just how true her denial had been. She'd told him she never expected anything from their relationship other than pleasure, so how did that explain the river of tears she'd cried when they'd made love for the very last time?

She needed to remember that. Every bit of it. To remind herself of just how ruthless Zuhal could be—and just how stupidly sensitive *she* could be. He had all the wealth and the power while she had none, but she had something far more precious: her gorgeous little black-haired baby who was the light of her life. She wasn't going to be unreasonable—just as long as Zuhal wasn't. He needed to understand that, despite the huge differences between them, in their roles as parents they would be equals.

She laid Darius down in his crib and went through the lullaby routine she'd begun after bringing him home from the hospital. She remembered how scared she'd been, yet determined to love her little baby with all her heart. But Darius had been easy to love. An easy baby all round. He hadn't cried incessantly at night, nor been difficult to feed. Had he somehow sensed that Jasmine had been having a tough time adapting to life as a single mum and, in some loyal baby way, had made it as simple as possible for her?

Her hair was still damp from bath-time play and she certainly hadn't got around to changing her clothes when Jasmine heard an authoritative rap on the door. But she wasn't planning on trying to make herself look presentable to Zuhal, was she? To slip into something glamorous so he might look at her with admiration rather than contempt. Apart from the fact that it was so long since she had dressed up for a night out, mightn't that send out the wrong message? Zuhal had one role to play in her life and that was as a father. She bit her lip. Which meant she needed to put all thoughts of the other stuff out of her mind. The kisses and the caresses and the scarily fast way he could always make her come. The way she'd almost succumbed in his arms earlier...

Even so, she couldn't quite block out her foreboding as she ran downstairs, because she suspected that remaining immune to Zuhal was going to be easier said than done. Heart racing, she pulled open the door to greet him, wishing his impact weren't always so overwhelming. But it was. Every time she saw him she felt as if someone had squeezed her heart within an iron fist and wouldn't let it go. Unlike her, Zuhal *had* changed his clothes—adopting the casual attire which occasionally permitted him to go as incognito as was possible when you were the possessor of such head-turning good looks. His soft black jacket meant he smelt faintly of leather, underpinned with that subtle scent of sandalwood which was so much a part of him. Dark jeans hugged the powerful length of his thighs and his jaw was shadowed with the new growth which appeared so soon after he'd shaved, reminding her of just how virile he'd always seemed to her innocent eyes.

But these were things she didn't need reminding of. Zuhal's allure and charisma had never been in any doubt. It was his other qualities she needed to remember right now. His ruthlessness and determination. His ability to cast something aside once he was bored with it. She needed to remind herself that she had simply been a diversion. A sexual plaything to amuse himself with before the time came to take a suitable bride.

There was no conventional greeting from him—no pleasant social niceties which other men might have felt duty-bound to make. He walked straight past her and, without warning or ceremony, slapped a Manila envelope down on the table before turning to look at her, his black eyes glittering. 'You might want to read this before we go any further,' he observed.

'What is it?' she questioned.

He hesitated—an uncharacteristic enough gesture for Jasmine to instantly be on her guard.

'In a nutshell?' he responded. 'It's a legal document which requires only your signature.'

Her crushed heart crashed against her ribcage. 'My signature?' she echoed.

'That's right.'

She blinked as she surveyed the envelope with the wariness of someone being presented with an unexploded bomb. 'What kind of legal document?'

Unbuttoning the soft leather jacket, he subjected

her to the full intensity of his ebony gaze. 'One which will make you a very rich woman, Jazz,' he said quietly. 'Giving you the kind of wealth which would make creating your own fashion label a reality rather than a hopeless dream.'

'Really?' she said, trying to stop her voice from sounding as if she were being strangled but wanting— no, *needing*—to hear the full extent of his heartlessness so she could remind herself of it if ever she was stupid enough to entertain a single tender thought about him. 'And what exactly would I have to do to get this money?'

There was a pause.

'I think you know the answer to that. You sign over all rights to my son.'

She'd known he was going to say something on those lines but she hadn't expected his statement to be quite so bald. It was shocking and it was unbelievable. In effect he was asking her to *sell her baby*! To sign over 'all rights' to him and make as if he hadn't grown in her womb for nine whole months before he'd finally flopped, red-faced and bawling, into the world, after a long labour which had had her screaming with pain and gripping onto the hand of the nearest midwife, because she had birthed Darius alone.

She remembered the kick of his little heel against her distended belly during the long, hot summer of her pregnancy. The sight of his little heart fluttering frantically during the ultrasound appointments at the hospital, when she had blinked at the rapidly moving image and thought how it seemed like magic. Could he really be asking her to just give her son up, to hand him over for an inflated sum of money?

She searched his face for some sign that he might feel bad about making his brutal request, but there was no guilt or shame on his hawk-like features. Nothing other than a grim determination to get what he wanted, as befitted an all-powerful sheikh. And even though she wanted to fly across the room and rake her fingernails down that hard face while demanding to know how he dared to be so cruel and ruthless, Jasmine resisted the urge to retaliate in anything other than a calm and reasoned manner. Because drama wouldn't serve her well. In fact, it wouldn't surprise her if he had one of his palace doctors listening at the door recording their conversation, waiting for the first opportunity to pronounce her as hysterical and unfit to care for the baby prince. A new determination began to rise up inside her, made stronger by her fierce and protective love for her little boy. 'You must know I could never agree to that, Zuhal,' she said, equally quietly.

He subjected her to an assessing look. 'I had hoped you might be reasonable, Jazz.' The tightening of his jaw was the only outward sign that he was irritated by her response. 'But if you really think that maintaining contact across two such dramatically different cultures would benefit the child's welfare, rather than unsettling the hell out of him—then we will have to negotiate some sort of visitation rights for you.'

Some sort of visitation rights? Had he taken leave of his senses? Jasmine stared at him in confusion before comprehension dawned on her and she gave a sudden laugh. 'Oh, I see,' she said slowly. 'That's the first rule of successful bargaining, isn't it? You go in high, then negotiate down. You make your initial proposition so outlandish that I'm then supposed to be grateful for every little concession you make afterwards. Isn't that right? But we aren't talking about oil or diamonds or territory here, Zuhal, or any of the things you usually bargain for—we're talking about a baby.' The breath felt thick and tight in her throat. She felt as if she could hardly get the words out. 'I'm not going to just hand him over to you and *visit* him! Apart from missing him more than I can imagine—I wouldn't put it past you to veto my visa and ban me from ever entering Razrastan! How can you possibly ask such a thing and claim to have any humanity in your heart? Every child needs its mother!'

Zuhal met her furious glare. She was wrong about that, he thought bitterly. No child *needed* a mother. He had managed well enough without his, hadn't he? Even though the Queen had been there *physically*—a glamorous and ethereal presence in the royal palace—she had never been there for him. Shamelessly devoted to his older brother, she had taken parental favouritism and elevated it to a whole new level. Many times he had thought it would be preferable growing up without her, for she used to look through him as if he were invisible. She had made him *feel* invisible.

'Having a mother isn't *necessary*,' he bit out. 'Many successful men and women have managed perfectly well without a maternal influence. You have only to examine the pages of history to realise that.'

In frustration she shook her head and a lock of buttery blonde hair fell against her flushed cheek. 'I'm not talking about mothers who die or who for some reason can't look after their children. I'm talking about mothers who have a choice. And I do have a choice, Zuhal. Oh, I may not have your money or power but I have something which is worth a whole lot more than any of those things, and that is love. I love Darius with all my heart and I would do anything for him. Anything. And I can tell you right now that, no matter what you say or try to do, you won't succeed in taking him away from me!'

Zuhal's eyes narrowed as he absorbed the passionate fervour of her words. She was daring to argue with him in a way she would never have done in the past, when her role in his life had been nothing more than his compliant mistress, whose role had been to bring him pleasure. She had become a lioness during their separation, he realised with grudging admiration, before wondering how he was going to talk her out of her convictions.

Once it would have been easy. A soft smile and seeking look would have been enough to get her to capitulate to his wishes. But back then their roles had been very different and no one would ever have described them as equals. And things had changed. She'd just told him she had no power but she was wrong. She had all the power because she had his son and it seemed he was going to have to move strategically to get what he wanted.

Taking a few moments' respite from the unresolved thoughts which were racing around his mind, he looked around her cramped cottage, registering again how cheap it looked. For the first time it occurred to him that, despite her earlier promise to 'rustle up' some food, there was no evidence of this. No table lovingly set with candles or flowers. No napkin elaborately folded to resemble a fan or some other such nonsense. In short, none of the lavish attention to detail he was used to whenever he had allowed a woman to cook for him.

'I mean what I say, Zuhal,' she continued, her terse words falling into the uneasy silence which had fallen. 'You're not rubbing me out of Darius's life and behaving as if I didn't exist.'

Turning away from his scrutiny of the decor, he fixed her with a steady stare. 'The alternative will not be easy,' he warned softly.

She blinked with incomprehension. 'What do you mean?'

'Having a child being brought up as half-royal, half-commoner. Half-English and half-Razrastanian.'

'Then let him be brought up as English.'

'No way,' he growled. 'He needs to be aware of his royal ancestry and the responsibilities which might one day rest upon his shoulders.'

She frowned at him. 'Surely you're not implying that Darius could one day be King—when he is illegitimate.'

Zuhal stilled as a sudden wave of cynical possibility washed over him. Was this what she had secretly hoped for all along? he wondered. She'd accused him of going in with high stakes, but perhaps she was doing the same thing in her determination to drive a hard bargain. Perhaps the reality was that she was ambitious for herself as well as for her son. Perhaps having had a little time to think about it, she was imagining what could be hers, if she went about it in the right way. Because what woman wouldn't want to be a queen of the desert, with jewels and palaces and unrivalled wealth? More than that, who wouldn't want to be married to *him*? Many had jockeyed for that position in the past, but none had succeeded.

'If you're trying to get me to marry you, I can tell you right now it's not going to happen.' His voice took on a harsh and forbidding note. 'Because nothing has changed, Jazz. You are still a foreign divorcee who would be totally unsuitable for the role of Queen. My people would never accept you. Which is why I must put duty first and continue my search to find a suitable bride. But that doesn't mean that Darius can't be my insurance policy—just in case I don't produce another male heir.'

Her look of quiet reflection was replaced by one of incredulity. 'Trying to get you to marry me?' she scoffed. 'Do you really think I'd want to marry a man who treats women like second-class citizens—who regards his little boy as nothing but an *insurance policy*?'

'Fortunately, that question is destined to remain academic, since I have no intention of doing so.' His smile was swift and dismissive. 'Which means we must come to an alternative arrangement which will satisfy all parties.'

'What kind of arrangement?' Defiantly, she tilted her chin. 'What do you want?'

There was a pause. 'Who knows his true identity?'

'Nobody—not even my cousin,' she answered truthfully. 'I couldn't see the point of people finding out his father was a sheikh.'

He nodded. 'Good.'

'I didn't do it in order to get your praise,' she objected. 'I did it because I wanted to be able to trust people's true motives for getting to know us. I didn't want us to stand out, or for Darius to be made into a talking point.'

'If my brother had not died then things would be very different,' he observed reflectively. 'But he did. One day I hope to have a legitimate heir, but if that doesn't happen, then Darius will be entitled to inherit the crown. And since you refuse to let me take him back to Razrastan, then it seems he must grow up here. With you.'

'Well, thank heavens for that,' she said, breathing out a sigh of relief. 'Because I can't think of anything worse for his welfare than being incarcerated in some gilded palace with an autocratic brute like you!'

His nostrils flared. 'Nobody else would dare speak to me in such a way,' he iced out.

'That's about the only piece of information which has given me pleasure during this entire meeting!'

'Enough!' he snapped. 'It is imperative Darius learns about the country he might one day rule, which is why I want him brought up in London, so he can be schooled at the Razrastanian embassy. In a city which is big, and anonymous. Where nobody is going to discover his true identity—not if you don't tell them.'

'But we don't live in London, Zuhal,' she pointed out. 'We live in Oxfordshire.'

'That is not a problem. You will move.'

'I am not a pawn on a chessboard! I will not move!'

His patience seemingly exhausted, he slammed his fist down on a flimsy-looking table which shivered beneath the force and when he looked at her, Jasmine could see a fire-like determination blazing from his black eyes.

'I will take no more of your futile arguments, Jazz— or your defiant show of so-called pride in refusing to accept my support,' he raged. 'Because there are some things you need to understand. And number one is that there is no way a royal prince will be brought up somewhere like this! Why, there is barely room to swing a cat!'

'We don't have a cat.'

'Will you stop interrupting me?' he raged. 'You will need to be rehoused somewhere befitting my son's status. Somewhere secure.' His gaze moved with withering precision to the crack in the peeling window-frame, which was currently sending a whistle of chilly air into the small room. 'A place which isn't offering an open invitation for thieves and has room for the bodyguards our son needs and which I will be providing, whether you like it or not. Money is obviously not a consideration and I imagine you will quickly discover that you'll enjoy living somewhere which is considerably different from this.' His mouth hardened into a cynical line. 'Most women find luxury addictive, in my experience.'

Jasmine felt a mixture of fury and pain—and his reference to the other women in his life wasn't helping matters. He was insulting her home and lifestyle and maybe she should take him to task for that. But couldn't part of her see the wisdom in what he said, much as she hated to admit it? The modest savings she'd accrued while working at the Granchester hadn't lasted nearly as long as she'd expected, and her sewing only brought in enough money for them to keep their heads above water. Life was often a struggle and it was only going to get worse. She knew what it was like to be the poor kid in school. The one who was forced to sign up for free school dinners. Who lived in fear of someone commenting about the too-small hand-me-down clothes or the shoes which badly needed heeling. The last thing she wanted was for Darius to grow up like that—so how could she let pride stand in the way?

She gave a reluctant shrug. 'I suppose what you say makes sense.'

Zuhal's eyes narrowed. It was not the gratitude he had expected—not by any stretch of the imagination. He inclined his head with regal solemnity, but behind the formal mask he seethed at her stubbornness and thanklessness. 'I will have my people arrange somewhere for you to live as soon as possible,' he said coolly. 'Just pack up the essentials and be ready to leave when you hear from my office.'

Again, she was shaking her head, the long plait swinging like a blonde pendulum, and Zuhal was suddenly filled with an urgent desire to see her newly long hair spread out over his pillow.

'Actually, I would prefer to have some choice in our new home,' she said.

He opened his mouth as if to object, before closing it again. 'Very well,' he agreed reluctantly. 'I will have a shortlist drawn up for you to consider. And you'll need a new wardrobe—not just for the baby, but for you.'

She gave a bitter laugh. 'I don't want your charity, Zuhal. I never did. I'll wear what I always wear and make my own clothes.'

'You will do no such thing,' he contradicted icily. 'Because you are no longer a shop-worker living in hotel accommodation, or a single mother struggling to get by. You will be living in an expensive part of the city and it will naturally arouse suspicion if you look out of place—which, given your current appearance, wouldn't be difficult.'

Jasmine might have objected if his words hadn't been painfully true. She'd always tried to keep herself looking nice but it wasn't as easy as it had been in the past. Darius took up a lot of her waking hours and there simply wasn't the time to make new outfits for herself. Or the money. She tucked a long strand of hair behind her ear. It was why she'd stopped going to the hairdresser—why she'd let her trademark bob grow out.

She chewed her lip. It would be awful if she refused Zuhal's charity—because that was essentially what it was—and then got mistaken for a cleaner or a nanny when she was stepping into the elevator in her smart new London home. Because she knew how money worked. She'd worked at the Granchester long enough to recognise that rich people were only really comfortable with people like themselves. Who looked like them and spoke like them. And she didn't. Not by any stretch of the imagination. Not in her cheap jeans and a thrift shop sweater from which no amount of washing could shift the stubborn stain of regurgitated carrot purée which sat on the shoulder like a faded epaulet.

And then something else occurred to her. 'What about you?' she questioned.

He had been gathering up the Manila envelope which he had dumped on the table on his arrival but he looked up when she spoke, his black eyes watchful. 'What about me?'

'Where will you be living?'

He shrugged. 'I shall make sure I have a base in London close enough to see my son, but for the rest of the time I shall be in Razrastan, preparing for my future. For the formal signing of government papers to allow me to rule until...' his voice faltered slightly '...until my brother can be legally declared dead.'

She nodded, forcing herself to remember the human tragedy which lay at the heart of all this. 'Of course,' she said, sympathy softening her voice despite his harshness towards her.

There was a pause. He seemed to hesitate. 'And of course, I have another important matter to consider.'

'Oh? What's that?'

'My marriage,' he stated coolly.

Jasmine started, her heart jolting as if someone had just pulsed an electric shock right through it. 'Your marriage?'

He nodded. 'I still need someone by my side to help me rule my country—and as soon as possible. Which is why I must find a suitable candidate. I just wanted to warn you in advance, in case the press start speculating.' His gaze seared over her like a dark laser. 'I know what you're thinking, Jazz. That the discovery of my son and heir is a complicating factor in my matrimonial plans, but I don't anticipate any problems.' He smiled. 'My future wife will need to be a very understanding woman, for that is one of my requirements. And during access visits, she will love our son and treat him as her own. I will make sure of that.'

Jasmine prayed her face wouldn't betray her feelings. Had he really said he knew what she was thinking? He didn't have a *clue*. The hurt. The anger. The shame. The *fear*. She told herself she didn't care what Zuhal did with his life or who he took as his wife. But she did. Of course she did. She wanted to rail against the thought of another woman becoming stepmother to Darius, but there wasn't a lot she could do about it. It was a fact of modern life. She'd had a stepmother herself, hadn't she?

And look how that had turned out. Her father's much younger wife had resented all evidence that he'd been married before. She hadn't even allowed Jasmine to play with her baby stepsister—though that had actually worked in everyone's favour, because Jasmine's mother had been hysterical at the thought her daughter might prefer her new 'blended' family.

Painful memories of the past dissolved and Jasmine met the ebony ice of Zuhal's stare. She wished she could tell him to go to hell and that she had no intention of letting him move her into an apartment in a strange city, no matter how luxurious it happened to be. But she couldn't do that, because she recognised that Zuhal wanted the best for his son and maybe anonymous London was a better option than a rural little village. But that didn't mean that she had to roll over like a puppy dog and accept whatever he was prepared to throw her way, did it? Which meant she didn't have to entertain him for a second longer than she needed to. This man who was impervious to her pain.

'Would you like to look in on Darius before you leave?' she questioned in a calm voice, slightly mollified by his look of bemusement.

'Leave?' He frowned. 'Weren't you supposed to be cooking me supper?'

Her expression didn't change. 'There's nothing on the go, I'm afraid. But even if there was, I seem to have lost my appetite. And quite frankly, you're the last person I feel like sharing a meal with right now, Zuhal.'

CHAPTER FOUR

'So.' ZUHAL'S DEEP voice was clipped and matter-of-fact. 'What do you think of your new home?'

Jasmine wasn't sure what to think. She was still whirling from the speed with which her move to London had happened, and, with Darius now fast asleep in his luxury new baby seat, this was the first chance she'd had to get her bearings since arriving in the city that morning. To get used to her new accommodation. Home, Zuhal had called it—yet it didn't feel a bit like home.

She glanced around the sitting room—trying to get used to a room the size of a football pitch, with its stunning views over the bright green treetops of Hyde Park. It was the place she'd liked best out of the shortlist of properties the Sheikh's office had drawn up, mainly because it was the only one which didn't make her feel as if she was hemmed in by other buildings. This high up the traffic was just a distant hum—like bees—so it almost felt as if you were in the country rather than in the middle of a city. Jasmine had seen the apartment when it had been empty and cavernous—but in the interim, it had been completely and luxuriously furnished by an unknown hand.

She would have liked some say in the furniture herself and although she couldn't fault the decor, it had a distinctly impersonal feel to it—as if some top-end designer had simply thrown a lot of money at it. Giant velvet sofas were coloured in shades echoing the soft hues of the silken rugs which adorned the gleaming wooden floors. Vibrant oil paintings hung on the pale walls and a bronze sculpture of a horse's head was silhouetted against one of the tall windows. There were even glossy unread magazines artistically placed on one of several coffee tables and coloured glass vases full of fragrant roses. It looked like a set from a film—a room designed in a single day—not built up with memories, bit by bit, like a normal home. But whoever had said any of this would be normal? It wasn't normal to have been whisked here by darkened limousine, was it? Nor to have been followed by a fleet of bodyguards who, as far as she knew, were still lurking outside with those suspicious-looking lumps beneath their loose jackets.

Zuhal had arrived soon afterwards, sweeping in without any of his usual coterie of aides, which meant she was now alone with him, something which was making her pulse race and her breasts to become engorged and she hated it. She hated her body's instinctive reaction to a man who had proved how cold and heartless he could be. Who had announced his intention to take a royal bride and who regarded his firstborn son as his 'insurance policy'. But she was trying her best not to pass judgement, because that wouldn't benefit Darius in the long run, would it?

She wondered if she would ever get used to living somewhere which had three bathrooms—three!—all gleaming white and flashing silver and now crammed with the same bath products she'd sold in the Granchester Hotel boutique, so she knew exactly how eye-watering their cost.

She had chosen her own bedroom after the most cursory of glances because she had no desire to be in any room containing a bed, not with Zuhal breathing down her neck and creating the kind of flashbacks she could have happily done without. The most beautiful room of all was the nursery, which had been prepared for Darius. There was a curved crib fashioned from wood which felt satin-soft to the touch and a mobile full of planets and stars dangling from the ceiling above it. On a pristine window sill was a line of toys—fluffy bears and a soft little monkey with bright eyes. And somehow, the simple comfort of this room made Jasmine feel that the decision to move here had been the right one, if only for her son's sake.

She walked over to the window—away from the subtle sandalwood of Zuhal's scent—and peered down into the park, where she could see people braving the light spring breeze and sitting on benches to eat their supermarket sandwiches. A teenage boy was doing gravity-defying things on a skateboard. Around the line of the lake, she could see the yellow blur of daffodils, all dancing and fluttering in the breeze—just like in the poem she'd learnt at school. She'd been hopeful back then—until her mother's final meltdown about her father's supposed sins had made schooling something she'd just had to fit in whenever she could, and attention to homework an impossible dream.

But something about that memory made her think about the future. Her own ambitions might have tumbled along the wayside, but Darius still had a lifetime to look forward to. Shouldn't she try to put a positive spin on everything which was happening, despite her many misgivings? To answer the Sheikh's question with enthusiasm rather than doubt.

'It's lovely,' she said, as she turned back to face him.

If he had been expecting a slightly more ringing endorsement, he made no reference to it. 'And do you think you can be happy here?' he persisted.

Happy? It was a funny question. Since Darius's birth, all Jasmine had wanted was to ensure security for him and now she'd done just that—even though she hadn't planned it. From now on the two of them were going to be living in unbelievable splendour, while Zuhal picked up all the bills. She should have been relieved, and yet…

How could she possibly be relieved—or relaxed— when part of her still wanted the Sheikh so badly, even though she knew it was wrong to feel that way? Her body ached whenever he was in the vicinity and she was poignantly reminded of how it had felt when he used to make love to her, and a big part of her wanted that to happen all over again. Yet he'd blithely told her he was going in search of a bride who would one day become her baby's stepmother. Wouldn't that kind of cold cruelty fill most people with anger instead of desire?

Unwillingly, she began to study him—wondering if she would be able to do that objectively. But for now, at least, objectivity was a fruitless expectation. His dark grey suit flattered his broad-shouldered body to perfection, subtly showcasing all the muscular power which lay beneath. He had been born to make women look at him, with those hawkish good looks and eyes of ebony fire. She remembered the way she used to stroke her fingers through his hair—giving him the Indian head massage which one of the spa therapists at the Granchester had taught her to do. She remembered what an overdeveloped feeling of pleasure it had given her—to have the powerful and alpha Sheikh purring like a pussycat and relaxing under her rhythmical ministrations.

With an effort she dragged her gaze away from him and glanced out of the window, where sunlight was bouncing off the fresh green leaves which were shimmering in the distance. 'I'm going to do everything in my power to be happy,' she said truthfully.

'Good. That is the kind of positive attitude I like.'

She shrugged as she turned to meet his eyes. 'I'm not doing it for your benefit, Zuhal. I owe it to my son.'

'Our son, Jazz. Please don't ever forget that,' he corrected smoothly, shooting a quick glance at his watch as the doorbell rang, its peal sounding unnaturally loud as it echoed through the spacious apartment. 'Excellent. Right on cue. Come with me, please.'

Jasmine blinked. Surely they weren't expecting visitors? During several heated debates about privacy during the choosing of this apartment, she'd got the definite message that she and Zuhal weren't going to be doing any socialising together. In fact, their relationship—such as it was—was very definitely to be kept under the radar. Which suited her just fine. She wanted to spend as little time with him as possible. No. Why not put it another way? She *needed* to spend as little time with him as possible, if she wanted to hang onto her sanity. 'Come where?' she questioned. 'Who's that ringing the doorbell?'

'Wait and see.'

Jasmine clamped her lips shut, annoyed at his high-handedness but, her curiosity alerted, she followed him past the blissfully sleeping Darius, towards the front door.

After a low-voiced command in his native tongue, the door was opened from the outside by a bodyguard, to reveal a woman standing there. Aged around thirty, she was dressed in what Jasmine recognised instantly as traditional Razrastanian robes and her hair was coiled on top of her head in an elaborate fretwork of black waves. She directed a kind smile towards Jasmine before bobbing a curtsey to Zuhal, who immediately indicated that she should stand at ease as he gestured for her to enter the apartment.

'Jazz, I'd like you to meet Rania,' he said. 'She is going to be helping you look after Darius. His new nanny.'

'I am very pleased to meet you, mistress,' said Rania in perfectly modulated English. 'And I am very much looking forward to meeting Darius.'

'Why don't you come and meet him right now?' suggested Zuhal smoothly.

'He's asleep,' said Jasmine quickly, still reeling from this latest development and yet another demonstration of Zuhal's high-handedness.

'I will not wake him, mistress,' said Rania softly.

What else could she do other than lead her to the baby? Jasmine told herself it was pitiful how hard her heart clenched as she watched the Razrastanian woman crouch down and fix her dark gaze on the sleeping Darius, as if committing every atom to memory.

'The son of the Sheikh is a truly magnificent baby,' said Rania at last, as she straightened up.

Jasmine couldn't fault the sentiment but her smile felt forced. She felt like a puppet. As if everyone were pulling her strings. Moving her this way, then that— leaving her with no idea of where she was or what she was doing. And all she could think of were the words Rania had spoken and which were now circling inside her head. *The son of the Sheikh. The son of the Sheikh.* Was the Razrastanian nanny, despite her kind smile and soft voice, planning to push Jasmine to the side-lines and edge her out of the picture, so that his royal father could assume complete dominance? She could feel her mouth growing firm with determination. Well, that was never going to happen.

Never.

'He bears such a strong resemblance to his father,' Rania was cooing.

Jasmine wished she could deny it. To say that, actually, the baby had *her* eyes or *her* hair—but there was no evidence of her features, or her hazel eyes or blonde locks. With his olive skin and black hair, there surely couldn't be another child on the planet who was more a mini-me of his darkly handsome father than Darius. His limbs were sturdy, his eyelashes outrageously long, and the baby clinic had already told her how tall he was going to be.

'Indeed he is, Rania,' Jasmine said, trying to regain her composure as she turned her attention to more practical matters. 'Whereabouts…um, where will you be staying?'

She could see Rania looking uncertainly towards Zuhal as if for guidance and the Sheikh interposed instantly.

'Rania has her own apartment, which is connected to this one,' he said, with the smooth assurance of a man who had thought of everything. 'I don't think you can have paid it very much attention during your first viewing.'

Jasmine's lips tightened. Obviously not.

'I was here yesterday, putting the final touches to it,' said Rania proudly. 'Would you care to see it, mistress?'

'I most certainly would,' said Jasmine, shooting Zuhal a furious glance. 'And really, there's no need to call me mistress. Jasmine will do just fine.'

'But—'

'*Please*,' said Jasmine firmly, wondering if Rania—despite all her linguistic skill—had any idea that the word mistress had a very different meaning in English. One which she definitely did not wish to be associated with *her*. She forced a new brightness into her voice. 'Let's go, shall we? I can't wait to see where you'll be living, Rania.'

In silence, the three of them walked along the long corridor, until they reached a door at the far end, which Jasmine hadn't noticed before. Or rather, it was the one thing the agent hadn't bothered to point out during an otherwise extensive tour—perhaps if she'd been feeling a little less dazed she might have discovered it herself. The Razrastanian woman pushed open the door and gestured for them to step inside, which Jasmine did—although she noticed that Zuhal remained standing broodily on the threshold.

Inside, was a separate and very beautiful little apartment, with a door leading to a bedroom and another to a neat kitchen. A sitting room with its own small terrace overlooked the park and on one of the walls was a framed poster of a place Jasmine instantly recognised. She felt as if someone were twisting a knife inside her as she studied the imposing building in the foreground of the picture. A golden palace with soaring towers and cobalt cupolas which glinted in the bright sunshine. Jasmine swallowed, for she knew that this was Zuhal's home. The home he would soon share with his royal bride.

And, for half the year—with Darius, too.

'What a beautiful view you've got, Rania,' she said weakly.

Did Zuhal guess how churned up she was feeling? Was that why he stepped forward, to take her by the elbow to support her, as if she were an old lady he was helping to cross a busy road. Quickly she brushed his hand away because she didn't want him touching her—and not just because she couldn't trust her body's reaction to him. Did he really think that an outward show of concern could make up for the fact that he was behaving like an overbearing brute? First, he'd announced that he intended marrying another woman—and now this!

'Why don't we let Rania get settled in?' he suggested smoothly. 'You can both talk baby routine later.'

Rania nodded, quietly closing the door as she disappeared into her rooms, and Jasmine waited until she and Zuhal were back in the sitting room before she said anything. Waited until they were completely out of earshot and made sure that Darius was still asleep—and that her breathing had settled down-so her words didn't come out in a senseless babble.

'You let me vet the apartment!' she accused him hotly. 'But you didn't think to give me the opportunity of telling you whether or not I liked the woman you have employed to help take care of our son?'

'Everyone likes Rania,' he said.

'That's not the point!' Dangerously close to yelling, Jasmine sucked in a deep, unsteady breath. 'And what's more—you know it! So don't give me that *I don't know what you're talking about* look and expect me to be taken in by it!'

Zuhal found himself taken aback by her rage and, in another situation, might almost have been amused by it—because didn't such passion always change into something much more agreeable when it was transferred to the bedroom? But that was never going to happen, judging by the way Jazz was glaring at him—with emerald fire spitting from her eyes.

Undeterred, he loosened his tie a fraction. 'He is a desert prince, Jazz,' he said. 'And having a nanny is a given for all royal children. He will be looked after by someone who speaks my language and who knows the myths and legends of my country. He will grow up bilingual, which is essential for a boy who might one day be King.'

'But I've only ever looked after him myself. I told you before—I've never left him with a stranger.'

'Rania is the daughter of my own nanny at the palace—my favourite, as it happens. She speaks perfect English and received her training at one of the finest establishments in England, one which provides childcare for your own royal family, just in case you're interested.'

'Not particularly. And that isn't the point. You should have asked me first.'

His patience was beginning to wear thin but Zuhal bit back the impatient retort which was on the tip of his tongue, telling himself to go easy on her. To treat her with impartiality as they negotiated their way through these tricky new waters. But how was such impartiality possible when his mind and his body had been in constant conflict, since he'd walked up the weed-strewn path of her little cottage less than a fortnight ago? When every night since he had been plagued by memories of her soft breasts and curvy hips. By the disturbing recall of the way she used to wriggle over his body like some kind of sexy eel, mounting him with a yelp of exultant pleasure as she rode them both to fulfilment. And then afterwards run her fingers through his hair, digging their firm tips into his scalp and massaging away the tension, so that he'd been left feeling almost *boneless* with pleasure.

The other day he'd kissed her and the kiss they'd shared had been as potent as any he could remember. Was that because it had been abruptly cut short and not allowed to proceed to its natural conclusion? Was that why his subsequent sense of frustration had been more pronounced than any he could remember? Zuhal acknowledged the hard jerk of his groin, feeling as if his body was somehow taunting him.

There were a million reasons why he shouldn't want her, even if you discounted her basic unsuitability. She had deceived him. Had tried to keep their child a secret from him. Why, even when Darius had cried out, when he had still been ignorant of his identity, Zuhal had seen the distress clouding her pale face—and then her deliberate manipulation as she had sought to distract him.

If she could have got him out of her cottage without disclosing he was a father, then she would have done, he reminded himself grimly.

But even that knowledge did not lessen her allure, or stop him from wishing he could carry her into one of those conveniently empty bedrooms to slake his hunger for her, once and for all. And then maybe rid her memory from his mind for ever.

He sighed. Compromise wasn't something he was often called upon to use, but maybe he should make an exception in this case. Slowly he inclined his head, determined to acknowledge her concerns. 'If, for any reason, Rania proves unsatisfactory...' he saw her visibly brighten '...any *sensible* reason,' he added swiftly, 'then we can use someone else. Do you think I would do anything to threaten or disrupt the life of my son, Jazz?'

'Now you're making me sound unreasonable.'

'That was not my intention. Darius needs someone in his life other than his parents,' he said. 'Someone to trust and feel safe with. Surely you must see that?'

She was nodding her head now, as if determined to match his own mood of compromise with one of her own. Smoothing her dress down with fingers he noticed weren't quite steady, she met his eyes with a rare expression of complicity. 'I suppose you're right.' She shrugged. 'Especially since he doesn't have any grandparents.'

Zuhal's mouth hardened, but he was unable to manufacture any sorrow that this was the case, for he had grown up without knowing his own grandparents, which might have helped dissolve some of the tensions which had existed in the palace. But he had survived, hadn't he? Deliberately, he focussed his gaze on Jazz because that was infinitely more pleasurable than thinking about the toxic environment in which he had been raised.

In just a fortnight the chill weather had turned into something more usual for this time of year and her simple cotton dress was sprigged with blossom—she had clearly made it herself—with her soft pink cardigan a shade lighter than the tiny flowers. She looked young, vibrant and utterly desirable and Zuhal was filled with a powerful desire to touch her. To crush his lips down on hers and to slide his fingers beneath her floaty skirt and touch her where she was warm and sticky. His throat thickened. Yet despite the undeniable allure of her appearance, she looked like a student on her way to lectures, not a young woman who now occupied one of the most expensive pieces of real estate in London.

'I thought I told you to buy yourself some new clothes,' he observed.

'What's wrong with what I'm wearing?'

'There's nothing *wrong* with them. But your clothes are not appropriate for your new position in life, Jazz,' he said softly. 'We both know that.'

She gave a quick nod of her head, as if she was preparing to say something difficult. 'And how exactly would you define that position, Zuhal—that's something we haven't discussed, have we?'

Zuhal tensed. Was this an invitation to be completely frank with her? To reach a new understanding which they could both enjoy to the max? What was it the English sometimes said? *To make hay while the sun shines.* He felt his pulse quicken. Her eyes were no longer flashing green fire, obscuring the golden lights which usually glinted there. But in place of the anger he could detect a distinct smokiness—and Zuhal had known enough women to recognise what that meant. Hadn't she made it obvious when he'd walked in here today and looked at him with desire in her eyes? When he had observed the instinctive hardening of her nipples beneath the cheap cotton of her dress.

'That's up to you, Jazz,' he said silkily. 'The decision is yours.'

Her eyes narrowed with suspicion. 'You're being very...oblique. I'm still not quite sure what you mean.'

'Then let me state my words plainly, so there can be no misunderstanding.' He paused, aware that his throat had dried, so that it resembled the dust of his beloved desert homeland. 'When we kissed the other day, there was no doubt that the passion which burns between us was as strong as before. I looked at you and I wanted you. I still do, despite your determination to keep my son from me and your subsequent defiant behaviour. But I am willing to overlook your stubbornness, because you were the best lover I've ever had.' He glittered her a smile. 'And I am eager to taste such pleasures with you again.'

She nodded her head solemnly, as if she was giving his words careful thought before responding to them. 'You're saying you want us to take up where we left off last time, is that it?'

He slanted her a smile. The kind of smile which women had told him was like being caught beneath the full force of the sun. 'I couldn't have put it better myself,' he said softly.

'Even though you are currently in the market for a royal bride?'

His smile died. 'That isn't going to happen overnight, Jazz. Even though speed is of the essence—I don't anticipate taking a wife before the end of the year.'

'And during that brief window of opportunity, we'll be lovers?'

'I knew you would understand,' he breathed.

'Oh, I understand all right.' The fire in her eyes was back and so too was the mulish tilt of her chin. 'I understand that you're an arrogant man with an overdeveloped sense of entitlement, who treats women like toys he can just pick up and toss away once he's had enough of them.'

She took a step closer, like a boxer squaring up to an opponent in the ring.

'Do you really think I'm going to hang around here, waiting for one of your rare visits—ready to drop everything when you deign to show your face-and then simply fall into bed with you?'

'How dare you speak to me this way?'

'While in the meantime,' she continued remorselessly, 'you're out there courting every eligible princess the desert region has to offer in order to find yourself a suitable bride?'

'That's a very extreme way of looking at it,' he bit out.

'It's the truth, Zuhal,' she said. 'What other way is there to look at it?'

He glowered at her. 'I have been completely straight with you, Jazz. Perhaps you would do me the honour of returning the favour. And if you don't want to be my lover, then how do you intend spending your time?'

Jasmine sucked in a deep breath, knowing she needed to be strong. Or at least she needed to *appear* strong. Zuhal didn't have to know she wanted intimacy just as much as he did—the difference being that for her it spelt emotional danger. 'You are planning to live your life as you see fit, Zuhal,' she said quietly. 'And I'm going to do exactly the same. I'm going to be the best mother I can, and to accommodate your wishes where Darius is concerned. But I'm also going to live my own life. I plan to make friends and forge a future for myself.'

'With a man?' he shot out instantly.

Jasmine couldn't deny the pleasure she got from the dark look of jealousy which crossed his features and made his shadowed jaw clench. And although the thought of being anywhere near any man other than Zuhal made her feel violently sick, he didn't have to know that.

'Who knows what I will do? I'm young and free and single,' she said, with a carelessness she hoped didn't sound faked. 'And this is England, Zuhal. Where men and women are equal.'

He gave an angry snort, a pulse flickering wildly at his temple as he walked away without another word, and Jasmine was surprised that the loud slamming of the front door hadn't woken the baby.

CHAPTER FIVE

'HIS ROYAL HIGHNESS is waiting for you in the drawing room, mistress.'

Pausing in the middle of unbuckling Darius from a buggy the size of a small car, Jasmine hid her frown as she was met by a nervous-looking Rania. She'd learnt it was pointless to ask the nanny not to call her 'mistress', just as she'd learnt she had absolutely no control over the Sheikh's movements in her life. That he turned up when he felt like it and, of course, could walk right in whenever he wanted to because there was always Rania or a bodyguard to let him in. And because he owned it, of course. She might be the one who was living here, but Zuhal was the one who had paid for the apartment and everything it contained. Sometimes it felt as if he *owned* her, too.

It wasn't an ideal situation, because every time he arrived she had to fight an instinctive urge to touch him—and how crazy was *that*? Just as she had to fight the desire to stare at him and drink in all his power and his hard, masculine beauty—because remembering just how good it felt to be in his arms would do her no favours at all. He flew into London once a week on business and Jasmine tried to make herself scarce whenever he arrived to see his son, although Rania was always on hand to meekly obey his orders. Because pretending they were a happy family was nothing but a mockery of the harsh reality.

And because she didn't want to get stuck into a doomed pattern of togetherness, which would be shattered when he found himself a royal bride.

But every time Zuhal left, she had to go through the process of eradicating him from her mind, telling herself that meaningless sex with her ex-lover was a bad idea in every respect, no matter how much her body craved it or how fierce the unspoken attraction which always seemed to sizzle between them. She'd had her chance and she'd done the right thing in turning it down. That ship had sailed.

Rania stepped forward. 'Let me take Darius for you, mistress.'

'Thanks, Rania—but I'll do it. I think he's teething because he was up for most of the night. He was a bit cranky in the clinic this morning, but the nurse said he's coming on leaps and bounds.'

Nervously, Rania cleared her throat. 'This is excellent news, mistress, but His Royal Highness will not enjoy being kept waiting.'

'I'm sure he won't,' said Jasmine, a renewed cheerfulness washing over her, despite her lack of sleep. 'But maybe it will do him good.'

'You think so?' A silken voice came filtering through the air and Jasmine felt all the little hairs on the back of her neck prickling in anticipation as Zuhal entered the hallway with noiseless stealth. She could sense his presence with every soft footstep he took towards her and it took a moment for her to compose herself so that her expression would register indifference, rather than desire. She looked up to meet his gleaming eyes as, pausing only to trace the tip of a finger over his son's soft cheek, he turned to the Razrastanian nanny. 'Rania, will you mind taking care of Darius so that I can speak to Jazz in private?'

'Certainly, Your Royal Highness.'

Eagerly, Rania complied, removing Darius from his buggy with the tender efficiency which Jasmine had grown to like and trust—although she didn't like the way the nanny always deferred to the Sheikh. She looked down at the baby's black curls with a rush of fierce, maternal love, but her heart sank a little as Zuhal gestured for her to accompany him to the sitting room, where, outside, the spring flowers in the park had given way to the bright blooms of early summer.

'You didn't think to warn me that you were coming?' she said, bending down to unnecessarily straighten a velvet cushion which the cleaner had placed at perfect right angles to the one beside it.

'Why would I do that?' he questioned blandly. 'Unless you were planning to do something which you know would anger me, should I walk in on you unexpectedly. Is that the case, Jazz?'

'Please don't talk in riddles, because I haven't got the energy to work them out, Zuhal,' she said. 'Like what?'

'Like being here with another man,' he accused, all

blandness gone now as a cold note of steel entered his voice.

'I don't know what you're talking about.'

'I think you do.' He began to pace the room, more agitated than she'd ever seen him. 'There was a man here yesterday.'

Jasmine narrowed her eyes as memory came flooding back to her. 'How on earth do you know that?'

'How do you think I know?' he demanded. 'Because my bodyguards informed me!'

'So you're having me *spied* on now, are you?' she returned. 'Bad enough you sent someone to investigate the playgroup I decided to join—as if I wasn't capable of making a judgement about it myself—but now I discover that I'm not even allowed to invite friends back to what is supposed to be my *home*, without your heavies reporting back to you!'

'Please don't be so naive, Jazz,' he hissed, his pacing footsteps coming to a halt as he turned round to fix her with a blistering stare. 'My son is currently under your care and naturally my staff keep me informed if anyone unknown to them should visit the apartment. You're lucky he wasn't stopped at the door and sent on his way. So I will ask you…who was he?'

For a moment Jasmine was tempted to call his bluff. To tell him that the man in question was her new lover and they'd both been eagerly waiting until the baby was fast asleep so that they could jump into bed together and enjoy a wild night of passion. But there was being independent and there was being downright stupid—and no way was she going to mess with Zuhal, not when he was in this kind of mood. When a dark and dangerous anger was radiating from his powerful body in waves which were almost tangible.

Reluctantly, she shrugged. 'He's an Italian waiter I used to know when I was working at the Granchester.'

'An Italian waiter?' he repeated, as if she had just told him she'd been entertaining a mass murderer. 'What the hell was he doing here, Jazz? Practising his silver service technique, or was he teaching you how best they like to kiss in Roma?'

'Don't be so ridiculous,' she answered stiffly. 'He's actually been getting experience—'

'What kind of experience?' he shot back immediately.

'*Work* experience—before he goes back to join his father's restaurant in Lecce—not Rome,' she completed witheringly. 'His sister is pregnant and he knew I liked to sew, so he asked if I would design something especially for the new baby which he could take back to Italy with him. Which I have, although it's not quite finished. Here...' She slipped from the sitting room to one of the unused bedrooms, which she had turned into a makeshift sewing room, before returning with a tiny, hand-smocked romper suit which she waved in front of him. 'See for yourself if you don't believe me.'

As she held up the impossibly small garment, Zuhal felt the tight knot of tension which had been building up inside him dissolve—to be replaced by the instant rush of relief. Had he really imagined Jazz in the arms of another man? But that was the trouble. Of course he had. Many times. Because he was frustrated. Because he felt powerless. Because for once in his life here was a woman refusing to do what he wanted her to do, which was to fall into bed with him. He'd tried telling himself he could understand why she no longer wanted to be his lover and, as the mother of his son, her proud morality should please him. He told himself it was better all round if their relationship entered a new, platonic phase, yet still he couldn't stop thinking about her—even though logic told him that her chilly refusal to resume her tenure as his lover was only feeding his desire. That same logic had convinced him that sex was the only way to get her out of his system for good—for what woman didn't lose her allure when a man was repeatedly exposed to her?

And perhaps he was going about it the wrong way.

'I have seen something like this before,' he said slowly, his eyes still on the impossibly small garment.

'Of course you have. Darius has one which is very similar—although his is a different colour. Here I've used boats rather than ducklings.'

He nodded. 'It is an exquisite piece of work,' he said, his gaze taking in the delicate blue and white embroidery.

She was looking at him expectantly, as if waiting for the punchline. 'And?'

'And…nothing.' He shrugged, before producing a smile. 'You obviously have great talent.'

She shook her head in self-deprecating denial. 'I wouldn't go that far.'

'No arguments, Jazz. Why not just accept the compliment in the spirit in which it was intended?'

'Okay,' she said cautiously. 'I will. Thank you.' Her cheeks a little flushed now, she regarded him warily. 'So what can I do for you today, Zuhal? Apart from giving you a platform to demonstrate your unreasonable jealousy?'

Trying not to focus on the fecund swell of her breasts, Zuhal attempted to put his jumbled thoughts into some kind of coherent order.

'There are a couple of things I need to discuss with you.'

'That's fine. Discuss away,' she said. 'But could you please do it quickly because I'm planning to take a walk in the park while the sun's still out.'

'But you've only just got back!'

'Rania will be here while Darius has his nap, so I thought I'd have a bit of a snooze in the fresh air, because your son kept me awake for a lot of the night. Forgive me for having such an outrageous plan for my afternoon—but I wasn't aware I had to clock in and out every time I left the apartment, although maybe that was stupid of me,' she added sarcastically. 'Perhaps the reason you bought the whole penthouse floor of this block was because it resembles a fortress.'

'You don't like living here?' he questioned. 'This was your favourite out of the shortlist, if you remember?'

Jasmine hesitated because usually he didn't ask her opinion—riding roughshod over her wishes was much more his style. She knew she really ought to count her blessings now that she had security for her son and no financial worries. But despite these things, she'd quickly found London very different from Oxford—especially when you had a baby in tow. When she'd been working at the Granchester she'd had no responsibilities and her time off had been her own. But not any more. Now she was achingly aware that her baby needed pals his own age, which was why she had joined an infant playgroup—the one Zuhal had insisted on vetting.

Darius loved it when they sang songs and jangled tambourines and she'd met plenty of other young women her age. But they'd all been nannies, not mothers, which had made Jasmine feel even more of an outsider. She'd made friends with a couple of them on a very superficial level, but hadn't dared ask them back to her home. Because if they saw all this wall-to-wall luxury, wouldn't they inevitably start asking questions? In fact, hadn't one of them—Carrie—already tried? Questions Jasmine couldn't possibly answer because then it would all come tumbling out that she was the one-time mistress of a future king, and mother to his illegitimate heir.

'It's very comfortable,' she said, in careful reply to the Sheikh's drawled query. 'But sometimes I get stir-crazy living all the way up here. I mean, I know there's the balcony to sit on but it's not quite the same as walking outside. Sometimes I feel...'

'What?' he prompted softly.

'Oh, I don't know...' She shrugged her shoulders. 'Trapped.'

His eyes narrowed. 'I can understand that. Very well. I will grant you your wish. We will take a walk together.'

Startled, she looked at him. 'And how's that supposed to work? I thought we weren't supposed to be seen together.'

'Nobody will notice us. We will simply be a couple out walking in the sunshine, one of many such couples. My military training taught me that I can always blend into the background if I try,' he explained. 'And my bodyguards have been trained to observe from the shadows.'

Blend in?

Jasmine stared at him. Was he deluded? Dominating the vast sitting room with his powerful presence, his outward appearance wasn't so very different from the other successful businessmen who frequented this part of the capital. In his exquisitely cut charcoal suit and a silk shirt the colour of buttermilk, he was certainly dressed like your average billionaire. But he *was* different, no two ways about it. He was a desert sheikh and that affected the way he did things. The way he thought about things. She didn't particularly want to go for a walk with him yet the alternative was being cooped up inside, with the four walls closing in on them and a sensory overload on both her imagination and her body, so Jasmine nodded her head.

'Okay,' she said.

While Zuhal spoke rapidly into his cell phone in his native tongue, she went off to get ready, checking Darius and assuring Rania she wouldn't be long. Pausing only to pull on a pair of espadrilles and cram a straw hat over her head, she exited her bedroom to find Zuhal waiting for her in the hallway, looking at his golden wristwatch with ill-disguised irritation. He had removed his tie and undone the top two buttons of his shirt, offering a distracting glimpse of dark chest hair just beneath the pale silk.

Did she imagine his jaw tightening when he caught sight of the summery espadrilles whose matching pink ribbons were criss-crossed over her lower legs like a wannabe gladiator? No, she didn't think so. She might have been innocent when she met him and been subsequently accused of naivety—but she wasn't deluded enough to deny the unmistakable sensual charge which entered the atmosphere whenever they were alone together. It was the same sensory overload which made her itch to touch the slashed angles of his darkly handsome face, and to cover his lips with hungry kisses. A response which she tried her best to batten down, usually with remarkably little effect—like today—when the tug of heat low in her belly was inconveniently reminding her how big he used to feel when he was inside her.

But it was strange and curiously satisfying being outside with him as Jasmine realised that fresh air or daylight had never really featured in their relationship. In some ways it had been more of a vampire affair. There had been those badly lit restaurants of their early dates, and afterwards her being smuggled into a borrowed mews house for snatched nights together. But the combination of blue sky and sunshine glittering on the water of the lake was making her feel curiously carefree, in a way she hadn't been for months. And Zuhal had been right about his bodyguards slipping into the shadows, because even when she looked very hard, she couldn't see them.

He hadn't exaggerated about blending in himself, either. Was it the fact that he had removed his tie, or was it just his unusually relaxed stance rather than his regal demeanour, which made him into just a spectacularly handsome man who was taking a summer stroll with his...?

What?

How would she describe her role in the future King's life? Not his girlfriend, that was for sure. Not even his lover—not any more. And mother of his child made it sound as if they'd been married, which of course they never had been. She bit her lip. She'd never had any status at all, really—which begged the question of why she had tolerated it so happily. Was that because her sexual awakening had been so powerful that it had rocked her world in a way which nothing else had come close to? Because she'd been so totally caught up in this new way of living and feeling—of being somebody's *lover*?

Or was it because at the time she'd thought herself in love with him? Crazy, really. How could you be in love with a man who treated you as a convenience— flitting in and out of your life as the mood took him? She hadn't really known him at all—and, as she was starting to get to know him now, she was seeing a ruthless side which he'd never shown before.

His deep voice broke into her reverie.

'I thought the whole point of a walk in the sunshine was that it was supposed to be relaxing, but instead you're looking as if you have all the cares of the world on your shoulders. Relax, Jazz. It's a beautiful day.'

Jasmine blinked to find the Sheikh's black gaze

trained on her. The edges of his lips were curved into a smile and silently she reproached herself. She had to stop analysing stuff and wishing for things which were never going to happen. Why couldn't she just live in the moment and enjoy it?

'You're right. It is. Gorgeous.' Tilting her hat back, she breathed in, half closing her eyes until a vaguely familiar tinkle of music made her open them again. There was an ice-cream van in the distance, with a small queue of children forming at the front, and maybe it was the powerful collision between difficult past and difficult present which made something hard and hurtful coil itself around her heart.

'Jazz? Is something wrong?'

Zuhal's deep voice snapped her back to reality and she blinked at him, momentarily disconcerted. 'Why?'

'You've gone pale.' His voice had become a silken whisper. 'As pale as milk.'

If she'd been in the apartment she would never have told him, but high up in that expensive citadel, he would never have asked. And maybe that was another thing which being outside did. It freed you from inhibition. It allowed memories to rush back and with them came all the feelings, so that in that moment she was no longer a puzzled new mother, but a bewildered little girl again.

'There was an ice-cream van outside my house when I was little,' she said, her voice sounding as if it were coming from a great distance away. 'I heard the music and went outside to listen—more to drown out the sound of my parents arguing than in any great hope of getting an ice cream.'

'And did you get one?'

'Actually, I did.' She gave a quick smile, because the Sheikh's calm question meant he was able to slip almost unnoticed into her memory. 'My father came outside and bought me a cone—the biggest I'd ever seen. A massive thing heaped with pink and white ice-cream with one of those flaky chocolate bars sticking out of the top. I was surprised because he would never normally have done that and it made me wonder why he was there, in the middle of the day, when he should have been at work. He kissed me on top of my head and said goodbye in a funny kind of voice, and I remember watching him walk down the road just as my mother came flying out of the house.'

'And?' he prompted, into the silence between them, which was broken only by the far-off sound of children playing.

She shrugged. 'My mother told me he was leaving. That he had another little girl with someone else—a new daughter he loved much more than me. She said some other stuff, too—stuff I've done my best to forget—and then she had a complete meltdown. Actually, so did my ice cream,' she added flippantly as she stared at the sun-scorched grass, willing her eyes not to fill with tears. 'Amid all the drama I'd completely forgotten about it and it fell off the cornet and lay on the pavement in a big, creamy puddle.' It had been the end of her childhood and the beginning of a new and very different phase, where she had become the mother, and her mother, the child.

'Jazz,' said Zuhal softly. 'Are you crying?'

She looked up, surprised by the sudden touch of his fingertips to her face. When had he moved close enough to touch her?

'No,' she answered proudly. 'Crying is a waste of time.'

Was she imagining the gleam of understanding in his black eyes, or was it a case of just seeing what she wanted to see? A pulse began to jump at her temple as he rubbed the pad of his thumb against her chin and that simple brush of skin against hers reminded her all too vividly of the days when their bodies had lain naked together. Jasmine swallowed, praying that he would continue, knowing that if he pulled her into his arms she would not resist. Because didn't she want that? More than anything? To feel his lips on hers and be locked in his embrace, so she could let his lovemaking melt away all her pain. Wasn't she sick and tired of the celibate stand-off which had sprung up between them?

The air between them seemed to shift and change. She could feel the sudden tension in her body as he took another step towards her. A flash of hope and longing swept through her as his hawk-like features clicked into focus, when the unexpected sound of her own name made Jasmine jump back in alarm.

'Jasmine! Hey, Jasmine!'

She turned around to see Carrie, the nosy nanny from the toddler group who today had neither of her twin charges with her. She was wearing cut-off denim hot pants which made the most of what was obviously a spray tan, and a T-shirt bearing the legend *Luscious* was stretched tightly across her generous chest.

Jasmine shot a swift look at Zuhal but he wasn't ogling the brunette stunner, unlike just about every other man in the vicinity. Instead, he was regarding Carrie with an expression of cool disdain.

'Well, hi. Fancy seeing you here,' said Carrie, looking him up and down, the gleam in her eye suggesting she found his disdainful expression both a turn-on and a challenge. 'You must be Mr Jasmine?'

'This is Zuhal,' said Jasmine quickly, only to see the Sheikh glare at her. 'We were just—'

'Leaving,' said Zuhal firmly, cupping Jasmine's elbow with the guiding clasp of his palm.

'Oh.' Carrie pouted. 'Must you? I see we're all childless. Thank. The. Lord. Why don't we go over to that Pimm's tent by the bandstand? It's a perfect day for getting sloshed in the sunshine.'

'I don't drink,' said Zuhal repressively.

Jasmine thought afterwards that it was a pity Carrie took a confident step towards him because her slightly predatory action was misinterpreted as one of aggression by his phalanx of bodyguards, who immediately swarmed from behind various trees, to surround them. Carrie was blinking at them in astonishment and Jasmine noticed that one of the bodyguards was having difficulty averting his gaze from her heaving breasts.

'Oh, wow,' breathed Carrie softly. 'Now I think I'm spoilt for choice!'

The next few minutes passed in a blur. Jasmine was aware of being virtually frogmarched out of the park and back to the apartment, with Zuhal's angry words ringing in her ears. And all that softness and understanding she'd thought she'd seen in his face had vanished, replaced by a cold censure which made his eyes glint like steel.

'I cannot believe that you associate with such people!' he stormed, as the elevator zoomed them up towards the penthouse.

'I don't think she meant any harm,' she defended. 'She's just...just a young woman who likes to work hard and play hard.'

'She is a predator!' debated Zuhal fiercely. 'Who dresses like a tramp! And I do not want my son associating with someone like her—that is simply not going to happen. Do you understand, Jazz?'

'What, are you planning to vet everyone I come in contact with?'

Grimly, he nodded. 'If I need to, then yes.'

She hated the way he just breezed in and out of her life, making changes as the mood took him, before waltzing back to Razrastan again. He needed to understand that although she was living in one of his properties, she was still a free agent and she would see whoever she wanted to see. But Jasmine clamped her lips shut, telling herself there was no point in discussing it now, not when he was in this kind of mood.

Yet she felt distinctly flat when he delivered her back to the apartment. His rugged features were still dark with rage as he bid her a terse farewell before striding out of the apartment without another word.

She stood in the empty sitting room after he'd gone, looking out as the golden sunlight bounced off the bright green of the treetops, realising how unsatisfac-

tory the situation had become. She wanted him, yes—
she had never stopped wanting him, if the truth were
known—but for reasons of pride and self-preservation,
she was no longer prepared to settle for what little he
was prepared to offer her.

CHAPTER SIX

JASMINE FIRST REALISED something was wrong when she got a call to her mobile phone from an unlisted number. Deciding it was probably a sales call, she nonetheless picked it up, mainly because it had been ages since anyone had rung her.

'Hello?' she said cautiously.

'Is that Miss Jones? Miss Jasmine Jones?' The caller's voice was female, smoky and very confident.

'Speaking.'

'Just a couple of questions for you, Miss Jones. Is it true that you're the mother of the Sheikh of Razrastan's baby?'

Jasmine nearly dropped the phone. 'Who is this, please?'

'My name is Rebecca Starr from the *Daily View*,' said the voice. 'And I notice you're not issuing a denial to my question.'

Jasmine cut the connection with shaking fingers, wondering how the smoky-voiced Rebecca Starr had got hold of her number and wondering how best to respond. She swallowed. If in doubt, do nothing—wasn't that what people always said? She certainly wasn't going to bother Zuhal with it—not when he had stormed out in such a bad mood yesterday after that incident in the park with Carrie and her hot pants.

The phone rang again and Jasmine snatched it up, afraid that the shrill ringtone would wake her sleeping baby.

'Miss Jones? It's Rebecca Starr again. Do you have any immediate plans to marry Sheikh Zuhal Al Haidar of Razrastan?'

'Where did you get this number from?' Jasmine demanded uselessly.

'Because we understand there is a vacant role for a new royal Sheikha,' continued the journalist smoothly. 'Now that Zuhal is to be crowned King.'

With an angry squeak, Jasmine cut the connection, resisting the temptation to hurl the phone against one of the velvet cushions which were lined up neatly on the nearby sofa, knowing that if she did someone would just put them right back again. That was the trouble with having a fleet of cleaners at your disposal, she thought—there was never any mindless domestic work with which to displace your angry thoughts. No floors to clean or cobwebs to flick away from the ceiling.

She tried to convince herself that the press would soon lose interest if she didn't fan the flames of their story but she still felt faintly uneasy as she went about her normal routine. When he woke from his nap, she took Darius out for a stroll in his buggy and the warm sun beat down on the bare skin of her upper arms. Trying to ignore the discreet presence of the accompanying bodyguards, she found herself hoping she wouldn't bump into Carrie again, dreading having to bat away a stream of curious questions about Zuhal. But sooner or later she was going to have to see her, wasn't she? And what then? She couldn't pretend he didn't exist and she couldn't spend the rest of her life avoiding questions because she wasn't sure how to answer them.

She was just rounding the path to skirt the edge of the glittering lake when she sensed movement nearby and, glancing up, saw a blinding flash. Blinking, she watched as the black blur of one of the bodyguards hurtled towards a copse of trees while three others hurried forward to surround her.

'What's going on?' she questioned.

'Paparazzi,' one of them answered succinctly.

'What do they want?'

'Photos of you. And of the royal Prince. We need to leave, Miss Jones.'

'But—'

'Right now, Miss Jones,' he interrupted.

Jasmine forced herself to stay positive as she was practically marched back to the apartment—because having a baby meant you couldn't afford to indulge in introspective gloom—but she was glad when Rania stepped in to take Darius for her. And once she was on her own, reaction set in and Jasmine could do nothing to stop the jittery feelings which flooded over her. Her skin felt cold. Her hands were shaking and her heart was racing like a train. She wondered if this was how the future was going to look, with her locked away in her luxury apartment, hiding from anonymous people who took photos of her baby son without anyone's permission.

She wanted to pace the room. To talk to someone, but mostly she wanted to talk to Zuhal—and that surprised her. Maybe it was because he was the only person who would understand. The only person who *could* understand, because Darius was his son too. She went into her bedroom—with its pristine bed and neatly folded nightdress on the pillow. The framed photos of Darius and the portrait study of her mother taken before disillusionment had set in were the sole signs that this room actually belonged to anyone. A single woman's bedroom, she thought, as she scrabbled around in one of the drawers for the phone number Zuhal had given her.

With fingers which were still shaking, she keyed in the numbers and Zuhal's almost instant pick-up brought her up with a start, because for some reason it hadn't occurred to her that he might give her his direct line. She pulled a face at her pale reflection in the mirror.

Did she really think so little of herself?

And why wouldn't she, when she had been cut so comprehensively from his life once before?

'Zuhal?'

'What's happening?' he demanded, his voice underpinned by something she'd never heard there before. 'Are you okay?'

'Yes. But I've been…been…' The words trembled on her lips and she found herself unable to say them.

'Ambushed by paparazzi?' he provided harshly.

She sucked in an audible breath. 'So your spies have already got back to you, have they?'

Amid the opulent surroundings of an aircraft which was more like a flying palace, Zuhal scowled. 'Of course they have,' he bit out. 'What do you think I pay my staff to do, Jazz? They are guarding my son. It's their duty to tell me exactly what's happening in his life at any given time and I gather someone was photographing you in the park.' Silently, he cursed the distance between them and her stubbornness in not having let him bring up Darius in a country where people would not have access to focus their long-range lens on an innocent little prince. And then he realised that she was ringing him and that was something new. Fear coursed through him in a way it had never done before. 'Has something else happened?' he demanded as dread rippled down his spine. 'Is Darius okay?'

'Darius is fine, but I...' He could hear her swallow. Could hear her try to piece her words together, even though her voice was shaking. 'I had a phone call from a journalist.'

He froze. 'Saying what?'

'Asking if I was the mother. Asking if...'

'If what, Jazz?'

He could hear the embarrassment in her voice. Or was it distaste? he wondered bitterly.

'If I was planning to marry you.'

Zuhal closed his eyes and allowed the prolonged silence to send its noiseless scream down the international phone line before hearing her cough.

'Zuhal? Are you still there?'

'Yes, I'm right here—but don't worry, I'll be with you very soon.'

'With me?' He could hear the confusion in her voice. 'But you told me you were going back to Razrastan.'

'I was,' he agreed grimly. 'But the moment I heard about the incident in the park, I had my jet made ready. I'm on my way back to London.'

'You're on your way back to London,' she repeated dully. 'And just what is that supposed to achieve?'

'I don't intend discussing it with you now, Jazz,' he snapped. 'I've always found the phone a particularly unsatisfactory form of communication.'

'Which is presumably why you avoided it in the past,' she said waspishly.

He scowled, but he wasn't going to get into an argument with her now. Especially not about things which had happened between them in the past. It was the future which needed addressing now, he thought grimly. 'Expect me in around three hours' time,' he said briefly, and cut the call.

Jasmine couldn't settle to anything as she waited for Zuhal to arrive. He didn't bother to ring the doorbell, he just let himself into the apartment—in a cruel parody of a husband returning home from work.

For a split second she almost didn't recognise him because for once he was wearing traditional robes and she'd only ever seen him dressed that way in photos. Her heart clenched in her chest and she felt a moment of aching awareness as she acknowledged his powerful and almost primitively alpha presence in the pristine apartment. His black hair was completely covered by a white silk headdress, knotted with a circlet of scarlet.

The stark lines made his hawkish profile appear more autocratic than usual, just as the flowing robes emphasised the hardness of his body, rather than disguising it with its swishing folds. Maybe it was because she was all too aware of what lay beneath—all that muscular physique honed by years of riding.

He flicked her an unfathomable look as he strode towards the sitting room and what choice did she have but to follow him? But Jasmine was aware of a new tension about him and something indefinable glittering from his black eyes.

'Is this what you wanted all along?' he queried silkily.

She blinked at him in confusion. 'What are you talking about?'

'I'm talking about the sudden press interest, which seems to have come out of nowhere.'

'And I'm supposed to have provoked it, is that it?'

He shrugged. '*You* were the one who wanted to walk in the park yesterday, remember?'

'Only because I was feeling positively claustrophobic stuck in here with you!'

His eyes grew hard. 'Did you set it all up so that we'd bump into that woman Carrie—who has clearly run straight to the newspapers about us?'

'How could I do that when I had no idea that you were going to take a walk with me?'

Zuhal sliced the condemnatory palm of his hand through the air. 'You could have phoned her when you were putting on your hat!'

'Well, I didn't!' she flared. 'I can't believe you'd

think me even capable of such a thing—of putting my son at risk like that. How dare you?'

Zuhal was so taken aback by the fury in her voice that he let his hand fall to his side. And the crazy thing was that all he wanted to do was to kiss her—long and hard and deep. He wanted to take her in his arms and strip them both bare and lose all this anger and these recriminations. He scowled, because now was not the time to be distracted by the lure of sex, no matter how much he ached to be inside her again. The whole situation had got completely out of hand and it was now time for him to rein it all in, using the most effective means at his disposal.

He was going to have to do what he should have done the moment he found out about his son.

'You will have to come back to Razrastan with me,' he said.

'I beg your pardon?'

His mouth twisted. 'I don't think my statement requires any clarification.'

'You don't think your statement requires any clarification?' she repeated. 'Well, I do! What happened to keeping me here, with Darius as your insurance-policy heir, while you went out seeking a suitable bride?'

'I'll tell you exactly what happened,' he gritted out. 'My son has been discovered by the press. It hasn't hit the newspapers yet because my lawyers currently have an injunction out—but it will, because the courts will probably throw it out on the grounds that it's in the public interest to announce that Razrastan has a new heir. Even if they don't you can't keep something like this quiet for ever. Which is why the best kind of damage limitation is for you to agree to return to the guaranteed safety of my homeland.'

She shook her head. 'I can't do that, Zuhal,' she whispered.

Beneath his silken robes, Zuhal's body stiffened. Was she really refusing the gift he could offer her—a place of sanctuary while he worked out some kind of future for them all, even though he didn't yet know what that future could possibly be? She was a mass of contradictions, he conceded unwillingly—a woman who continually perplexed him. Who kept him at arm's length with a determination which was in itself a turn-on.

Yet he found himself remembering that moment in the park when he'd touched her and had seen her whole demeanour soften. Her green eyes had blazed with something passionate and unspoken. If that woman— Carrie—had not burst in on them, might he not have taken Jazz into his arms and kissed her? Brought her back here and spent the rest of the day having sex with her, so that once again she would become his compliant lover of old, eager to agree with whatever he suggested? When, instead, she was returning his gaze with a cool confidence which was making him seethe. So how best to proceed? He couldn't exactly drag her kicking and screaming back to Razrastan, could he? No matter how vivid *that* particular fantasy was turning out to be!

'You must realise that now I have discovered the existence of my son, nothing can ever be the same, Jazz.'

'You didn't discover him,' she answered. 'You came across him by chance.'

'However you care to define it,' he iced out, 'the facts remain the same. You are the mother of the Sheikh's son and you both remaining here in England is no longer a satisfactory option. You have no experience of press harassment but I do. You will be given no space until you provide them what they want, which is a story.'

She tipped her head back, her green eyes on a collision course with his. 'You really think I'd sell a story to the papers?'

'Actually, no. I don't.' He shook his head. 'But the story won't go away and in the meantime rumours will abound.'

'Rumours?' she questioned wryly. 'Or the truth?'

'The fact of our son is undeniable.' He gave a heavy sigh. 'I just need to figure out the best way to present it to my people and I can't do that if I'm constantly worried about you being besieged by all and sundry.'

'I don't know,' she hedged.

Sensing weakness, he swooped. 'Come back to Razrastan with me, Jazz,' he urged. 'Which will at least give us the space to think about the future.'

Jasmine turned away, touching her tongue to her dust-dry lips, her heart pounding as she acknowledged his words. He was promising nothing—certainly not on the emotional front. He'd spoken as if she were a plant he was eager to pluck from her native soil, to transplant her in his own, but with no assurances that she could thrive there. He wanted her to go to *his* palace and *his* country—where he literally ruled the roost. She would have absolutely no power there, and very little say in matters. And all this was complicated by her feelings for him, which wouldn't seem to go away. Because she still wanted him. Not just her body, but her heart, too. She wanted him in a way which was never going to happen and she knew that to go to his desert home would be to make herself vulnerable.

But what alternative did she have? Staying here and playing a constant cat-and-mouse game with the press? Continuing to obsess about him finding himself a suitable wife—a scenario which made her want to batter her fists against the walls of this elegant apartment which still didn't feel like home.

Would the royal palace feel any different?

She bit her lip.

The chances were that it wouldn't but, for her son's sake, shouldn't she give it a *try*? To see if Zuhal's suggestion was in any way workable, even if she had no real faith in the idea?

'Very well,' she said slowly. 'I will bring Darius to Razrastan and we will consider our options.'

Zuhal nodded, but there was no sense of triumph or satisfaction in his heart at having won round one of what he suspected was going to be a difficult battle. Was he going to have to make Jazz his bride in order to get her to comply with his wishes?

His mouth hardened. She was not the kind of woman he had ever imagined marrying and he did not know if his people would accept her—but Razrastan required an heir, just as it required a king.

His country had never needed him before but it seemed that, suddenly, it did now.

CHAPTER SEVEN

ZUHAL WALKED INTO the lavishly appointed drawing room and suppressed a rising feeling of apprehension as he thought of what lay ahead. Forty-eight hours had passed since he'd arrived here in the palace, with the blonde Englishwoman and her son in tow. A child who was very obviously the fruit of his loins, although nobody had dared comment on that fact to his face. He'd been aware that his courtiers and staff were buzzing with questions they wouldn't dream of asking their ruler, but he also knew that sooner or later the subject would need to be addressed.

And this morning, he had done just that. He paced the room, the silk of his robes rippling over his bare flesh. His meeting with his closest advisors had concluded there was only one satisfactory way to provide the best possible future for his son.

Zuhal's throat constricted. His son. The small but sturdy scrap of humanity who bore his genes. He'd thought the disappearance of his elder brother had been the most seismic thing which could happen to him but he had been wrong. Becoming the unexpected ruler of this vast desert kingdom was certainly momentous but the thought of fatherhood was far more significant and he was still processing it.

His jaw tightened. During the flight here he had surreptitiously observed Darius during those moments when Jazz had been sleeping. Registering the coal-black curls and golden dark skin of the baby, he'd felt an unexpected thrill of accomplishment and pride shivering through his veins. He had managed to produce an heir to continue the powerful Al Haidar line, without even trying. And in that moment he had vowed that whatever happened between him and Jazz he would never allow her to remove Darius from the country he would one day rule.

Did she realise that?

He heard the sound of footsteps and looked up. Her footfall was soft on the marble floor and as he saw the pale gleam of her hair in the distance, he felt the instinctive jerk of his groin. He ran his gaze over her as she approached and found himself approving her unfamiliar appearance, thinking how perfect she looked in the part of would-be desert Queen. Surprisingly, she had made no resistance to the assortment of 'appropriate' clothes he had insisted on providing for her—as if recognising the need for the kind of high-specification wardrobe required of his fiancée. Her measurements had been dispatched to one of the palace couturiers and an array of soft silken robes in a muted spectrum of colours had been waiting on her arrival in the capital city of Dhamar. With a compliancy he hadn't been expecting, she had also approved the exquisite garments which had been procured for the infant Prince, despite her own ambitions in that particular area. In fact, the only things she'd brought with her from England were something called a baby monitor, which she had insisted on being installed as soon as they arrived, and a soft toy monkey, with bright eyes.

'Ah, Jazz,' he said, as she grew close and he could not help his gaze from drinking her in, as a thirsty man might drink after a long day in the desert. She was wearing a silky gown the colour of a ripe mango, which brought out the golden lights in her unusual eyes. He could see the luscious thrust of her breasts as their curved weight pushed against the fine material and he thought longingly of the way he used to trace patterns on them with his fingertips, before taking her nipple into his mouth and teasing it until she gasped aloud. He felt the rush of lust and it was with an effort that he dragged his eyes away to meet her gaze. 'I trust you've settled in well?' he questioned benignly. 'And that your quarters meet with your satisfaction.'

She gave a flicker of a smile. 'That's a bit of an understatement. They're absolutely amazing. I've never seen anything quite like them. Not even when I worked at the Granchester.'

Zuhal didn't like the implication that a hotel—no matter how grand—could possibly be compared to his royal palace, but he made no comment. She would soon learn what were and were not acceptable topics of conversation, but now was not the time for a short lesson in diplomacy! He inclined his head. 'I'm glad you think so,' he said. 'And now, we will feast. I trust you have some appetite tonight, Jazz—for the servants inform me that you have eaten remarkably little since our arrival.'

She raised her eyebrows. 'Does that mean I'm still being spied on—despite living in your palace with practically no contact with the outside world?'

'I prefer to think of it as looking out for your welfare,' he corrected spikily. 'So why don't you sit down over there?'

The sweeping movement of his hand indicated an ornate table which had been laid up in one of the recessed windows overlooking the floodlit rose garden. On golden platters were elaborate displays of glistening fruits and savoury dishes, as well as tall decanters of iced fruit juice. Since he'd dispensed with all his servants, it meant Zuhal now found himself in the highly unusual position of having to serve her with food and drinks himself. And he thought she seemed completely oblivious to the honour he was affording her.

'Thank you,' she replied, perching on one of the gilt-edged chairs, before accepting the glass he was offering. 'Mmm... Delicious,' she added, as she sipped at the iced pomegranate juice.

He sat down opposite her and spooned some stewed aubergine onto her plate. 'How is Darius settling in?' he questioned.

'Better than I thought he would,' she said, as she lifted up her fork. 'Even the change in climate and the fact that we've leapt ahead by a few hours doesn't seem to have perturbed him. He's just had his bath and I've read him a story and now he's fast asleep. He won't wake until morning.'

'How can you be so certain?'

'Because that's his routine.' She hesitated for a moment, as if gauging his interest was genuine, before forging on. 'It's a routine I deliberately established, because I knew I'd never get time to get any sewing done otherwise. He's broken it a few times of course and once, when he was running a temperature, he was awake all night long.'

'And what was that like?' he questioned, his curiosity aroused.

'It was a nightmare,' she admitted. 'He screamed from dusk to daybreak. It was...' she gave a rather helpless shrug '...a long night.'

'I'm sure it was.' He realised with a start how much she'd had to deal with. That, despite Darius being an easy child, there had been nobody else for her to turn to—and surely that must have been hard, to have done it all on her own. Unexpectedly, he felt the stir of his conscience and suddenly he found himself wanting her to relax. To lose that pinched look which was making her face seem so pale. To become more like the Jazz of old, rather than this new, wary version. With this aim in mind, he coaxed her with food and watched as she tried a thimble-sized glass of Razrastan's famous lychee dessert wine, and it was with pleasure that he saw some of the tension leave her. 'Is there anything else you require?' he questioned solicitously. 'Anything my staff can help you with?'

Jasmine tried to concentrate on his question, but it wasn't easy. All she could think about was how frustrating it was to be within touching distance, when they hadn't actually touched at all. And while she knew this was probably the most *sensible* outcome—it certainly wasn't what her body wanted.

She couldn't seem to stop staring at his olive-dark face, wishing she could tug off that cream headdress and tangle her fingers in the rich blackness of his hair. She could feel her breasts tightening beneath her robe and the insistent tug of desire low in her belly as she surreptitiously ran her gaze over him. Suddenly it seemed like an awfully long time since she'd had sex. Well, it was. Over eighteen months, to be precise—and increasing exposure to the father of her child was reminding her all too vividly that she was a healthy young woman with physical needs of her own.

She found herself wanting to touch him—just as she had done when he had unexpectedly reappeared in her life again and had kissed her so passionately in her run-down little Oxford cottage. Maybe even more, because being with him again reminded her just how much she had always fancied him. And it wasn't his royal status which set her heart racing, or the fact that he was one of the wealthiest men on the planet. To her he was the man who had awoken her sexuality—the only man she had given her heart and her body to—and a woman never forgot something like that.

This was the man who used to flutter soft kisses over her belly before licking his tongue between the eager parting of her thighs. Who had brought her to orgasm that way, his hungry lips drinking in every shuddered spasm she made. The first time he'd done that she'd been incredibly nervous—self-conscious, even.

But Zuhal had taught her that sex was a gift to be enjoyed and there should be no barriers between consenting lovers. He had known her body inside and out, and sometimes, when he'd been deep inside her, it had been difficult to know where he began and she ended.

But she hadn't been thinking about that when she'd reluctantly agreed to come to Razrastan. She'd been thinking about her son. And now all her guilt about Darius not having had a father figure had been replaced by the fear that she'd walked into some sort of gilded trap. From the moment she'd entered the palace, the glittering walls seemed to enclose her with all their heavily guarded splendour. She'd looked around the vast and ornate citadel, slightly dazed to realise that Zuhal owned everything as far as the eye could see.

But he didn't own her, and that was what she needed to remember.

He had brought her and Darius here to get them away from a curious press and work out some kind of plan for the future—even though he had given her no indication of what that plan might be. He'd made it clear about the kind of woman he expected to marry and it certainly wasn't her—not that she'd want to marry such a cold-hearted brute in any case. Surely he wasn't expecting her to stay here indefinitely, while they lived separate lives?

She sighed, knowing she was going to have to make an effort. She needed to get on with the father of her child, no matter what happened between the two of them. So she nodded in response to Zuhal's unusually solicitous questions. 'There's nothing more we need,' she told him. 'Our rooms couldn't be any more comfortable and the view over the palace gardens is breathtaking. I had no idea that you could grow so many flowers in such a hot climate.'

'Fortunately, we do have access to water,' he commented sardonically, a dismissive wave of his hand indicating he was done with horticultural small-talk. 'And what of the nursemaids who will assist Rania? I trust they also meet with your approval, Jazz.'

It was a statement rather than a question and Jasmine hesitated, recognising once again that negotiation was better than confrontation. 'I have no complaints,' she said. 'They seem very...capable.'

'They are,' he agreed. 'Like Rania, many of them are the daughters of the women who used to care for Kamal and I when we were young.'

Jasmine nodded, his words reminding her that his upbringing was a million miles away from hers—a young prince surrounded by an army of servants. She realised she'd hardly ever heard him mention his own mother, not even when they'd been at their most intimate—actually, he'd barely mentioned his early years and neither had she. But back then their focus had been solely on pleasure, rather than the exchange of confidences which might have brought them closer as a couple. She met the black burn of his eyes. 'I wanted to talk to you about that,' she said hesitantly. 'You know, there's no need for a nurse to sit in the same room, watching Darius while he sleeps. I'm sure Rania and I can manage perfectly well on our own.'

'But I want something more for my son than just

managing,' he bit out. 'Darius will one day be King, and will need to get used to the presence of servants.'

Jasmine narrowed her eyes. 'You can't just come out and say things like that,' she objected, all thoughts of compromise forgotten. 'He might want to be a bank manager, living in the English countryside.'

He shook his head. 'No, not that. Not ever that. He will be King of Razrastan.'

'And how is that ever going to happen?' she demanded baldly.

His lips twisted into an odd kind of smile. 'I think you know the answer to that, Jazz,' he said softly. 'Darius will be my legitimate heir—and in order for that to happen, you must become my wife.'

A brittle silence entered the atmosphere as Jasmine stared at Zuhal with disbelieving eyes. 'Become your wife?' she repeated faintly.

'Surely the idea doesn't come as a complete shock to you?' he suggested sardonically. 'I have spoken with my closest advisors and government this very morning. They think my people will accept you, since you are the mother of my son. And, if the subject is handled with delicacy and tact, see no reason why we shouldn't marry. In fact, they concluded that marriage is the only appropriate solution to this particular dilemma.'

'*Dilemma?*' she echoed, outrage beginning to bubble up inside her. 'Is that how you see me?'

'Please don't fixate on the words I'm using but think instead about the meaning of what I'm saying, Jazz,' he continued remorselessly. 'I am proposing marriage. I, the Sheikh, am asking you, the commoner, to be my bride. Don't you realise what a great compliment that is?'

Jasmine shook her head. It didn't feel like a compliment. It felt like...

As if Zuhal was being forced into doing something he didn't want to do. As if he had been backed into a corner with no other way out. And wasn't that the truth of it? He didn't love her. He'd never loved her—so what were the chances of having a successful marriage? She thought about her own parents. About her mother's reaction when the relationship had started to crumble and the desperate way she'd tried to cling on. *I don't want to become like my mother,* Jasmine thought suddenly. And I don't want an uncaring sheikh's power to diminish me as a person, just because he wants to claim Darius as his rightful heir.

'It's too early to talk about marriage,' she said, quickly getting up from the table, unwilling to be subjected to Zuhal's look of disbelief as she gave him her answer. Resolutely, she walked over to one of the huge windows, glancing up at an indigo sky and thinking how far away the spatter of silver stars looked. 'Way too early.'

'Your attitude is more than a little *insulting*, Jazz,' he said, and she could hear the scrape of his chair and the sound of his footsteps as he walked over to join her. 'Don't you realise that most women would be eager to become my Queen?'

He was standing beside her—so close that they were almost touching. The warmth of his body was almost palpable and his presence was so powerful that Jasmine could scarcely breathe as raw longing clogged in her throat. 'Maybe they don't know you as well as I do!' She turned her head to look at him, detecting a brief flicker of outrage in the inky blaze of his eyes. 'I think we should take things slowly. I think, right now, that caution is probably the wisest choice.'

He gave a low laugh, which trickled over her skin like warm honey. 'Forgive me if I disagree,' he murmured, 'but I think a little recklessness might work better in our favour.'

She saw something in his eyes which was achingly familiar, as was the sudden tension which entered his hard body. And then suddenly Jasmine was in his arms and she never knew which of them instigated it, only that it seemed as inevitable as the rising of the giant moon outside the window, which was bathing them with a strange, silvery light. The Sheikh's mouth hovered briefly over hers and Jasmine gave a yelp as he brought it down hard to kiss her—before kissing him back with an urgent hunger which seemed to make her world spin. It felt as if she were falling. Or drowning. Drowning in a sweet, molten tide of desire.

Last time he'd kissed her, she'd felt a certain amount of restraint for all kinds of reasons, but mainly because she'd been concealing the knowledge of her son. Now she was concealing nothing. Not a single thing. She felt naked—despite the flowing material of the robes which covered her. She could feel the shameless spring of his erection pushing hard against her belly and felt the corresponding opening of her thighs as if she were silently girding herself to accommodate him. She heard his soft laugh as he acknowledged her submission, and his arms tightened around her back.

And Jasmine hugged him back because, oh, how she wanted this.

Now.

Here.

Just like this.

The real world retreated and all that mattered was the incredible sensation Zuhal was provoking by the tantalising whisper of a fingertip which traced its way down her spine. It was a gesture which felt almost innocent, yet how could it possibly be innocent when her nipples were hardening into tight buds which felt as if they were about to explode? He gave a low laugh of pleasure as he tilted her chin so that she was dazzled by the close-up fire of his eyes.

'Oh, Jazz,' he said softly. 'You want me, don't you? You want me so much, baby. You always did.'

His mocking smile dared her to deny it, but how could she deny it when it was the truth? When she'd dreamed and fantasised about this in weak moments when her defences had been down. Gazing up into the hectic gleam of his eyes, Jasmine was aware of her almost imperceptible nod of consent and the Sheikh's low growl of pleasure before he bent his dark head to kiss her again.

CHAPTER EIGHT

His hungry hands were on her breasts, her bottom and her belly as sexual heat ripped through Jasmine like a desert storm. Zuhal's fingers were moving urgently over her as if he couldn't wait to reacquaint himself with every inch of quivering flesh. She clung to his shoulders for support as he pulled her closer with a possessive mastery which made her feel weak with desire.

'Zuhal,' she breathed, the warmth of her breath mingling eagerly with his, the heat in her lower body starting its restless throb.

He didn't reply. Not at first. His only response was to deepen the kiss—his tongue exploring her with breathtaking intimacy. Her heart was racing like a piston as her fingers touched the unfamiliar headdress and she gave an impatient little tug to remove it. It slithered redundantly to the marble floor and suddenly his head was bare, just like in the old days. Exultantly, her fingertips explored the thick silk of his hair, before kneading at the base of his neck in a way which made him give an instinctive murmur of appreciation. Her hands moved to his biceps—powerful and supremely strong beneath his desert robes. She began to massage the rippling flesh and felt a familiar tension enter his body as he circled his hips in a way which made her intensely aware of his erection.

Jasmine closed her eyes as she felt that steely column pressing into her belly, suddenly aware of everything which had happened since they'd last made love. She recognised that her body had done some amazing things during that time. It had grown and given birth to a baby—an accomplishment which seemed both unreal and marvellous. But this was different. This was hunger. Sexual hunger. A raw and primitive need which was fierce and all-consuming. It was eating her up from the inside and igniting a yearning so powerful that she felt almost unable to stand.

Did Zuhal realise that? Was that why he drew back and stared down at her for a long moment—his eyes glittering like polished jet—before scooping her up into his arms with a moan which called out to her aching heart? When for a moment he seemed like the embodiment of all things alpha as he towered over her, dark and strong and vital as he carried her across the shiny marble floor towards an arched entrance at the far end of the vast chamber, his robes flowing like liquid silk as he walked.

'Where are we going?' she gasped, as he dipped his head to enter a narrow corridor, whose ceiling gleamed with exquisite inlaid tiles depicting erotic scenes of cavorting lovers.

'Somewhere where we'll be more comfortable.'

She looked up into the hectic gleam of his black eyes. 'Somewhere?'

'My bedroom,' he clarified unsteadily. 'It is connected to your apartments through this passageway, which is unseen by anyone else and which only the King is permitted to use. But I grant you my permission to use it any time you wish, Jazz.'

They emerged into a room which was way more magnificent than the suite which had been assigned to her and Darius, but for once Jasmine wasn't daunted by the size or splendour of the accommodation. Exquisite furniture and several statues swam in and out of focus, but all she could see was the vast bed, which Zuhal was striding towards.

Dimly she became aware of him impatiently brushing aside a litter of cushions before laying her down on it, his black gaze raking over her with a look of hungry speculation. Her hands were lying above her head and her legs were splayed out beneath the soft silken robes. And in that moment she felt like a sacrifice about to be offered up to the gods—a feeling which should surely have repelled the modern woman she was—yet the expression on his face spoke to some deep need inside her and she knew there was no power on earth which could have made her resist him.

'Oh, Jazz,' he groaned as he lay down beside her, his lips at her neck, his practised hand already rucking up the slippery fabric of her gown as his mouth drifted to her ear. 'You look so beautiful lying there.'

'D-do I?'

'Utterly.' he husked. 'Do you know how much I want you?'

'I think…' She closed her eyes as he began to drift kisses over her neck. 'I think I can just about work it out.'

'Then double it,' he growled. 'Better still, triple it.'

His hungry words thrilled her—they made her heart race even harder. She remembered the first time he'd taken her to bed, when her heart had swelled up with so much joy. When she'd cried—she wasn't quite sure why—when he had taken her virginity, and he had dried away her tears with a touch which had seemed almost tender.

And although some tiny voice in her head was telling her this was different—was urging her to employ caution—Jasmine refused to listen. Because how could she possibly be cautious when Zuhal's fingers were at her breasts? When they were cupping each swollen mound so that the mango silk appeared bright against his burnished flesh. And now his hand was inching its way up her leg, his featherlight fingertips brushing against the silky flesh of her inner thigh so that goosebumps were flowering beneath his touch. She could feel a syrupy rush soaking her panties and Jasmine closed her eyes before opening them again. 'Zuhal,' she said weakly, and just saying his name out loud was making her even more excited.

'Do you like that?'

'You…you know I do,' she managed to say, but only just—because now he had reached her panties and his finger was tracing a teasing path over the delicate fabric, which stretched tightly over her aching mound. Jasmine swallowed. How could she have forgotten that her body could ever feel like *this*?

'And this?' he questioned, almost carelessly.

She almost shot off the bed as skilfully he targeted her quivering clitoris. 'Oh, yes,' she groaned. '*Yes.*'

'How much do you like it?' he murmured.

'A…a lot,' she breathed.

'Then let's see if we can do something you like even more, shall we? Any ideas, Jazz?'

'I'll… I'll leave those to you,' she gasped. 'You were always the one with the ideas.'

Pushing aside the damp fabric, he began to thrum his finger against her moist flesh and Jazz began to quiver as his hand took on that slick rhythm she hadn't felt for so long. Already she felt crazily close to coming, knowing that if she let him continue she would succumb to the intense orgasm which was building up inside her. And wasn't that what she wanted? Wasn't that *all* she wanted? A quick, physical release to satisfy her aching body—with no danger of compromising her heart. Fractionally she lifted her hips and squirmed, her silent invitation to continue with his ministrations all too obvious. But Zuhal obviously had other ideas. Pulling his hand away and allowing it to rest indolently against the springy curls of her pubic hair, he pressed his lips into her ear.

'No,' he breathed hotly. 'Not like that. Not the first time. I want to feel myself inside you again, Jazz. Deep inside you, where I belong.'

His erotic words rocked her. They set up an answering clamour in her body which made her long to accommodate him. But even as her trembling thighs were spreading open to welcome him, that cautious voice of earlier was louder now, and less easy to ignore. It was reminding her that his words weren't true. That this wasn't the *first time*. Far from it. She was countless episodes and almost two years away from that initial deflowering, which had taken him by surprise. She was no longer the virgin divorcee he had rapturously introduced to sex. Nor was she the idealistic innocent who believed that just because a man groaned out heartfelt words of desire when he was orgasming inside you, it meant any more than just physical satisfaction. With Zuhal it had only *ever* been about physical satisfaction. But now there was something else he wanted even more badly. His baby son. Was that what this was all about? Softening her with seduction while he plotted to take what he saw as rightfully his?

Did he think that if she had sex with him now she would instantly agree to marriage?

Because that had been part of the trouble before—she'd allowed passion to sweep her away, so that she wasn't really thinking straight. Was that why she had tolerated her very part-time role as his mistress and been content to live in the shadows of his life? Maybe that was what amazing sex did to you…it robbed you of your strength and logic—and she needed both those things like never before. For her son's sake, but also for her own.

Her thoughts blurred as he slipped a finger inside her panties and she knew that if she didn't stop him soon, she would be past the point of making a rational decision…

Wriggling free of his intimate caress, she somehow managed to scramble off the day-bed, steeling herself against the sight of Zuhal still lying there in his rumpled robes, two high lines of colour flushed across his autocratic cheekbones, his black eyes burning with an expression she couldn't quite work out.

'Was it something I said?' he questioned mockingly.

Flattening her fingers against her heaving breasts, Jasmine struggled to get her breath back. 'That…that wasn't supposed to happen!'

'No?' He raised his black brows. 'So just what did you *think* was going to happen when I carried you in here, Jazz? Did you think we were going to have a discussion about world politics, or that I was about to start regaling you with stories of Razrastanian history?'

She realised that although outwardly he appeared cool and in control, his sarcastic words were underpinned with unmistakable irritation as he folded his arms behind his head to cushion it. She couldn't blame him.

'I'm sorry.' Distractedly, she shook her head. 'I wasn't thinking.'

There was a pause as his black eyes bored into her. 'Why don't you want to have sex with me, Jazz?'

She could feel the burn of her cheeks. She shouldn't have allowed him to bring her in here, putting herself in a situation she couldn't handle. Because wasn't the truth that she wanted to go right back over there and have him touch her with all that sweet unerring accu-

racy again? Didn't she long to feel him inside her—
deep inside her—as he himself had groaned out a few
minutes ago?

But a few moments of pleasure weren't powerful
enough to make her forget why she was here. He'd offered her marriage but she was still unsure of what
her answer was going to be. Because surely she could
only accept if she felt equipped enough to cope with
a loveless union. The last thing she needed was to be
blinded by desire. 'Because sex will just complicate
things. Surely you can see that.'

'You're saying you don't want us to be intimate?' he
queried softly.

Her voice was stiff as she tried to give an honest answer. 'I'd be a liar if I said I didn't want it. I just…just
don't feel ready for it at the moment.'

'Maybe that's something you ought to think about
next time you start batting those big green eyes at me,'
he observed, a little pulse hammering frantically at his
temple.

She gave an awkward nod of acknowledgement. 'We
were both responsible for what just happened, not just
me. We got…carried away.'

'And then some,' he agreed drily.

Attempting to put some space between them, Jasmine walked across the room to stand beside a marble
statue of a winged creature which was half-falcon, half-
goat—before turning back to face him. But he was still
tempting her. She suspected that he always would. 'I'll
try to be more circumspect in future,' she said.

There was a pause. 'Even if that means resisting your own desires?'

She met the curious question gleaming in the depths of his ebony eyes. Could she explain what was making her so cautious, without coming over as vulnerable or needy in the process? 'Here in your lavish palace, the only thing I have is my integrity and I don't intend to compromise it,' she said. 'I won't be able to think straight if we become intimate again. I'm afraid that desire will cloud my judgement and I can't afford to let that happen.'

'These are fighting words, Jazz,' he observed softly.

'They aren't meant to be. I don't want to fight with you, Zuhal.' She drew in a deep breath, praying her new-found conviction wouldn't leave her. Praying she wouldn't morph back into that docile Jasmine of old who had been content with the crumbs of affection the powerful Sheikh had thrown her way. 'We're no longer two occasional lovers who can't keep their hands off each other. We're parents. We have a lifetime bond through our son. We rushed into a relationship once before without really getting to know one another. This time, I think we should take things more slowly—to decide whether or not we could make a marriage work.'

'And am I supposed to admire your reluctance?' he questioned. 'Is your elusiveness part of some complex female game of playing hard to get in order to make yourself seem more of a prize?'

'I can assure you I'm not playing games, Zuhal. This is much too important for that. I have to believe that there's a basic compatibility between us before I agree to become your wife—otherwise it's just a recipe for disaster.'

Zuhal shook his head, unable to believe that Jazz of all people was turning him down. A woman who had been eager to learn all he could teach her—who had been the most delightful of all his lovers. Was she holding out for what women always demanded—words of love he would not provide? *Could* not provide, he reminded himself bitterly. If Jasmine wanted violins and moonlight she was doomed to be disappointed.

He looked at her. During that tantalising tumble which had just taken place on his bed, her hair had come free from its ribbon and was now tumbling down in waves of golden silk. She looked like an angel, he thought reluctantly, her long lashes shuttering the verdant beauty of her green eyes. He watched her smoothing down her robes as she struggled to catch her breath and in that moment she looked like the Jasmine he remembered—young and wild and passionate. But this Jasmine had just pushed him away in a way she would never have done before.

For a moment he was tempted to walk over there and attempt to change her mind. Would she have the strength to resist him a second time? He suspected not as for a moment he imagined being inside her again, his length encased inside her molten tightness as he rocked them both towards that blissful goal.

But he wasn't going to do that. She would regret soon enough having turned him down and discover that he had no intention of chasing after her all the way to the altar. Did she really think a man in his position would ever have to grovel to a woman? His lips hardened into a smile.

Let her come to him.

'So what exactly is it you want of me, Jazz?' he enquired casually.

It was a question Jasmine had never thought he'd ask. She knew what she'd wanted when they'd been together before but had accepted she was never going to get it. Because you couldn't demand love when instinct told you that love was an alien concept to a man like Zuhal. But she could discover more about the man who had always been a closed book to her when they had been casual lovers, couldn't she?

'Obviously, I'd like to learn about your country and your culture, Zuhal. But I'd also like to learn more about you.'

'Even though you've just turned down a method guaranteed to do exactly that?'

'I didn't find out much about you in all the time we were together, did I? And we were having plenty of sex back then.'

He raised his eyebrows. 'There are official biographies you can look at,' he said coolly. 'Which have always been in the public domain. We even have the authorised versions here in the palace library, which you are perfectly at liberty to read.'

She shook her head. 'That's not what I meant.'

'Oh?'

It was the most forbidding of looks and maybe if so much hadn't been at stake, Jasmine might have heeded its silent warning. But there was a potential marriage to consider, and it had to have the makings of a good one for her to risk putting Darius at its centre. And how could she consider marrying a man who remained little more than a stranger?

'I want to hear it from you, Zuhal,' she said. 'From your lips, not somebody else's.'

She saw his face darken with frustration, irritation and then a grim kind of acceptance. 'Very well,' he said at last, bending to pick up the discarded headdress which she had pulled from his head. 'You'd better speak to my diary secretary.'

'Your diary secretary?' she echoed in confusion.

'Of course.' He gave the flicker of a smile edged with undeniable *triumph*. 'How else did you think I was going to find time to see you? I am King now, with many demands on my time. Speaking of which…' he glanced at his watch '… I must leave you now, since I have work to do.'

She blinked. 'What, now?'

His black eyes glittered. 'There is always work to do, Jazz, no matter what the clock says. And since the evening has fallen far short of my expectations, I might as well put what remains of it to good use. I will show you back to your rooms and anything you require, just ring and one of the servants will attend to you.'

A peremptory wave of his hand indicated she should precede him. But it did more than that—it made it very clear who was in charge.

Jasmine opened her mouth to object before shutting it again, because what could she say? She had turned down his proposal and now he was suggesting she make an appointment to see him, in the same way he might schedule in an appointment with his dentist! And meanwhile that vast and rumpled bed was mocking her with all its unused promise.

The bubble of the evening seemed to have burst. She walked ahead of him, hearing the soft shimmer of his robes brushing over the marble floor as he followed her. And all she could think about was the powerful perfection of his brooding body and the way it had felt when he'd held her in his arms again, as she tried to quash a deep and overwhelming sense of regret.

CHAPTER NINE

IT SHOULD HAVE been a fairy tale. At least, that was how it might have looked to an outsider. A one-time single mother plucked from her humble abode and transplanted into a glittering, golden palace by a sheikh who was eager for her to be his bride.

A lump rose in Jasmine's throat. Because this was no fairy tale. This was living in a gilded prison.

It was true she'd been meeting all kinds of new people—from royal monarchs who ruled neighbouring countries to the noblemen and women of Razrastan itself. She'd sat beneath sparkling chandeliers, wearing a fortune in diamonds around her neck—while discussing with the American ambassador the proposed trip by the President of the United States of America!

Those were the facts.

The irrefutable facts.

But facts only told you so much. They only showed you the supposedly smooth surface—not the dark undercurrents which were swirling beneath. She might be the mother of the Sheikh's baby, and they might be polite and perfectly civil with each other in public. But in reality they'd barely spent any time alone since she had rejected Zuhal's sexual advances, and the subject of marriage was still unresolved.

She'd wanted to get to know him before making any firm commitment, but how was that possible when palace life seemed the enemy of intimacy? When meals were distinctly formal and featured guests Zuhal thought it prudent she meet. During course after endless course, streams of servants weaved their way in and out, bearing extravagant dishes heaped with Razrastanian specialities, whose very names dazzled her. None of the servants ever met her eyes. They seemed to look right through her. She suspected they disapproved of this Englishwoman who had entered their royal palace with an illegitimate baby in tow. Maybe they were glad there had been no official acknowledgement of her role in the Sheikh's life.

And none of these functions offered any opportunity for private conversation with Zuhal because he was always sitting at the far end of the table, looking impossibly aloof and regal. Why, the physical distance between them was so great, that just getting him to hear her meant she almost had to shout. Just as there had been no shared moments of parenting with him. It seemed he made time to see his son only when he was certain Jasmine wasn't around and she wondered if he was punishing her for refusing his proposal, by deliberately keeping his distance. On more than one occasion, she had emerged from her dressing room, her hair still damp from the shower, to see the silky shimmer of the Sheikh's pale robes disappearing through the tall, arched doorway.

Sometimes she would wake early when the baby was still asleep and the palace all but silent. Once, unable to get back to sleep, she had gone to the stable complex, just as Zuhal was dismounting from his horse after his morning ride. Hidden away in the shadows, he hadn't seen her, but Jasmine had watched as he'd peeled a silk shirt from his torso. Like a woman hypnotised, she had observed his slow striptease with a racing heart which had threatened to burst out of her chest. With hungry eyes she'd drunk in the gleam of his burnished skin and bronzed definition of his powerful physique. There wasn't an inch of surplus flesh on his hard body and his washboard abs were glistening like the cover shot of a fitness magazine. She'd found herself wanting to run over and to slowly slide her way down over his body. To lick her tongue over his chest, revelling in the taste of each salty bead of sweat, knowing they were all a part of him. And then to unzip his jodhpurs and feel his proud length springing free, first against her fingers and then into the moist and waiting cavern of her lips.

She began to question if she'd been too hasty. If she had driven him away with her proud stance, which had masked her fears about getting intimate with him again. Yet how was she ever going to find out whether they were compatible if they were never alone? When the days were ticking away, bringing closer the formal signing of the papers which would make Zuhal the official ruler of Razrastan. She hadn't actually ruled out marriage, had she? She'd just told him she wanted to get to know him better before she committed. So maybe it was time for action instead of all these fractured thoughts. Maybe she should take Zuhal at his word and book herself an appointment to see him, since he obviously had no intention of backing down himself.

Which was how one sun-dappled morning she found herself in Zuhal's offices in the south-west corner of the palace, which overlooked a sylvan courtyard of trees. At its centre was a cool pond, in which red-gold fish swam—giving the place a curiously peaceful feel. Inside, it was completely different—a modern hive of activity hiding behind the ancient doors. Assistants tapped feverishly at the keyboards of sleek computers and rows of clocks indicated different time zones from around the world. She was asked to wait in an anteroom, before being shown into an inner sanctum for a meeting with Zuhal's chief aide—a shuttered-faced man in traditional Razrastanian robes, who looked up from his desk as she was ushered in.

'Miss Jones,' he said smoothly, rising to his feet to greet her. 'My name is Adham. This is an unexpected pleasure.'

Jasmine recognised his voice instantly. She would never forget it, not in a million years. A chill rippled down her spine. This was the same aide who had blocked her attempt to tell Zuhal she was pregnant all those months ago. Was that why his face was so unfriendly when he looked at her? Why she detected a glimmer of darkness in his expression as she entered his plush office? Or was he just more open about expressing what she suspected most of the palace staff really felt about her? Quashing down her instinctive apprehension, Jasmine composed her face into a look of polite enquiry. 'I hope I'm not disturbing you?'

'Not at all, Miss Jones,' he said, his forced smile seeming to contradict his benign words. 'What can I do for you this morning?'

Jasmine felt the sudden pounding of her heart, recognising that this was the moment. She was here to try to deepen her relationship with the father of her child and to address seriously the possibility of being a future queen. So maybe it was time to start acting like one. To show Adham that she was no longer some inconvenient lover he could dismiss as if she didn't matter, but part of Zuhal's life, whether he liked it or not.

Adopting the wide smile which had always been super-effective when dealing with tricky customers at the Granchester boutique, she gestured towards the sunlit garden outside. 'It is an exceptionally beautiful morning, isn't it?' she observed, with diplomatic politeness.

'Indeed. The weather in Razrastan is especially temperate at this time of year,' Adham answered, the faint elevation of his eyebrows silently urging her to get to the point.

Jasmine did exactly that. 'I'd like to see the Sheikh, please.'

'I'm afraid that won't be possible, Miss Jones. His Royal Highness is busy at the moment. I'm sure you are well aware of the demands on his time at this key stage in the country's future,' he said, his tone smooth and pleasant, although the icy gleam of his eyes suggested a certain insincerity. 'In fact, he is on the phone to the Sheikh of Maraban, as we speak.'

'Oh, I didn't mean *right now*,' said Jasmine quickly. 'Obviously, he's tied up most of the time. I appreciate that. I just wondered if you could make an appointment for me to see him.'

A flicker of incredulity passed over the shuttered features. 'An appointment, Miss Jones?'

'If you would. Zuhal did say we should coordinate our diaries in order to make time for one other.'

'His Royal Highness mentioned nothing to me.'

'Does Zuhal run everything past you, then, Adham?' questioned Jasmine innocently.

It was the first time in her life that she'd ever pulled rank—not that she'd ever had any rank to pull before now—and to her astonishment it worked. As if realising that this time she wouldn't be thwarted, the aide reluctantly bent his head to study the leather-bound diary in front of him before returning his shuttered gaze to hers. 'Very well. I believe I can fit you in, if you are prepared to be flexible. Shall we say tomorrow morning at ten o'clock? His Royal Highness has a window of thirty minutes he can allot to you, after his morning ride.'

Thirty minutes! Not even an hour alone with the man who had asked her to marry him! And just around the time when Darius would be having his post-breakfast playtime, which wasn't what you'd call convenient. But if this was the best she could hope for, then she was going to grab it with both hands. 'Perfect,' she said brightly.

The aide consulted some sort of grid chart in front of him. 'If you would like to make your way to the Damask Room at the allotted time, His Royal Highness will join you there.

Jasmine nodded. 'Thank you, Adham.'

Despite the somewhat lukewarm response she'd received, Jasmine felt a fizz of excitement as she returned to her suite, where Darius was waiting with Rania. The baby gurgled with pleasure as she held out her arms to him and her mind was buzzing as she wondered how to make the most of her time alone with Zuhal tomorrow.

Was that being super-needy?

No, she told herself, as she waved a noisy rattle in front of the baby's nose. Not needy at all. It was being grown-up and sensible. Accepting that she wasn't dealing with just *any* man. She closed her eyes with pleasure as Darius wrapped his chubby little arms around her neck and snuggled up close. Zuhal was a man who would soon be King and she needed to make allowances for that.

But that night, during a pre-dinner drinks reception for a cluster of visiting Argentinean diplomats, she looked up to find the Sheikh's eyes fixed on hers more often than usual. The expression in their ebony depths was one she couldn't decipher, but it was enough to set her heart racing as she walked forward to meet the line of guests.

She had decided to treat these functions in the same way she used to regard shopping evenings at the Granchester boutique, trying to put people at their ease—and for the most part this made them bearable. Yet tonight it felt different. Or maybe it was just she who felt different. She'd broken the deadlock and from tomorrow, she would start learning more about the Sheikh whose narrowed gaze was currently sweeping over her like a dark spotlight. She wished he wouldn't look at her like that in public. Making her dress feel as if it had suddenly become two sizes too small. Making her brow break out into tiny little beads of sweat beneath her carefully coiffed hair.

As usual, she and Zuhal left the reception at exactly the same time but tonight, instead of going to his own suite, he insisted on accompanying her to Darius's room where he remained while she checked on him, before dismissing Rania for the night. The main reception room of her private suite seemed very large and echoing as she shut the door to the nursery and turned to Zuhal, realising that, for the first time in a long time, they were completely alone. She swallowed. She could detect the subtle yet very masculine scent of sandalwood radiating from his powerful body, making her uncomfortably aware of his raw virility as she regarded him with cautious question in her eyes.

'I understand you paid a visit to Adham this morning,' he said, without prompting.

'I did.'

'And insisted on a meeting with me tomorrow morning.'

Wasn't his expression more than a little *smug*? Jasmine wondered, with a touch of indignation. 'Insist?' she echoed lightly. 'I thought that's what we agreed. Appointments in the diary. A rather unconventional way of a couple getting to know each other, it's true, but that was the only way you could guarantee allotting me any time.'

'It's true, that's what we agreed,' Zuhal conceded, feasting his gaze on her luscious body and letting it linger there. He'd said it to make her realise that he had neither the time nor the inclination to play games with her. He'd imagined his cool indifference might make her reconsider her foolishness in rejecting him and bring her running into his arms. That without further prompting she would slip along the secret corridor to his bed and seek the pleasure she was guaranteed to find there.

But it hadn't worked out that way.

His remoteness hadn't had the desired effect of taming her or bringing her into his bed. There had been no delicious blonde lying waiting for him between the slippery silk of his sheets, eagerly taking him into her arms before spreading those delicious thighs for him. Instead, she had remained as prim as a maiden aunt and ironically this had only increased his hunger for her. His mouth dried. As if he needed any more hunger than was already coursing around his frustrated veins!

'So you've got what you wanted,' she observed thoughtfully.

A pulse flickered at his temple as she tilted her chin with faint challenge. 'On the contrary, Jazz,' he demurred softly. 'I'm still waiting for the thing I want most.'

Her eyes narrowed as she looked at him and suddenly all that old sexual shorthand was back. The flush to her cheeks and the darkening of her eyes. The spring of her nipples against the silk of her robes and quick writhe of the hips, which was almost imperceptible to anyone else but him.

'Jazz,' he said, on a throaty note of hunger he couldn't disguise and he heard her answering intake of breath. Did she move first or did he, and wasn't that something he needed to know—in order to establish whose victory this was? But suddenly Zuhal didn't care—not about the method, only the result. He didn't care which of them had backed down as, with a hungry moan, he closed his arms around her and desire reverberated through him as never before.

Her mouth opened beneath his kiss and her moan echoed his as he explored her with his tongue. Sweet heaven, but she tasted good. So good. His shaking hands were on her robes, tugging at them impatiently with none of his usual restraint, and she was doing the same thing to him—touching his body through the delicate material as if she were discovering it for the very first time. But this was nothing like the first time. Back then she had been a virgin and now she was a sexually experienced woman who knew exactly what she wanted. And so did he.

Her hand pressed boldly against his erection as he deepened the kiss and, urgently, he backed her up against the wall, peeling off her tunic and flinging it aside before dispensing with his own the same way. He ripped off her panties so that they fluttered onto the Persian rug, his fingers quickly finding the moist heat now exposed to him and beginning a deliciously familiar rhythm. The scent of sex filled the air as he strummed against the warm syrupy feel of her and she bucked immediately.

'Yes,' she gasped, brokenly, and suddenly she forgot everything. Forgot that she probably shouldn't be doing this and that Zuhal wasn't using any protection. All she could think about was it. And him. The word burst out of her lips again. 'Yes.'

His hands clamped around the cool flesh of her buttocks, he lifted her up so she could lock her thighs around his hips, positioning herself perfectly for that first, deep thrust which made her gasp in the way he remembered so well For a moment he had to still in order to compose himself, terrified he would come straight away—like some over-keen schoolboy whose wildest fantasy had just been realised.

'*Oh*,' he breathed, as control returned to him and he resumed his thrust. Each. Hard. Hungry. Thrust. 'Isn't that good, Jazz?' he demanded unsteadily. 'Isn't it the best thing you ever felt?'

Her breath was hot against his neck, her words slurred with pleasure. 'Is it praise you're seeking, Zuhal?'

No, it wasn't praise. He told himself it was orgasm he wanted—all he had ever wanted—but orgasms were easily attained, weren't they? And then he stopped thinking altogether, focussing instead on how tight she felt as his balls slapped softly against her molten heat. On how his heart was pounding like a regimental drum as he increased his speed. He drove into her while doing all the things he knew she liked best. Grazing her nipples with his teeth—so that she was balancing on the fine edge between pain and pleasure. Stroking his thumb down the enticing valley which cleaved between her buttocks, so that she moaned softly with pleasure.

When she came, he followed almost immediately, kissing away her shuddering moans as his seed spurted long and deep into her body and he felt the inexplicable clench of his heart. Long minutes passed as her head flopped against his shoulder and he could hear her breathing fanning his neck. At last she unfolded her legs and slid them down so that she was standing again, her weight now pressed against the wall instead of into his body. But when he tilted her chin to stare into her eyes, she was having none of it and shook her head.

'No. Don't say anything,' she said.

'Not even to ask you whether you'd like to do it all over again?'

Her emerald gaze was very clear. 'And if I did, would you use some protection this time?'

He nodded. 'Of course I would. I wasn't thinking. At least, not about that.'

There was a fraction of a pause. 'Neither was I. But I need to do some thinking now, so will you please go?' She shook her head as if to pre-empt further argument. 'I mean it, Zuhal. Just go.'

It took a moment or two for him to realise she meant it and slowly he expelled a long breath. It was the first time he'd ever been ejected from a woman's bedroom but to Zuhal it suddenly felt more like a reprieve than a punishment. Because wasn't it a relief to be spared the inevitable analysis of what had just happened, in that tedious way women had of always overthinking things?

They both knew exactly what had just happened.

Sex. Amazing sex—nothing more and nothing less.

His lips curved into a satisfied smile as he allowed himself the brief luxury of a stretch. 'Sure,' he said, as he bent to retrieve his discarded robes.

CHAPTER TEN

THE SUN WAS rising in the dawn sky as Zuhal headed towards the stables next morning. He felt the tension leaching from his body—something he attributed to the amazing sex he'd had with Jazz last night, an erotic encounter which was making him grow hard just thinking about it. Because tension was an integral part of his life now, he recognised. It went hand in hand with the many new challenges facing him as monarch. Yet he found himself relishing those challenges in a way he hadn't been anticipating, because he had never imagined he would be King. To rule had never been his destiny, but already his people were beginning to accept him, even to warm to him, and he was confident that he would be able to do his best by them.

Wasn't that the silver lining to the dark cloud which had descended on him when Kamal had disappeared? The realisation that he no longer felt the outsider in the country of his birth?

The distant sky was a flamboyant display of flamingo-pink and orange as he swung himself into the saddle and urged his horse forward. Last night had been pivotal in all kinds of ways. He had spent the evening watching Jazz perform admirably as Queen-in-Waiting and her subsequent sexual capitulation boded well for the future. Surely now there was no further barrier stopping him from making her his bride? No reason for her to keep him dangling while she tantalisingly refused to give him her answer.

His mouth curved into a speculative smile. He remembered the way he had ripped the robes from her body and the way she had moaned as his fingers found her wet heat. Pride was all very well, but sexual satisfaction was a far more powerful motivator. Wouldn't that fast and furious encounter encourage her to go ahead with the marriage as quickly as possible, so that they could become husband and wife?

He rode for nearly an hour and was galloping back towards the stables when, suddenly, he caught sight of the gleam of blonde hair in the distance. Jazz. He felt his groin tighten as his gaze drank her in. In the light desert breeze, the folds of her robes had moulded themselves to her delectable body and he was reminded of clasping those luscious curves before bringing them both to orgasm. Was she eager for an early replay? he thought with hungry amusement Was that why she was here? Perhaps she wanted him to tumble her onto the stable floor and take her amid all the bales of hay, rutting into her like a stallion?

'So this time you don't mind being seen?' he questioned as he slowed his horse and drew up beside her.

She blinked up at him in alarm. 'Seen?'

He jumped down onto the dusty ground. 'Didn't I

once observe you watching me from afar? Standing in a corner of the stables and watching while I took off my clothes?' Her answering colour told him that her shadowed presence hadn't been a figment of his over-heated imagination and, although she was now glaring at him, he smiled. 'Don't worry, I rather liked you in the role of voyeur.'

'I'm not worried!' she flared back at him, her cheeks still flushed and pink.

'So why are you here?' he mused softly. 'As far as I'm aware, we aren't supposed to be meeting for another hour and I need to shower first. Unless what happened last night means you're thinking you might like to join me? I'm quite happy for you to soap me off, my beauty. It's far too long since we had a shower together.'

Jasmine wished he would stop making sexual allusions every time he opened his mouth because they were drawing her attention to his body, which she'd been trying very hard to forget. But how could she forget when the memory had kept her awake most of the night, as she'd recalled the way he had driven into her. Her cheeks grew hotter as she remembered her eagerness to have sex with him—backed up against one of the palace walls, of all places, with her legs wrapped tightly around his bare back as he had taken her on a quick trip to paradise. What had happened to her determination to keep things on an impartial footing until she had discovered whether she wanted to marry him? It had vanished the moment he had taken her in his arms and kissed her.

'I don't want to talk about that,' she said. 'Last night shouldn't have happened.'

His eyes glittered. 'Are you quite sure?'

'Quite sure. I'm supposed to be getting to know you,' she continued. 'In a rather more formal way than that.'

'As you wish. I've never had to beg a woman for sex before, Jazz—and I'm certainly not going to start now.'

'It was usually the other way round, was it?' she queried mischievously.

He gave a brief smile as they began to walk towards the stables, and Jasmine suddenly became aware of a sense of wistfulness as she breathed in a long-forgotten fragrance. 'I love that smell,' she said suddenly.

He turned to look at her. 'What smell?'

'You know. Horses. Leather. Dust. Sweat. The whole thing. Stables, I guess.' She gave a sigh, which seemed to bubble up out of nowhere. 'You're very lucky to be able to ride out in the desert with no fences or houses or roads to get in the way. You must get a real sense of freedom out here—the kind you don't really get back in England.'

He narrowed his eyes, as one of the grooms led his horse away. 'You sound as if you know what you're talking about.'

'You seem surprised.'

'Maybe I am. I thought you were the quintessential city girl. Are you telling me you can ride, Jazz?'

'Yes, I can ride,' she said quietly. 'I used to love all things equestrian until the age of ten. Or did you think I'd always been poor and that riding is a rich person's sport?'

He lifted his hand by a fraction, but the quirk of his lips indicated a signal of acknowledgement rather than command.

'So what happened when you were ten?' he continued curiously as they began to walk back towards the palace.

Jasmine tried to avert her gaze from the thrust of his thighs against his jodhpurs, but it wasn't easy—particularly when she thought of her fingers roving over their hair-roughened power last night and the memory of what lay at their apex. She cleared her throat. 'It was a continuation of the fallen-ice-cream episode,' she said.

'The fallen ice cream?' he repeated blankly.

'You remember. I told you about it in London. When my father left home.' She gave an impatient shake of her shoulders. 'Weren't you listening?'

'Yes, of course I was listening. Forgive me. I am feeling a little *distracted*. You can't blame me for that, in view of what happened between us last night.' With what looked like an effort, he dragged his gaze from her torso to her face. 'So what happened—after your father left home?'

He had stopped walking and was looking at her, waiting for her answer.

'We had to sell the house and the car,' she explained. 'And my pony was the first thing to go, obviously.'

'Why?'

Jasmine felt a flicker of irritation at his incomprehension. Did he really lack the imagination to work it out for himself, or was he just incapable of putting himself into the shoes of a normal person? She stared down at her feet, aware of a fine layer of dust from the yard which was now covering her toes and wishing she'd worn something more substantial than beaded flip-flops.

She lifted her gaze to his. 'Because as well as making his much younger secretary pregnant and causing a scandal at work, my father had also been living beyond his means—and once it was discovered, everything started to tumble down. The banks needed to be paid and there was no money to pay them. It meant my mum was left with very little. In fact, with almost nothing. We had to start renting a tiny apartment.' She sucked in a deep breath. 'And Mum had to go back out to work—but the only work she could get was cleaning. Overnight she went from being a middle-class wife to what she called a "skivvy" and she never got over it, really. She got ill soon after that. Perhaps the two things were related.'

Zuhal met the sombre expression clouding her green-gold eyes. It must have been tough, he acknowledged, as they resumed their step and the soaring blue cupolas of the palace swam into view. Maybe everyone's childhood was tough, he concluded grimly as several servants spotted him and lowered their gazes in natural deference. Or maybe it was family life itself which created all the problems. He thought about his own parents. About the so-called 'love' which had corrupted the atmosphere with so much poison. His mouth twisted. Who needed it? Surely mutual tolerance and good sex were a better long-term bet than all the chaos wreaked by love?

He observed the glint of sunlight on Jazz's pale hair and imagined her as a horse-mad young girl. He could picture her in a smart jacket, her hair in a net and a crop in her hand. A bright rosette pinned to her pony as she leaned forward to pat the forelock. It must have hurt to have lost all that, he realised with a sudden flash of insight, which wasn't usually his thing. Because although he didn't have quite the same affinity with horses as his brother did—*had done*—he corrected painfully, he still valued his daily ride above most things.

'Would you like to ride out with me tomorrow morning?' he said as she began to move away from him.

She turned back and he could see the uncertainty on her face. 'I haven't been on a horse for years,' she said. 'I don't know if I can still do it.'

'There's only one way to find out.'

'I don't know, Zuhal.'

'Is that a yes?' he prompted softly, and suddenly it mattered. It mattered a lot.

There was a pause and then she nodded, her blonde ponytail shimmering like the tail of a horse in the early-morning haze as her green eyes met his. 'It's a yes. And thank you. But there's no way I'll be able to keep up with you. Give me the most gentle horse in your stable and I'll be happy just trotting around the yard.'

'You will do no such thing,' he vowed. 'You can have my undivided teaching skills, if you like.' He felt the flicker of a pulse at his temple and the more insistent one which was throbbing deep in his groin. 'And don't they say it all comes rushing back, the moment you're back in the saddle?'

'I guess they do,' she said and the smile she gave him lingered long after he had watched her retreating into the palace.

He spent longer in the shower than usual—mainly because his newly ignited sexual hunger refused to be doused, even by the prolonged jets of icy water over his heated skin. He found himself bemused and intrigued by her determination to ignore what had happened last night. Unless her prudishness was all for show and she was planning to seduce him during their ten o'clock appointment in the Damask Room. Yes, that could work. That could work very well. He felt the flicker of a pulse at his temple and ordered Adham to ensure that he was not disturbed for the duration of the meeting, telling him it was possible it might run over.

But his anticipation was dampened the moment Jazz was shown into the room and he saw a new light of purpose glinting from her green-gold eyes. She was wearing a demure cream gown which covered her from head to ankle and his heart sank. Sinking down gracefully into one of the soft chairs, she pressed her knees together and he couldn't help contrasting her demure image with the wildcat lover who had greedily met his urgent thrusts last night.

'I'd like to discuss bringing the high chair into the dining room,' she began, without any kind of fanfare.

He narrowed his eyes. 'Excuse me?'

'I think it's best if we make some attempt to live as a normal family, even if these surroundings are far from normal, and neither is our situation. But I think it would benefit Darius if he joined us at lunchtime. That's all.'

Zuhal frowned. 'Have you forgotten that we often have international delegations with officials present during lunch?' he demanded.

'No, I haven't forgotten. But it will do them good to see the powerful King living as other men do. It would make you seem more…approachable.'

'You think I'm unapproachable?' he demanded.

She hesitated. 'I think as King you're still an unknown factor and interacting with your son will show people a softer side of you. Can you see any reason why we shouldn't give it a trial run, Zuhal?'

He met the determination in her eyes and felt a smile begin to build. 'I guess not,' he said, as grudging admiration for her sheer tenacity washed over him.

Then followed a debate about the installation of a small sandpit—'It's not as if we're short of the raw material, Zuhal!'—and before he knew it the half-hour was up. The meeting had not gone as he had hoped and yet, for some reason, he found himself whistling softly underneath his breath as he went off to his next appointment.

Next morning she joined him at the stables and he discovered that she was a good rider who possessed a natural affinity with the horse he had chosen especially for her. At first their routes were slow and unambitious—rarely venturing too far from the palace, until Zuhal was confident that Jazz herself was at ease. He watched her walk and canter and gallop with a growing feeling of satisfaction. He observed her increasing confidence as she and the horse became better acquainted before increasing the scope of their rides by taking her a little further into the desert.

And the stream of questions she'd implied she'd wanted the answers to had somehow failed to materialise. Maybe the sheer physicality of riding demanded all her attention, or maybe she was cleverer than he'd given her credit for by not pushing him into a corner. Her occasional queries were light—like butterflies dropping onto a blossom rather than rocks falling into a well. They seemed to encourage confidences rather than making him clam up, as had happened so often in the past whenever women had tried to delve beneath the surface. Once or twice, he found himself offering an opinion which hadn't been asked for. Like the time he'd admitted missing the banter and friendly rivalry he'd shared with his brother. Or confessing that being a ruler was harder than he'd envisaged and perhaps he had judged Kamal too harshly—something which troubled him now. He didn't tell her that for the first time ever he felt as if his life had true meaning. That he was no longer just the royal 'spare', and as ruler he found he had the power to make a difference.

But after an entire fortnight of uneventful rides, Zuhal had decided that enough was enough. He wanted her in his arms again and her body language was sending out a silent message that she wanted him just as much. This celibate existence had gone on long enough. He would put her in a position where she couldn't distract herself with horses or babies and this time *demand* she marry him!

The ride they embarked on the following day was

their most ambitious yet and for most of it he rode beside her, his headdress streaming in the wind as they tracked the golden sands in silence, the pounding of hooves and the snort of the horses the only sounds to be heard.

'Look over there,' he said after a while, slowing down to point into the distance. 'See anything?'

Screwing up her eyes, Jasmine noticed a tiny dot on the horizon which was growing bigger as they rode towards it, until she saw the outline of a large tent with a conical roof. Nearby was an unexpected copse of trees and a group of smaller tents. In the shade of the trees they dismounted and Zuhal tethered the horses before two male servants appeared from one of the smaller tents, bringing bowls of water for the animals to drink.

'Is this what you call an oasis?'

'Ten out of ten, Jazz,' he murmured.

He motioned for her to follow him into the cool interior of the largest tent, which stood some distance away. Dipping her head to enter, she gave an audible gasp as she gazed around the deceptively vast interior where intricate bronze lamps hung from the ceiling and silken rugs were scattered over the floor. A large day-bed of silver brocade stood beside an exquisitely carved table, on which reposed tiny glasses studded with the rainbow colours of what looked like real jewels.

'Oh, Zuhal—it's beautiful,' she breathed, unable to conceal her wonder or her delight. 'I don't think I've ever seen anything quite so beautiful.'

'Not even at the Granchester Hotel,' he questioned sarcastically.

A smile played at the edges of her lips. 'Not even there!'

He inclined his head in acknowledgement. 'Please, sit,' he said formally.

A little saddle-sore after the long ride, Jasmine obeyed, sinking into the heap of cushions he was indicating, while Zuhal called out something in his own language before lowering himself down beside her.

'What is this place?' she asked, as one of the servants appeared at the door of the tent, bearing a large stone jug and dispensing cool liquid into two tiny jewelled glasses.

'It is my refuge,' he said slowly, once the servant had left. 'It was my brother's refuge too, and our father's before him. It is traditionally the place where kings have come to escape from the pressures of court and palace life.'

Jasmine nodded as she took a sip of the refreshing drink. She had been treading on eggshells for days, afraid of driving him away with her curiosity and trying to establish some kind of trust between them, but something told her that now was the time to dig a little deeper. 'What was it like?' she asked, putting her glass down and leaning back against the soft nest of cushions.

'What?' he queried obliquely.

'Growing up in a palace.'

'You've experienced something of that yourself,' he answered carelessly. 'You will have noted the presence of servants. Of days which are governed by form and by structure. Of the innate need for formality—despite your single-handed mission to disrupt that formality by having our son eat his lunch with us.'

Jazz felt an inner glow because it was the first time he'd ever said *our* son. 'You can't deny that he's been very well behaved!' she defended.

'No, I cannot deny that,' he agreed gravely.

There was a pause before, encouraged by his relaxed demeanour, she asked a little more. 'So how did being a royal impact on your family, when you were a child?'

He shrugged. 'I never knew anything different. My blood is blue on both sides. My father came from a long line of desert kings and my mother was a princess from the neighbouring country of Israqan.'

Her voice was cautious. 'So was it an arranged marriage?'

'Unfortunately, no. It was not,' he answered repressively. 'If it had been there might have been a chance it might have worked. As it was, they met at the Razrastanian embassy in New York and *fell in love.*'

Jasmine registered the unmistakable contempt which had coloured those last three words. 'And was that so bad?'

'It was disastrous,' he said, his lips twisting with derision. 'Experience has taught me that love is nothing but an illusion which justifies desire and such...*passion* cannot possibly be sustained. At first it is an explosion—but explosions inevitably destroy whatever is around them. And then there is drama. Endless drama—with scenes and fights and tears. How I hate drama,' he added bitterly.

'And is that what happened—to your parents?'

'That is exactly what happened.' His black eyes glittered. 'It quickly burnt itself out and all that was left were two people who were essentially incompatible and who hated one another.'

'I'm sorry to hear that,' she offered, pausing for a moment before asking, 'So how did they deal with it?'

Again, he shrugged. 'My father sought comfort elsewhere and my mother threw all her energies into preparing my brother for his accession to the throne, in order to make him the finest ruler this land has ever known.'

'Did she indulge him?' she asked sharply.

'You could say that.' He took a last mouthful of juice before putting the jewelled beaker down. 'He grew up feeling he was capable of anything. That he was indestructible.'

'And where did you come in all this?' she questioned suddenly. 'Where did you fit in, Zuhal?'

Zuhal's eyes narrowed. Perceptive of her. But also perhaps a little too close to the bone. He prepared to bat away her question with flippancy before something stopped him and he frowned as he became aware that he had never admitted this to anyone. He'd never really been in a position to before, because he hadn't seen the point in confiding in any of his lovers, knowing that to do so would have been a potential security breach.

Yet suddenly the desire to connect was stronger than his innate desire to conceal. Was that because, as his potential wife, Jazz needed to know what kind of man he really was—so she didn't foster any unrealistic fantasies which could never be met? 'I didn't fit in anywhere,' he grated. 'Not then. I was the forgotten son. The invisible son. There's no need to look so shocked, Jazz. Don't they say every mother has her favourite? Well, it wasn't me. But I was well fed and well cared for and that was enough.' He saw the pain in her eyes and reached out to tilt her chin with his finger. 'Have I told you enough for one day? Don't you find the discussion of dysfunction a little...tedious? Surely you can think of a more pleasurable way of passing the time other than talking about a past which is lost to us for ever?'

The air between them thrummed. The breath left her lungs. Glancing up into the inky gleam of his eyes, Jasmine felt an erratic quickening of her pulse. She wanted to know more but she sensed that now was not the time, just as she sensed that Zuhal needed her now in a way he hadn't needed her before.

'I can think of several things,' she said huskily. 'It depends which one you're referring to.'

'You know exactly what I'm talking about.' He sprung to his feet to close the tent flaps, so that the interior instantly grew dim and mysterious. Now the cavernous space was lit only by the silvery brocade of the day-bed, the silky colours of the rugs and the bright sheen of metal lamps as he returned to join her on the floor and pulled her into his arms again. 'This,' he breathed. 'I'm talking about this.'

Jasmine knew he was going to kiss her but underpinning her desire was an overwhelming rush of emotion as he put his arms around her, as she thought about the little boy who nobody had wanted. But then he sank her into the soft cushions and her thoughts were forgotten as their mouths met in a hard and hungry kiss which left them gasping for oxygen.

His fingers were unsteady as he unbuttoned her shirt and tugged it from her shoulders, so that she was lying there in just her jodhpurs, riding boots and a black lacy bra. 'That's better,' he murmured.

'Do you—?'

'No. No more words, Jazz,' he said, with a shake of his head as he bent to pull off her riding boots. The jodhpurs were next to go, each movement a sensual torture as he slowly stroked them down her thighs, his fingers whispering tantalisingly over the black lace wisp of her panties. She gasped as he unclipped her straining bra, so that her breasts spilled out—one nipple finding itself positioned perfectly for his waiting lips to suck on.

'Oh!' she gasped.

'I thought I said no words.'

'I couldn't help myself.'

His eyes swept over her, as he swiftly removed his own clothes before taking her hand in his. 'Is this what you want?' he questioned, directing her fingertips to his groin. 'I think it is. It's certainly what *I* want.'

And Jasmine needed no further guidance as she wrapped her trembling fingers around his mighty shaft, enjoying the sound of his murmured pleasure as she began to slide them up and down the silken skin. Lying down beside her, he kissed her until she was quivering—touching every inch of her with a taunting skill, until she was making strangled little pleas. At last he positioned himself over her and she could feel the heaviness of his body and the hard brush of his erection between her thighs. And then he gave one hard, long thrust, to tunnel up deep inside her—and as he did so, another rush of emotion threatened to overwhelm her. Closing her eyes, Jasmine sank her lips against his sweat-sheened shoulder. Because this wasn't some *wham-bam* bout up against the wall. This was heart-stoppingly intimate and terrifying in its implications. And only Zuhal could make her feel like this. Respond like this.

'Zuhal,' she said brokenly, but maybe he didn't hear. Maybe he was so intent on giving her pleasure that he was oblivious to her turbulent feelings—or maybe he just preferred to ignore them. And then everything was forgotten as her body began to spasm helplessly around him.

She was dimly aware of the choked cry he gave as her back arched and the spurting rush as he filled her with his seed. When the world came back into focus at last, it was for her to find his dark head resting on her breast, one bent arm around her neck, his breath warm against her damp skin. And wasn't it infuriating how stupidly *mushy* she felt? Wasn't she in danger of falling for him all over again, despite his emotional distance and his obvious mistrust of anything to do with love? But then something occurred to her—something which drove all these thoughts clean from her mind.

'That's the second time we've omitted to use any protection,' she said.

He stirred and yawned. 'Doing it with you as nature intended just seems to come naturally to me,' he admitted. 'Do you mind?'

Jasmine hesitated, aware that something had shifted and changed between them. Say it, she urged herself. Don't expect him to guess what you're thinking and then be angry when he gets it wrong. 'I think it's better if we decide if and when to have another baby,' she said carefully. 'Rather than just leaving it to chance.'

'Do you want another baby, Jazz?'

There was a long segment of silence. 'If we're to be married, then yes, I think I do,' she answered eventually.

'You mean the marriage you've been dragging your feet about?'

She didn't deny his accusation, just shifted her weight a little as she looked up into his eyes. 'Because up until now, we've seemed more like strangers than anything else.'

His black gaze burned into her. 'But now we're no longer "strangers"—you're happy for it to go ahead?'

Happy? It seemed a strange word to use in the circumstances. It felt a long time since she'd experienced that particular emotion. When she'd found herself alone and pregnant, it had been independence which Jasmine had strived for and, against all the odds, she had achieved it. Even though it had been a bit of a struggle, she had forged a decent life for herself and Darius. She had been her own woman—in charge of her own destiny—and she recognised that her growing feelings for Zuhal threatened to destabilise everything she had achieved.

She met the dark gleam of his eyes. Yet today he had shown a chink in his armour and a vulnerability she hadn't expected. He'd described the awful atmosphere in the palace when he'd been growing up. He'd described how his parents had made a mockery of love and how he despised and mistrusted the word and all it stood for as a consequence. She got that. But she could show him by example that it didn't need to be like that, couldn't she? She loved Darius and maybe Zuhal would come to realise that love wasn't always a dirty word. And if that happened, then couldn't they learn to love each other—or was that a wish too far?

'Yes,' she said gravely. 'I am. And I'm prepared to give our marriage my very best shot.'

'Good.' He inclined his dark head. 'Then it is agreed. We will wed as soon as possible. We will become husband and wife and have shared goals for a stable future, not just for the monarchy, but for Darius—and for any brothers and sisters he may have.'

She thought how business-like they both sounded—as if they were dealing with a business merger rather than a relationship. But his mouth was soft as he reached out for her and most of her misgivings melted away beneath the sensual onslaught of another heady kiss.

She kissed him back with a fervour which matched his own and his face was tight as he lifted her up and brought her down onto his aching shaft, groaning as she began to ride him. And suddenly it was all happening so fast. Indecently fast. She felt that first sweet clench which began to dominate her world as she began to come, aware that he was watching her closely. His fingers were tight on her breasts as her back arched and she threw her head back with a fierce shout which was quickly echoed by his own.

Afterwards they lay there very quietly, and it was with a beat of something which felt like hope for the future that Jasmine agreed to Zuhal's suggestion that they head back to the palace. With a sense of torpor, they dressed and drank some juice before going back outside, where the rested horses seemed infected by their laziness, making the return ride slow and leisurely.

Zuhal wasn't quite sure at which point he noticed that something was different. Was it the barely perceptible flash from one of the palace windows, as if someone was looking out for them, which made his body grow tense? Or was it just the sight of three of his aides waiting for them in the stable yard—Adham among them, which was highly unusual?

There was an expression on his chief aide's face which he'd never seen before—one he couldn't quite decipher—and Zuhal's heart gave a lurch of foreboding as he tried to work out exactly what was going on. But then he saw a rare smile break out on Adham's face as he rushed forward to greet the Sheikh.

'Your Royal Highness!' exclaimed the aide, not even waiting until Zuhal had leapt from his horse. 'I have wondrous news! Your brother is returned. The King is alive!'

CHAPTER ELEVEN

'WHERE THE HELL have you been?'

Zuhal stared into the face of his brother—a brother he hardly recognised. Kamal's face was gaunt, his eyes sunken, and his ragged clothes unlike any he would usually wear as royal regalia. He must have lost at least twenty pounds, and his black hair flowed down past his shoulders. Only his proud deportment betrayed the fact that this was no ordinary man who had been lost in the desert for months and months, but in fact a desert king.

'Well?' Zuhal's demand rang out through the echoing Throne Room. The blonde gleam of Jasmine's hair reminded him she was sitting in the window seat, but he barely noticed her—his only focus on the brother he had thought was dead. Utter relief at seeing his only sibling alive suddenly transformed itself into righteous anger. 'Are you going to give me some kind of explanation about how you've just miraculously returned, after we've spent months sending search parties out for you?'

Kamal nodded, his gaunt expression becoming tight and tense, as if he had no desire to relive what had happened to him. 'The sandstorm came down on us suddenly and my horse and I were lost—'

'That much I know,' Zuhal interrupted impatiently. 'And if you'd bothered letting someone know where you were going then we could have found you.'

'No. You could never have found me,' said Kamal, his voice suddenly bleak. 'For I was swallowed up in the most inaccessible part of the desert, heavily concussed, with my leg broken.'

'Oh, my brother,' said Zuhal, his voice suddenly trembling with an emotion he did not recognise.

'Were it not for the nomadic tribe from the Harijia region who found me and took me in and helped me back to health, I would surely have died.' Kamal looked down at his hands. 'I lived in their tents as one of them for many months and they taught me much about the land I thought I knew. I liked living there.' He lifted his gaze to his brother. 'For a while I thought I wanted to stay. Maybe a part of me didn't want to come back and continue to be King.'

There was a silence.

'So what changed your mind?' asked Zuhal slowly.

There was silence. 'I heard you were getting married to the Englishwoman.' Another pause. 'And that she had a child.'

Noiselessly Jasmine rose to her feet and left the Throne Room, but nobody noticed her go. Of course they didn't. Ever since they'd returned to the palace she'd felt invisible to the man she'd spent the afternoon having sex with and the reason for that was as plain as the nose on her face. The King had returned and her place here was now redundant.

* * *

An exhausted Kamal retired early and Jasmine spent that night in Zuhal's bed, but his lovemaking—although satisfying—felt almost *perfunctory* and he resolutely refused to discuss the impact of the King's return on their future. The following morning he had already left for his early ride when she woke and Jasmine was aware of a sharp sense of disappointment that he hadn't taken her with him, as was usual. Had he only tolerated her accompanying him on his daily ride because he'd wanted her to marry him?

But now there was no longer any need for him to marry her, was there?

Jasmine found herself in a strange position. She felt alone and scared—more scared even than when she'd found herself pregnant. She didn't want to put any more pressure on Zuhal but this sense of being in limbo wasn't doing her any good. She needed to face up to the facts and calmly ask the Sheikh what he really wanted now that his brother had returned—perhaps when they were in bed, soft and satiated by sex. Perhaps when her arms were around his waist and he was nuzzling her neck in a way which made her shiver with something deeper than desire. Or would it be easier if they were face to face across a table, so that she wasn't naked and vulnerable? So that she could calmly get up and leave and go and cry with dignity and in private…

Trying to work out the best way to approach such a delicate matter, she took Darius out for an afternoon stroll, planning to sit in the palace rose garden and sing him the soft lullabies he loved. Rainbow light arced through the spray of the ornate fountains, and the blousy blooms of perfumed flowers made her feel as if she'd tumbled into a kaleidoscopic fantasy-land as she walked through the spacious gardens. She was going to miss this beautiful place, she thought, with a sudden clench of her heart.

The air was soft and drowsy with the buzz of bees and Jasmine thought she heard the drift of voices coming from the interior of the rose garden. She wondered who it might be as her sandaled feet moved silently towards the sound, until the familiar velvety caress of her lover's voice indicated he was deep in conversation with his brother.

She didn't mean to eavesdrop. In fact, she was just about to turn away and go somewhere else in order to give them peace, when she heard her name mentioned. She told herself afterwards that it was only human nature to stand there for a moment or two. To want to know what was being said about her. She told herself it was a good thing she *did* listen—because otherwise, how would she have known the truth? Wouldn't she just have carried on weaving impossible dreams about the future and hoping that one day Zuhal might learn to love her, if only a little?

'Jazz?' Zuhal's voice was drawling. 'What about her?'

'Won't she mind not being Queen—now that I'm back?'

'It is not in her remit to *mind*.'

'But she is a woman, Zuhal—and women are notoriously ambitious for their men.'

'Not Jazz.' There was a pause. 'We don't have that kind of relationship.'

'What kind of relationship *do* you have, then?'

'It defies definition,' said Zuhal flippantly.

'Oh?' Kamal's voice probed further. 'Are you still going to marry her, now that I'm back?'

'I haven't decided.'

Jasmine bristled at his arrogance—his innate certainty that *he* was the one who called the shots—when Kamal's next question made her heart pound violently against her breastbone.

'Do you love her?'

There was another pause, during which Jasmine could hear some unknown bird singing high from one of the treetops, and its sweet, drenching song sounded unbearably poignant.

'No,' said Zuhal, in a hard, empty voice. 'You must realise by now that I don't do love, Kamal.'

She'd known that all along, but even so Jasmine was surprised by the fierce intensity of the pain which ripped through her as she registered that cold and unequivocal statement. She wanted to gasp with shock and pain—but somehow she held it back, because now was not the time. And really, she'd learned nothing new, had she? Because nothing had changed.

Zuhal had told her he didn't do love. He mistrusted it and didn't want it—for reasons which were perfectly understandable. He'd told her that emphatically and now he was stating it loud and clear to his brother. Perhaps he was doing her a favour. Would she really have been content to spend her life here with him, not daring to show her feelings for fear it would make him angry, or suspicious that she had started to love him again? What kind of an example would that set to Darius?

She was trembling as she silently turned the pram and pushed it away as fast as she dared go, knowing that there was only one solution which lay open to her—and she took the baby to Rania, before going to Zuhal's offices to find him. Ignoring Adham's protest, she walked straight into the Sheikh's office without knocking to find him talking on the phone. Something in her face must have sent out an unspoken warning because he uttered a few terse words in his native tongue before terminating the call and rising slowly to his feet.

'This is unexpected,' he said, a faint note of reproof in his deep voice.

'I overheard you,' she said.

His brow darkened. 'What are you talking about?'

'In the garden, talking to your brother. I heard you say you didn't love me.'

He didn't look in the slightest bit abashed. 'But you knew that already, Jazz. I've never lied to you about that.'

'No, I know you haven't.' She drew in a deep breath. 'And while part of me respects you for your honesty, I've realised I can't live like that. It's not good for our son to live like that either.'

'So what do you expect me to say in response to this?' he demanded. 'To tell you that I didn't mean it?'

'No. I don't expect that, Zuhal. If you must know I admire your honesty and the fact that you've never spun out lies or empty promises.' She took a deep breath. 'But

I just want you to arrange for me and Darius to return to England, and as soon as possible.'

He raised his dark brows. 'To do what?'

She shrugged. 'To live somewhere—not London, but close enough for you to be able to access us easily. And a house, I think—not an apartment—because I want Darius to have a garden of his own. I'd like to go back to Oxfordshire until I can find something which meets with your approval. You can even appoint your body-guards if you wish—since I recognise that as Darius is your son we need protection. But I want to go back, Zuhal.' Her voice suddenly became low. Urgent. 'And as soon as possible.'

Zuhal's mouth hardened with anger and contempt as he acknowledged Jazz's manipulative demands. Well, if she was hoping he would start grovelling in an attempt to persuade her to stay, then she was in for a disappointment. He didn't argue with her, because this kind of conversation felt like one he'd had too often with women in the past—though never with Jazz, he conceded. It was emotional blackmail. She was making a statement. She was leaving.

And she was taking their son with her.

He kept his cold resolve through all the arrangements for their departure and maintained it as he saw her and Darius off from the airfield. But he couldn't deny the inexplicable lurch of his heart as he saw her disappearing inside the private jet, his son's dark curly head bobbing over her shoulder. It felt as if a dark cloud were descending on him as he recalled saying goodbye to his child, who'd naturally been too young to realise what was happening. But *he* had known, hadn't he? Had known and felt guilty and resentful, all at the same time—half tempted to tell Jazz that he wouldn't allow her to take his progeny from the country, but knowing deep down that the child needed his mother.

The powerful engines roared but he turned away so that his back was to the plane during take-off, mainly because he'd got a damned speck of dust in his eye and infuriatingly, it was watering. On returning to the palace, he worked solidly for the rest of the day, checking his phone with unusual regularity.

But the only thing he heard from Jazz was after she'd touched down in England and sent a miserable little text saying, I'm back. Which, of course, he had already known, because his security people had alerted him.

He sent back an equally bald text:

I will be in touch to discuss arrangements about Darius.

But she didn't reply, which infuriated him even more.

His handover to Kamal almost complete, he decided to reward himself with some extra riding, deciding that some hard physical exercise was exactly what he needed to rid himself of this strange frustration which was burning away inside him. But for once the exertion and beauty of the desert failed to work their magic and he realised he was missing Darius more than he would ever have imagined. His mouth thinned. He would travel to Europe and see him, but he would do it in his own time and on *his* terms.

Stopping in Paris en route for a long-overdue meeting, he checked himself into a sybaritically indulgent hotel with glittering views over the river Seine, for an overnight stay. He wasn't really in the mood for socialising but unexpectedly ran into the dashing ex-polo player, Alejandro Sabato, and agreed to have dinner with him. He'd forgotten how the charismatic Argentinean attracted women like wasps buzzing towards uncovered food and several times their meal was interrupted while one of them gushingly requested a selfie with the ex-world champion. And then, much to Zuhal's annoyance, they were papped leaving the upmarket restaurant.

Zuhal's eyes were gritty when he woke next morning and, although he tried ringing Jazz from his plane before he touched down in England, the call went straight to voicemail. But she didn't bother ringing back and neither did she pick up the second call he made as his limousine—with diplomatic flag flying—sped from the airfield towards Oxfordshire.

A house had been purchased for her, not far from where she'd lived before—but her new home was a world away from her old, rented cottage. Set like a jewel in an acre of walled garden, the detached villa had mullioned windows which glinted like diamonds in the sunshine and a soft grey front door. Two bright pots of scarlet geraniums stood on either side of the front door and the sporty little saloon he'd insisted on buying for her was parked in front of the garage. But when Zuhal lifted the shiny bronze knocker to sound out a summons through the house, nobody came to the door. He tried again with the same result and he scowled.

Where the hell *was* she?

His anger grew as he waited in his limousine, drumming his fingers against his knees and glancing out at the lonely lane, wondering if she was safe and wondering why he had allowed her to live this kind of existence in the English countryside. By the time she returned, a bag bulging with groceries on the bottom of the pram, he was seething, as his eyes raked over her.

She was back to wearing jeans and a shirt, and her hair was twisted into a plait as she returned his gaze with shuttered eyes. She couldn't have looked less like the perfumed Queen she'd been poised to become, yet something twisted deep inside him as he stared at her. Something he didn't want to acknowledge for fear of where it would take him.

'Wouldn't it be more sensible to have one of the bodyguards do your shopping for you?' he demanded, as he carefully helped her manoeuvre the pram into the spacious hallway of the house to avoid waking the baby. 'Rather than struggling like this on your own?'

'Not if I want to have any semblance of living a normal life,' she responded. 'I thought you were coming yesterday.'

'I tried to ring but you didn't pick up.'

'And? You could have left a message.'

'I don't like leaving messages.'

'We all have to do things we don't like, Zuhal— but it would have been common courtesy to have informed me that you weren't going to be here when you said you were. I have to be able to rely on you. Darius is too young to know the difference right now, but in the future he needs to know that you're going to turn up when you say you are.'

He frowned, knowing that she had a point and realising that nobody—nobody—had ever spoken to him quite so caustically before. 'I had business to attend to in Paris.'

'So I saw in the papers.'

His eyes narrowed as he detected a faint crack in her voice. 'I thought you didn't read the papers.'

'I…' She seemed a little lost for words at this and swallowed, before tilting her chin with the stubborn gesture he had grown to recognise. 'Why are you here, Zuhal? If it's to see Darius then perhaps you'd like to wait in the sitting room until he's awake? If it's to organise access arrangements, then wouldn't it be better if it was done officially, through your office and your lawyers?'

He studied her. 'And that's what you want, is it?'

She swallowed again, but even so when her words came out they still sounded as if she had a foreign body lodged in her throat. 'Yes, that's what I want.'

Zuhal stilled as something inside him twisted. Something which felt like pain. Not the brutal kind, which came from a cut or a blow, but something much more insidious—and yet it was sharp. Crushingly sharp. He held his palm over his chest, as if that might steady the erratic beat of his heart as he looked into green-gold eyes which contained the hint of unshed tears.

'Jazz?' he said huskily, even though he wasn't really sure what it was he was asking.

'I'm not sure I can deal with this,' she said, with a brisk shake of her head. 'Not right now. I'm not in the mood. You told me you didn't like drama—that you saw enough of it during your childhood to put you off it for ever—well, neither do I. I wasn't expecting you and I'm not…prepared.'

'Why do you need to be prepared for my visit?'

She shook her head. 'It doesn't matter.'

'It does. It matters to me.'

Jasmine stared at him. Was he completely *stupid*? Didn't he realise that since returning she'd realised just how much he'd burrowed his way underneath her skin? That the memory of his proud hawkish features swam into her mind at pretty much every opportunity? That she missed him. She missed him more than she had any right to miss him.

But why tell him any of that? Why *should* she admit her weakness—and her love—for a man who didn't want it? That would completely disrupt the delicate balance of power which existed between them, which they needed to maintain in the future. It wasn't as if they weren't ever going to see each other again. Because of Darius there were bound to be lots of times over the years when they would bump into one another and she needed to ensure things stayed dignified and civilised between them. And that was never going to happen if Zuhal thought she was pining for him. Suddenly Jasmine could picture him laughing about her behind her back, perhaps when he was lying in bed with a new lover. Could imagine his drawled, cruel words as he dissected their relationship with forensic accuracy.

Jazz? Oh, she's nobody special. Just the mother of my child. There's nothing between us. The pregnancy was a mistake. Does she love me? She could even imagine his arrogant smile. *Yeah. I guess she does.*

Well, she wasn't going to give him that pleasure. Pointedly, she looked at her watch. 'So which is it to be, Zuhal? Either way, I need to get on, so you must excuse me. I've got someone coming over to look at some of my baby designs.'

Zuhal frowned and still he felt a burst of dark restlessness as something occurred to him. He remembered one morning when he'd found Jazz in the nursery, just before Kamal had returned. She'd been sitting on the floor flicking a balloon in front of their gurgling son, while dappled sunlight from the rose garden had streamed in on them both. She'd looked up at him and smiled, with a look of simple joy in her eyes, and he had smiled back. His heart pounded as he remembered going off to his office, whistling softly beneath his breath. He thought about the hard morning rides he'd taken since she'd gone, which had failed to work their magic, mainly because she hadn't been there to talk to. The space at the lunch table, which seemed so bare without her. The high chair which had been put away, as if Darius had never even been there.

His jaw clenched and the pain which had been twisting inside him grew unbearable. He knew he could walk away after he'd seen his little boy. He could agree that all such future meetings would probably be best conducted on neutral territory, through their respective lawyers. Or he could tell her the truth, which was only just beginning to dawn on him. A shocking truth which seemed to have come at him out of nowhere.

He thought back to when he'd discovered he had a son and told Jazz he would continue to seek a suitable bride, before blithely announcing that Darius would be his 'insurance policy' in case his new wife proved infertile. Suddenly he recognised just how wickedly cruel his words had been, though he'd never really stopped to consider the consequences of saying them before now. He thought how tolerant she had been, even in the face of all that heartlessness. How strong and brave in withstanding the undoubted suspicion and coolness of the palace servants when he'd first taken her to Razrastan. And determined, too. She had rejected his advances when they'd arrived at the royal palace—with a single-mindedness he suspected most other women wouldn't have displayed in her place. Didn't that make him respect her even more?

'Jazz, listen to me.'

'We've said everything we need to say.'

'But that's where you're wrong. I haven't even started but I need to start now by telling you just how much I miss you—'

'No!' she butted in, urgent desperation in her voice, as if she couldn't bear to hear what he was about to say. 'One thing I've always admired about you is your honesty—so please don't ruin that by telling me lies!'

'Not lies but the truth,' he argued doggedly, as the certainty inside him grew. Like when your plane dropped down, out of the cotton-wool blur of the clouds—and suddenly there was a whole clear landscape below you. 'I've realised why I ended my relationship with you the first time round—long before I planned to.'

'Don't,' she whispered, with a shake of her blonde head. 'Just *don't.*'

'It was because you used to make me *feel* stuff,' he continued, undeterred. 'Stuff I didn't want to feel. I listed all the reasons why you were unsuitable for any kind of future and I forced myself to believe them. But I never forgot you, Jazz. Not ever. Why else do you think I chose to come to you when I needed comfort and succour after my brother disappeared?'

'Because you thought I would be a walkover?'

He shook his head. 'No,' he said simply. 'Not that. And not just because you were the best lover I've ever had but because something told me that with you I would be able to break the rule of a lifetime, and talk. Why else did I never...' his voice deepened, and cracked '...take another woman to my bed, since parting from you?'

She was staring up at him, disbelief widening her green-gold eyes. 'Are you trying to tell me you haven't had sex with anyone else since we split up?'

'I am telling you, because it's the truth,' he clarified unsteadily. 'And I'll you another. That my morning rides haven't been the same without you by my side to talk to. That the palace has seemed empty without you there. But I'll tell you something else, something which eclipses all those other realisations and that is that I love you. I love you, Jazz. I love you so very much.'

She shook her face from side to side, her expression disbelieving and mulish. 'But you don't want love. You don't do love.'

'That's what I thought and that's what I said—only now I discover I was wrong. Because I don't want to live without it. Without you. Without Darius. My family—the most precious thing in the world, which I almost let slip through my fingers.' He reached out and took her hands in his, and even though they lay there—inert and cold—she didn't pull them away. 'Will you forgive me for all the cruel and unthinking words I've said to you, my beautiful Jazz? Will you give me another chance to show you that I am capable of change, and of love? Will you allow me to become the husband you deserve? To cherish you and protect you for as long as I live?'

There was a pause during which she shook her head again as she stared down at the exquisite silken rug he'd had shipped here from Razrastan. But when at last she lifted her gaze to his, he could see bright tears brimming over in her extraordinary eyes, making them look like new leaves which were drenched with the morning dew.

'Yes,' she whispered, at last. A tear was trickling down her cheek but her fingers were curling into his. 'How could I refuse when I love you, too? When I've never stopped loving you, no matter how hard I tried.'

He smiled but it took an effort as he realised just how close he'd come to losing her. And as he pulled her close, he discovered that the wetness on her cheek was mingling with tears of his own. 'But now you don't have to try any more, my love. The only thing you have to do right now is to seal our love in the most traditional way of all.' His words grew unsteady as he positioned her face so that her mouth was within claiming distance. 'So kiss me, Jazz. Kiss me and convince me all this is real.'

EPILOGUE

It was a perfectly warm English evening. The sinking sun was gilding the edges of the sky as dusk glimmered on the horizon. On the veranda of their large, white house overlooking green hills and rolling countryside, Jasmine kicked off her shoes, which were sinfully high to walk in, but which were her husband's undoubted favourite, which was why she wore them. Briefly, she closed her eyes because she still got a sharp hit of pleasure whenever she thought about those two words.

My husband.

The man she had married and the man she loved. The man who loved her back and who had no qualms about showing her just how much.

As if on cue, Zuhal emerged from the house where he had been kissing their three children goodnight after reading them one of the many Razrastanian fables which Jasmine was eager to see translated into English because they were just so *good*. Darius particularly liked the one about the desert falcon who discovered the lost rubies before turning into a prince and marrying the Princess. Unbelievably, their son was nearly five now and a bright tearaway who loved teasing his twin sisters, Yasmin and Anisa—eighteen months old and the apples of their father's eye.

She looked up at him and smiled. 'Everything quiet?'

Zuhal's answering smile was slow, the glint in his eyes provocative and his murmured reply contented. 'Fast asleep. Which means we have the whole evening ahead of us. What would you like to do, my love?'

What Jasmine sometimes wanted was to pinch herself, to ask herself whether this could really be happening, if life could possibly be this good. But it could, and it was. From difficult and rocky beginnings there had emerged the kind of relationship she had never imagined would exist between her and the Sheikh of Razrastan.

She and Zuhal had married in a lavish ceremony in his country, attended by the great and the good from around the globe and, in the absence of a father, his brother Kamal had consented to give her away. She had become close to the King in the time leading up to their wedding and during their subsequent visits, though, as she sometimes said to Zuhal, he had hinted at something which had happened to him during his period away from the palace—something to do with a woman, which had not yet been resolved.

And then something else wonderful had happened. Her ex-husband had seen the reports of her marriage in the newspapers and had wished her every happiness, telling her that he had remarried himself. In fact, Richard and David had managed to track down a rare, first edition of Razrastanian poems and had sent it to her and Zuhal as a wedding present and, with that simple gesture, yet another scar of the past had been healed.

As newly-weds, she and the Sheikh had decided to settle in England, moving to an enormous estate in the beautiful county of Sussex, where Zuhal had achieved a lifetime ambition and, in addition to his thriving property and shares portfolio, had opened up his own polo club, which was currently breaking all records. It had taken him a while to adjust from the idea of being a prosperous king to being a prosperous businessman again, but he had seen the many benefits his new life offered him. And these days he articulated all his hopes and fears to his beloved wife.

In the early days of the polo club, he had received practical advice from the dashing ex-player Alejandro Sabato, who had assured Jasmine that Zuhal had played no part in the photograph which had been plastered all over the press, of the two men emerging from a restaurant with several blonde women in pursuit that night in Paris.

'He was unusually quiet that night,' Alej had mused. 'And several times he mentioned your name. I knew then that he was in love with you.'

Jasmine smiled, as Zuhal walked over to her and began to massage her shoulders. In love. Yes. Her previously closed-up lover had become the most demonstrative and affectionate of men.

'You haven't answered my question,' Zuhal murmured, as he bent to kiss her neck. 'About what you'd like to do tonight?'

She turned her head a little, so that she could catch the ebony gleam of his dark eyes. 'Any suggestions?'

'Plenty,' he murmured. 'But you are a remarkably difficult woman to please. I try to shower you with jewels, but you aren't interested.'

She held up her left hand as she surveyed the rare blue stone which had been purloined from the palace vaults in Razrastan. 'That's because one diamond is enough.'

'And I offer to fly you to Paris for the weekend, but you refuse.'

'That's because there's no place like home.'

He smiled. 'You didn't even want to go out for dinner tonight, despite the fact that the chef of the restaurant I was planning to take you to has just won his third Michelin star. Which makes me wonder what exactly you would like to do tonight, my beautiful Sheikha Al Haidar?'

With a soft laugh Jasmine rose to her feet, wiggling her now bare toes against the cool tiles as she looped her arms around her husband's neck and planted her lips just a few centimetres away from his. 'I think I'd like to take you to bed,' she murmured. 'To show you and tell you just how much I love you, and how much I value having you in my life.'

Zuhal nodded, his throat suddenly constricting. 'And I shall tell you yet again that I became the luckiest man in the world all those days ago, when I walked into a hotel boutique and saw you standing there, blushing and not quite meeting my eyes.'

Her beautiful face was so close to his. And, as he always did in times of great emotion—which he no longer attempted to bury or deny—Zuhal used the poetic words of his native tongue, a language which Jazz was gradually coming to understand.

'If I stood you next to all the planets which glow in the mighty desert sky,' he said huskily, 'then you would be the very brightest, my darling Jazz.'

He lowered his head to hers and began to kiss her—tenderly at first, but with a fast-growing passion which soon had her moaning with pleasure. And the stars were shimmering like diamond dust in the darkening sky by the time Zuhal lifted his wife into his arms and carried her into the bedroom.

* * * * *

CASTIGLIONE'S PREGNANT PRINCESS

LYNNE GRAHAM

CHAPTER ONE

'COME ON,' ZAC DA ROCHA chided his brother. 'There's got to be some room for manoeuvre here, something that you want more than that car. Sell it to me and I'll buy you anything you want.'

Fierce hostility roared through Prince Vitale Castiglione because his Brazilian half-brother irritated the hell out of him. The fact that they were both luxury-car collectors had to be the only thing they had in common. But no didn't ever mean no to Zac; no only made Zac raise the price. He couldn't seem to grasp the reality that Vitale couldn't be bribed. But then, Zacarias Da Rocha, heir to the fabled Quintel Da Rocha diamond mines and fabulously wealthy even by his brothers' standards, was unaccustomed to refusal or disappointment and constitutionally incapable of respecting polite boundaries. His lean, strong face grim, Vitale shot a glance at the younger man, his brilliant dark eyes impassive with years of hard self-discipline.

'No,' Vitale repeated quietly, wishing his older brother, Angel Valtinos, would return and shut Zac up because being rude didn't come naturally to Vitale, who had been raised in the stifling traditions and formality of a European royal family. A lifetime of rigid conditioning invariably stepped in to prevent Vitale from losing his temper and revealing his true feelings.

Of course, it had already been a most unsettling morning. Vitale had been disconcerted when his father, Charles Russell, had asked both him and his two brothers to meet him at his office. It had been an unusual request because Charles usually made the effort to meet his sons separately and Vitale had wondered if some sort of family emergency had occurred until Charles had appeared and swept his eldest son, Angel, off into his office alone, leaving Vitale with only Zac for company. Not a fun development that, Vitale reflected before studiously telling himself off for that negative outlook.

After all, it wasn't Zac's fault that he had only met his father the year before and was still very much a stranger to his half-brothers, who, in spite of their respective parents' divorces, had known each other since early childhood. Unhappily, Zac with his untamed black hair, tattoos and aggressive attitude simply didn't fit in. He was too unconventional, too competitive, too *much* in every way. Nor did it help that he was only a couple of months younger than Vitale, which underlined the reality that Zac had been conceived while Charles Russell had still been married to Vitale's mother. Yet Vitale could understand how that adulterous affair had come about. His mother was cold while his father was emotional and caring. He suspected that while caught up in the divorce that had devastated him Charles had sought comfort from a warmer woman.

'Then let's make a bet,' Zac suggested irrepressibly.

Vitale was tempted to roll his eyes in comic disbelief but he said nothing.

'I heard you and Angel talking earlier about the big palace ball being held in Lerovia at the end of next month,' Zac admitted softly. 'I understand that it's a very formal, upmarket occasion and that your mother is expecting you to pick a wife from her selection of carefully handpicked female guests...'

Faint colour illuminated Vitale's rigid high cheekbones and he ground his even white teeth. 'Queen Sofia enjoys trying to organise my life but I have no current plans to marry.'

'But it would be a hell of a lot easier to keep all those women at bay if you turned up with a partner of your own,' Zac pointed out without skipping a beat, as if he knew by some mysterious osmosis how much pressure Vitale's royal parent invariably put on her only child's shoulders. 'So, this is the bet... I bet you that you couldn't transform an ordinary woman into a convincing socialite for the evening and pass her off as the real thing. If you manage that feat, I'll give you my rarest vehicle but naturally I'll expect an invitation to the ball. If your lady fails the test, you hand over your most precious car.'

Vitale almost rolled his eyes at that outrageously juvenile challenge. Obviously he didn't do bets. He raked his black glossy hair back from his brow in a gesture of impatience. 'I'm not Pygmalion and I don't know any *ordinary* women,' he admitted truthfully.

'Who's Pygmalion?' Zac asked with a genuine frown. 'And how can you not know any ordinary women? You live in the same world I do.'

'Not quite.' Vitale's affairs were always very discreet and he avoided the sort of tacky, celebrity-chasing women likely to boast of him as a conquest, while Zac seemed to view any attractive woman as fair game. Vitale, however, didn't want to run the risk of any tabloid exposés containing the kind of sexual revelations that would dishonour the Lerovian throne.

In addition, he was an investment banker and CEO of the very conservative and respectable Bank of Lerovia, thus expected to live a very staid life: bankers who led rackety lives made investors unprofitably nervous. Lerovia was, after all, a tax shelter of international repute. It was a small country, hemmed in by much larger, more powerful countries, and Vitale's grandfather had built Lerovia's wealth and stability on a secure financial base. Vitale had had few career options open to him. His mother had wanted him to simply be the Crown Prince, her heir in waiting, but Vitale had needed a greater purpose, not to mention the freedom to become a man in his own right, something his autocratic mother would never have willingly given him.

He had fought for his right to have a career just as he now fought for his continuing freedom of choice as a single man. At only twenty-eight, he wasn't ready for the responsibility of a wife or, even more depressingly, the demands of a baby. His stomach sank at the prospect of a crying, clinging child looking to him for support. He also knew better than anyone how difficult it would be for any woman to enter the Lerovian royal family and be forced to deal with his domineering mother, the current Queen. His unfortunate bride would need balls of steel to hold her own.

At that point in Vitale's brooding reflections, Angel reappeared, looking abnormally subdued, and Vitale sprang upright with a question in his eyes.

'Your turn,' his older brother told him very drily

without making any attempt to respond to Vitale's unspoken question for greater clarification.

Angel was visibly on edge, Vitale acknowledged in surprise, wondering what sensitive subject Charles Russell had broached with his eldest son. And then Vitale made a very good guess and he winced for his brother, because possibly their father had discovered that Angel had an illegitimate daughter he had yet to meet. That was Angel's biggest darkest secret, one he had shared only with Vitale, and it was likely to be an inflammatory topic for a man as family-orientated as their parent. It wasn't, however, a mistake that Vitale would ever make, Vitale thought with blazing confidence, because he never ever took risks in the birth-control department. He knew too well how narrow his options would be in that scenario if anything went wrong. Either he would have to face up to a colossal scandal or he would have to marry the woman concerned. Since the prospect of either option chilled him to the bone, he always played safe.

A still-handsome middle-aged man with greying hair, Charles Russell strode forward to give his taller son an enthusiastic hug. 'Sorry to have kept you waiting so long.'

'Not a problem,' Vitale said smoothly, refusing to admit that he had enraged his mother with his insistence on travelling to London rather than attending yet another court ceremonial function. Even so, his lean muscular length still stiffened in the circle of the older man's arms because while he was warmed by that open affection he was challenged to respond to it. Deep down somewhere inside him he was still the shrinking little boy whose mother had pushed him away with distaste

at the age of two, telling him firmly that it was baby-
ish and bad to still seek such attention.

'I need a favour and I thought you could deal with
this thorny issue better than I could,' Charles admitted
stiffly. 'Do you remember the housekeeper I employed
at Chimneys?'

Vitale's eloquent dark eyes widened a little in disconcertion, lush black gold-tipped lashes framing his
shrewd questioning gaze. He and Angel had spent
countless school vacations at their father's country
house on the Welsh border and Vitale had cherished
every one of those holidays liberated from the stuffy
traditions and formality of the Lerovian court. At Chimneys, an Elizabethan manor house, Vitale had been free
as a bird, free to be a grubby little boy, a moody difficult adolescent, free to be whatever he wanted to be
without the stress of constantly striving to meet arbi-
trary expectations.

'Not particularly. I don't really remember the staff.'

His father frowned, seemingly disappointed by that
response. 'Her name was Peggy. She worked for me for
years. She was married to the gardener, Robert Dickens.'

A sliver of recollection pierced Vitale's bemused
gaze, a bubble of memory about an old scandal finally
rising to the surface. 'Red-haired woman, ran off with
a toy boy,' he slotted in sardonically.

His tone made his father frown. 'Yes, that's the one.
He was one of the trainee gardeners, shifty sort with
a silver tongue,' he supplied. 'I always felt responsible
for that mess.'

Vitale, who could not imagine getting involved or
even being interested in an employee's private life,
looked at the older man in frank astonishment. 'Why?'

'I saw bruises on Peggy on several occasions,' Charles admitted uncomfortably. 'I suspected Dickens of domestic abuse but I did nothing. I asked her several times if she was all right and she always assured me that she was. I should've done more.'

'I don't see what you could have done if she wasn't willing to make a complaint on her own behalf,' Vitale said dismissively, wondering where on earth this strange conversation could be leading while marvelling that his father could show visible distress when discussing the past life of a former servant. 'You weren't responsible.'

'Right and wrong isn't always that black and white,' Charles Russell replied grimly. 'If I'd been more supportive, more encouraging, possibly she might have given me her trust and told me the truth and I could have got her the help she and her daughter needed. Instead I was polite and distant and then she ran off with that smarmy little bastard.'

'I don't see what else you could have done. One should respect boundaries, particularly with staff,' Vitale declared, stiffening at the reference to Peggy's daughter but striving to conceal that reality. He had only the dimmest memory of Peggy Dickens but he remembered her daughter, Jazmine, well but probably only because Jazz figured in one of his own most embarrassing youthful recollections. He had little taste for looking back to the days before he had learned tact and discretion.

'No, you have to take a more human approach, Vitale. Staff are people too and sometimes they need help and understanding,' Charles argued.

Vitale didn't want to help or understand what motivated his staff at the bank or the palace; he simply wanted them to do their jobs to the best of their ability. He didn't get involved with employees on a personal level but, out of respect for his father, he resisted the urge to put his own point of view and instead tried to put the dialogue back on track. 'You said you needed a favour,' he reminded the older man.

Charles studied his son's lean, forbidding face in frustration, hating the fact that he recognised shades of his ex-wife's icy reserve and heartless detachment in Vitale. If there was one person Charles could be said to hate it would have to be the Queen of Lerovia, Sofia Castiglione. Yet he had loved her once, loved her to the edge of madness until he'd discovered that he was merely her dupe, her sperm donor for the heir she had needed for the Lerovian throne. Sofia's true love had been another woman, her closest friend, Cinzia, and from the moment Sofia had successfully conceived, Charles and their marriage as such had been very much surplus to requirements. But that was a secret the older man had promised to take to the grave with him. In the divorce settlement he had agreed to keep quiet in return for liberal access arrangements to his son and he had only ever regretted that silence afterwards when he had been forced to watch his ex-wife trying to suck the life out of Vitale with her constant carping and interference.

'Yes…the favour,' Charles recalled, forced back into the present. 'I've received a letter from Peggy's daughter, Jazmine, asking for my help. I want you to assess the situation and deal with it. I would do it myself but I'm going to be working abroad for the next few months and I don't have the time. I also thought you would handle it better because you knew each other well as children.'

Vitale's lean, strong, darkly good-looking face had tensed. In truth he had frozen where he stood at the threat of being forced to meet Jazz again. 'The situation?' he queried, playing for time.

The older man lifted a letter off the desk and passed it to him. 'The toy boy ripped Peggy off, forged her name on a stack of loans, plunged them into debt and *ruined* their financial standing!' he emphasised in ringing disgust. 'Now they're poor and struggling to survive. They've tried legal channels and got nowhere. Peggy's ill now and no longer able to work.'

Vitale's brow furrowed and he raised a silencing hand. 'But how is this trail of misfortune your business?' he asked without hesitation.

'Peggy Dickens has been on my conscience for years,' Charles confided grudgingly. 'I could have done something to help but I was too wary of causing offence so... I did nothing. All of this mess is on me and I don't want that poor woman suffering any more because I failed to act.'

'So, send her a cheque,' Vitale suggested, reeling from the display of guilt his father was revealing while he himself was struggling to see any connection or indeed any debt owed.

'Read the letter,' his father advised. 'Jazmine is asking for a job, somewhere to live and a loan, not a cheque. She's proud. She's not asking for a free handout but she's willing to do anything she can to help her mother.'

Vitale studied the envelope of what was obviously a begging letter with unconcealed distaste. More than ever he wanted to argue with his father's attitude. In Vitale's opinion, Charles owed his former employee and her daughter absolutely nothing. By the sound of it, Peggy Dickens had screwed up her life; however that was scarcely his father's fault.

'What do *you* want me to do?' Vitale asked finally, recognising that how he felt about the situation meant nothing in the face of his father's feelings.

Yet it amazed Vitale that his father could still be so incredibly emotional and sentimental and he often marvelled that two people as ridiculously dissimilar in character as his parents could ever have married.

'I want you to be compassionate and kind, *not* judge-mental, *not* cynical, *not* cold,' Charles framed with anxious warning emphasis. 'And I know that will be a huge challenge for you but I also know that acknowledging that side of your nature will make you a better and stronger man in the process. Don't let your mother re-make you in her image—never forget that you are *my* son too.'

Vitale almost flinched from the idea of being compassionate and kind. He didn't do stuff like that. He supported leading charities and always contributed to good causes but he had never done anything hands-on in that area, nor had he ever felt the need to do so. He was what he was: a bred-in-the-bone royal, cocooned from the real world by incredible privilege, an exclusive education and great wealth.

'I don't care what it costs to buy Peggy and her daughter out of trouble either,' his father added expansively. 'With you in charge of my investments, I can well afford the gesture. You don't need to save me money.'

'I'm a banker. Saving money and making a profit comes naturally,' Vitale said drily. 'And by the way, my mother is *not* remaking me in her image.'

Charles vented a roughened laugh. 'It may be grave-yard humour but I wouldn't be a bit surprised if you find yourself engaged by the end of that ball next month! Sofia is a hell of a wheeler dealer. You should've refused to attend.'

'I may still do that. I'm no pushover,' his son stated coldly. 'So you want me to stage a rescue mission in your name?'

'With tact and generosity,' the older man added.

Exasperation leapt through Vitale, who used tact every day of his life because he could never be less than courteous in the face of the royal demands made of him. But no matter how onerous the demand Charles had made struck him, there was, nevertheless, a certain pride and satisfaction to the awareness that his father was *trusting* him to deal with a sensitive situation. He realised that he was also surprisingly eager to read Jazz's letter.

Jazz, a skinny-as-a-rail redhead, who had developed a massive crush on him when she was fourteen and he was eighteen. He had been wildly disconcerted that he rather than the friendlier, flirtier Angel had become the object of her admiration and he had screwed up badly, he acknowledged reluctantly, cracking a wounding joke about her that she had sadly overheard. But then Vitale had never been the sensitive sort and back then he had also essentially known very little about women because he had stayed a virgin for many years longer than Angel. But, not surprisingly, Jazz had hated him after that episode and in many ways it had been a relief to no longer be the centre of her attention and the awful tongue-tied silences that had afflicted her in his presence. In the space of one awkward summer, the three of them had travelled from casual pseudo friendship to stroppy, strained discomfiture and then she and her mother had mercifully disappeared out of their lives.

Compassionate... Kind, Vitale reminded himself as he stood outside his father's office reading Jazz's letter, automatically rating it for use of English, spelling and conciseness. Of course it had been written on the computer because Jazz was severely dyslexic. Dyslexic and clumsy, he recalled helplessly, always tripping and bumping into things. The letter told a tale of woe that could have featured as a Greek tragedy and his sculpted mouth tightened, his momentary amusement dying away. She wanted help for her mother but only on her own terms. She wanted a job but only had experience of working as a checkout operator and a cleaner.

Per carita...for pity's sake, what did she think his father was going to find for her to do on the back of such slender talents? Even so, the letter was pure Jazz, feisty and gauche and crackling with brick-wall obstinacy. An ordinary woman, he thought abstractedly, an ordinary woman with extraordinarily beautiful green eyes. Her eyes wouldn't have changed, he reasoned. And you couldn't get more ordinary than Jazz, who thought a soup spoon or a fish fork or a napkin was pure unnecessary aristocratic affectation. And she *was*, evidently, badly in need of money...

A faint smile tilted Vitale's often grim mouth. He didn't need a stunning beauty to act as his partner at the palace ball and he was quite sure that if he hired the right experts Jazz could be transformed into something reasonably presentable. Having a partner for the ball to

fend off other women would make sense, he acknowledged reluctantly. But shooting Zac down in flames
would undeniably be the most satisfying aspect of the
whole affair. Jazz might be ordinary and dyslexic but
she was also clever and a quick study.

Vitale strolled back to his younger brother's side
with a rare smile on his wide sensual mouth. 'You're
up next but before you go…the bet,' he specified in an
undertone. 'Remember that blonde waitress who wanted
nothing to do with you last week and accused you of
harassment?'

Zac frowned, disconcerted colour highlighting his
high cheekbones at that reminder of his rare failure to
impress a woman.

'Bring her to the ball acting all lovelorn and clingy
and suitably polished up and you have a deal on the
bet,' Vitale completed, throwing down the gauntlet of
challenge with pleasure while recalling the very real
hatred he had seen in that woman's eyes. For once,
Zac, the smooth-talking seducer, would have his work
cut out for him…

Jazz straightened her aching back at the checkout because she had worked a very long day. Her schedule had
kicked off at dawn with a cleaning shift at a nearby hotel
and then she had got a call to step in for a sick work-
mate at the till in the supermarket where she earned
extra cash on a casual basis. Both her jobs were casual,
poorly paid and unreliable. But some work was better
than no work, she reminded herself doggedly, better
than living on welfare, which would have distressed her
mother more even though that choice would have left
mother and daughter somewhat better off.

But while Peggy Dickens had raised her daughter to be a worker rather than a whinger or a freeloader, Jazz still occasionally let her thoughts drift into a dream world where she had got to complete the education that would have equipped her with a degree that enabled her to chase better-paid jobs and climb an actual career ladder. Unfortunately, the chaos of her private life had prevented her from, what was that phrase…achieving her full potential? Her full pink mouth curled at the corners with easy amusement for who was to say that she was worth any more than the work she was currently doing? No point getting too big for her boots and imagining she might have been more, not when she came from such humble roots.

Her mother had been a housekeeper, who married a gardener and lived in accommodation provided by their employer. Nobody in Jazz's family tree had ever owned a house or earned a university degree and Peggy had been bemused when her daughter had chosen to continue her education and aim so much higher than any of her ancestors, but her mother had been proud as well.

And then their lives had gone down the tubes again and Jazz had had to put practicality first yet again. Unfortunately, it was virtually impossible to regain lost ground. Jazz had almost had a nervous breakdown studying to overcome the drawbacks of changing schools three times over during her teen years. She had not wept when her parents' unhappy marriage had finally broken down because her father had often beaten up her mother and had hurt Jazz as well when she had been foolish enough to try and intervene. She had grieved, though, when her father had died unexpectedly only a couple of years afterwards without having once tried to see her again. Evidently her father had never much cared for his only child and that knowledge had hurt. She had been sincerely aghast, however, when her mother, Peggy fell in love with Jeff Starling, a much younger man.

Love could be the biggest risk out there for a woman, Jazz reflected with an inner shiver of repulsion, most especially the kind of love that could persuade an otherwise sensible woman into jumping straight out of the frying pan into the fire.

But there were other kinds of love as well, she reminded herself comfortingly, life-enriching family connections that soothed and warmed, no matter how bad life got. When Jeff's bad debts had ensured that Peggy and her daughter couldn't even get a lease on a rental property, Peggy's kid sister, Clodagh, had given them a home in her tiny apartment. When Peggy had been diagnosed with breast cancer, Clodagh had stepped back from her little jewellery business to shepherd her sister to her appointments and treatments and nurse her tenderly while Jazz tried to keep on earning what little money she could.

Bolstered by those more positive thoughts, Jazz finished her shift and walked home in the dusk. Her phone pinged and she dug it out, green eyes widening when she read the text with difficulty. It was short and sweet, beginning, *re: letter to Charles Russell*.

Holy Moses, she thought in shock, Charles Russell was actually willing to meet her to discuss her mother's plight! Ten o'clock tomorrow morning, not much notice, she conceded ruefully, but beggars couldn't be choosers, could they?

In desperation, she had written to her mother's former employer pleading for help. Charles was a kind man and generous to a fault but almost ten years down the road from Peggy's employment, Jazz had not even expected to receive a reply. That letter had been a long shot, the product of a particularly sleepless night when she was stressing about how she could best help her mother with the stable, stress-free existence she needed to recover from what had proved to be a gruelling treatment schedule. After all, they couldn't live with Clodagh for ever. Clodagh had sacrificed a lot to take them in off the street, not least a boyfriend, who had vanished once the realities of Clodagh's new caring role had sunk in. Ironically, Jazz had not thought that there was the remotest possibility that her letter to Charles Russell would even be acknowledged...

A hot feeling of shame crept up inside her, burning her pale porcelain skin with mortified heat because the instant she had posted that letter, she had squirmed with regret over the sacrifice of her pride. Hadn't she been raised to stand on her own feet? Yet sometimes, no matter what you did and no matter how hard you worked, you needed a helping hand to climb up out of a ditch. And evidently, Charles Russell had taken pity on their plight and maybe, just maybe, he had recognised that he could offer his assistance in some way. With somewhere to live? With employment? Hope sprang high, dousing the shame of having written and posted a begging letter. Any help, no matter how small or seemingly insignificant, would be welcome, she told herself sternly.

Stuffing her phone back in her pocket, Jazz unlocked the door of the apartment, suppressing a sigh when she saw the mess in the living and kitchen area. Clodagh wasn't tidy and she wasn't much for cleaning or doing dishes or laundry but Jazz did what she could to pick up the slack, always conscious that she lived in Clodagh's home while remaining equally aware that her neat freak of a mother found it depressing to live in such messy surroundings. But there wasn't much that could be done to make a one-bedroom apartment stretch to the occupation of three adults, one of whom was still struggling to regain her strength. The treatments might have concluded but Peggy was still in the recovery phase. Clodagh shared the bedroom with her sister but when Peggy had a restless night, Clodagh took the couch and Jazz slept in a sleeping bag on the floor.

'I had a good day,' Peggy announced chirpily from in front of the television, a thin-faced, pale and still-frail-looking woman in her forties. 'I went for a walk in the park after mass.'

'That's brilliant,' Jazz said, bending down to kiss the older woman's cheek, the baby fine fuzz of her mother's regrown hair brushing her brow and bringing tears to her tired eyes. The hair had grown again in white, rather then red, and Peggy had refused to consider dying it as Clodagh had suggested, confessing that as far as she was concerned any hair was better than no hair.

Jazz was intensely relieved that her mother was regaining her energy and had an excellent prognosis. Having initially faced the terrifying prospect that she might lose her mother, she was merely grateful to still have her and was keen to improve the older woman's life as much as possible.

'Hungry?' Jazz prompted.

'Not really,' Peggy confessed guiltily.

'I'll make a lovely salad and you can do your best with it,' Jazz declared, knowing it was imperative to encourage her mother to regain some of the weight she had lost.

'Clodagh's visiting her friend, Rose,' Peggy told her. 'She asked me to join them but I was too tired and I like to see you when you come in from work.'

Suppressing her exhaustion, Jazz began to clean up the kitchen, neatly stowing away her aunt's jewellery-making supplies in their designated clear boxes and then embarking on the dishes before preparing the salad that was presently the only option that awakened her mother's appetite. While she worked, she chattered, sharing a little gossip about co-workers, bringing her working day home with her to brighten her mother's more restricted lifestyle and enjoy the sound of her occasional chuckle.

They sat down at the table to eat. Jazz was mentally running through her tiny wardrobe to select a suitable outfit for her morning appointment with Charles Russell. Giving up the luxury of their own home had entailed selling off almost all their belongings because there had been no money to spare to rent a storage facility and little room for anything extra in Clodagh's home. Jazz had a worn black pencil skirt and jeans and shorts and a few tops and that was literally all. She had learned to be grateful for the uniform she wore at both her jobs because it meant that she could get by with very few garments. Formality insisted on her wearing the skirt, she conceded ruefully, and her only pair of high heels.

She had not mentioned her letter to either her mother or her aunt because she hadn't expected anything to come of it and, in the same way, she could not quite accept that she had been given an appointment. Indeed, several times before she finally dropped off to sleep on the couch that evening, she had to dig out her phone and anxiously reread that text to persuade herself that it wasn't a figment of her imagination.

Early the next morning, fearful of arriving late, Jazz crossed London by public transport and finally arrived outside a tall town house. She had been surprised not to be invited to the older man's office where she had sent the letter, but perhaps he preferred a less formal and more discreet setting for their meeting. She was even more surprised by the size and exclusive location of the house. Charles Russell had once been married to a reigning queen, she reminded herself wryly. A queen who, on her only fleeting visit to her former husband's country home, had treated Jazz's mother like the dirt beneath her expensively shod feet.

But Charles had been infinitely kinder and more gracious with his staff, she recalled fondly, remembering the older man's warm smiles and easy conversation with her even though she was only his housekeeper's daughter. Unlike his royal ex-wife and second son, he was not a snob and had never rated people in importance solely according to their social or financial status. A *kind* man, she repeated doggedly to herself to quell her leaping nervous tension as she rang the doorbell.

A woman who spoke little English, and what she did speak was with an impenetrable accent, ushered her into an imposing hall furnished with gleaming antiques and mirrors. Scanning her intimidating surroundings and feeling very much like an interloper, Jazz began to revise up her estimate of Charles Russell's wealth.

Another door was cast open into what looked like a home office and a man sprang up from behind the solid wooden desk.

Jazz was so aghast by the recognition that roared through her slender frame that she froze on the threshold of the room and stared in dismay, all her natural buoyance draining away as though someone very cruel had stabbed a pin into her tender flesh and deflated her like a balloon. It was Vitale, not his father, and that had to be… Her. Worst. Nightmare. *Ever…*

CHAPTER TWO

VITALE STARED, TAKEN aback by the woman in the doorway because she was a knockout, the kind of vibrant beauty who turned male heads in the street with her streaming red-gold curls and slender, supple body. About the only things that hadn't changed about Jazz were her eyes, green as jade set in a triangular face, skin as translucent as the finest pale porcelain and a surprisingly full pink mouth, little white teeth currently plucking at her lower lip as she gazed at him in almost comical horror.

'Come in and close the door,' Vitale urged smoothly, wondering how on earth he was going to teach her to stop wearing her every thought on her face while also wondering why he found that candidness attractive.

Jazz made a valiant attempt to stage a recovery even though every ounce of her hard-won confidence had been blown out of the water. Shock waves were travelling through her slight body. One glimpse of Vitale and her brain was mush at best and at worst sending her back in time to a very vulnerable period she did not want to remember. But there Vitale was, as sleek and drop-dead gorgeous as he had ever been and so compelling in his undeniable masculine beauty that it took terrible effort to even look away from him.

What was it about Vitale, what crazy weakness in her made him seem so appealing? His brother, Angel Valtinos, had been too pretty and vain to draw her and she had never once looked at Angel in *that* way. But then, Vitale was a much more complex and fascinating creature, all simmering, smouldering intensity and conflicts below the smooth, sophisticated surface he wore for the world. Those perfect manners and that cool reserve of his couldn't mask the intense emotion he held in restraint behind those stunning dark golden eyes. And he was *so* sexy. Every sinuous movement of his lean, muscular body, every downward dip of his gold-tipped, outrageously thick black lashes, and every quirk of his beautifully shaped sensual mouth contributed to his ferocious sex appeal. It was little wonder that when she had finally been of an age to crush on a man, her attention had immediately locked onto Vitale, even though Vitale had found it quite impossible to treat her like a friend.

Jazz closed the door in a harried movement and walked towards the chair set in front of the desk. You're a grown-up now. The embarrassing stuff you did as a kid no longer matters, her defences were instructing her at a frantic pitch, and so intent was she on listening to that face-saving voice that she didn't notice the edge of the rug in front of her. Her spiky heel caught on the fringe and she pitched forward with a startled cry.

And Vitale was there at supersonic speed, catching her before she could fall and steadying her with a strong arm to her spine. The heat of his hand at her waist startled her almost as much as his sudden proximity. She jerked skittishly away from him to settle down heavily into the chair but her nostrils flared appreciatively. The dark sensual scent of his spicy cologne overlying warm earthy male plunged her senses into overdrive.

Vitale had finally touched her, Vitale, who avoided human contact as much as possible, she recalled abstractedly, striving not to look directly at him until she had got her stupid brain back on line. He would be smiling: she *knew* that. Her clumsiness had always amused him because he was as lithe and sure-footed as a cat. Now he unnerved her more by not returning to the other side of the desk and instead lounging back against it with unusual casualness, staying far too close for comfort, a long, muscular, powerful thigh within view that did nothing to restore her composure.

Her fingertips dug into her palms as she fought for calm. 'I was expecting to meet with your father,' she admitted thinly.

'Charles asked me to handle this,' Vitale confided, barely resisting the urge to touch the wild corkscrew mane of flaming ringlets tumbling across her shoulders with gleaming electric vigour. So, he liked the hair and the eyes, he reasoned, wondering why he had abandoned his usual formality to sit so close to her, wondering why the simple smell of soap that she emanated was so surpassingly sexy, wondering why that slender body with its delicate curves, tiny waist and shapely legs should suddenly seem so very tempting a package. Because she wasn't his type, not even remotely his type, he told himself sternly. He had always gone for tall, curvy blondes, redheads being too bright and brash for his tastes.

On the other hand he had never wanted so badly to

touch a woman's hair and that weird prompting unnerved him into springing upright again and striding across the room. The dulled throb of awakening desire at his groin inspired him with another stab of incredulity because since adulthood he had always been fully in control of that particular bodily affliction.

'I can't think why,' Jazz said, dry-mouthed, unbearably conscious of him looming over her for that split second before he moved away because he stood well over six feet tall and she barely made a couple of inches over five foot.

'I assure you that the exchange will work out very much to your advantage,' Vitale husked, deciding that his uncharacteristic interest had simply been stimulated by the challenge that he now saw lay ahead of him: the transformation of Jazz. Number one on the agenda would be persuading her to stop biting her nails. Number two would be ditching the giant fake gold hoop earrings. Number three would be avoiding any shoe that looked as if a stripper might wear it.

Jazz let slip a very rude startled word in response to that unlikely statement.

And number four would be cleaning up her vocabulary, Vitale reflected, glad to so clearly see her flaws so that he could concentrate on the practicalities of his challenge, rather than dwell on any aspect that could be deemed personal.

'Don't swear,' Vitale told her.

Jazz reddened as high as her hairline because she could remember him saying the same thing to her when she was about twelve years old while warning her that once she became accustomed to using such words, using them would become an embarrassing habit. And being

Vitale, he had been infuriatingly bang on target with that advice. Using curse words had made her seem a little cooler at school back then…well, as cool as you could be with bright red hair and a flat chest, puberty having passed her by for far longer than she cared to recall, making her an anomaly amongst her peers.

'You need financial help,' Vitale pointed out with undiplomatic bluntness, keen to get right to the heart of the matter and remind her of her situation. If he neglected to remind her of her boundaries, Jazz would be a stubborn, defiant baggage and hard to handle.

Living up to that assessment, Jazz flew upright, earrings swinging wildly in the torrent of her burnished hair, colour marking her cheekbones, highlighting eyes bright with angry defensiveness. 'I did *not* ask for money from your father!' she snapped back at him.

'Employment, a home, the settlement of outstanding loans?' Vitale reminded her with cruel precision. 'How could any of those aspirations be achieved without someone laying out a considerable amount of money on your behalf?'

The angry colour drained from her disconcerted face, perspiration breaking out on her short upper lip as he threw her crash-bang up against hard reality, refusing to allow her to deny the obvious. She stared back at him, trapped like a rabbit in headlights and hating him for it. Mortification claimed her along with a healthy dose of shame that she should have put herself in such a position and with Vitale of all people. Vitale, who had never treated her like an equal as Angel had done, Vitale who had never for one moment forgotten that she was essentially a servant's child, thrown into the brothers' company only by proximity.

Vitale watched Jazz crash down from fury to bitter, embarrassed acceptance. *Sì*…yes, he told himself with satisfaction, that had been the right note to sound. She dropped back into the chair, sunset heat warming her cheeks and bowing her head on her slender neck.

'And the good news is that I'm willing to provide that money *if*…in return, you are willing to do something for me.'

'I can't imagine anything that I could do for you,' Jazz told him truthfully.

'Then listen and learn,' Vitale advised, poised by the window with the light glimmering over his luxuriant blue-black hair, the suave olive planes of his cheekbones taut. 'At the end of next month my mother is throwing a ball at the palace. Her objective is to match me up with a future bride and the guest list will be awash with young women who have what the Queen deems to be the right pedigree and background.'

Jazz was staring at him now in wide-eyed wonderment. 'Are you kidding me?'

His sculpted mouth quirked. 'I wish I was.'

Her smooth brow furrowed as she collided with hot dark golden eyes and suddenly found it fatally difficult to breathe. 'You're angry about it.'

'*Oviamente*…of course I am. I'm nowhere near the stage in life where I want to get married and settle down. But having considered the situation, it has occurred to me,' Vitale murmured quietly, 'that arriving at the ball with what appears to be a partner, whom I'm seriously involved with, would be my best defence. I want you to be that partner.'

'*Me?*' Jazz gaped at him in disbelief, green eyes a pool of verdant jade bemusement as she gazed up at him, soft full pink lips slightly parted. 'How could *I* be your partner? I couldn't go to a royal ball!'

'Suitably gowned and refined, you could,' Vitale disagreed, choosing his words with care because the throb below his belt went up tempo when he focused on that soft, oh, so inviting full lower lip of hers. 'But you would have to be willing to work at the presentation required because you would have to both *look* like and *act* like the sort of woman I would bring to a royal ball.'

'Impossible,' Jazz told him. 'It would take more than a fancy dress and not swearing.'

'It would but, given that we have several weeks at our disposal in which to prepare, I think you could easily do it,' Vitale declared, shocking her even more with that vote of apparent confidence. 'And whether you successfully contrive the pretence or fail it, I will still pay you well for trying to make the grade.'

'But why me?' Jazz spluttered in a rush. 'Why someone like me? Surely you have a friend who could pretend to be something more for the evening?'

'Why you? Because someone bet me that I couldn't pass off an ordinary woman as a socialite at a royal ball,' Vitale delivered, opting for the truth. 'You fit the bill and I prefer to *pay* for the pretence rather than ask anyone to do me a favour. In addition, as it will be in your best interests to succeed, you will make more effort to meet the standard required.'

Jazz was transfixed by his admission. 'A bet,' she echoed weakly. 'To go to all that effort and put out money simply to win a bet…it would be absurd.'

Vitale shrugged a wide shoulder, sheathed in the finest silk and wool blend, the jacket of his exquisitely well-tailored suit sliding open to reveal his torso, lean, strong muscles flexing below the thin cotton shirt. Her mouth ran dry because he was a work of art on a physical level, every silken, honed line of his lean, powerful physique hard and muscular and fit. 'Does the absurdity of it have to concern you?'

'I guess not...' she said uncertainly, knowing that what was what he wanted her to say, playing it sensibly by ear and reluctant to argue while momentarily lost in the dark, exciting challenge of his hard, assessing gaze.

She had almost forgotten what that excitement felt like, had never felt it since in a man's radius and had been much too young and naïve to feel its mortifying bite at the age of fourteen. She had experienced what felt like all the sensations of a grown woman while still trapped in the body of an undeveloped child. Unsurprisingly, struggling to deal with that adolescent flood of sexual awakening had made her so silent, so awkward and so wretched around Vitale that she had been filled with self-loathing and shame.

Now that same excitement was curling up hot in the pit of her stomach and spreading dangerous tendrils of awareness to more sensitive places. She felt her nipples pinch tight below her tee shirt and her small breasts swell with the shaken breath she snatched in as she willed the torture to stop. But her body's reaction to Vitale had never been something she could control and the inexorable pulse of that heat between her thighs made her feel murderously uncomfortable and foolish.

A bet, she was still thinking with even greater incredulity, desperate to stop thinking about her physical reaction to him. Vitale was willing to invest good money in an attempt to win a bet. That was beyond her capacity to imagine and she thought it was very wrong. In her experience money was precious and should be reserved to cover the necessities of life: rent, heat and food. She had never lived in a world where money was easily obtained or where there was ever enough of it. Even when her parents had still been together, having sufficient money simply to live had been a constant source of concern, thanks to her father's addiction to online betting.

But Vitale lived at a very different level, she reminded herself ruefully. He took money for granted, had never gone without and could probably never understand how bone-deep appalled she was by his light-hearted attitude and how even more hostile she was to any form of gambling.

'I don't approve of gambling,' she admitted tightly, thinking of the families destroyed by the debts accrued and the addicts who could not break free of their dream of a big win.

'It's *not*—'

'It *is* gambling,' Jazz cut in with assurance. 'You're betting on the outcome of something that can't be predicted and you may make a loss.'

'That's my problem, not yours,' Vitale delivered without hesitation. 'You need to think about how this arrangement would benefit you. I would settle those loans and find a place of your choosing for you and your mother to live. I don't know what I could offer on the employment front but I'm sure I could provide some help. The decision is yours. I'll give you twenty-four hours to think it over.'

Her green eyes flared in anger again. 'You haven't even told me what would be involved if I accepted!'

'Obviously you'd have to have a makeover and a certain amount of coaching before you could meet the demands of the role,' Vitale imparted, marvelling that she hadn't eagerly snatched at his offer straight away. 'Right now you're drowning in debt and you have no options. I can *give* you options.'

It was the bald truth and she hated him for spelling it out. If wishes were horses, then beggars would ride, she chanted inside her head. Being badly in debt meant that she and her mother had virtually no choices and little chance of improving their lot in life. She swallowed hard on that humiliating reality that put Vitale squarely in the driver's seat. A makeover, *coaching*? Inwardly she cringed but it was no surprise to her that she would not do as she was. She would never be good enough for Vitale on any level. She didn't have the right breeding or background and found it hard to credit that even a makeover would raise her to the standard required by a highly sophisticated royal prince, who couldn't even drink beer out of a bottle without looking uncomfortable.

'Yes, if I can trust you, you could give us options,' she conceded flatly. 'But how do I know that you will keep your promises if this doesn't work?'

Vitale stiffened as though she had slapped him. 'I give you my word,' he bit out witheringly. 'Surely that should be sufficient?'

'There are very few people in this world that I trust,' Jazz admitted apologetically.

'I will have a legal agreement drawn up, then,' Vitale breathed with icy cool. 'Will that satisfy you?'

Jazz lifted her head high, barely able to credit that she was bargaining with Vitale. 'We don't need a legal agreement for something this crazy. You get rid of the loans first as a show of faith,' she dared. 'I'm fed up trying to protect my mother from debt collectors.'

'I don't understand why you're even trying to repay loans that were fraudulently taken out in your mother's name.'

'It's incredibly difficult to prove that it *was* fraud. Jeff died in an accident last year and he wasn't prosecuted. A solicitor tried to sort it out for Mum but we didn't have enough proof to clear her name and she won't declare herself bankrupt because she sees that as the ultimate humiliation,' she explained, wanting him to know that they had explored every possible avenue. 'She was ill and going through chemo at the time and I didn't want to put any more pressure on her.'

'You give me all the paperwork for the loans and I will have them dealt with,' Vitale asserted. 'But if I do so, I will own you body and soul until the end of next month.'

'Nobody will *ever* own me body and soul.'

'Apart from me for the next couple of months,' Vitale contradicted with lethal cool. 'If I pay upfront, I call the shots and you do as you're told, whether you like it or not.'

Jazz blinked in bewilderment, wondering how she had got herself into the situation she was in. He thought he had her agreement and why wouldn't he when she had bargained the terms with him? Even the prospect of those dreadful loans being settled knocked her for six. A visit or a phone call from a debt collector upset her mother for days afterwards, depriving her of the peace of mind she needed to rebuild her life and her health. How could Jazz possibly turn her back on an offer like Vitale's? Nobody else was going to give them the opportunity to make a fresh start.

'You haven't given me a chance to think this through,' she argued shakily.

'You were keen enough to set out your conditions,' Vitale reminded her drily.

And her face flamed because she was in no position to protest that assumption. The offer of money had cut right through her fine principles and her aversion to gambling. The very idea that she could sort out her mother's problems and give her a happier and more secure future had thoroughly seduced her.

'You'll move in here as soon as possible,' Vitale decreed.

Her head flew up, corkscrew curls tumbling across her shoulders, green eyes huge. 'Move in here? With *you*?'

'How else can we achieve this? You must be readily available. How else can I supervise? And if I take you to the ball it will be assumed we are lovers, and should anyone do a check, it will be clear that you were already living here in my house,' Vitale pointed out. 'If we are to succeed, you have to consider little supporting details of that nature.'

Jazz studied him, aghast. 'I can't move in with you!' she gasped. 'What am I supposed to tell my mother?'

Vitale shrugged with magnificent lack of interest. 'Whatever suits. That I've given you a job? That we're having an affair? I don't care.'

Her feathery lashes fluttered rapidly, her animated face troubled as she pondered that problem. 'Yes, I could admit I sent the letter to your father and say I've been offered a live-in job and my aunt would look after Mum, so I wouldn't need to worry about her,' she reasoned out loud. 'Would I still be able to work? I have two part-time jobs.'

'No. You won't have the time. I'll pay you a salary for the duration of your stay here,' Vitale added, reading her expression to register the dismay etched there at the news that she would not be able to continue in paid employment.

'This is beginning to sound like a very expensive undertaking for you,' Jazz remarked uncomfortably, her face more flushed than ever.

'My choice,' Vitale parried dismissively while he wondered how far that flush extended beneath her clothing and whether that scattering of freckles across the bridge of her nose was repeated anywhere else on her delicate body. He wondered dimly why such an imperfection should seem even marginally appealing and why he should suddenly be picturing her naked with all the eagerness of a sex-starved teenage boy. He tensed, thoroughly unsettled by his complete loss of concentration and detachment.

'I'll say you've offered me a job,' Jazz said abruptly, her thoughts leaping ahead of her. 'Are there many art works in this house?'

Vitale frowned and stared enquiringly at her. 'Yes, but—'

'Then I could say that I was cataloguing them or researching them for you,' Jazz announced with satisfaction. 'I was only six months off completing a BA in History of Art when Mum's life fell apart and I had to drop out. I may not have attained my degree but I have done placements in museums and galleries, so I do have good working experience.'

'If what you're telling me is true, why are you working in a shop and as a cleaner?'

'Because without that degree certificate, I can't work in my field. I'll finish my studies once life has settled down again,' she said with wry acceptance.

Vitale struggled to imagine the added stress of studying at degree level in spite of her dyslexia and all its attendant difficulties and a grudging respect flared in him because she had fought her disability and refused to allow it to hold her back. 'Why did you drop out?'

'Mum's second husband, Jeff, died suddenly and she was inconsolable.' Jazz grimaced. 'That was long before the debt collectors began calling and we found out about the loans Jeff had taken out and forged her name on. I took time out from university but things went downhill very quickly from that point and I couldn't leave Mum alone. We were officially homeless and living in a boarding house when she was diagnosed with cancer and that was when my aunt asked us to move in with her. It's been a rough couple of years.'

Vitale made no comment, backing away from the personal aspects of the information she was giving him, deeming them not his business, not his concern. He needed to concentrate on the end game alone and that was preparing her for the night of the ball.

'How soon can you move in?' he prompted impatiently.

Jazz stiffened at that blunt question. 'This week sometime?' she suggested.

'I'll send a car to collect you tomorrow at nine and

pack for a long stay. We don't have time to waste,' Vitale pronounced as she slid out of the seat and straightened, the pert swell of her small breasts prominent in a tee shirt that was a little too tight, the skirt clinging to her slim thighs and the curve of her bottom, the fabric shiny with age. Her ankles looked ridiculously narrow and delicate above those clodhopper sandals with their towering heels. The pulse at his groin that nagged at his usually well-disciplined body went crazy.

'Tomorrow's a little soon, surely?' Jazz queried in dismay.

Vitale compressed his lips, exasperated by his physical reaction to her. 'We have a great deal to accomplish.'

'Am I really that unpresentable?' Jazz heard herself ask sharply.

'Cinderella *shall* go to the ball,' Vitale retorted with diplomatic conviction, ducking an answer that was obvious to him even if it was not to her. 'When I put my mind to anything, I make it work.'

In something of a daze, Jazz refused the offer of a car to take her home and muttered the fiction that she had some shopping to do. In truth she only ever shopped at the supermarket, not having the money to spare for treats. But she knew she needed time to get her head clear and work out what she was going to say before she went home again, and that was how she ended up sitting in a park in the spring sunshine, feeling much as though she had had a run-in with a truck that had squashed her flat.

'She's as flat as an ironing board, not to mention the hideous rag-doll hair but, worst of all, she's a *child*, Angel…'

Vitale's well-bred voice filtered down through the

years to sound afresh inside her head. Angel spoke Greek and Vitale spoke Italian, so the brothers had always communicated in English. Angel had been teasing Vitale about her crush and of course Jazz had been so innocent at fourteen that it had not even occurred to her that the boys had noticed her infatuation, and that unwelcome discovery as much as Vitale's withering description of her lack of attractiveness had savaged Jazz. She had known she wasn't much to look at, but knowing and having it said out loud by the object of her misplaced affections had cut her deep. Furthermore, being deemed to be still a child, even though in hindsight she now agreed with that conviction, had hurt even more at the time and she had hated him for it. She still remembered the dreadful moment when the boys had appeared out of the summerhouse and had seen her standing there, white as a sheet on the path, realising that they had been overheard.

Angel had grimaced but Vitale had looked genuinely appalled. At eighteen, Vitale hadn't had the ability to hide his feelings that he did as an adult, and at that moment Vitale had recognised how upset she was and had deeply regretted his words, his troubled dark golden eyes telegraphing that truth. Not that he would have admitted it or said anything, though, or even apologised, she conceded wryly, because royalty did not admit fault or indeed do anything that lowered the dignified cool front of polished perfection.

"Cinderella shall go to the ball," he had said as if he were conferring some enormous honour on her. As if she cared about his stupid fancy ball, or his even more stupid bet! But she *did* care about her mother, she reminded herself ruefully, and if Vitale was willing to

help her family, she was willing to eat dirt, strain every sinew to please and play Cinderella…even if the process did sting her pride and humiliate her and there would be no glass slipper waiting for her!

CHAPTER THREE

'I'M ONLY WORRIED because you had such a thing for him when you were young.' Peggy Starling rested anxious green eyes on her daughter's pink cheeks. 'Living in the same house with him now, working for him.'

'He's a prince, Mum,' Jazz pointed out, wishing her colour didn't change so revealingly, wishing she could honestly swear that she now found Vitale totally unattractive. 'I'm not an idiot.'

'But you were never really aware of him being a royal at Chimneys because Mr Russell wanted him treated like any other boy while he was staying there and his title was never used,' her mother reasoned uncomfortably. 'I just don't want you getting hurt again.'

'Oh, for goodness' sake, Peggy, stop fussing!' Clodagh interrupted impatiently, a small woman in her late thirties with the trademark family red hair cut short. 'Jazz is a grown woman now and she's been offered a decent job and a nice place to live for a couple of months. Don't spoil it for her!'

Jazz gave her aunt a grateful glance. 'The extra money will come in useful and I'll visit regularly,' she promised.

Her possessions in a bag, Jazz hugged her mother and

her aunt and took her leave, walking downstairs, because the lift was always broken, and out to the shabby street where a completely out-of-place long black shiny limousine awaited her. Amusement filtered through her nerves when she saw that the muscular driver was out patrolling round the car, keen to protect his pride and joy from a hovering cluster of jeering kids.

Vitale strode out of his office when he heard the slam of the front door of the town house because somewhere in the back of his mind he couldn't quite credit that he was doing what he was doing and that Jazz would actually turn up. More fool him, he thought sardonically, reckoning that the financial help he was offering would be more than sufficient as a bait on the hook of her commitment.

He scanned her slim silhouette in jeans and a sweater, wondering if he ought to be planning to take before and after photos for some silly scrapbook while acknowledging that her hair, her skin, her eyes, her truly perfect little face required no improvement whatsoever. His attention fell in surprise to the bulging carrier bag she carried.

'I told you to pack for a long stay,' he reminded her with a frown. 'I meant bring everything you require to be comfortable.'

Jazz shrugged. 'This *is* everything I own,' she said tightly.

'It can't be,' Vitale pronounced in disbelief, accustomed to women who travelled with suitcases that ran into double figures.

'Being homeless strips you of your possessions pretty efficiently,' Jazz told him drily. 'I only kept *one* snow globe, my first one…'

And a faint shard of memory pierced Vitale's brain. He recalled her dragging him and Angel into her bedroom to show off her snow globe collection when they must all have been very young. She had had three of those ugly plastic domes and the first one had had an evil little Santa Claus figure inside it. He and Angel had surveyed the girlie display, unimpressed. 'They're beautiful,' Vitale had finally squeezed out, trying to be kind under the onslaught of her expectant green eyes, and knowing that a lie was necessary because she was tiny, and he still remembered the huge smile she had given him, which had assured him that he had said the right thing.

'The Santa one?' he queried.

Disconcerted, Jazz stared back at him in astonishment. 'You remember that?'

'It stayed with me. I've never seen a snow globe since,' Vitale told her truthfully, relieved to be off the difficult subject of her having been homeless at one stage, while censuring himself for not having registered the practical consequences of such an upsetting experience.

'So, when do the lessons start?' Jazz prompted.

'Come into my office. The housekeeper will show you to your room later.'

Jazz straightened her slender spine and tried hard not to stare at Vitale, which was an enormous challenge when he looked so striking in an exquisitely tailored dark grey suit that outlined his lean, powerful physique to perfection, a white shirt and dark silk tie crisp at his brown throat. So, he's gorgeous, *get over it*, she railed inwardly at herself until the full onslaught of spectacular dark golden eyes heavily fringed by black lashes drove even that sensible thought from her mind.

'First you get measured up for a new wardrobe. Next you get elocution.'

'*Elocution?*' Jazz gasped.

For all the world as though he had suggested keelhauling her under Angel's yacht, Vitale thought helplessly.

'You can't do this with a noticeable regional accent,' Vitale sliced in. 'Stop reacting to everything I say as though it's personal.'

'It *is* freaking personal when someone says you don't talk properly!' Jazz slashed back at him furiously, her colour heightened.

'And the language,' Vitale reminded her without skipping a beat, refusing to be sidetracked from his ultimate goal. 'I'm not insulting you. Stop personalising this arrangement. You are being prepared for an acting role.'

The reminder was a timely one, but it still struck Jazz as very personal when a man looked at her and decided he had to change virtually everything about her. She compressed her lips and said instead, '*Freaking* is not a bad word.'

Vitale released a groan, gold-tipped lashes flying high while he noticed the fullness of her soft pink lips even when she was trying to fold them flat, and his body succumbed to an involuntary stirring he fiercely resented. 'Are you going to argue about everything?'

Common sense assailed Jazz and she bent down to rummage industriously in her carrier bag. 'Not if you settle these loans,' she muttered in as apologetic a tone as she could manage while still hating him for picking out her every flaw.

Vitale watched her settle a small heap of crumpled papers on his desk while striving to halter her temper, a battle he could read on her eloquent face. He supposed he could live with 'freaking' if he had to. For that matter he knew several socialites who swore like troopers and he wondered if he was setting his expectations rather too high, well aware that if he had a flaw, and he wasn't willing to acknowledge that he *did*, it was a desire for perfection.

'After elocution comes lessons in etiquette,' he informed her doggedly, suppressing that rare instant of self-doubt. 'You have to know how to address the other guests, many of whom will have titles.'

'It sounds like a *really* fun-packed morning,' Jazz pronounced acidly.

Amusement flashed through Vitale but he crushed it at source, reluctant to encourage her irreverence. Of course, he wasn't used to any woman behaving around him the way Jazz did. Jazz had smoothly shifted straight back into treating him the same way she had treated him when they were teenagers and it was a disorientating experience, but not actively unpleasant, he registered in surprise. There was no awe or flattery, no ego-boosting jokes or flirtatious smiles or carefully choreographed speeches. In the strangest way he found her attitude, her very refusal to be impressed by his status, refreshing.

Later that same day, Jazz got a break at lunchtime. She heaved a sigh over the morning she had endured; lessons had never before made her feel so bored and fed up because all the subject matter was dry as dust. For the first time, however, she was becoming fully aware that Vitale occupied a very different world from her own and the prospect of having to face weeks of such coaching sessions made her wince. But if that was what rescuing her mother demanded from her, she would knuckle down and learn what she had to learn, she conceded reluctantly. A sheaf of supporting notes in front of her, she stroked coloured felt-tipped pens through salient points to highlight them, a practice she had used at university to make reading less of a challenge for her dyslexia. It would be easier for her to ask for spoken notes that she could listen to but she absolutely hated asking for special treatment that drew attention to her learning disability, particularly when it would only remind Vitale of yet another one of her flaws.

Her room, however, was beautiful, she allowed with a rueful smile that took in her silk-clad bed, the polished furniture and the door into the en-suite bathroom. She might as well have been staying in a top-flight exclusive hotel because her surroundings were impossibly luxurious and decidedly in the category of a major treat. The lunch, served in a fancy dining room, had been excellent as well, she was thinking as she sped downstairs for the afternoon session of coaching, wondering what was next on the agenda.

'*Jazz?*' a voice said in disbelief.

Jazz stopped dead mid-flight and stared down at the tall dark man staring up at her from the foyer, swiftly recognising him from his high public profile in the media. 'Angel?' she queried in shock.

'What the hell are you doing in my brother's house?' Angel demanded bluntly, scanning her casual jeans-clad appearance with frowning attention.

Trying to think fast, Jazz descended the stairs, wondering what she was supposed to say to Vitale's half-brother. Were the two men still as close as they had been as kids?

'I think that's a secret so I'd rather not go into detail,' she parried awkwardly. 'How are you?'

'That's OK, Jenkins,' Angel addressed the older man still standing at the front door as if in readiness for the Greek billionaire's departure. 'You can serve coffee in the drawing room for Jazz and I.'

'Where's Vitale?' Jazz enquired nervously.

'Out but we *must* catch up,' Angel said with innate assurance while the older man spread wide the door of what she assumed to be the drawing room.

'Who's Jenkins?' she asked to forestall further questions when the door was closed again.

'Vitale's butler. This is a pretty old-fashioned household,' Angel told her cheerfully. 'Now tell me about the secret because I know my brother better than anyone and Vitale does not *have* secrets.'

'I can't… Don't push me,' Jazz protested in desperation. 'My mother and I are in a bit of a pickle and Vitale is helping us out.'

'Charitable Vitale?' Angel inclined his head thoughtfully. 'Sorry, that doesn't wash.'

'I contacted your father first,' Jazz admitted, hoping that fact would distract him, because Angel was displaying all the characteristics of a terrier on the scent of a juicy bone.

'Tell me about your mother,' Angel invited smoothly.

Jazz gave him a brief résumé of their plight and confided that she had told her family that she was working for Vitale even though she strictly wasn't. 'But if it hadn't been for the *b-bet*—' she stumbled helplessly at letting that word escape '—Vitale wouldn't have needed me in the first place.'

'Bet,' Angel repeated with a sudden flashing smile of triumph. 'Zac, our kid brother, I surmise. And what *is* the bet? Vitale tells me everything.'

And since she had already given away half the story she gave him the whole. Angel gave her a shattered appraisal before he dropped down beside her on the sofa and burst out laughing, so genuinely amused at the prospect of her being coached for a public appearance at a royal ball that she ended up laughing too. Angel had always been so much more down-to-earth than his brother.

That was the point when Vitale entered the room, seeing his brother and Jazz seated close and laughing in a scene of considerable intimacy. That unanticipated sight sent a current of deep-seated rage roaring through Vitale like a hurricane.

'Jazz…you're supposed to be with Jenkins right now, not entertaining my brother!' he bit out rawly, dark golden eyes scorching hot with angry condemnation on her flushed face.

'Jenkins?' she queried, rising upright.

'Table manners,' he extended crushingly, sending a tide of red rushing across her stricken face and not feeling the slightest bit guilty about it.

Jazz fled, mortified that he would say that to her in front of Angel as if she were a half-bred savage, who didn't know how to eat in polite company. Was she? Ridiculous tears prickled at the backs of her eyes and stung. Did Vitale remember her as having had dreadful table manners when she was younger? It was a deeply embarrassing suspicion.

'Well, wasn't that unroyal eruption educational?' Angel quipped as he sprang upright and studied Vitale with a measuring scrutiny. 'Yes, she's turned out quite a looker, our childhood playmate.'

Jazz was only a little soothed to learn that Vitale's butler had been co-opted into teaching her about the right cutlery to use, rather than her manners. Furthermore, for once, she was receiving a lesson she needed, she acknowledged grudgingly, when she was presented with a formal table setting in the dining room that contained a remarkably bewildering choice of knives, forks and spoons. When that was done, she returned to her room and was seated against the headboard, reading a book she had got in a charity shop, when the door opened with an abrupt lack of warning.

It was Vitale and he was furious, as she had never seen him before. A dark flush lay along his high cheekbones, only contriving to accentuate the flaming gold of his spectacular eyes. 'You spilled it all like an oil gusher!' he condemned wrathfully. 'Don't you have any discretion?'

Stiff with discomfiture, Jazz scrambled off the bed in haste. 'I let one word slip and then there didn't seem much point in holding back,' she admitted ruefully. 'I'm sorry if you didn't want him to know.'

'You were too busy flirting with my brother to worry about what you told him!' Vitale accused fiercely.

Jazz was stunned by that interpretation, particularly when her response to Angel had always been more like a sister with a big brother than anything else. She had never felt the smallest spark in Angel's radius, while Vitale could set her on fire with a careless glance. 'I wasn't *flirting* with him!' she replied forcefully. 'That's nonsense.'

'I know what I saw,' Vitale sliced in with contempt. 'You were all over him like a rash!'

Anger began to stir within Jazz as she stared up at Vitale, who was towering over her like a particularly menacing stone wall. 'I didn't even touch him, for goodness' sake! What the hell are you trying to imply?' she demanded.

Already struggling to master a fury unlike any he had ever experienced, Vitale stared down at her, his lean brown hands clenched into fists because he felt incredibly violent. Angel was an incorrigible flirt and women went mad for him. Vitale had never had that freedom, that ready repartee or level of experience, and suddenly that lowering awareness infuriated him. His attention zeroed in on Jazz's luscious pink mouth and suddenly he wanted to taste that mouth so badly it hurt, his body surging in a volatile wave straight from rage to sexual hunger. His brain had nothing to do with that unnerving switch.

Vitale snatched her up off her feet and kissed her in a move that so disconcerted her she didn't fight, she only gasped. A split second on, the punishing, passionate force of his hard mouth was smashing down on hers, driving her lips apart, his tongue penetrating that moist and sensitive internal space. She shuddered with reaction, her arms balancing on his shoulders, her hands splaying round the back of his neck, fingers delving into the luxuriant depths of his black hair. A tsunami of excitement quivered through Jazz with every deeply sensual plunge of his tongue. It was like nothing she had ever felt in a man's arms before and the very intensity of it was mind-blowing because it was everything she had ever dreamt of and nothing she had ever thought she could feel. He could certainly kiss, she thought helplessly, awash with the stimulation spreading through her heated body.

Without warning, it was over and Vitale was setting her back down on the floor, swinging on his heel and walking out again without a word, even closing the door behind him. Jazz almost laughed, her fingers rising to touch her tingling mouth, wild butterflies unleashed in her tummy. Vitale hadn't said a word, which was *so* typical of him. He would walk away and refuse to think about it or talk about it, as if talking about it would make it more damaging.

But Vitale was genuinely in shock, throbbing with such raw sexual arousal he was in pain, dark golden eyes burning with the self-discipline it had taken to tear himself away. She tasted like strawberries and coffee but she had engulfed him like too much alcohol in his veins. He felt strangely disconnected from himself because his reactions, his very behaviour, were unacceptable and abnormal. He could barely credit that he had been so angry that he had wanted to smash his brother through the wall, couldn't begin to explain what had awakened that anger. He loathed every one of those weird feelings and fought to suppress them and bury them deep. He stripped where he stood in his bedroom before heading for the shower.

In comparison, Jazz lay on top of her very comfortable bed and thought about that kiss, the ultimate kiss, which had shot her full of adrenalin, excitement and longing. She felt as if she had been waiting half her life to discover that a kiss could make her feel like that, but it was a terrible disappointment that Vitale had achieved that feat because there would be no interesting future developments happening in that quarter, she reflected wryly. It was just sex, stupid, confusing sexual urges that had neither sense nor staying power, and she should write it off to a silly impulse and a moment of forgetfulness. He wasn't even the sort of guy she wanted in her life and he never would be. He was too arrogant, too reserved, too quick to judge…but, my goodness, he knew how to kiss…

Fate had short-changed her, she thought resentfully. She was still a virgin because she had always been waiting to meet a man, who would make her crave more of his touch. She had wanted her first lover to be someone whom she desired and cared about. Unfortunately, desire had evaded her in the invasive groping sessions that had been her sad experience as a student. Even worse, she still remembered the emotional hurt inflicted by her father's abuse. How could she trust any man when her own father had attacked her? Jazz had been wary of the opposite sex ever since, even though she was now wishing she had a little more sexual experience because then she would have had a better idea of how to read Vitale and deal with him.

Had her crush on Vitale at fourteen made her more vulnerable? Jazz cringed at the suspicion and dismissed it because she hadn't actively thought about Vitale in years and years. He had only come to mind when she'd seen him in some glossy magazine, squiring some equally superior beauty at some sparkling celebrity event and, like Cinderella in real life, she thought sadly, she had known how impossible her dream had been at fourteen. He was what he was: a prince, born and bred to a life so different from hers that he might as well have been an alien from another planet. He wasn't a *happy* prince either, she thought with unwilling compassion. Even as an adolescent she had recognised that Vitale didn't really know what being happy was.

When she was informed that she had another coaching session late that afternoon, she was incensed to learn that it was in deportment. She put in the time with the instructor and then knocked on Vitale's office door.

'Yes?' Vitale looked up from his laptop and then sprang upright with the perfect courtesy that was engrained in him. Woman enters room: *stand*, she reflected ruefully, and it took just a little bit of the edge off her temper and the faint unease she had felt at seeing him again so soon after that kiss. It definitely didn't help, though, that he still looked gorgeous to her from the head of his slightly ruffled black hair down to his wonderful dark deep-set eyes that even now were clearly registering wariness. She knew exactly what he was thinking and almost grinned. He was still waiting to be attacked over the kiss.

'Deportment?' she queried drily instead. 'Don't you think that's overkill? I don't slouch and I can walk in a straight line in heels. What more do you want?'

His dark eyes flared gold and he tensed, reining back all that leaping energy of his. 'I thought it might be necessary but if it's not—'

'It's not,' Jazz cut in combatively.

'Then we can wave goodbye to that session,' Vitale conceded mildly, watching her walk across his office to look out of the window. She was wearing that damnably ugly skirt and heels again, but had he been of a literary bent he could have written a poem along the lines of what that cheap fabric did to the curve of her little rounded bottom where he had had both hands clasped only hours earlier. It had felt every bit as good and femininely lush as it looked, he acknowledged, thoroughly unsettled by that thought and the pulse at his groin. The effect she had on his body was like a kind of madness, he decided then in consternation.

'I have some questions about this bet and you may not think I'm entitled to answers,' Jazz remarked stiffly. 'Who are you planning to say I am at the ball?'

His winged ebony brows drew together in bewilderment. 'What do you mean?'

Jazz threw her shoulders back. 'Well, I assumed you'd be giving me a fake name.'

Vitale frowned, currently engaged in noticing how red and full her lips seemed, wondering if he had been rough because he had *felt* rough, drunk on lust and need, out of control. 'Why would I give you a fake name?'

'Because if I'm pictured with you anywhere the press might go digging and wouldn't they just love pointing out that the Prince has a housekeeper's daughter on his arm?' Jazz extended stiffly, gooseflesh rising in the claustrophobic atmosphere and the intensity of his gaze.

'*So?*' Vitale prompted thickly, acknowledging that kissing her had been one of the most exhilarating encounters he had ever had and cringing at the awareness. He was an adult man with a great sex life, he reminded himself doggedly. As Angel would say, he really needed to get out more.

'Doesn't that bother you?' Jazz asked in surprise.

'No. Why would it? I'm not foisting a fake personality or some sort of scam on the public. This bet is for private consumption only,' Vitale explained. 'There's nothing wrong with being a housekeeper's daughter.'

'No, there's not,' Jazz agreed with the glimmerings of her first real smile in his presence and the startling realisation that Vitale was not quite the snob she had believed he was. It was as if a giant defensive barrier inside her dropped and, disturbed by the discovery, she quickly turned to leave him alone again.

'Jazz…once you get clothes delivered tomorrow we'll be going out to dinner in the evening,' Vitale informed her, startling her even more. 'Your first public appearance.'

Dining out with Vitale, Jazz ruminated in wonder as she returned to her room, planning an evening composed of a long luxurious bath, washing her hair and watching something on TV.

CHAPTER FOUR

JAZZ COULDN'T SLEEP. Accustomed to a much more physically active existence, she wasn't tired and at two in
the morning she put the light back on and tried to read
until hunger took over and consumed her. She knew she
shouldn't but she loved a slice of toast and a hot drink
before bed and the longer she lay awake, the more all-
consuming the craving became. Inevitably she got up,
raising her brows at her appearance in the faded long
tee shirt she wore to bed. No dressing gown, no slip-
pers in her wardrobe but so what? If she was quiet she
doubted if she would wake up the very correct Jenkins.

The stairs creaked and she didn't like moving round
in total darkness but a light could rouse someone likely
to investigate. By touch she located the door at the
back of the hall and through that a flight of stairs,
which ran down into the basement area where she assumed the kitchen lay. Safely through that door, she
put on lights and relaxed. The kitchen was as massive
as a hotel kitchen and she padded about on the cold
tiles, trying not to shiver. She located bread and the
toaster and milk and then, wonder of wonders, some
hot-chocolate powder to make her favourite night-time
drink. Jazz was grateful she wasn't like her aunt, who

joked that she only had to look at a bar of chocolate to gain an inch on her hips.

Her toast ready, she sat down at the table to eat with appetite, eyes closing blissfully as she munched hot butter-laden toast, which was the first glimpse Vitale had of her as he strode barefoot through the door.

'You can't wander round here in the middle of the night!' he began impatiently. 'My security team wakened me.'

'Your security... *What?*' Jazz gasped, startled out of her life by the interruption and even more startled by the vision Vitale made bare-chested and barefoot, clad only in a pair of tight jeans. He was completely transformed by casual clothing, she conceded in awe.

Vitale groaned out loud. 'The whole house is wired with very sensitive security equipment and I have a full team of bodyguards who monitor it.'

'But I didn't see anything and no alarm went off.'

'It's composed of invisible beams and it's silent. As soon as the team established that it wasn't an intrusion but a member of the household they contacted me, not wishing to frighten you.'

'Well, I'm not frightened of you,' she mumbled round a mouthful of toast that she was trying to masticate enough not to choke when she swallowed because, in reality, Vitale was delicious shorn of his shirt and her mouth had gone all dry.

He was a classic shape, all broad shoulders, rippling muscular torso sprinkled with dark curls of hair leading down into a vee at his hips and a flat, taut stomach. Clothed she could just about contrive to resist him, halfnaked he was an intolerable lure to her eyes.

'They saw you on camera, realised that you weren't

fully dressed and surmised that the sudden intrusion of a strange man could scare you.'

'On *camera*?' she repeated in horror, striving to recall if she had scratched or done anything inappropriate while she was in the kitchen, bracing her hands on the table top to rise to her feet and move away from it.

Vitale shifted lean dark hands upward in a soothing motion. 'Relax, they've all been switched off. We're not being monitored right now.'

'Thank goodness for that,' she framed tremulously, the perky tips of her nipples pushing against the tee shirt below Vitale's riveted gaze. 'I only got up to get something to eat.'

'That's perfectly all right,' Vitale assured her thickly, inwardly speculating on whether she was wearing anything at all below the nightshirt or whatever it was. 'But for the future, I'll show you a button you can press just to let security know someone's wandering around the house and this won't happen again.'

'OK,' Jazz muttered, still shaken up at the idea that she had been watched without her knowledge by strange men.

Vitale ran a surprisingly gentle hand down the side of her downturned face. 'It's not a problem. You haven't done anything wrong,' he murmured sibilantly, his accent catching along the edges of his dark, deep, masculine voice.

A shocking flare of heat rose up from the heart of her as he touched her face and Jazz threw her head back in mortification, her green eyes wide with diluted pupils.

'Don't look at me like that,' Vitale framed hoarsely. 'You have the most beautiful eyes... You always did.

And I didn't intend to say that, don't know which random brain cell it came from.'

An overpowering need to smile tilted Jazz's tense lips because he sounded so stressed and so confounded by his own words. Beautiful eyes, well, that was something, her first and probably only ever compliment from Vitale, who worked so hard at keeping his distance. But he had touched her first, she reminded herself with faint pride in what felt vaguely like an achievement. Her body was taut as a bowstring and breathing was a major challenge as she looked up into dark, smouldering golden intensity. Ditto, beautiful eyes, she labelled, but she didn't really think women were supposed to say things like that to men so she kept quiet out of fear that he would laugh.

'*Troppa fantasia*... I have too much imagination,' Vitale breathed, being steadily ripped in two by the conflicting impulses yanking at him. He knew he should let her go and return to bed but he didn't want to. He was ridiculously fascinated that, even in the middle of the night and fresh from her bed with tousled hair, she looked fantastic. And so very different from the women he was used to, women who went to bed in make-up and rose before him to put on another face to greet the dawn, and his awakening, plastic perfect, contrived, artificial, everything that Jazz was not. Jazz was *real* right down to her little naturally pink toenails and that trait was incredibly attractive to him. With Jazz what you saw was literally what you got and there were no pitfalls of strategy or seduction lined up to trip him.

'I would never have thought it,' Jazz almost whispered, so painfully conscious of his proximity that the little hairs were rising on the back of her neck. 'You're a banker.'

'And I can't have an imagination too?' Vitale inserted with a sudden flashing smile of amusement that would have knocked for six the senses of a stronger woman than Jazz.

'It's unexpected,' she mumbled uncertainly, all of a quiver in receipt of that mesmerising, almost boyish grin. 'You always seem so serious.'

'I don't feel serious around you,' Vitale admitted, tiring of looking down at her and getting a crick in his neck. In a sudden movement that took her very much by surprise, he bent, closed his hands to her tiny waist and lifted her up. He settled her down on the end of the table. He was incredibly, ferociously aroused but Jazz seemed curiously unaware of the chemistry between them, almost innocent. No way could she be *that* innocent, he told himself urgently, because he would never touch an innocent woman and he desperately needed to touch her. His lovers were always experienced women, who knew the score.

'But then you never know what you're feeling,' Jazz quipped. 'You're not into self-analysis.'

'How do you know that?' Vitale demanded with a frown.

'I see it in you,' Jazz told him casually.

Vitale didn't like the conversation, didn't want to talk either. He spread his hands to either side of her triangular face and he tasted that alluring pink mouth with unashamed passion.

Jazz was afraid her heart was about to leap right out of her chest, her breathlessness as physical as her inability to think that close to him. She felt nebulously guilty, as if on some level her brain was striving to warn her that she was doing something wrong, but she absolutely refused to listen to that message when excitement was rushing like fire through her nerve endings. Her nipples tightened, her slender thighs pushing firmly together on the embarrassing dampness gathering at the apex of her legs.

'*Per l'amor di Dio...*' Vitale swore, fighting for control because he was already aching. 'What do you do to me?'

'What *do* I do to you?' Jazz whispered, full of curiosity.

She excited the hell out of him but he was too experienced to let that salient fact drop from his lips. 'You tempt me beyond my control,' Vitale heard himself admit regardless and was shocked by the reality.

'That's all right,' Jazz breezed, one hand smoothing up over a high cheekbone, the roughness of his stubbled jaw lending a brooding darkness to his lean, strong face in the dimly lit kitchen, her other hand tracing an exploring path up over the sweep of his long, smooth back. 'Are you sure those cameras are all off?' she framed, peering anxiously round the brightly lit kitchen.

'*All* of them,' Vitale stressed, but he strode back to the door to douse the strong overhead illumination, plunging them into a much more welcoming and more intimate space only softly lit by the lights below the cupboards.

Her hand slid back to his spine. His skin was hot, faintly damp but it was his eyes she was watching and thinking about, those beautiful black-fringed eyes singing a clear song of stress and bewilderment and the glorious liberating message that he wasn't any more in charge of what was happening between them than she was.

'I want you, *bellezza mia*,' he growled all soft and rough, sending shimmying awareness right down her taut spine just as he reached down and lifted her tee shirt and whipped it off over her head.

Jazz loosed a startled yelp and almost whipped her hands up to cover her naked body, but in that same split second of dismay she asked herself if she wanted to be a virgin for ever and if she would ever have the chance to have such a skilled lover, as Vitale was almost certain to be, again. And the answer to both questions was no. He wasn't going to want a shy woman, was he? And he had to know all the right moves to ensure the experience was good for her, hadn't he?

'You are *so* beautiful,' Vitale almost crooned, his hands rising to cup her delicate little breasts, which were topped with taut rosy tips that he stroked appreciatively with his thumb.

And that fast, Jazz had no desire to either cover up or breathe because the fabulous joy and satisfaction of being deemed beautiful by Vitale overwhelmed her. In gratitude, she stretched up to find his mouth again for herself, nibbling at his lower lip, circling slowly with newly discovered sensuality while all the time he was stroking and rolling and squeezing the peaks of her breasts that she had never known could be so responsive to a man's touch. Little fiery arrows were travelling down to the heart of her, making her hips shift and squirm on the table as the heat and tightness increased there. And then, with what felt like very little warning to her, a climax shot through her like an electric charge, making her cry out in surprise and pleasure.

'And as responsive as my most erotic dream,' Vitale husked, wrenching at the zip of his jeans.

A lean brown hand pried her legs apart while she was still in a sort of blissful cocoon of reaction. Vitale pulled her closer and tipped her back to facilitate his intentions. A long finger traced her entrance and eased inside. He uttered a hungry groan of appreciation because she was very wet and tight and then he froze. 'I'll have to take you upstairs to get a condom,' he bit out in frustration.

'I'm on birth control,' Jazz muttered helpfully. 'But are you...safe?'

'Yes because I've never had sex without a condom,' Vitale confided, but the temptation to try it without that barrier was huge. He tried to argue with himself but, poised between her legs, craving the welcome her slender, lithe body offered his raging arousal, he realised it was a lost battle for him before it even started.

With strong hands he eased her closer still and she felt him, hard and demanding against her most tender flesh, and both nerves and eagerness assailed her. Her whole body came alive with electrified longing as if that first redemptive taste of pleasure had ignited an unquenchable fire of need inside her. He sank into her by easy degrees, groaning something out loud in Italian as she buried her face against a satin-smooth brown shoulder, barely crediting she was making love with Vitale, every sense she possessed rioting with sensation, the very smell and taste of his skin thrilling her.

And then he slammed right to the heart of her and a stinging pain made her grit her teeth and jerk in reaction. Withdrawing a little, Vitale paused for an instant, pushing up her face and looking down at her with what appeared to be brazen incredulity, and she knew then that at the very least he suspected he had been her first lover and he wasn't pleased. But she ignored that unwelcome suspicion and wriggled her hips with feminine encouragement, watching him react and groan with a newly learned sense of empowerment.

'Don't stop,' she told him.

And for the very first time ever, Vitale did exactly as she told him. He sank deeper again, stretching the tender walls of her heated core with hungry thoroughness and, that instant of pain forgotten, Jazz craved his contact. He gave her more, picking up speed, hard and fast until he was pounding into her and her excitement climbed with his every fluid, forceful thrust. It was much wilder and infinitely more uninhibited than she had dimly expected from a man as reserved as Vitale; indeed it was passionately explosive. She reached another climax and her body convulsed around his, the whole world, it seemed, erupting around her as he shot her into a deeply erotic and exhilarating release. A faint ache pulled at her as he withdrew and zipped his jeans.

'Diavolo!' Vitale exclaimed, stepping back from her while she fumbled for her tee shirt and hurriedly pulled it on over her head with hands that felt clumsy and unable to do her bidding. 'Why the hell didn't you tell me you were a virgin?'

Fixing her face to a determined blank, Jazz slid off the table, only just resisting a revealing moan as discomfort travelled through her lower body. 'We're not having a post-mortem,' she parried sharply, mortification engulfing her in an unanticipated tide that threatened to drown her. 'You're not entitled to ask nosy questions.'

She had had sex on a kitchen table with Vitale and she couldn't quite believe it but she certainly knew she didn't intend to linger to discuss it!

For a split second of frustration, Vitale wanted to strangle her. Her hectically flushed face was mutinous and furious and she was pointedly avoiding looking at him, which annoyed the hell out of him even though he didn't understand why. After all, he didn't want a post-mortem either, didn't have a clue why or how what they had just done had happened and could think of at least ten good reasons why it *shouldn't* have happened.

He watched her limp across the tiled floor as if she had had a run-in with a bus instead of her first experience of sex and he felt hellishly guilty and responsible. He experienced a sudden, even more startling desire to scoop her up and sink her into a warm reviving bath... and then have sex with her again? As if that were likely to improve anything, he reflected sardonically, raking unsteady fingers through his tousled black hair. What the hell was wrong with him? His brain was all over the place and he couldn't think straight but he knew he had just enjoyed the best sex of his life and that was downright terrifying...

Jazz had informed Vitale that there would be no post-mortem but, seated in a bath at three in the morning, Jazz was unhappily engaged in staging her own. Had she actually thought of what they had done as 'making love'? Yes, she had and she was so ashamed of herself for that fanciful label because she really wasn't *that* naïve. It had been sex, pure and simple, and she knew the difference because she wasn't a dreamy teenager any longer, she was an adult. Or *supposed* to be, she thought with tears stinging the backs of her eyes and re-gret digging wires of steel through her shrinking body.

Of course, they would both pretend it hadn't hap-pened...a moment of madness, the mistake swiftly bur-ied and forgotten. After all, this was Vitale she was dealing with and he wasn't going to want to talk about it either. On that front, therefore, she was safe, she as-sured herself soothingly. It was his fault in any case—he had had no business parading around half-naked in jeans and tempting her into that insanity. She hugged her knees in the warm water and sighed. She had done a stupid, stupid thing and now she had to live with it and with Vitale for weeks and weeks, being all polite and standoffish, lest he think she was up for a repeat encounter. Running away or hiding wasn't an option.

A knock sounded lightly on the door and she almost reared out of the bath in her horror because she abruptly appreciated that Vitale was *not* running true to form. In a blind panic she snatched at a towel and wrapped it round her, opening the door the merest chink to say discouragingly, 'Yes?'

Vitale discovered that he was immediately pos-sessed by an impossibly strong urge to smash the door down and he gritted his teeth on yet another unfamil-iar prompting to act unreasonably and violently. 'Will you please come out? You have been in there for ages.'

From that point he wasn't the only individual val-iantly gritting teeth. Her flushed face frozen as he had never seen it before, Jazz emerged from the bathroom, noting that he had put on a black shirt. 'I didn't know you were waiting,' she said dulcetly, leaning heavily on her one and only elocution lesson.

'Look, don't go all girlie on me. I don't expect that

from you,' Vitale countered crushingly. 'I only want the answer to one question.'

Jazz tried to unfreeze a little and look normal, or as normal as she could feel being confronted by Vitale when she was wearing only a towel. 'OK.'

'Why is a virgin on birth control?' he asked gravely.

'I don't really think that's any of your business. It was for…well, medical reasons,' she told him obliquely, unwilling to discuss her menstrual cycle with him, her colour heightening until she felt like a beetroot being roasted and wanted to slap him for it.

'It will be very much my business if you get pregnant,' Vitale breathed witheringly.

'It's so like you to look on the dark side and expect the very worst,' Jazz replied equally witheringly. 'It's not going to happen, Vitale. Relax and go back to bed and please forget this ever happened for both our sakes.'

'Is that what you want?' Vitale wanted to rip off the towel and continue even though he knew she was in no condition to satisfy him again. It had nothing whatsoever to do with his brain. It was pretty much as if his body had developed an agenda all of its own and he couldn't control it.

'We just had a sleazy encounter on a kitchen table in the middle of the night. What do you think?' Jazz enquired saccharine sweet.

Vitale was receiving a strong impression that anything he said would be taken down and held against him. *Sleazy?* That single descriptive word outraged him. He swung on his heel, his lean, powerful body taut, and left the room and just as quickly Jazz wanted to kick him for giving up on her so easily. Her thoughts were a turbulent sea of conflict and confusion and self-loathing, sending her seesawing from one extreme to the other. No sooner was he gone than she wanted him back and she flung off the towel and climbed into bed, hating herself. It was so typical of Vitale to worry about the fact that he hadn't used contraception. Now he would be waiting on that axe to fall and that was a humiliating prospect, even though it also reminded her that she hadn't yet taken her daily pill. She dug into her bag and took it before switching off the light.

What was done was done and it had been amazing, she thought ruefully, but it was better not to think about that imprudent sudden intimacy that had changed everything between them. Now she was no longer thinking about Vitale as the boy he had once been, but Vitale, very much a man in the present and that switch in outlook disturbed her, made her fear that somewhere deep down inside her there was still a tiny kernel of the fourteen-year-old who had believed the sun rose and set on Prince Vitale Castiglione…

CHAPTER FIVE

'WOMEN MY AGE don't wear clothes like this,' Jazz was saying by late morning the next day, appalled by the vast collection of garments, all distinguished solely by their lack of personality. 'I'm not your future wife or one of your relatives. I'm supposed to be only a girl-friend. Why would I be dressed like an older woman?'

'I want you to be elegant,' Vitale responded, unimpressed by her reasoning. He wanted every bit of her covered up. He didn't want her showing off her shapely legs or her fabulous figure for other men to drool over. Recognising Angel's appreciation of the beauty Jazz had become had been quite sufficient warning on that score. 'I imagine you would prefer to show more flesh.'

That was the last straw for Jazz after a trying few hours of striving to behave normally when she did see Vitale between coaching sessions. Temper pushed up through her like lava seeking a crack to escape. 'Where do you get all these prejudices about me from?' she demanded hotly. 'I don't wear revealing clothes. I never have. And as you know I haven't got much to reveal!'

'You have more than enough for me, *bellezza mia*,' Vitale breathed half under his breath, heat stirring at his groin as he thought about the delectable little swells he had explored the night before.

Jazz flinched and acted studiously deaf in receipt of that tactless reminder. He was no good at pretending, she recognised ruefully. 'This stuff is all so bland,' she complained instead, fingering a pair of tailored beige trousers with a curled lip. There was a lot of beige, a lot of navy and a lot of brown. He was even biased against bright colour. 'If this is your taste, you certainly didn't miss out on a chance of fame in the fashion industry.'

Vitale reached a decision and signalled the stylist waiting at the far end of the very large room. 'Miss Dickens is in charge of the selections. By the sound of it, she will be ordering a more adventurous wardrobe,' he declared, watching the slow smile that lit up Jazz's piquant little face while smoothly congratulating himself on knowing when to ease up on exerting control. 'But pick out something here to wear tonight.'

Jazz chose a fitted navy dress and shoes and lingerie as well as a bag.

'Thanks!' she called in Vitale's wake as he left her alone with the stylist to share her own likes and dislikes.

His arrogant dark head turned in acknowledgement, brilliant dark-fringed eyes a fiery gold enticement, and desire punched her so hard in the chest that she paled, stricken that she could have made herself so vulnerable. Putting such pointless thoughts from her mind, she concentrated on choosing clothes and particularly on the necessary selection of a spectacular gown for the royal ball.

After asking for lunch to be served in her room she was free to go home and visit her family for a few hours, and it was a welcome break from the hothouse atmosphere of Vitale's imposing London home. Her mother and her aunt were baking and Jazz sat down with a cup of tea and tried to feel normal again.

But she didn't feel normal after she had put on the navy dress over the silk lingerie, her feet shod in hand-stitched leather sandals with smart heels. Although she had never bothered much with make-up she made a special effort with mascara and lipstick, knowing that that was one thing she did need that Vitale probably hadn't thought about: make-up lessons.

'No, I like you the way you are,' Vitale asserted, startling her in the limo on the way out to dinner. 'Natural, healthy. You have beautiful skin... Why cover it?'

Jazz shifted an uncertain shoulder. 'Because it's what women do... They make the most of themselves.'

Vitale studied her from his corner of the limo. She looked stunning, the dark dress throwing her amazing hair into prominence and emphasising her delicate figure and long slender legs. He willed his arousal to subside because he had made decisions earlier that day. He was going to step back, play safe, ensure that there was no more sex, no more blurring of the lines between them, but he only had to look at her to find his resolution wavering.

That had never happened to Vitale before with a woman. He had never succumbed to an infatuation, had always assumed that he simply wasn't the emotional type. His affairs were always cool and sexual, nothing extra required or needed on either side. Naturally he had been warned since he was a teenager that he would, in all likelihood, have to marry for dynastic reasons rather than love and he had always guarded himself on the emotional front. What he felt for Jazz was desire, irresistible burning desire, and there was no great mystery about that when it was simply hormones, he told himself soothingly.

A current of discreetly turned heads and a low buzz of comment surrounded their passage to their table in the wildly exclusive restaurant where they were to dine. Vitale's gaze glittered like black diamonds when he saw other men directing lustful looks at Jazz. For the moment, Jazz was *his*, absolutely his, whether he was having sex with her or otherwise, he reasoned stubbornly.

Jazz sat down, surveying the table to become belatedly grateful for Jenkins's lesson in cutlery clarification. 'So, tell me what you've been doing since you left school?' she invited him cheerfully. 'Apart from being a prince and all that.'

They talked about being students. Vitale admitted that banking had been the only viable option for him. He also told her that he had a house in Italy where he planned to take her before the ball.

'For how long?' she asked, her lovely face pensive in the candlelight, which picked up every fiery hue in her multi-shaded red mane of hair for his appreciation. 'I like to see my mother regularly.'

'A couple of weeks, no more. When this is over, *after* the ball—' Vitale shifted a fluid, lean brown hand in emphasis '—I will pay for you to finish your degree so that you can work in your chosen field.'

'That's a very generous offer but you're already covering quite enough in the financial line,' she began in surprise and some embarrassment.

'No. I tricked you,' Vitale divulged, disconcerting her even more with that abrupt confession of wrongdoing. 'My father is settling your mother's loans. He wanted to. It makes him feel that he has helped her.'

'You...*tricked*...me?' Jazz gasped in disbelief that he could quietly admit that.

'Being a bastard comes naturally. I needed you to accept the bet and I used *your* need for money to win your agreement,' Vitale pointed out levelly. 'I feel that I owe you that amount of honesty because you have been honest with me.'

'So, you're saying your father would *always* have helped?' Jazz prodded in even greater surprise because she wasn't, once she thought about it, that shocked to discover that Vitale could be extremely calculating and shrewd. She didn't, however, feel that she was in a position to complain or protest because if he had used her to suit his own purposes, she was also most assuredly using *him*. Having already received a discreet cheque in payment for her supposed salary, she had given it in its entirety to her mother. No, she wasn't proud that she had accepted money from a man she had also slept with, but she really could not bear to watch her mother scrimp and struggle. Being seriously poor had taught Jazz a lot of tough life lessons.

'Papa feels very guilty about your mother. He was concerned that there was a possibility of domestic abuse in your parents' marriage...' Vitale volunteered very quietly after their plates had been cleared away.

Jazz turned sheet white and her fingers curled into the tablecloth, scrunching it. 'There was,' she conceded, thrown back in time to a period she rarely revisited. 'My father was violent when life didn't go his way and he took it out on us.'

Vitale was appalled and then shocked that he was

appalled because he had heard of such situations, but then he had never personally known anyone who confessed to being a victim of domestic abuse. 'You…as well as your mother?'

'On several occasions when I tried to protect Mum. Poor Mum got the worst of it,' Jazz conceded heavily. 'Dad was hooked on online gambling and when he lost money he took it out on his family with his fists.'

A very real stab of anger coursed through Vitale at that news. He was remembering Jazz as a tiny child and a skinny teen and realising that she knew what it was to live in fear within a violent home where she should have been safe. His strong jawline was rigid. 'I'm sorry you had to go through that experience.'

Jazz pursed her lips and sighed. 'I think that was why Mum ran off with her second husband, Jeff. He was supposed to be her escape but he was more of a dead end. He wasn't violent, just dishonest. But you know, the older I get, the more I realise that many people have had bad experiences when they were young,' she told him in an upbeat tone. 'It doesn't have to define you and it doesn't have to hold you back and make you distrust everyone you meet. You can move beyond it. I know I have.'

Vitale stretched out a hand and squeezed hers to make her release the tablecloth and she laughed and let go of it when she appreciated what she had been doing, her lack of self-pity and her strength delighting him.

'I have the mother from hell,' he confessed unexpectedly. 'Controlling, domineering, very nasty. If she has a heart, I've never seen it. All she cares about is the Lerovian throne and all the pomp and ceremony that go with it.'

Jazz smiled, pleased that he trusted her enough to

admit that. 'You're very lucky to have such a pleasant father, then,' she pointed out.

'Sì...' Vitale confirmed, startled that he had spoken ill of his mother for the first time ever and quite unable to explain where those disloyal words had come from. There was something odd about Jazz that provoked him into acting against his own nature, he decided darkly. Maybe it was simply the fact that she was so relaxed in his company that she broke through his reserve. Was that why he was acting out of character?

As for the problem that was his mother, he had only told the truth, he reasoned ruefully. Sofia Castiglione was feared even by the royal household. It was not disloyalty to tell the truth, he acknowledged then, while marvelling that in admitting that salient fact to Jazz he felt some of his tension drop away.

Outside the restaurant, the limousine awaited them, two security guards forcing a man with a camera to back off. The flash of a photo being taken momentarily blinded her as Vitale guided her at speed back into the limo.

'Who is she?' another voice shouted.

'Who am I?' she teased Vitale with amusement as she settled back into her seat.

'A mystery redhead. I will not give out your name. I have no intention of doing the work of the paparazzi for them,' Vitale supplied, his attention locked to her small, vivid face, so pale against the backdrop of that mass of vibrant hair, fine freckles scattered across her diminutive nose. Hands off, he reminded himself doggedly even as he ached.

'Do you want a drink?' he enquired as they entered the house.

'No, thanks. I'm sort of tired,' she admitted, because she had had little sleep the night before, but she was not about to allude to that reality when Vitale was behaving like a perfect gentleman who had never once touched her. 'Goodnight.'

She kicked off her shoes inside her room, feeling oddly lonely, and wriggled down the zip on her dress to peel it off and hang it up with the care demanded by a superior garment. She stripped and freshened up before reaching for the silky robe she had taken from the clothes selection earlier that day and that was when someone rapped on the door and it opened almost simultaneously.

Vitale strode in, leant back against the door to close it again and said thickly, 'I don't want to say goodnight...'

Surprised in the act of frantically tying the sash on her robe closed, Jazz literally stopped breathing. Smouldering dark golden eyes assailed hers in an almost physical assault and her heart started banging inside her chest like a drum. 'But we—'

'We are both single, free to do whatever we like,' Vitale incised, suppressing every thought he had had, every decision he had made only hours earlier in favour of surrendering to the hunger that had flamed up inside him the instant she'd tried to walk away from him.

Air bubbled back into her lungs and she snatched in a sudden deep breath. *'But,'* she started afresh, inexplicably feeling that *she* had to be the voice of reason.

Vitale prowled forward with the grace of a jungle cat. 'Is there anyone else in your life?'

'Of course not. If there had been, last night wouldn't have happened,' she protested.

'Then I don't see a problem, *bellezza mia*,' Vitale proclaimed in a roughened undertone as he teased loose the knot in the sash in a very slow way. 'Let's keep it simple.'

Simple? But it *wasn't* simple, she wanted to scream while knowing that he was taking his time with the sash to give her the opportunity to say no if she wanted to. But she didn't want to say no, didn't want him to leave her again and that disturbing awareness shook her up. Her heart was thumping so hard she could've been in the last stage of running a marathon and all she could see was Vitale ahead of her, those scorching dark golden eyes with a black fringe of gold-tipped lush lashes that a supermodel would have envied. Somehow, *he* was her finishing line and she couldn't fight that, didn't have that amount of resistance when he was right there in front of her, wanting her, *needing* her, Jazmine Dickens, against all the odds...

He eased the robe off her slight shoulders and let it drop and when her hands whipped up to cover herself, he groaned and forestalled her, trapping her small hands in his. 'I want to see you, *all* of you.'

Her hands fell away, green eyes wide with uncertainty, and he lifted her up, threw back the covers on the bed and laid her down.

'You're wearing too many clothes,' she told him shakily.

Vitale dealt her a slanting grin that lit up his lean, darkly handsome features like the sunrise. He undressed with almost military precision, stowing cuff links by the bed, stacking his suit on a chair, peeling off snug black briefs that could barely contain his urgent arousal. A slow burn ignited in her pelvis, her nipples tinging into tight buds, a melting sensation warming between her thighs.

It was only sex, she bargained fiercely with the troubled thoughts she was refusing to acknowledge, only sex and lots of people had sex simply for fun. She could be the same, she swore to herself, she would *not* make the mistake of believing that what they had was anything more serious than a casual affair. That was what Vitale had meant when he said, 'Let's keep it simple…'

He joined her on the bed, all hair-roughened brown skin and rippling muscle, so wonderfully, fundamentally different from hers, the sexual allure of his body calling to her as much as her body seemed to call to him. He kissed her and the fireworks started inside her, heat and longing rising exponentially with every searing dip of his tongue inside the moist interior of her mouth.

Her entire body felt sensitised, on an edge of unbearable anticipation.

'I want to show you the way it should have been last night,' Vitale husked. 'Last night was rough and ready.'

'But it worked,' she mumbled unevenly, running a forefinger along the wide sensual line of his lips, revelling in the freedom to do so.

'You deserve more,' Vitale insisted, bending his arrogant dark head to catch a swollen pink nipple in his mouth and tease it. 'Much more…'

And much more was very much what she got as Vitale worked a purposeful passage down over her slender length, pausing in places she hadn't even known had nerve endings and dallying there until she was writhing in abandonment, before finally settling between her spread thighs and addressing his attention to the most sensitive place of all.

Self-consciousness was drowned by excitement, sheer physical excitement that she could not restrain. He used his mouth on her, circling, flicking, working her body as though it were an instrument and her pleasure grew by tormentingly sweet degrees until the tightness banding her pelvis became a formless, overwhelming need she could no longer withstand. When he traced the entrance to her lush opening, her spine arched and she cried out as a drowning flood of pleasure surged through her slight body and left her limp.

'Much better,' Vitale pronounced hoarsely, staring down at her enraptured expression with satisfaction. 'That's how it should have been the first time and if you'd warned me—'

'You probably wouldn't have continued,' Jazz interrupted, tying him back down to earth again with that frank assessment.

'You don't know that,' Vitale argued fierily, pushing back her slim thighs and sliding between them, the urgency in his lean, strong body unashamed.

Jazz looked up at him, wondering how she knew it, but know it she did even though it wasn't very diplomatic to drop it on him like that when he was so hopeless at grasping the way his own mind worked. 'I suspected it,' she admitted.

'Nothing short of an earthquake would have stopped me last night!' Vitale swore vehemently, finally surging into her moist, tender sheath with a bone-deep groan of appreciation. 'You feel glorious, *bellezza mia*...'

And the powerful surge of his thick, rigid length into her sensitive core felt equally glorious to Jazz, stretching the inner walls, filling her tight. Her eyes closed and her head rolled back on the pillow as she let the pulsing pleasure consume her. Ripples of delight quivered through her and she arched up her hips, helpless in the grip of her need. Nothing had ever felt so right or so necessary to her. He ground his body into hers and she saw stars behind her lowered eyelids. She began to move against him, hot and frenzied as he slammed into her, primal excitement seizing her with his heart thundering over hers. And then she reached a ravishing peak and rhythmic convulsions clenched her womb as he shuddered over her with an uninhibited shout of satisfaction. A rush of sensation washed her away in the aftermath of lingering pleasure.

'It's amazing with you,' Vitale gritted breathlessly, releasing her from his weight.

Jazz stretched out her arms and tried to snatch him back. 'Don't move away.'

'I'm not into hugging.'

'Tough,' Jazz told him, snuggling up to him regardless. 'I need hugs.'

Vitale's big body literally froze, tested out of his comfort zone.

'It's called compromise and we are all capable of it,' Jazz muttered drowsily against his chest, one arm anchoring round him like an imprisoning chain. 'I'm not telling you I love you because I *don't*. I'm just fond of you, so don't make a fuss about nothing.'

In a quandary, Vitale, who had been planning to return to his own room, lay staring up at the ceiling. He had to stretch away from her to switch off the light, but she hooked him back with the efficiency of a retriever picking up game even though from the sound of her even breathing he knew she was definitely asleep.

She was so blunt, he reflected helplessly, wondering if he should simply push her away to make it back to his own bed. He was relieved that she had no evi-

dent illusions about their relationship and wasn't thinking along the lines of love because he didn't want to
hurt her. Seducing a virgin was a dangerous game, he
acknowledged, wondering why she had still been un-
touched, wondering why he was even interested because
his interest in his lovers was usually very superficial.
He didn't quite know how he had ended up having sex
with her again and wondered if it mattered. He decided
it didn't and if he slept with her, he could have her again
in the morning, so staying put made very good sense...

'Could we just rough it for a night?' Jazz asked hopefully a week later.

Vitale frowned. 'Rough it?'

'Instead of going to some very fancy restaurant, we
could go to a supper club I know that does ethnic dishes.
It's cheap but the food's great.' Studying his unenthusi-
astic expression, Jazz grimaced. 'Vitale, just for once
can we go off the official map?'

'I don't follow an official map,' Vitale argued, meeting hopeful eyes and simply wanting to see the liveli-
ness return to her lovely face, which was telegraphing
her conviction that he would refuse her suggestion. 'All
right, just this once but if either of us get food poisoning, you're dead!'

'We're not going to get food poisoning,' she assured
him with a confident grin.

They ate a delicious and surprisingly elaborate five-
course meal in a private city garden and Vitale drank
out of a bottle without complaint and watched Jazz sparkle across the table. He was more relaxed than he could
ever remember being with a woman. She had so much
verve and personality he couldn't take his eyes off her

and the awareness that he was taking her home to bed gave him a supreme high of satisfaction.

A week later she dragged him out to the flower market on Columbia Road and he took a photograph of her, her slender figure almost lost in the giant armful of flowers he had bought her. They walked along the South Bank and he watched street performers entertain for the first time ever, laughing when she called him a stuffed shirt for admitting that.

'You can't always have been so sensible, so careful about everything you do and say,' she remarked with a frown.

'I learned to consider everything I did and said when I was very young,' Vitale confided. 'As a child, I was always trying to please my mother but eventually I gave up. I don't think she much likes children...or maybe it was only me.'

Jazz was shocked. 'You don't think she liked you even as a child?'

Vitale frowned. 'If being a queen hadn't demanded that she produce an heir I don't think she would ever have had children. I was a typical little boy—noisy, dirty and always asking inconvenient questions. She often cut short the time she was supposed to spend with me because I irritated her.'

'But you were only being a normal kid,' Jazz contended feelingly, catching his taut fingers in hers to squeeze them and gazing up at his shadowed features. 'That wasn't about you, it was about her and her flaws, not yours. Obviously she didn't enjoy being a mother but that wasn't your problem and you shouldn't let it make you feel guilty or responsible. You're an adult now and you don't need her the same way.'

That was certainly true, Vitale conceded, thinking back to his cold, distant relationship with his mother and his once childish efforts to improve it and win her approval. But as an adult he *knew* Sofia Castiglione now and he no longer expected her to change or tried to please her. Maturity had taught him that he was tough enough to get by on his own.

'I don't feel guilty,' he told Jazz, 'but I do get embarrassed when she treats people badly. When you're born into a privileged life like ours, you can't take it for granted and you can't afford to forget that you rule, not just by right of birth but only with the agreement and the support of the people.'

He was a deeper thinker than she had ever acknowledged and she was impressed by that distinction that he made. By the sound of it, his mother was a right old horror, she thought ruefully, annoyed that Vitale had clearly been so damaged by the wretched woman's inability to love her son. That night she lay awake for a long time, secure in the circle of Vitale's arms, thinking with warm appreciation of how tender he could be with her even though he had evidently had very little tenderness shown to him. He was so much more than he seemed on the outside...

'But I can't be... I'm flying to Italy tomorrow,' Jazz framed without comprehension because what she had been told had come as such a gigantic shock that every scrap of natural colour had drained from her rigid face.

'You're pregnant, around six weeks along,' the brisk female doctor repeated quietly.

'But I'm on the pill!' Jazz exclaimed shakily. 'How can I be pregnant?'

The doctor consulted her computer screen. 'I see you've been taking the mini pill for menstrual irregularity. Have you been careful to take it at the same time every day? It can be a little less effective as birth control than other methods. For contraceptive purposes, I would have recommended an implant.'

'The *same* time every day?' Jazz gasped in dismay.

'That information would've been in the instruction leaflet with the tablets.'

Jazz winced, acknowledging an own goal. 'I didn't read it.'

The doctor gave her a résumé of the various conditions that could make the birth-control pill less reliable and then added that nothing was one hundred per cent guaranteed to prevent pregnancy and that there was always a tiny proportion of women who still conceived regardless.

Jazz was in so much shock that she collided with someone as she left the surgery and spluttered an apology before she wandered aimlessly down the street into a café to sit with a cup of tea and contemplate her predicament. Vitale would go spare, that was all she could initially think. He might even think she had done it deliberately and had lied about being on the pill. Vitale was a naturally suspicious man when it came to women.

Other thoughts began to intrude. She was pregnant. She hadn't thought she could be when the nurse had asked for samples on her first visit to the surgery. No chance, she had cheerfully told the nurse, secure in her conviction that she could not conceive. But she had gone to the surgery in the first place because she was having troublesome symptoms. Very tender breasts, heartburn, occasional bouts of dizziness, increasing nausea and a sensitivity towards certain smells. Ironically she had suspected the pill, the only medication she took, might be causing those effects and had thought she might be offered another brand to try. Oh, dear heaven, what was she going to tell her mother? Her mother would be so disappointed in her daughter when she became a single parent...

Jazz heaved a distraught sigh, her eyes stinging madly. Peggy Dickens had always been very frank about the reality that *she* had had to get married back in the days in Ireland when a man was still expected to marry a pregnant girlfriend. She had admitted that she would never have married her daughter's father otherwise because she had already seen worrying evidence of his violent temper. Well, there would be no question of marriage to worry anyone, Jazz reflected limply. Vitale was highly unlikely to propose to a housekeeper's daughter, whom he had hired to fulfil a bet.

But Jazz also knew that she wanted her baby. Her baby, part of her *and* Vitale, which was an unexpectedly precious thought, she acknowledged. And it would be a royal baby too, she reflected, because Vitale *was* a prince. Although maybe her baby wouldn't be royal, she reasoned hesitantly, because their child would be born illegitimate. They were only involved in a casual sexual affair, she reminded herself with painful honesty, because on some level that truth made her feel ashamed, as though she secretly thought she had traded herself too cheaply. There was, after all, nothing solid or secure about their current intimacy. For the sake of the bet, Vitale had trotted her out to dinner several times and once to a West End showing of a new film. Only it still wasn't a *real* relationship, was it?

For six weeks, she had suppressed the wounding fear that she was merely a convenient sexual outlet for Vitale because she was living in the same house. The only time he didn't share her bed was when he was travelling on business or returning to Lerovia to appear at some royal function. Should she have kicked him out of bed?

A rueful smile tilted Jazz's generous mouth. Pride said one thing, her heart said another. She loved having Vitale in her bed and his uninhibited hunger for her delighted her. Was that why she had never once said no? He behaved as though he needed her and that made her feel special and important. Perhaps that fiery sexual intimacy wasn't very much to celebrate but it was certainly more than she had ever hoped to have with Vitale and it made her happy.

Now it seemed that she was paying the price for that freewheeling happiness. She must have conceived right at the beginning of their relationship, she reckoned heavily, to be already six whole weeks along. What was she going to do if he asked her to have a termination? She would simply have to tell him that she was very sorry but, while her pregnancy might be unplanned and inconvenient, she still wanted her child. *His* child too, she conceded wretchedly, digging out her phone to text him.

We need to talk when you get back tonight.

Problem?

Don't try to second-guess me.

She knew that if she wasn't careful he would dig and dig by text until he got it out of her, and it really wasn't something she was prepared to divulge remotely.

The phone pinged and kept on pinging with more texts. More questions for clarification, Vitale getting increasingly impatient and annoyed with her for her lack of response. Maybe she shouldn't have said anything at all, maybe that would have been more sensible. But Jazz had always suffered from the kind of almost painful honest streak that made immediate confession a necessity. She ignored her phone and stared down into her tea, feeling as if the world had crashed down on her shoulders because her discovery meant that she and Vitale were already over and done.

The end, she thought melodramatically because what little they had would not survive the fallout from a pregnancy that she already knew he didn't want.

'Leave your phone alone!' Sofia Castiglione, the Queen of Lerovia, snapped furiously at her son in the office of the royal palace. 'I want you to look at these profiles.'

Vitale resisted even glancing fleetingly down at the women's photographs lined up on his mother's glass desk and the neatly typed background info set beside each. Even a glance would encourage his mother's delusions and he refused to be bullied by her. 'I've already made it clear that I have no intention of getting married *any* time in the near future. It's pointless to play this game with me. It's not as though you want to step down from the throne. It's not as though we are in need of another generation in waiting,' he intoned drily.

'You are almost thirty years old!' his mother practically spat at him. 'I married in my twenties.'

'And think of how well that turned out,' her son advised sardonically, recognising that his mother appeared to dislike him even more now than she had disliked him when he was a child and wondering if that was his fault.

As a little boy he had found her scorn and constant criticism profoundly distressing. He had soon discovered that even when he excelled at something he did not receive praise. For a long time he had struggled to understand what it was about him that evidently made him so deeply unlovable. Did he remind her of his father? Or was it simply that she would have resented any son or daughter waiting in the royal wings to become her heir? Or was Jazz right and was it simply that his mother disliked children?

'Don't you *dare* say that to me!' the older woman launched in a tone of pure venom, her heavily Botoxed and still-beautiful face straining with rage. 'I did my duty and produced an heir and I expect *you* to do your duty now as well!'

'No, possibly in another ten years, *not now*,' Vitale spelt out with emphatic finality and strode out of the room to continue texting Jazz, whose refusal to reply was seriously taxing his already shredded temper.

CHAPTER SIX

'I SAW IT at the airport,' Vitale lied, because for some reason Jazz was staring at the very expensive snow globe he had bought her as though it had risen up out of hell accompanied by the devil waving a pitchfork.

Jazz could feel silly tears flooding her eyes, knew it was probably another side effect of pregnancy and inwardly cringed. Why now? Why now, this evening of all evenings, did he have to do something really thoughtful and generous? It was the snow globe to top all other snow globes too, she acknowledged numbly, large, gilded and magnificent, full of little flying cupids, whose wings looked suspiciously diamond-studded and, when you shook it, it rained golden snow rather than white. It put her Santa globe to shame, lowering it to plastic bargain-basement level.

'It's really, really beautiful,' she told him chokily because it was, it was divine, but even if it had been hideous she would have said the same because she was so touched that he had bought her a personal gift. The globe, unlike the new wardrobe and the jewellery he had purchased and insisted she wear, had not been given to facilitate her leading role in a bet to be staged at a royal ball. All of that was fake, like the fake accent she had picked up from the elocution and the knowledge of how to curtsy to royalty that she had learned. She was to pretend to be something she was not for Vitale's benefit.

'What's the matter with you?' Vitale demanded with a raw edge to his dark, deep voice. 'And why did you send me that weird text?'

Jazz's legs turned all weak and she dropped down abruptly on the edge of a sofa in the big imposing drawing room where she never ever felt comfortable because it was stuffed with exceedingly grand furniture and seats as hard as nails. 'Something's happened, well, actually it happened weeks ago although I didn't know it then,' she muttered in a rush. 'You should sit down and take a very deep breath because you're going to be furious.'

'Only my mother makes me furious,' Vitale contended impatiently, studying her with keen assessing eyes, picking up on her pallor and the faint bluish shadows below her eyes. 'Are you ill?'

Jazz focused on him, poised there so straight and tall and gorgeous with his blue-black hair, arresting features and wonderful eyes, and she snatched in a very deep breath. 'Not ill...*pregnant*,' she told him with pained reluctance.

Vitale froze, engulfed in a sudden ice storm. He stared back at her, his eyes hardening and narrowing, and she watched him swallow back hasty words and seal his mouth firmly shut again.

'No, you can say what you like,' Jazz promised him ruefully. 'No offence will be taken. Neither of us were expecting this development and I know it's bad news as far as you're concerned.'

'*Very* bad news,' Vitale admitted in shock, paler than she had ever seen him below his naturally bronzed complexion. 'You said you were on birth control. Was that a lie?'

'No, it wasn't,' Jazz assured him. 'But for whatever reason, although I didn't miss taking a single pill, I've conceived and I'm about six weeks in.'

'And we've only been together around seven weeks!' Vitale thundered, cursing in Italian only half under his breath, his lean hands coiling with tension. 'Right, the first thing we will do is check this out in case it's a false alarm.'

'It's *not* a false alarm,' Jazz argued but Vitale had already stalked angrily to the far end of the room to use his phone, where she listened to him talking to someone in fast and fluent Italian.

All of a sudden even the sound of his voice was grating on her because, within the space of a second, everything had changed in his attitude to her. His voice was now ice-cool and his gaze had blanked her because he was determined to reveal no normal human reaction beyond that '*very* bad news', which really, when she thought about it, said all that she needed to hear and know. He had seemed so relaxed with her before and now that was gone, probably never to return.

Vitale studied Jazz while he spoke to his friend and discomfiture lanced through him. No, it wasn't a deliberate conception, and he knew that because he trusted her, and there she sat as if the roof had fallen in on top of her and she wasn't a skilled enough actress to look like that if that wasn't how she truly felt. Pregnant? *A baby?* Vitale was shattered but, unlike his brother Angel, he wouldn't make the mistake of running away from his responsibilities. He also knew that Jazz was a devout churchgoer from a rural Irish Catholic background and that a termination was a choice she was unlikely to make. He would be a father whether he liked it or not. But, before he agonised over that truth and its consequences, he was determined to take her to see a gynaecologist, who was a close friend and could be trusted to be discreet.

'Giulio Verratti is a close friend, whom I've known since my teens,' he volunteered stiffly. 'He also has a private practice as a consultant gynaecologist here in London.'

In silence, Jazz nodded, resigned to his need for a second opinion.

'I'll feel happier if he confirms it,' Vitale completed grimly.

Jazz thought that that was the wrong choice of words because the taut, forbidding lines of Vitale's lean, strong face suggested he might never be happy again. Regret filled her to overflowing. Her announcement had destroyed their affair. It would have ended anyway after the royal ball, she reminded herself ruefully. There had always been a clock ticking on their relationship and the ball was now only a week away.

'Let's talk about something else,' Vitale suggested as he steered her out to the waiting limo.

'How can we?' Jazz exclaimed.

'How do you feel about this situation?' he shot at her without warning.

'I was devastated at first,' Jazz confided. 'But now I can't help being a little bit excited too… Sorry.'

'You don't need to apologise,' Vitale intoned. 'Obviously you like children.'

'Don't you?'

'It's not something I've thought about. It's something I assumed was light years away in the future,' he breathed tautly.

He had defrosted a tad and she wanted to reach for his hand but resisted the temptation, recognising that it was not a good moment. Only two nights back, he had slept with her in his arms all night, but those days were over, she thought sadly. In a casual affair, a pregnancy was divisive, a source of concern rather than celebration. He would want their child to remain a secret as well, she mused unhappily. He wouldn't want the existence of an illegitimate kid splashed all over the media. Would he want to be involved in their child's life in any way? Or would he hope that giving her money would keep her quiet and persuade her to accept that he could not play *any* sort of active paternal role?

Giulio Verratti was a suave Italian in his thirties with prematurely greying hair. They didn't even have to sit down in the waiting room before a nurse swept them into the consulting room and the gynaecologist explained the tests that could be done on the spot. The nurse shepherded Jazz off to perform the tests before Jazz returned to the plush consulting room where the results were passed to Giulio.

'You're definitely pregnant,' he announced.

Vitale's shuttered expression betrayed nothing to her anxious glance.

'I'm a little concerned by a rather high reading in your hCG,' he confided and he went on to offer her a transvaginal ultrasound, which could be more accurate at an earlier stage than a normal scan.

Vitale flinched. 'No. We won't put her through that unless it is strictly necessary for her health.'

'Are there any twins in your family?' Mr Verratti asked smoothly.

'Several,' Jazz volunteered. 'My grandmother and some cousins.'

'There's a strong possibility that this could be a multiple pregnancy and I'll do an ordinary ultrasound now to see if I can pick up the heartbeat or heartbeats yet,' the older man informed them calmly and he called the nurse to help Jazz prepare for the scan.

Gel was rubbed on her abdomen and a hand-held scanner was run over her. Eyes wide, she stared at the monitor and then she heard the very fast sound of the foetal heartbeat and Mr Verratti laughed with satisfaction. He pointed at the monitor to indicate two blurred areas that he said were her babies. 'You do indeed carry twins,' he assured her.

Twins? Vitale had never worked so hard at controlling his expression. *More* than one child? The bad news just got worse and worse, he conceded helplessly. But every cloud had a silver lining, he instructed himself grimly. There had to be a plus side to even this disaster, although he had yet to see it. He would gain the heir his mother was so keen for him to produce but to achieve that he would have to marry Jazz, an alliance that Queen Sofia, the supreme elitist, would never agree to. But then he was fortunate that he did not actually require his mother's consent to marry. She had always assumed that, somewhere in the Lerovian tomes of royal dynastic law, such a prohibition existed but Vitale knew for a fact that it didn't. He was free to marry whomever he liked even if, at that precise moment, he hadn't the slightest desire to get married to Jazz or any other woman.

And he blamed himself entirely for taking on that crazy competitive bet with his younger brother, Zac. What insanity had possessed him? Of all three of the brothers, Vitale was indisputably the sensible, steady one and yet look at the mess he was in now! Somehow, he had contrived to choreograph his own downfall by moving a young woman into his home, whom he couldn't keep his hands off, he thought with raw self-loathing and distaste. He had known from the outset that Jazz attracted him and he had still gone ahead, believing that he had vast self-discipline and learning differently very, very quickly.

And it was hardly surprising that it threatened to be a multiple pregnancy, he conceded even more grimly, considering that they had been having sex every night for weeks on end. Not once had he used a condom as an extra safeguard. His *own* mistakes, his own indefensible errors of judgement, piled up on top of Vitale like a multiple road crash and plunged him into brooding silence.

Jazz lay awake alone most of that night. Vitale had barely spoken after leaving Mr Verratti's surgery. He hadn't even come to say goodnight to her, indeed had been noticeably careful not to touch her again in any way. It was as if she now had a giant defensive forcefield wrapped round her. Or as if her sudden overwhelming attraction had just died the very instant he'd realised she was pregnant with twins. The truth of their predicament was finally settling in on him and of course, he was upset. But she had kind of—secretly—hoped he would come to her if he was upset, as he had one other night after a more than usually distressing argument on the phone with his shrewish mother. He had shared that with her and she had felt important to him in a different way for the first time.

A little less fanciful now, she sat up in bed and put on the light to study her gilded and very ornate snow globe and her eyes simply overflowed again, tears trickling down her cheeks while she sniffed and dashed them away and generally hated herself for being such a drip. She had got attached to him, hadn't she? She was *more than fond* of Vitale after so many weeks of living with him.

How had she felt as though they were tailor-made for each other when that was so patently untrue? She, a housekeeper's daughter, he, a royal prince? Would he even continue with the bet now? He wouldn't want her in the public eye again, she reckoned, wouldn't wish to be associated with a woman who would be looking very pregnant in a few months' time. When Mr Verratti had mentioned that provocative word, 'twins', Vitale had looked as though he had been hand sculpted out of granite. She had practically heard Vitale thinking that *one* child would have been quite enough to contend with. She recognised that she was getting all het up with no prospect of calming herself down again. Eventually sheer exhaustion made her sleep.

First thing the next morning, she found herself in the bathroom being horribly sick and that shift from nausea to actual illness felt like the last straw. Washing away the evidence, she examined her wan reflection in the mirror and decided she had a slight greenish cast that was not the tiniest bit attractive. The sore boobs squashed into a bra that had become too small didn't help either, she thought miserably as she got dressed, selecting jeans and a colourful top in the hope of looking brighter and less emotionally sensitive than she actually felt.

She walked slowly downstairs. Vitale appeared in the dining-room doorway.

'Breakfast… Join me,' he suggested in that same hatefully distant tone.

'I didn't want this development either,' she said in her own defence as she moved past him, avoiding looking at him quite deliberately.

'I think I know that,' he conceded curtly.

Her bright head flew up and she looked at him. *'Do you?'*

Exasperation flared in his forbidding gaze. 'Yes, but it doesn't change the situation.'

She supposed it didn't. He accepted that she wasn't guilty of intent but somehow she still felt that she was being held to blame. And possibly she *was* to blame, thinking about the instructions she had failed to read because at the time contraception had not been an issue she'd cared about or needed. She had assumed she was safe from conception when she wasn't but he had made the same assumption. What did it matter now anyway? He was right. A lack of intent didn't change anything.

She lifted a plate and helped herself to toast and butter, her unsettled stomach cringing at the prospect of anything more solid.

'Shouldn't you be having something more to eat?'

'I'm nauseous. That's why I went to the doctor in the first place,' she admitted stiltedly as Jenkins poured tea and coffee while Vitale simply ignored the older man's presence.

When the butler had closed the door on his exit, Vi-tale studied her and said flatly, 'We have to get married and quickly.'

Jazz stared back at him wide-eyed and stunned by incredulity at that declaration. 'That's ludicrous!' she gulped.

'No, it isn't. There is another dimension to this issue which you are ignoring but which I cannot ignore,' Vitale imparted coolly. 'The children you carry will be heirs to the throne of Lerovia with the firstborn taking precedence. If they are born illegitimate they *cannot* be heirs and I know that I don't want a child of mine in this world that feels cheated of their birthright because I failed to marry you.'

He was quite correct. Jazz had not considered that issue in any depth or how any such child would feel as he or she grew up and realised the future they had been denied by an accident of birth. She swallowed hard but still said, 'Be sensible, Vitale. You can't marry someone like me. You're a prince.'

'I don't think we have a choice. We'll get married very discreetly and quietly in a civil ceremony and keep the news to ourselves until after the ball,' Vitale informed her.

'You're still taking me to the ball?' she murmured in surprise.

'If you're going to be my wife, why wouldn't I take you?'

'But you don't *want* to marry me,' she pointed out shakily. 'And feeling like that it would be all wrong for both of us.'

Vitale dealt her a cool sardonic appraisal. 'We don't have to stay married for ever, Jazz. Only long enough to legitimise our children's birth.'

'Oh…' Jazz reddened fiercely, feeling foolish for not having recognised the obvious escape clause in his startling announcement that they should marry. He wasn't talking about a normal marriage, of course he wasn't. He was suggesting a temporary marriage for their children's sake followed by divorce, a relationship that would be, in its own way, as false as the role he had already prepared her to play at the ball as his partner.

'And there *is* a plus side for me,' Vitale continued smoothly. 'I get the heir my mother so badly wants me to have and there will be no pressure on me to marry a second time.'

Jazz had lost colour as the true ramifications of what he was proposing slowly sank in, but pride made her contrive an approximation of a smile. 'So, everybody gets what they want,' she completed tightly.

Everybody but me, she conceded painfully, forced to listen to how he wanted to marry her and then get rid of her again after profiting from her unintentional fertility. She was seeing the side of Vitale that she hated, that sharp-as-knives, cold, calculating streak that could power him in moments of crisis. And it chilled Jazz right down to the marrow bone.

Inside her chest her heart felt as though he had stuck an actual knife in it. Over the past weeks, she had become attached but *he had not*. For Vitale, she had been a means to an end, a convenient lover, not someone he valued in any more lasting way. Now he planned to make the best of a bad situation and marry her to legitimise the children she carried. That would benefit him and it would benefit their children as well. But there would be no benefit for Jazz in becoming Vitale's temporary wife. Continued exposure to Vitale's callous indifference would only open her up to a world of hurt. And what on earth would it be like for her to become a member of a *royal* family? Ordinary women like her didn't marry princes, she reflected with a sinking stomach. How the heck could she rise to the level of a royal?

But, seriously, what choice did she have? She didn't have the luxury of saying no to what was surely the most unromantic proposal of marriage that had ever been voiced by a man. How could she deny her unborn twins the right to become accepted members of the Lerovian royal family? That would be a very selfish thing to do, to protect herself instead of securing her children's future. And she could see that Vitale had not a doubt that she would accept his proposal, which made her want to throw a plate of really messy jelly at him. All those years being chased by princess-title-hunters hadn't done him any favours in the ego department. Evidently, he believed he was a hell of a catch, even on a temporary basis. Below her lowered lashes, her green eyes flared with slow-burning anger. He was rich and handsome and titled. He put in a terrific performance in bed and bought a good snow globe. But really, what else did he have to offer? Certainly not sensitivity, anyhow.

'We'll be married within a few days.'

Vitale dealt her an expectant appraisal as if he was hoping she would jump about with excitement or, at the very least, loose an unseemly whoop of appreciation. Cinderella got her Prince Charming—*not*, she recognised angrily. He hadn't even asked her if she wanted to marry him because he took assent for granted. And why not? The marriage wouldn't last any longer than possibly eighteen months and then he would be free again, free of the housekeeper's daughter and her baggage.

'My babies live with me,' Jazz declared combatively, lest he be cherishing any other sort of plan for their children. 'I raise my children.'

Vitale lifted and dropped a broad shoulder, the very picture of nonchalance. 'Of course. I believe you have an elocution lesson now.'

Jazz flushed in surprise. 'I'm to continue with those lessons?'

'Naturally. For a while at least you'll have public appearances to make in your role as my wife. Your pregnancy, though, will eventually make it easier to excuse you from such events,' he pointed out calmly.

'You really do have it *all* worked out.' Jazz rose stiffly from her seat and walked out of the room without a backward glance.

Vitale gritted his even white teeth in frustration. He would never understand women if he lived to be a thousand! What was wrong with her now? Why was she sulking? Jazz didn't sulk. She was never moody. He liked that about her. So, what was the problem?

During a long, sleepless night he had contrived to find the silver lining in their predicament and he had been satisfied with the solution he had chosen. Why wasn't *she* delighted? He was willing to marry her, jump through all the hoops he had always avoided, just for her benefit and the twins'. OK, his wide sensual mouth curled, he wasn't saying that there wasn't *anything* in the arrangement for him. Jazz officially in his bed would be a personal gain, a sort of compensation for the pain and sacrifice of getting shackled at a mere twenty-eight years old to a woman his mother would despise and attack for her commonplace background. Anger flooded him. What more could he do in the circumstances?

On the morning of Jazz's wedding day, three days later, sunshine flooded into the apartment living area but she still didn't feel the slightest bit bridal. Sworn to secrecy, her mother and her aunt were attending the ceremony, but the very fact that Vitale had not asked to meet her family beforehand only emphasised to Jazz how fake their wedding would be. Angel and his wife, Merry, were to attend as witnesses.

In the preceding three days, Jazz had gone shopping for the first time armed with a credit card given to her by Vitale. She had got fitted for new bras and had picked an off-white dress and matching jacket to wear. But it had not been a happy time for Jazz. Her mother, Peggy, had been distraught when Jazz had announced that she had fallen pregnant by Vitale. It had taken her daughter and her sister's combined efforts to persuade the older woman that Jazz's pregnancy did not have to be viewed as a catastrophe when Vitale was about to marry her. Naturally Jazz had not even hinted to either woman that Vitale was not planning on a 'for ever' marriage.

That, for the moment, was her secret, her private business, she thought ruefully, but pretending for the sake of her mother and her family that Vitale genuinely cared enough about her to *want* to marry her cost her sleep. Her bouts of sickness had become worse and when, the second evening, Vitale had walked into her bedroom and found her being horribly ill in the bathroom he had insisted on asking his friend, Giulio, to make a house call. Mr Verratti had told her that the excessive sickness was probably the result of her twin pregnancy, warned her about the danger of dehydration and given her medication that would hopefully reduce the nausea. None of those experiences had lifted Jazz's low spirits or the horrible feeling of being trapped in a bad and challenging situation over which she had no control.

'How do you feel?' was Vitale's first question when they met at the register office, because Peggy Dickens had begged her daughter to spend that last night at home in her aunt's apartment, which had meant, traditional or otherwise, that Jazz had had very little sleep resting on a lumpy couch after having enjoyed the luxury of a bed of her own for weeks.

'I'm fine,' she lied politely, turning to greet Angel, who was smiling, and then be introduced to his glowing dark-haired wife, who was wonderfully warm and friendly. But Jazz went red, just knowing by the lingering look Angel gave her that he knew she was pregnant as well and she felt humiliated and exposed while wondering if Angel's wife was being so nice because she pitied her.

'I should have said that you look amazing in cream,' Vitale said hastily, as if belatedly grasping that that was more what people expected from a bridegroom than an enquiry about her health.

Not so amazing that he had felt any desire to so much as kiss her since her pregnancy announcement, Jazz reflected bitterly. But then Vitale, trained from childhood to say the right thing at the right time, couldn't always shake off his conditioning. In the future, she expected him to treat her with excessive politeness and distance, much as he had been treating her since she had told him she had conceived. And it hurt Jazz, it hurt much more even than she had thought it would to live with that forbidding new chill in his attitude towards her. It was as if Vitale were flying on automatic pilot and she was now a stranger because all intimacy between them had vanished.

If only she could so easily banish her responses, she thought unhappily, studying Vitale where he stood chatting with his brother and his wife. Vitale was a devastatingly handsome male distinguished by dark golden black-fringed eyes that sent heat spiralling through her pelvis, which made her avert her eyes from him uneasily. Her body still sang and tingled in his presence, all prickling awareness and sensual enthusiasm, and it mortified her, forced her to crave the indifference he seemed to have embraced with ease.

The wedding ceremony was short and not particularly sweet. For the sake of their audience, Jazz kept a determined smile on her lips and studied the plain platinum ring she had been fitted for only the morning before. She was also thinking about the very comprehensive prenup she had signed an hour after that ring fitting and her heart was still sinking on that score. That document had even contained access arrangements for their unborn children and a divorce settlement. Reading that through to the end had been an even more sobering experience. Vitale had thought of everything going into their temporary marriage and he had taken every possible precaution, so it was hardly surprising that any sense of being a bride escaped her.

'Give him time,' Angel urged her in an incomprehensible whispered aside before he departed with his wife, after a brief and extremely formal lunch at an exclusive hotel with her family. 'He's emotionally stunted.'

Vitale joined his bride in the limo that was taking them to the airport and their flight to Italy for a long weekend preceding the ball and said, 'It's completely weird seeing Angel like that with a woman.'

'Like what?' Jazz prompted.

'Besotted,' Vitale labelled with a grimace. 'Didn't you notice the way he kept on touching her and looking at her?'

'I noticed that they seemed very happy together.'

'They started out like us. Merry had Angel's daughter last year and at first Angel didn't want anything to do with either of them and now look at them,' Vitale invited in apparent disbelief. 'Already hoping for another child some day, he told me...'

Jazz perked up... Well, it was an encouraging story. 'Fancy that,' she remarked lightly.

'I wouldn't ever want to feel that way,' Vitale admitted.

'Why not?' she asked boldly.

The silence dragged and she thought she had got too personal and that he wasn't going to answer her.

But Vitale was grimacing. 'I saw my father crying once. I was very young but it made a big impression on me. He explained that he wouldn't be living with my mother and I any longer. They were splitting up. At the time, I didn't really understand that but later, when I looked back, I understood. I don't know why they divorced but I don't think it was related to anything Papa did. He was heartbroken.'

Jazz winced but persisted. 'Didn't you ask him why they broke up?'

'I never liked to. I was afraid of upsetting him. He's a very emotional man.'

But Jazz was thinking of Vitale as a little boy seeing his father distraught over the loss of a woman. Had that disturbing glimpse put Vitale off falling in love? After all, he already had a mother in his life who must surely have damaged his ability to trust women. Exposed to Charles's heartbreak, Vitale must always have tried to protect himself from getting too attached to a woman. After all, the very first woman he had been attached to, *his mother*, had rejected him.

'I should have invited Papa today and he'll be hurt that I left him out but I didn't want to get him involved in our predicament,' Vitale continued.

And that's the reward you get for digging where you shouldn't, Jazz told herself unhappily. Vitale knew their marriage would be a short-lived thing and that was why he had left his father out. 'Did you tell Angel the truth?' she asked, even though she felt that she already knew the answer to that question.

'*Sì...*' Vitale confirmed quietly. 'I have no secrets from Angel.'

'Apart from the bet,' she reminded him.

And disconcertingly, Vitale laughed at that reminder with genuine appreciation. 'I felt it was so juvenile to try and one up Zac that I was embarrassed. I don't know what got into me that day at my father's office. Or that day when you told Angel about the bet. I was in a very bad mood.'

In the days that followed that meeting with Angel at Vitale's house Jazz had come to suspect that Vitale had been angry because he had misinterpreted her friendly ease with his older brother as flirtation, forgetting that when they were kids Angel had been as much her play-mate as he had been. She had thought, even *hoped* that Vitale was possessive of her attention and jealous. Now she knew better, she thought wryly.

Feeling like a wet weekend, she stepped onto her first private jet, stunned by the opulent interior and the spaciousness of the cabin.

'There's a bedroom you can rest in at the far end,' Vitale told her helpfully as he opened up his laptop, evidently intending to work.

'I might just do that,' she said tartly since it seemed to her that he was hoping to be left in peace.

She kicked off her shoes, and removed her jacket and lay down on the comfortable bed and slept like a log. Vitale remembered it was his wedding day when he was warned that the flight was about to land and he strode into the sleeping compartment to wake Jazz.

She looked so small and fragile lying there that he was taken aback because Jazz always seemed larger than life inside his head. Not since she got pregnant though, he reflected grimly. That had changed every-thing for them both as well as adversely affecting her health. Giulio had advised him to be very careful be-cause a multiple pregnancy was both more dangerous and more likely to result in a miscarriage and one could not be too careful either with one's wife or with chil-dren, one of whom would be the next heir to a throne. Blasted pregnancy, Vitale thought bitterly, because he could see how wan and thin she was already. Her ap-petite was affected…her mood was affected. Nothing was the same any more and he missed her vivacity and spontaneity.

Jazz wakened with a start to find Vitale bent over

her, his stunning dark golden eyes grim as tombstones.
In haste, she edged back from him and sat up.

'We're about to land. You'll have to come back out,'
he warned her.

'I must've been more tired than I appreciated,' she
muttered apologetically while wondering if her absence
had even registered with him.

CHAPTER SEVEN

ONE OF VITALE'S security team drove the four-wheel-drive up what Vitale assured her was the very last twisting, turning road because Jazz was carsick and they had to keep on stopping lest she throw up. It made her feel like an irritating young child and the politer Vitale was about the necessity, the more exasperated she suspected he was. So much for the honeymoon she had assured her family he was taking her on, even if events had conspired to ensure they only got to take a long weekend in Italy before the royal ball in Lerovia. It would be the honeymoon from hell, she decided wretchedly.

And then the car turned down a leaf-lined lane and way at the top of that lane lay the most beautiful house she had ever seen. Not as big as she had expected, not extravagant either. It was a sprawling two-storey farmhouse built in glorious ochre-coloured stone that was colouring into a deeper shade below the spectacular setting sun above. It was surrounded, not by a conventional garden, but by what looked very like a wildflower meadow and the odd copse of leafy trees.

'It's gorgeous,' she said, speaking for almost the first time since she had left the plane about something other than an apologetic reference to the reality that she felt ill again.

Vitale sprang out of the car and opened the passenger door with a flashing smile that disconcerted her, his lean, darkly handsome features appreciative. 'I thought you mightn't like it,' he admitted. 'It's not luxurious like the town house or the palace. It's more of a getaway house.'

'It'll probably still be fancier than I'm used to,' Jazz pointed out, simply relieved that he was acting human again instead of frozen.

A light hand resting at her spine, Vitale walked her down the path and into a hall with a polished terracotta tiled floor. Jazz shifted away from him again to peer through open doors, registering that the furnishings were simple and plain, not a swag nor any gilding in sight, and she relaxed even more, smiling when Vitale called her back to introduce her to the little woman he called Agnella, who looked after the house. Jazz froze to the floor when Agnella curtsied to her as if she were royalty.

'Why did she do that?' she asked Vitale as they followed their driver and their luggage up the oak staircase.

'Because you're my wife and a princess even though I don't think you quite feel like one yet,' Vitale suggested. 'I'm afraid you'll have to curtsy to my mother every time you see her because she's a stickler for formal court etiquette. When I'm King, which is a very long way away in my future,' he admitted wryly, 'I will modernise and there will be a lot less bowing and scraping. Unfortunately, the Queen enjoys it too much.'

'Is that so?' Jazz encouraged, stunned by his sudden chattiness.

'Yes, the monarchy in Lerovia would never be described as one of the more casual bicycling royal families,' Vitale admitted with regret. 'Life at the palace is pretty much the same as it must have been a couple of hundred years ago.'

Jazz pulled a face. 'Can't say I'm looking forward to that. How on earth is your mother going to react to me?' she prompted anxiously.

'Very badly,' Vitale told her bluntly. 'I intend to break that news by degrees for your benefit. You'll be attending the ball as my fiancée.'

'Fiancée?' Jazz repeated in surprise. 'How… For *my* benefit?'

'My mother is likely to go off in an hysterical rant and she can be very abusive. I don't want to risk her throwing a major scene at the ball and I'm determined to protect you from embarrassment. I'll tell her after the ball that we are already married but not with you present. Be assured that, whatever happens, *I* will deal with the Queen.'

Merely inclining her head at that unsettling information about the kind of welcome she could expect from his royal mother, Jazz walked into a beautiful big bedroom with rafters high above, a stripped wooden floor and an ancient fireplace at the far end. In the centre a bed festooned in fresh white linen sat up against an exposed stone wall while a windowsill sported a glorious arrangement of white lilac blossoms. 'I really love this house. Can't you just imagine that fire lit in winter? You could add a couple of easy chairs there and use that chest by the wall as a coffee table.'

Vitale blinked in bewilderment, stealing a startled glance at her newly animated face. 'What a great idea,' he intoned, although he had never in all his life before thought about interior décor or furniture. 'We could go shopping for chairs.'

'Could we?' A little of her animation dwindling, Jazz wondered why she was rabbiting on as if he were truly her husband and the farmhouse their home and her colour heightened with embarrassment. 'I was just being silly and imaginative,' she completed, kicking off her shoes and settling down on the side of the low bed because she was tired, worn down by her stress and her worries.

'We'll look for chairs. I hired a designer to do the basics here and never added anything else,' Vitale repeated a shade desperately, keen to keep the conversation afloat even if he had to talk about furniture to do it. He could not stand to see Jazz look so sad and her interest in the farmhouse had noticeably lifted her mood for the first time that day. Considering that it had been their wedding day, Vitale felt very much to blame. 'I didn't really have the time to think about finishing touches but I'm grateful for any advice.'

'I'm sure you could hire another interior designer,' Jazz told him quellingly, recalling the wealth of the male she was addressing and feeling even more foolish.

'I'd prefer you to do it,' Vitale asserted in growing frustration, having watched her face dim again as though a light had been switched out. 'You won't make it too grand.'

'Well, no,' Jazz agreed dulcetly. 'I have no experience of grand, so I could hardly make it that way.'

He watched her slight shoulders slump again and

strode forward. 'Would you like to wear your engagement ring?' he asked with staggering abruptness.

'My...*what*?'

Eager to employ any distraction available to him,
Vitale dug a ring box out of his pocket and flipped it
open, it being his experience that women loved jewellery. Although, as he extended the opulent emerald and
diamond ring, he was belatedly recalling that Jazz had
been annoyingly reluctant even to accept the basics like
a gold watch and plain gold stud earrings from him.

'Lovely,' Jazz said woodenly, making no move to
claim the ring.

Vitale's strong jawline squared with stubborn determination. He lifted her limp hand and threaded the
diamond ring onto her finger until it rested up against
her wedding ring. 'What do you think?' he was forced
to prompt when the silence stretched on even after she
had snatched her hand back.

'Stunning,' Jazz said obediently since she could see
it was expected of her.

'It is yours. I'm not going to ask for it back!' Vitale
launched down at her with sudden impatience, wondering if that was the problem. 'When we split up, everything I have given you is yours!'

Instead of being reassured, Jazz flinched and rose
upright in a sudden movement, colour sparking over
her cheekbones. 'And isn't that a lovely thing to say to
me on our wedding day?' she condemned sharply. 'Of
course, it wasn't a *real* wedding day, was it?'

Thoroughly taken aback by her angry, aggressive
stance, Vitale stared at her with bemused dark eyes. 'It
felt real enough to me.'

'But it *wasn't* real! Did you think I was in any danger of forgetting that for a moment? Well, don't worry yourself! I wasn't in danger of forgetting for a *single* moment. I had no wedding dress. You haven't touched me since I told you I was pregnant, not even to kiss the bride! I know it's all fake, like the stupid wedding ring and the ceremony and now an even stupider engagement ring. You don't *want* to be engaged or married to me. Did you think that little piece of reality could possibly have escaped my notice?' she demanded wrathfully at the top of her voice, which echoed loudly up into the rafters.

'I didn't want to be engaged or married to anyone,' Vitale confessed in a driven undertone while he tried to work out what they were arguing about. 'But if I have to be, you would definitely be my first choice.'

'Oh, that makes me feel *so* much better!' Jazz flung so sarcastically that even Vitale picked up on it.

Instantly Vitale regretted admitting that he hadn't wanted to be engaged or married to anyone. Was that quite true though? He had looked at Jazz throughout the day and had felt amazingly relaxed about their new relationship. But obviously, not kissing his bride had gone down as a big fail, but then Vitale had never liked doing anything of that nature in front of other people.

'I was trying to compliment you.'

'News flash…it didn't work!' Grabbing up a case from her collection of brand-new matching designer luggage, Jazz plonked it down on the bed.

'You're pregnant and you're not supposed to lift heavy things!' Vitale raked censoriously at her.

Jazz ignored him, ripping into the case, carelessly tossing out half the contents and finally extracting a robe. 'There'd better be a bath in there for me to soak

in,' she muttered, stalking across the floor to the ajar
door of the en suite, checking that there was and then
recalling that she didn't have her toiletries.

In a furious temper she went back to check the luggage and, still finding the all-important bag missing,
left the bedroom to go back downstairs and see if it had
been left in the car.

Vitale released his breath in an explosive surge, genuinely at a loss. Somehow everything was going wrong.
He had been too honest with her. He should never have
mentioned splitting up or her keeping the jewellery.
Angel had said women were sentimental and sensitive
and all of a sudden that prenuptial agreement he had
settled in front of her loomed like a major misjudge-
ment. He had to turn things around but he hadn't a clue
how and he sprang up again, concentrating on the overwhelming challenge of needing to please a woman for
the first time in his life.

The bath, he thought, and then he had it, the awareness of her love of baths prompting him. He grabbed
the flowers on the window sill up and strode into the
bathroom like a man on a mission.

Hot, perspiring and cross as tacks after having to lo-
cate their driver and interrupt him at his evening meal
to gain access to the bag that had been left in the car,
Jazz made it back into the bedroom, which was comfortingly empty because she had had enough of Vitale for one day. She got to keep the jewellery, yippee,
big wow there if she was a gold-digger but, sadly, she
wasn't. She had wanted to keep *him*, not the jewellery,
which was the sort of thought that tore Jazz apart inside and made her feel humiliated because Vitale had

made it very clear that *he* did not want to keep *her*. She undressed and slid on the robe.

Entering the bathroom, Jazz was sharply disconcerted to find it transformed. The bath had already been run for her and candles had been lit round the bath, turning it into a soothing space while the lilac blossoms exuded a pale luminous glow in one corner. Rose petals floated on the surface of the water and she blinked in disconcertion at the inviting vision. Vitale? No, she decided. He wasn't capable of making that kind of romantic effort. She tested the water, found it warm and, with a shrug, she dropped the robe and climbed in.

Vitale pushed open the door, relieved she hadn't locked it, and extended a wine glass to her.

At the intrusion, Jazz jerked in surprise, water sloshing noisily around her slight body as she raised her knees automatically to conceal herself in a defensive pose. 'What are you doing?' she exclaimed, her voice sharp, accusing.

'Trying,' Vitale retorted curtly. 'Maybe I'm not very good at this.'

'*You* ran my bath, lit the candles?' Jazz gasped, wide-eyed with astonishment.

Vitale crouched down by the side of the bath, far too close for comfort, dark golden eyes enhanced by curling gold-tipped lashes stunningly intent on her flushed face. 'You're my wife. This is our wedding day. You're sick and you're unhappy. Isn't it believable that I would try to turn that around?'

Her soft pink mouth opened uncertainly and then closed again, her lashes fluttering up on disconcerted green eyes. 'You don't usually make any effort,' she pointed out somewhat ungraciously.

'Situations change,' Vitale reasoned, speaking as though every word he spoke might have a punitive tax imposed on it and he were being forced to keep speech to the absolute minimum.

'I suppose they do,' Jazz muttered, accepting the glass. 'You know I can't drink this?'

'It's non-alcoholic,' he informed her.

Jazz sipped the delicious ice-cool drink and suddenly laughed with real amusement, startling herself almost as much as him. 'It's homemade lemonade!'

'My cousins visit me here occasionally. They have children and Agnella always likes to be prepared. She was my nurse when I was a child,' he confided. 'My mother sacked her when she reached a certain age because she prefers a youthful staff but Agnella wasn't ready to be put out to grass. She and her husband look after this place for me.'

'You're making your mother sound more and more like an evil villain,' Jazz whispered, for the bathroom with little flames sending shadows flickering on the stone walls was as disturbingly intimate as Vitale's proximity.

Vitale lifted and dropped a wide shoulder in silent dismissal. His jacket and tie had vanished but he hadn't unbuttoned his collar and, without even thinking about it, Jazz stretched out her hand and loosened the button, spreading the edges apart to show off his strong brown throat. 'There, now you look more relaxed,' she proclaimed, colouring a little at what she had done. 'Everything's changed, Vitale.'

'*Sì*…but we're in this *together*,' Vitale reminded her with gruff emphasis.

'Obviously,' she conceded. 'But I don't know where we go from here.'

'*We* don't have to change,' he argued with a sudden vehemence that disconcerted her. 'We can go on exactly the way we were in London.'

'I don't think so,' Jazz declared, her heart quickening its beat with a kind of panic at how vulnerable that would make her, to continue as though she didn't know her happiness was on a strict timeline with a definite ending. She had to protect herself, be sensible and look to the future. Continuing what they had shared before now looked far too dangerous. 'I mean, since the moment I announced that I was pregnant, you backed off like I'd developed the bubonic plague.'

'Giulio warned to be careful with you.'

'Giulio? Mr Verratti?' she queried. 'He *told* you not to touch me? That we couldn't have sex?'

Vitale frowned. 'No, only to be *careful* and you were so obviously tired and unwell I respected the warning. Naturally, I left you alone,' he confided grittily. 'I didn't want to be selfish and I am naturally selfish and thoughtless. I was raised to always put myself first in relationships, so I have to look out more than most to avoid that kind of behaviour.'

He was so serious in the way in which he told her that that it touched Jazz. He knew his flaws, strove to keep them under control, didn't trust in his senses to read situations, never thought of explaining himself, simply strove to avoid the consequences of doing something wrong. It was a very rudimentary approach to a relationship and almost certain to result in misunderstandings. Jazz studied the disturbingly grave set of his lean, darkly handsome features and stroked her fingers down the side of his sombre face, fingertips brushing through a dark shadow of prickly black stubble.

'If you're coming to bed with me, you need a shave,' she told him softly, knowing she couldn't fight the way she felt at that moment, the yearning that was welling up from deep inside her to be with him again.

Right at this moment, Vitale was hers, and maybe she would never have more than a few fleeting moments feeling like that but did that mean she shouldn't have him at all? Yes, it would hurt when it ended but why shouldn't she be happy while she still could be? Wasn't trying to prepare for the end of their relationship now simply borrowing trouble?

Stark disconcertion had widened Vitale's dark gaze, letting her know that sex had not actually been his goal for once and Jazz smiled sunnily, replete with the feminine power of having surprised him.

'OK, *bellezza mia…*' His dark deep masculine drawl was slightly fractured and he vaulted back upright, sending her a flashing brilliant smile that made her tummy perform a somersault. 'I'll shave.'

And away he went to do it, where she had no idea, as she lay back in her candlelit bath, full of warm fuzzy feelings powered only by lemonade and candlelight. He had surprised her too and she was genuinely amazed by that reality. Vitale could be so very conservative and polite that it was often hard to catch a glimpse of what lay beneath. A man who was worried and concerned enough about their troubled relationship to run her a bath and put candles and flowers around it. Only a little thing though, much like her snow globe but it showed her the other side of Vitale, the side he worked so hard to hide and suppress, the sensitive, caring side. That could be enough for her, she told herself firmly, that could be enough to make the risk of loving him worthwhile even if it couldn't last for ever. Not everyone got a happy-ever-after.

He had said he was 'trying'. Well, she could try too, no shame in that, she told herself urgently, blowing out the candles and drying her overheated skin with a fleecy towel before walking naked into the empty bedroom to climb into the bed and rejoice in the cool linen embrace of the sheets.

Vitale reappeared, closed the door and surveyed her where she lay, Titian ringlets spilling across the white pillows like a vibrant banner. Hunger leapt through him with a ferocity that still disturbed him. His motto was moderation in all things but there was nothing moderate or practical about his desire for Jazz. It was a need that took hold of him at odd times of the day even when she wasn't in front of him, a kind of craving that had creeped him out when he'd first learned that she was pregnant because what had been going on inside his head should, in his estimation, have killed all desire for her, not fuelled it. But now he didn't even have to think about that anomaly, he told himself with fierce satisfaction. They had reached an accord, he didn't know how and he didn't *need* to know, did he? How wasn't important; that the accord existed was enough for him.

'Jazz…' he breathed hoarsely, standing beside the side of the bed, wrenching at his shirt.

Jazz sat up abruptly. 'Come here,' she told him with a sigh. 'You just ripped a button off your shirt.'

And he dropped down on the edge of the bed and she unbuttoned the shirt, full pert little rose-tipped breasts shifting beneath his mesmerised gaze with every movement. He tossed the shirt, stood up, unzipped his pants, thrust it all down, ran irritably into shoes and socks while wondering how any male could be so impatient for one woman that he forgot how to undress.

Jazz spread herself back luxuriantly against the pillows.

'What are you smiling at?' Vitale enquired almost curtly, feverish colour scoring his high cheekbones.

'You look gorgeous,' she told him truthfully, admiring every long, lean, powerfully muscular line of his big body and most particularly the potent proof of his hunger for her.

Vitale could feel his face burn because no woman had ever said that to him before. He had never encouraged that kind of familiarity in the bedroom but that would not inhibit Jazz, who would say exactly what she felt like saying. There was something wonderfully liberating about that knowledge. He didn't know what it was, but it put to flight the stress of the long day and the very uncomfortable phone call he had just shared with his father.

'You *married* Jazz?' he had said. 'Your mother will throw a fit.'

But Vitale could not have cared less at that moment as he hauled Jazz up to meet his mouth, all dominant male powered by seething hormones. His hunger currented through her like a wake-up call, setting every skin cell alight with his passion. And Jazz revelled in that awareness of his desire for her. It acted as a soother for other slights and insecurities. Nobody had ever wanted her the way Vitale seemed to want her. True, she hadn't given any other man the chance, she conceded, but Vitale's passion made her feel ridiculously irresistible. His sensual mouth greedily ravished hers, a knot of warmth already curling at the heart of her in welcome.

And then his hands roved over her, those sure skilled hands, fingertips plucking gently at her swollen nipples, stirring an ache between her slender thighs that dragged a moan from her because her whole body felt amazingly sensitised, amazingly eager, over-the-top eager, she adjusted in shame, squirming below his caresses, back arching as he began to employ his carnal mouth in a sweet tormenting trail down over her twisting length.

'Don't stop...' she exclaimed helplessly, her narrow hips writhing and rising until he caught them in firm hands and stilled her to withstand the onslaught of his sensual attention.

'Per l'amor di Dio,' Vitale groaned against her where she ached unbearably. 'If I had known I was this welcome, I'd never have kept my distance—'

'Pregnancy hormones,' Jazz cut in shakily. 'That's all it is.'

'Possibly multiple pregnancy hormones,' Vitale teased with unholy amusement dancing in his stunning eyes. 'Bring it on, *bellezza mia*. That aspect went unmentioned on the website I read.'

'Maybe it's just me,' she mumbled uncomfortably, her face hot as fire.

'No, it's intriguing to know a piece of me is in there,' Vitale growled, splaying his fingers across her stomach. 'It makes me feel like you really belong to me...weird,' he added for himself.

'All of it feels weird because it's wonderfully new to us,' Jazz reasoned, her fingers delving through his luxuriant black hair. 'I still can't quite believe it.'

Vitale let a fingertip trace lower and her head fell back, the power of speech stolen by an unexpectedly powerful flood of sensation that made her legs tremble.

He bent his head and employed the tip of his tongue and her entire body jerked and shifted, little sounds of delight breaking from her throat that she couldn't hold back. And then there was no more talking because she was trapped in the relentless need for fulfilment, need controlling her, hunger roaring through her like a greedy tempest, craving more and crying out in wonder as he gave her more and the all-consuming clenching of her body powered her into an unstoppable climax.

'In bed, you're my every dream come true,' she whispered shakily, still rocked by the final waves of pleasure.

'It's the same for me,' Vitale admitted raggedly as he rose over her, forging a strong path into the tender flesh he had prepared to take him. 'It's never been this good for me.'

He plunged into her and withdrew in a timeless rhythm as old as the waves in the sea. Erotic excitement gripped her as she gripped him, little gasps racking her, tiny muscles convulsing around him. She quivered with sheer anticipation as his pace quickened, stirring every atom of her being, driving her back up to the heights with every thrust until the bands low in her body began to tighten and she strained until he drove her over the edge again into glorious release. She watched him reach the same satisfaction as he shuddered over her, his lean, muscular body taut and damp and beautifully virile as he lifted himself at the last possible moment, striving not to crush her with his weight.

'I feel good now,' Vitale husked, sliding off her and pausing to drop a kiss on her brow before moving away.

'I'm so pleased about that,' Jazz said laughingly.

'You can hug me if you want. I've got used to it,' Vitale assured her arrogantly.

Jazz rolled her eyes at the ceiling. There he was making allowances for her again but not actively joining in. She had taught him to tolerate being hugged but it wasn't enough for her. She needed *him* to grab *her* and hold her close and he wasn't going to do that. But at the same time she couldn't be a gift that kept on giving for ever. Shows of such affection from her would be thin on the ground from here on in, she told herself firmly.

'Are you in a mood?' Vitale asked quietly, leaning over her and gazing down at her with a very wary cast to his lean dark features.

'No.' Jazz stretched slowly and smiled. 'I'm hungry.'

'Agnella is holding dinner for us,' he volunteered.

'Holding it? You mean it's ready?' Jazz exclaimed in dismay. 'Why didn't you tell me?'

'It's fine. I told her you were in the bath,' Vitale explained with the carelessness of a male accustomed to staff who worked to his timetable rather than theirs.

'And how long ago was that?' Jazz groaned, sliding hurriedly out of bed to head for the bathroom at speed. 'We should be more considerate, Vitale.'

'It's our wedding night,' Vitale reminded her, stepping into the spacious shower with her. 'That's different.'

'Don't you dare get my hair wet,' Jazz warned him as he angled the rainforest spout. 'It takes for ever to dry.'

Vitale laughed out loud and watched her wash at speed and step back out again.

'You know there are other pastimes you can enjoy in the shower,' he husked, humour sparkling in his dark eyes.

'We're going downstairs for dinner,' Jazz told him squarely, leaving the bathroom to root through the tangle of garments she had tossed out of her case earlier and find fresh comfortable clothing.

Their evening meal was served on an outside terrace shaded by vine-covered metal arches. A silver candelabra illuminated the exquisitely set table in a soft glow of light.

The first course arrived and Jazz tucked in with appetite, conscious of Vitale's scrutiny. 'What?' she finally queried in irritation.

'I like the fact that you enjoy food. So many women don't.'

'No, I think there's a certain belief out there that a healthy appetite in a woman is a sin and that it's somehow more feminine to pick daintily at food,' she told him, watching and copying what he did with his bread roll, still learning the little things she knew she needed to learn before she appeared at the fancy dinner that would precede the ball. Without warning, the concept of doing anything that could embarrass Vitale in public made Jazz cringe.

'You must have been appalled by my table manners when we were children,' she remarked uncomfortably.

'No. You were always dainty in your habits. But I will admit that I envied your freedom. You did as you liked and you said what you liked, just like Angel,' Vitale pointed out ruefully. 'I only ever had that luxury during those holidays. My childhood was in no way normal at the palace. My mother expected me to have the manners and outlook of an adult at a very early age.'

'I don't want our children growing up like that,' Jazz told him bluntly.

Vitale lounged back in his chair, all sleek, sophisticated male in the candlelight and devastatingly handsome. 'In that aim, we are in complete agreement,' he admitted. 'I want them to enjoy a normal happy childhood, free of the fear that they have to be perfect to be loved.'

'Does it matter to you whether they are boys or girls or even one of each?' she asked curiously.

'No. I have no preference. I will be very honest...' Vitale regarded Jazz with cautious dark golden eyes surrounded by gold-tipped lush black lashes. 'I have never wanted children but I have always accepted that I would have to have at least one for the sake of the throne. You have already achieved that requirement for me and to some extent, I can now relax, duty done...'

So, now I'm rent-a-womb, Jazz reflected, struggling not to react in too personal a way. He had told her the truth and she should respect that. *Duty done?* But he had *never* wanted children? That really worried her. His tender preparation of her bath had touched her heart and revitalised her but that blunt admission about never having wanted a child simply upset her again. All right, he was making the best of a bad job, as the saying went, but, as the woman playing a starring role and being made the best of, she felt humiliated and utterly insignificant in the grand scheme of Prince Vitale Castiglione's life...

CHAPTER EIGHT

JAZZ WAS UNPREPARED for the barrage of journalists and photographers who awaited their arrival at the airport in the capital city of Lerovia, Leburg. The amount of interest taken in her arrival with Vitale was phenomenal and she was no longer surprised by his request that she remove her wedding ring before their flight landed. Amidst the shouted madness of questions, flash photography and outright staring, Jazz felt as though she had briefly strayed into some mirror world, terrifyingly different from her own.

'The press know about the ball and my mother is too outspoken for there to be much doubt about its purpose, which was to find me a wife,' Vitale told her very drily when they had finally escaped into the peace of a limousine with tinted windows and a little Lerovian flag on the bonnet. 'So, obviously my arrival in Leburg with a woman is a source of great speculation.'

'But surely you've brought other women here?' Jazz exclaimed, still a little shaken up by her first encounter with the press en masse.

'You're the first. My affairs have always been kept off the radar and discreet,' Vitale explained reluctantly. 'Unlike Angel, I was never an international playboy and until today I have not been much troubled by the attentions of the paparazzi.'

'Did I hear someone shout a question about the engagement ring?'

'There were several, some in Italian and German,' Vitale advanced. 'That's why I gave it to you.'

'No, you gave it to me when you did because I was in a funk and you were trying to distract me,' Jazz told him wryly. 'Although I've no doubt you planned for me to arrive here flashing it.'

She liked the last word. His mother did as well. But somehow when Jazz cut in with one of her cute little last words, it didn't annoy him to the same degree, although her ability to read his motives unsettled him and made him feel tense. His lean, strong face clenched hard because he had already been tense. He hated conflict with Queen Sofia because it was a challenge to fight back when he was forced to give his aggressor the respect and obligation due to his monarch. It could never be a fair battle.

Jazz was merely relieved that she had put on an elegant dress and jacket for her arrival in Lerovia and had braided her hair, which left loose could look untidy. It had not escaped her attention that Vitale had grown steadily grimmer the closer they got to the country of his birth. Did he hate living in Lerovia, she wondered, or was it simply the problems he had dealing with his mother, the Queen?

She peered out at the city of Leburg, which appeared to have a skyline that could have rivalled Dubai's. It was an ultramodern, fully developed European city and a tax haven with very rich inhabitants, which she had learned from her own research on the internet. Furthermore, the man she had married, the father of her unborn twins, might be the heir to the Lerovian throne but he was also the CEO of the Bank of Lerovia. He hadn't told her any of that but then Vitale had never been much of a talker when it came to himself, so she wasn't the least offended by his omissions. In any case, she was perfectly capable of doing her own homework concerning the country where she was to live for the foreseeable future. Italian, German and English were widely spoken in Lerovia and many residents were from other countries.

The royal family had ruled Lerovia since the thirteenth century, which had disconcerted Jazz because for some reason she had always assumed that the Castiglione family were more recent arrivals. The ruling family, numbering only mother and son, lived in Ilrovia Castle, a white, much turreted and very picturesque building in the hills just outside the city.

Stealing a glance at Vitale's taut bronzed profile, she suddenly found herself reaching for his hand. 'You're not on your own in this,' she reminded him quietly. 'We got married for the sake of the children. I'm as much involved as you are.'

'No, you won't be. I won't put you in the path of my mother's spite. The Queen is my cross to bear,' he said very drily, quietly easing his fingers free. 'In any case, you're pregnant and you shouldn't be upset in *any* way.'

'Nonsense!' Jazz parried roundly, her backbone of steel stiffening but her pride and her heart hurt by the way he had instantly freed her hand. She gritted her teeth, inwardly urging herself to be patient and not to expect change overnight.

But even so, Vitale had been very different over their Italian weekend. He had been relaxed, not once retreating into the reserved and rather chilly impersonal approach that she was beginning to appreciate was the norm for him in public places or with strangers. Change had loomed only when they had landed in Lerovia, which really said it all, she thought ruefully. In her very bones, she was aware that she was soon to meet the mother-in-law from hell and that she had absolutely no defensive armour with which to fight back.

After all, she *was* the daughter of a humble housekeeper with no impressive ancestors, a little better educated than those ancestors but still without the official sanction of a degree even if she had almost completed one. And she was pregnant into the bargain, she conceded ruefully. She didn't qualify as an equal in Vitale's world. To put it bluntly, and Clodagh had, Jazz had married *up* in her aunt's parlance and Vitale had married *down*. Well, she was what she was and perfectly happy on her own account but it seemed only reasonable to expect the Queen of Lerovia to be severely disappointed in her son's choice of bride.

The car purred through a medieval stone archway guarded by soldiers, who presented arms in acknowledgement of Vitale's arrival. Jazz struggled not to feel intimidated as they entered a giant, splendidly furnished hall awash with gleaming crystal chandeliers and grand gilded furniture. Vitale immediately turned left to head up a staircase to one side.

'I have my private quarters in the castle. The Queen lives in the other wing and the ground houses the royal ceremonial apartments where official events are held and where we entertain,' Vitale told her on the stairs.

'You do realise that that is the only information you have ever given me about Lerovia?' Jazz remarked drily.

Vitale paused on the landing, dark golden eyes visibly disturbed by that observation.

'Oh, don't worry. The internet made up for your omission,' Jazz assured him ruefully. 'I've picked up the basics. It was interesting. I had no idea your family had been ruling here for so many generations or that gay people still live a restricted life here.'

He clenched his jaw. 'The Queen will countenance nothing that goes against church teaching. Unfortunately, the monarch in Lerovia also still has the right to veto laws proposed by parliament,' he admitted. 'I wasn't joking when I warned you that we lived in the past here.'

'Some day you'll be able to shake it up a little,' Jazz pointed out as he guided her through a door into a hallway that was surprisingly contemporary in contrast to the rather theatrical ground-floor décor.

'That day is a long way off,' Vitale intoned with firm conviction. 'The Queen will never voluntarily give up power.'

Jazz wandered round her new home, followed by two members of Vitale's domestic staff, Adelheid the housekeeper and Olivero, the butler. Both spoke excellent English and she learned that Vitale's wing had originally been the nursery wing devoted to his upbringing and in complete isolation from his mother's living accommodation. Obviously, the Queen was not the maternal type, Jazz acknowledged, knowing that she would never accept her children being housed at such a distance from her and solely tended to by staff. The more little glimpses she gained of Vitale's far from sunny childhood, the better she understood him.

Their spacious home stretched to three floors and steps led down from the big airy drawing room to the gardens. Jazz was smothering yawns by the time the official tour reached the master bedroom, which was decorated in subtle shades of green and grey. She was introduced to *her* maid, Carmela, who was already unpacking her luggage to fill the large, well-appointed dressing room off the bedroom. A maid, her own *maid*, she thought in awed disbelief.

Vitale entered after the maid had gone and found Jazz lying down on the bed with her shoes and jacket removed.

'I thought I'd go for a nap before I start getting ready for the ball. I'm really quite sleepy,' she confided, pushing herself up on her elbows, the braid she had undone to lie down now a tumbling mass of vibrant tresses falling over one shoulder, the arch of her spine pushing her breasts taut up against the fine silk bodice of her dress.

Vitale studied her with brutally male appreciation and a heat she was instantly aware of, his dark eyes scorching hot with the thought of possibilities, and something clenched low in her body, the stirring primal impulses of the same hunger.

'I'll leave you in peace,' he began.

'No,' Jazz countered, reaching out her hand to close into his sleeve. 'I'm not *that* tired.'

Vitale dealt her a sizzling smile that sent butterflies tumbling in her tummy and bent his head to kiss her, both his hands sinking into the torrent of her hair. Excitement leapt into her slender body like a lightning bolt and then just as suddenly the bedroom door burst noisily open. Vitale released her instantaneously and Jazz thrust herself up on her hands, her face flushed with annoyance and embarrassment as she focused on the woman who had stalked into their bedroom without so much as a warning knock. Even worse, a gaggle of goggle-eyed people were peering in from the corridor outside.

'Close the door, Vitale,' Jazz murmured flatly, staring at the enraged blonde, garbed in a stylish blue suit and pearls, standing mere feet away. 'We don't need an audience for this—'

'Oh, I think we do, leave the door wide, Vitale,' Queen Sofia cut in imperiously. 'I'd like an audience to see your red-headed whore being thrown out of the palace.'

Vitale closed the door and swung round. 'I will not tolerate so rude an intrusion, nor will I tolerate such abuse.'

'You will tolerate whatever I ask you to tolerate because I am your *Queen*!' the blonde proclaimed with freezing emphasis. 'I want this creature gone. I don't care how you do it but it *must* be done before the ball this evening.'

'If my fiancée leaves, I will accompany her,' Vitale parried.

'You wouldn't *dare*!' his mother screeched at him, transforming from ice to instant fiery fury.

A woman with no volume control, Jazz registered, only just resisting the urge to physically cover her ears. The Queen shot something at Vitale in outraged Italian and the battle commenced, only, frustratingly, Jazz had no idea what was being said. Vitale's mother seemed to be concentrating on trying to shout him down while Vitale himself spoke in a cool, clipped voice Jazz had never heard him employ before, his control absolute.

'Jazz will be my partner at the ball this evening,' Vitale declared in clarifying English. 'Nothing you can say or do will change that.'

'She's a servant's daughter... Oh, yes, I've found out all about you!' Queen Sofia shot triumphantly at Jazz, her piercing pale blue eyes venomous.

Jazz slid off the bed and stood up, instantly feeling stronger.

'You're a nothing, a nobody, and I don't know what my son's doing with you because he *should* know his duty better than anyone.'

'As you have often reminded me, my duty is to marry and produce a child,' Vitale interposed curtly. 'Jazz is the woman I have chosen.'

'I will not accept her and therefore she has to go!' The older woman cast the file she had tightly gripped in one hand down on the bed beside Jazz. 'Have a look at the candidates I selected. You couldn't compete with a single one of those women! You have no breeding and no education, none of the very special qualities required to match my son's status.'

'Get out,' Vitale breathed with chilling bite, closing a firm hand to the older woman's arm to lead her back to the door. 'You have said what you came to say and I will not allow you to abuse Jazz.'

'If you bring her to the ball, I will not acknowledge her!' Queen Sofia threatened. 'And I will make your lives hell!'

'I imagine Vitale is quite used to you making his life hell,' Jazz opined dulcetly, her head held high as the older woman stared at her in disbelief, much as though a piece of furniture had moved forward and dared to address her. 'And as long as I have Vitale by my side, you will not intimidate me with your threats either.'

'Are you going to let this interloper speak to your Queen like that?' his mother raged.

In answer, Vitale strode forward and addressed his mother in an angry flood of English, a dark line of colour edging his hard cheekbones. The older woman tried to shout him down but Vitale slashed an authoritative silencing hand through the air and continued in the same splintering tone, 'You will not call my fiancée vile names *ever* again. You will not force your way into my private quarters again either. I am an adult, not a child you can bully and disrespect. Other people may tolerate such behaviour from you but I no longer will. Be careful, Mother, *very* careful because your future plans could easily fall apart. Your insolence is intolerable and if it continues I will leave the palace and I will leave Lerovia,' he completed harshly. 'I will not live anywhere where my fiancée is viciously abused.'

The Queen was pale and seemed to have shrunk in size. She opened her mouth but then just as suddenly closed it again, visibly shattered by his threat to leave the country. As she left, Vitale shut the door firmly again.

For an instant there was complete silence. Jazz was shaken by his vigorous defence but still unconvinced by his decision not to tell the whole truth immediately.

'You should have told your mother that the deed was already done and that you are married,' Jazz told him unhappily. 'Why wait to break that final bit of news when she's already in such a snit?'

'I have my own ways of dealing with my mother,' Vitale countered curtly. 'Don't interfere and give her another excuse to attack you.'

'There's more than one way of skinning a rabbit!' Jazz tossed back at him, determined to fight her corner as best she could. 'Could you have my cases brought back in?'

Vitale froze, a winged ebony brow lifting. 'Why would you want your cases?'

'Because if your mother is free to walk into our bedroom any time she likes, I'm not staying,' Jazz told him bluntly.

'Dannazione...' Vitale swore with clenched fists of frustration. 'You heard what I told her.'

'I just witnessed a grown woman throwing a tantrum and hurling outrageous insults with apparent impunity. Being royal, being a queen, does not excuse that kind of behaviour.'

Vitale ground his teeth together and raked long brown fingers through his cropped blue-black hair. 'I agree,' he conceded. 'But I threatened to leave this country if she interferes again and that shocked her.'

'Ask for my cases, Vitale,' Jazz urged, refusing to listen. 'We could have been *in* bed when your mother walked in and she wouldn't have cared.'

In a provocative move, Vitale settled his broad shoulders back against the door and braced his long powerful legs. 'You can't leave. I won't let you,' he told her lethally.

'If you can't protect me in your own home, I'm leaving.'

'Over my dead body,' Vitale murmured, dark eyes glittering with challenge even as he stood his ground. 'You *will* be protected. I will accept nothing less.'

In reality Jazz was more incensed by his stubborn refusal to take her advice. 'I still think you need to tell the Queen now that we are married, I'm pregnant and that the marriage is only a temporary measure,' she countered between stiff lips.

'You don't know what you're talking about!' Vitale could feel his temper suddenly taking a dangerous and inexplicable leap forward again.

Jazz angled her head back, aware of the flare of angry gold brightening his forceful gaze but quite unafraid of it. 'Well, of course I don't… You don't tell me anything. It's all too personal and private for you to share, so you hoard all your secrets up like a miser with treasure!' she condemned resentfully.

'Don't be ridiculous!' Vitale shot back at her quellingly.

But Jazz was in no mood to be quelled. 'You had no problems telling *me* that I would only be your wife until the twins are born, so I can't understand why you would be so obstinate about sharing that same information with your mother! After all, she'll undoubtedly be delighted to hear that I'm not here to stay.'

At that unsought reminder of the terms he himself had laid down, Vitale's lean, strong features set like a granite rock and the rage he was struggling to control surged even higher. 'Now you are making a most inappropriate joke of our situation, which I intensely dislike.'

Jazz's green eyes took on an emerald glow of rage at that icily angry assurance because if there was one thing that drove her mad, it was Vitale aiming that icy chill at her. She had been proud of him when he'd targeted his mother with that chill though. 'Oh, do you indeed? I intensely dislike a stranger blundering into what is supposed to be the marital bedroom when we're on the bed! She's the kind of royal who gives me Republican sympathies! I will never *ever* forget that woman calling me a whore and I won't forgive her for it either, no, not even if she apologises for it.'

'The Queen does not do apologies. You are safe from that possibility,' Vitale derided. 'Now, you will calm down and have lunch, which is being prepared.'

'You will not tell me to calm down!' Jazz raged back at him. 'I will shout if I feel like it.'

'You're pregnant. You need to keep calm,' Vitale proclaimed.

'That is not an excuse to shut me up!' Jazz hissed back at him.

Vitale startled her by striding forward without warning and lifting her off her feet to settle her down squarely on the bed she had only recently vacated. 'It is the only excuse I need. Lunch will wait until you have rested.'

'Do I look like I'm in the mood to rest?' Jazz argued fierily.

'No, but you know it's the sensible option and you have to think about *them*.' Vitale unsettled her even more by resting his hand with splayed fingers across her stomach. 'Neither of us want you to run the risk of a miscarriage by getting overexcited and pushing yourself too hard when you're already exhausted and stressed. The ball tonight will tire you even more,' he reminded her grimly.

Jazz had paled and she closed her eyes, striving for self-control, but she was still so mad at him and frustrated that it was an appalling struggle to hold back the vindictive words bubbling on her tongue. And then her green eyes flew wide again, crackling with angry defiance. 'Surely a miscarriage would *suit*—'

Vitale froze, wide sensual mouth setting hard, dark golden eyes flashing censorious reproach. 'Don't you *dare* say that to me!' he breathed in a raw undertone. 'They are my children too and I want them, no matter how inconvenient their timing may be! No matter how much trouble their conception may have caused us!'

Jazz had stilled, her anger snuffed out at source by the wrathful sincerity she saw in his gaze and heard in his voice. 'I thought you didn't want children,' she reminded him.

'I thought so too but for some reason I'm getting excited by the idea of them now,' Vitale admitted reluctantly.

Surprisingly, a kind of peace filtered in to drain away her anger. She was ashamed of what anger had provoked her into saying to him but soothed too by her first real proof that Vitale truly *did* want their unborn children, regardless of their situation. Given sufficient time, he too had adjusted his attitude and his outlook had softened, readying him for change. She closed her eyes again, drained by the early morning start to the day, the travel and all that had followed their arrival at the palace. Fit and healthy though she was, the exhaustion of early pregnancy was pushing her to her limits and the imminent prospect of the ball simply made her suppress a groan.

Vitale glowered down at her prone figure. She had lost her temper, lost control, he reasoned grimly, had barely known what she was saying. Wasn't that why he guarded his own temper? But during that scene with his mother one unmistakable reality had powered Vitale. His wife and his children *had* to come first because they depended on him. His mother, in comparison, was surrounded by supporters comprised of flattering subordinates and socially ambitious hangers-on, not to mention her chief lady-in-waiting, the Contessa Cinzia, who had never been known to contradict her royal mistress.

Jazz only stirred when a maid entered the room bringing a tray and she sat up with a start, blinking rapidly while wondering what was crackling beneath her hips. Her seeking hand drew out a file and a dim memory of the Queen tossing it there surfaced.

'Thank you,' she told the maid. 'I'll eat at the table.'

She settled the file down on the table by the window. Carmela informed her that her hair and make-up stylist would be arriving in half an hour and, killing the urge to roll her eyes at that information, Jazz lifted her knife and fork and then paused to open the file…

CHAPTER NINE

'BUT IF THIS belonged to your grandmother that means it's royal, so how can I wear it?' Jazz protested as she held the delicate diamond tiara that shone like a circlet of stars between her reverent fingers.

'You're my wife and my grandmother bestowed her jewellery on me in her will for my wife's use,' Vitale explained. 'And if that is still not sufficient reason for you, think of how it will enrage my mother to see you draped in her mother's fabulous diamond suite.'

Her green eyes glinted with amused appreciation of that sally and she sat down by the dressing table to allow Vitale to anchor the tiara in her thick hair. With careful hands, she donned the earrings and the necklace from the same box and forced a smile, refusing, absolutely refusing to think about what she had read in that ghastly file that very afternoon. She needed to be confident for the ball, was determined to look as though she belonged at such a glittering event purely for Vitale's sake. The prospect of doing anything so-cially wrong in his mother's radius literally made her stomach clench with sick horror.

'You look wonderful,' Vitale husked as she rose again, a slim silhouette sheathed in a green gown that glistened with thousands of beads. Cut high at the front, it bared her slender back, skimming down over her narrow hips to froth out in sparkling volume round her stiletto-clad feet.

'Wonderful enough to win your bet?'

Vitale, designer chic in a beautifully tailored evening jacket and narrow black trousers, groaned out loud. 'I couldn't care less about that bet now and you know it. Accepting that bet was a foolish impulse I now regret.'

Jazz smiled, the generous curve of her lush mouth enhanced by soft pink, and Vitale shifted forward, dark golden eyes flaring. 'No,' she said succinctly. 'If you knew how long it took the stylist to do my make-up, you wouldn't dare even *think* of kissing me.'

Vitale laughed, startling himself, it seemed, almost as much as he startled her, amusement lightening the forbidding tension that had still tautened his strong features. 'You're good for me,' he quipped.

But nowhere near as good in the royal wife stakes as Carlotta, Elena or Luciana or their equivalents would have been, a rebellious little voice remarked somewhere down deep inside her where the file had done the most damage by lowering her self-esteem and making her feel almost ashamed of her humble background. Shutting off that humiliating inner voice, Jazz drank in a deep steadying breath and informed him that she was ready to leave.

The female staff had assembled to see her ball gown and Jazz smiled, pleased by their approbation, secure in her belief that she had chosen well when she'd decided not to pick the plain and boring black dress that Vitale would have selected. With diamonds sparkling at her every step, she caught a glimpse of her reflection in a tall hall mirror and barely recognised that glitzy figure.

Vitale's arm at her back, they entered a vast reception room on the ground floor where pre-dinner drinks were being served. Glorious landscape paintings of Lerovia lined the walls. Waiters in white jackets served drinks below the diamond-bright light of the gleaming crystal chandeliers twinkling above them. Angel and Merry headed straight for them and relief washed through Jazz the minute she saw their familiar faces.

'Super, *super* dress,' Merry whispered warmly.

'And yours,' Jazz responded, admiring the elaborate embroidery that covered her sister-in-law's pale gown. 'Vitale didn't tell me you'd both be here.'

'Vitale's on another planet when the Queen Bee is around,' Angel remarked very drily. 'One thing you will learn about Charles's sons, Jazz. He didn't pick our mothers very well.'

'But Charles is so lovely that he makes up for that,' Merry chipped in soothingly into the rather awkward silence that had fallen, because Jazz would not risk uttering a single critical word about the Queen, lest she be overheard and embarrass Vitale.

'Yes,' Jazz agreed as Angel roamed off to speak to his brother.

Place cards were carelessly swapped at the dining table to ensure that they sat with Angel and Merry and Jazz tucked into the first course with appetite, striving not to look in the direction of the Queen at the top of the exceedingly long table.

'Why's Zac not here?' Jazz asked curiously. 'I was hoping to meet him.'

'He'll be at the ball. He's not a fan of formal dinners,' Angel explained. 'He hates restrictions of any kind.'

'Very different from Vitale then… Interesting,' Jazz mused, incredibly curious about the third brother and already conscious that although Vitale hadn't actually admitted it, he didn't seem to like his Brazilian sibling much.

An hour later, Jazz was busily identifying the women in the ball room from their photographs in Queen Sofia's file, the 'suitable wives' file as she thought of it. And not a plain face or a redhead amongst the six candidates, all of them terrifyingly well-born, several titled, all possessed of the ability to speak more than one language, a high-flying education and a solid background of charitable good works. None of them would have required lessons on how to use cutlery or how to address an ambassador or curtsy to a reigning monarch. By the time she had finished perusing that damning file Jazz had felt horrendously inadequate. She had also felt ashamed that she had instinctively resented Vitale's certainty that theirs could only be a temporary marriage.

Of course, he didn't want to keep her when she was so ill-qualified for the position of a royal wife. Obviously, he would want a bride with all the accomplishments that he himself took for granted. Like with like worked best even in nature. It didn't mean that she was something lesser than the male she had married, she reasoned painfully, it only meant that they were too different.

'Zac's around here somewhere but I keep on missing him,' Vitale breathed impatiently, a lean bronzed hand settling to her slender spine as he walked out to the grand foyer where guests stood in clusters served by another army of waiters bearing drinks trays.

An older man intercepted them and urged Vitale to introduce him to his fiancée. 'Jazz.'

'Short for?'

'Jazmine,' she slotted in with a smile, because it was the first time she had been asked. 'My father registered my birth and he spelt it with a *z* rather than an *s*, which is how I became Jazz.'

'And a very good friend in the media told me that you've known each other since you were children,' the older man filled in with amusement. 'That's one in the eye for your mother,' he pronounced with satisfaction before passing on.

'Who was that?'

'My mother's younger half-brother, Prince Eduardo.'

'Your *uncle*?' Jazz repeated in surprise.

'My mother wouldn't even let him live here after she was crowned. She has always behaved as though she were an only child refusing to share the limelight...'

Jazz's attention had strayed to the male exiting from a room further down the hall, smoothing down his jacket, running careless fingers through his long black hair, his light eyes bright beneath the lights. 'Is that Zac?' she asked abruptly, recognising the resemblance.

Two giggling women, one blonde, one brunette in rather creased ball gowns emerged from the same room only one telling step in the man's wake.

'*Sì*...that's Zac,' Vitale confirmed with audible distaste. 'I wonder what he did with his partner while he was in there.'

A moment later, Zac answered that question for himself. 'Well, obviously you win. Jazz is amazing and I came alone,' he spelt out with a surprisingly charismatic grin of acknowledgement. 'My car is already in transit.'

While the brothers chatted, Jazz wandered off. Her mother-in-law was talking to a bunch of people at the far end of the hall and Jazz tactfully avoided that area.

Vitale rejoined her by sliding his arm round her back and she smiled. 'So, you won,' she commented.

'I set Zac up to fail. I feel a little guilty about doing that now,' Vitale confided in an undertone. 'But even so, this evening you have been a triumph of cool and control and I'm proud to be with you.'

Jazz gazed up at him in shock.

Vitale sighed. 'It needed to be said and I'm sorry that it took my kid brother to say it first,' he admitted.

'Who were those women Zac was with?'

'Willing ladies?' Vitale suggested.

'Don't be so judgemental!' Jazz urged. 'Nothing may have happened between them and Zac.'

'They're both on my mother's staff. I'm not in a charitable mood,' he admitted wryly. 'In any case, Zac is a player with the morals of an alley cat.'

Recognising that Vitale's judgemental streak ran to both sexes, Jazz almost laughed. She wondered if he had ever resented his inability to behave the same way. Of course, he had, she decided, of course he must have envied his brothers' freedom. Zac and Angel had freely chosen their lifestyles but birth had forced a rigid framework of dos and don'ts on Vitale and choice had had nothing to do with it.

'Did you ever just want to walk away from being royal?' Jazz asked him as he whirled her onto the dance floor for the opening dance beneath his mother's freezing gimlet gaze. But the ballroom was so colourful that

Jazz was entranced as more and more couples joined them on the floor, the ladies clad in every colour of the rainbow, their dresses swirling gracefully around them, the men elegant in black or white dinner jackets.

'Frequently when I was a child, more often as an adult,' Vitale confided, surprising her with that frankness. 'But a sense of duty to our name must be stamped into my DNA. Although I consider the idea, I know I won't actually *do* it.'

And it finally dawned on her that the unhappiness she had sensed in Vitale even as a child had been genuine and that acknowledgement saddened her. Shortly after midnight, soon after the Queen's regal exit from the ball, Vitale accompanied her up to the door of their apartment and she knew he intended to go and tell the older woman that he was a married man.

'If you're going to confront your mother,' she had argued all the way up the winding staircase. 'I should come with you.'

'There's no reason for you to be subjected to hours of her ranting and raving. For a start, she will initially insist that my having married without her permission makes the ceremony illegal,' Vitale retorted crisply. 'I'm used to her hysterics and she won't even listen until she calms down. Don't wait up for me.'

Thinking about Vitale poised like a soldier, icily controlled in the face of his Queen's wrath, made Jazz's hands clench into angry fists of frustration. She had arrived in Lerovia with an open mind concerning Queen Sofia but that single scene in their bedroom had convinced her that Vitale's mother was a despotic monster. And she cared, of course she *cared*, she reflected as she got ready for bed and finally climbed into that bed alone.

She loved Vitale. Oh, she hadn't matched the word to the feelings before in an effort to protect herself from hurt, but the hurt would come whether she labelled her emotions or not. She loved the male who had lit her candles round her bath, who had held her close all night before they travelled to Lerovia. He was amazingly affectionate when he thought she was safely asleep, she conceded with tender amusement, but wary of demonstrating anything softer during the hours of daylight.

Angel had deemed his younger brother 'emotionally stunted', but he had been wrong in that assessment. Vitale bore all the hallmarks of someone damaged in childhood. He had taught himself to hide his emotions, had learned to suppress his pain and his anger to the extent that he barely knew what he felt any more. Yet he was working so hard at protecting her from his horrible mother, she thought fondly before she drifted off to sleep.

Breakfast was served to her in bed late the next morning and her phone already carried a text from Vitale, letting her know that he was attending a board meeting at the bank and would be out most of the day. She ate sparsely, awaiting the nausea that often took hold of her but evidently it was to be one of her good days and she could go for a shower and dress, feeling healthy and normal for once instead of simply pregnant.

Clad in an unpretentious white sundress, she went down the stone steps into the gardens to explore and enjoy the early summer sunshine. She was slightly unnerved to be closely followed by the housekeeper, Adelheid, and introduced to the very large plain-clothed man with her as her bodyguard. Striving to forget that she had company, Jazz went for a walk and then phoned her mum to catch up. She was sitting on a bench beside an ornamental stone fountain when a young woman approached her with a folded note on a silver salver.

'It is an invitation to lunch from the Queen, Your Highness,' the woman informed her with a bright smile.

Shock both at the form of address and the explanation of the note engulfed Jazz. Obviously, Vitale had spoken to his mother after the ball and the royal household were now aware that she was a wife rather than a fiancée. Even so, Jazz had expected the Queen to react with rage to the news that her son was married to his red-headed whore rather than a luncheon invite, and she was perplexed, lifting the note from the ludicrous salver and opening it while struggling to control her face.

Yes, she had also noted that the young woman delivering the note had been one of the women who had been in that room the night before with her brother-in-law, Zac. She concentrated, however, on the single sheet of notepaper and its gracious copperplate written summons and gave her consent to lunching with Vitale's mother even though she would much have preferred to say no. Vitale would probably want her to say no, but then Jazz was made of much tougher stuff than the man she had married seemed willing to appreciate. Sticks and stones would not break her bones, indeed they only made her stronger. In fact, if *she* could for once take a little heat off Vitale, Jazz was delighted to take the opportunity.

'My dear,' Queen Sofia purred, rising to greet Jazz as if she were a well-loved friend as soon as she entered the imposing dining room with a gleaming table that rejoiced in only two place settings set directly opposite each other. 'Vitale shared your *wonderful* news with me.'

And the wonderful news, Jazz learned in disbelief, was that she was pregnant with twins. The Queen also trotted out that old chestnut about the heir and a spare with a straight face. In fact, she seemed to be, at that point, an entirely different woman from the one Jazz had met so unforgettably the day before. Sadly, though, that impression was to be a transitory one.

'Of course, Vitale has left me to organise the royal wedding,' the older woman continued smoothly.

'Wedding?' Jazz echoed in astonishment.

'You may legally be married now but for the benefit of our country and the dignity of the family there must be a religious ceremony in which you are *seen* to get married,' Queen Sofia clarified. 'Didn't my son explain that to you?'

'No,' Jazz admitted, thoroughly intimidated by the prospect of a royal wedding.

'Of course, you probably think it is a great deal of fuss over nothing when you and Vitale will not be together very long,' the older woman continued in a measured tone of false regret that told Jazz all she needed to know about why she was currently receiving a welcome. 'But our people expect a wedding and a public holiday in which to celebrate the longevity of the Castiglione family's rule.'

Jazz was holding her breath after that stabbing little reminder that as a wife she would not be enjoying family longevity. 'Of course,' she said flatly, because clearly her private wants and wishes were not to be considered in the balance of royal necessities.

'We are so fortunate that Vitale married you quickly and that your condition is not obvious yet,' the Queen carolled in cheerful addition.

My goodness, the prospect of a couple of babies truly transformed Vitale's mother, Jazz thought limply.

'Obviously we will announce that a civil ceremony took place in London some weeks ago,' the older woman assured her. 'Not that I think these days people will be counting the months of your pregnancy, but it will add to what my PR team regard as the romantic nature of this whole affair.'

'*Romantic?*' Jazz exclaimed, wondering if she would ever work up the nerve to say more than one word back to the Queen.

The Queen waved a dismissive hand. 'Your low birth. Your having known my son from childhood. His apparent decision to marry out of his class,' she pronounced with unconcealed distaste. 'We know that is not the true story. *We* know he *had* to marry you but our people will prefer the romantic version—the totally ridiculous idea that he could have fallen madly in love with you!'

Jazz was now pale as death with perspiration beading her short upper lip. She could no more have touched the plate of food in front of her than she could have spread wings and flown out of the window to escape the spite of the woman opposite her. She swallowed hard on her rising nausea, determined not to show weakness or vulnerability. She pushed her food around the plate while the Queen chattered about how very quickly the wedding could be staged and about how she would have Jazz's measurements taken immediately for her dress. After the meal, she was shown into another room where a dressmaker did exactly that and then she escaped back up to the apartment feeling as battered and bruised as though she had gone ten rounds with a champion boxer.

Jazz now understood exactly why the Queen of Lerovia was willing to make her the reluctant star of a royal wedding. The twins would be Vitale's heirs and that was seemingly important enough to the Castiglione dynasty to counteract his bride's notoriously humble beginnings. Jazz tried to comprehend her mother-in-law's unreservedly *practical* viewpoint. Vitale could have married a woman who did not conceive or a woman who had other difficulties in that field. Instead his heir and a spare were already on the way. The Queen despised her lowborn daughter-in-law but would tolerate her because Jazz was not in Lerovia to stay. Evidently, Vitale had told his mother the whole truth about his marriage and Jazz could not work out why she felt so wounded and betrayed by that reality when she had urged him to do exactly that.

There were no more secrets now and it was better that way, she told herself over a lonely dinner. The Queen would throw no more tantrums and would play along for the sake of appearances until Vitale and Jazz broke up. Everyone could now relax—everyone could be happy.

'You're having a bad dream… Wake up!' Vitale shook her shoulder.

In the darkness, Jazz blinked rapidly, extracted from a nightmare in which she was fleeing from some menace in a haunted castle remarkably similar to Vitale's home. 'I'm fine,' she whispered shakily. 'When did you get back?'

'Midnight.' His lean, powerful body perfectly aligned to hers. 'I let you down by not being here. I didn't expect my mother to invite you for lunch. I *told* her to stay out of my life. What the hell is she playing at?' he demanded in furious frustration.

'She's crowing about the twins.' Jazz sighed, drowsily stretching back into the reassuring heat of him. 'And organising a royal wedding.'

'You should never have joined her for lunch,' Vitale declared rawly. 'You should've said you were ill and left me to deal with her.'

'I managed. It was OK,' Jazz lied.

'I don't believe you,' Vitale admitted, flipping her over onto her back and leaning over her, his lean, darkly beautiful face shadowed by moonlight into intriguing hard edges and hollows. 'She would've been poisonous. Don't treat me like I'm stupid!'

'For goodness' sake…' Jazz faltered as he stretched over and switched on the light to stare down at her accusingly. 'She was a bit bitchy, little jibes…you know…'

'Of course I know,' Vitale asserted grimly, his strong jaw clenching hard. 'I've seen her in action many times when she wants to punish those who have crossed her. What did she say to you?'

'Nothing that wasn't the truth,' Jazz dismissed. 'That you *had* to marry me. Well, can't argue with that.'

Vitale swore long and low in Italian. 'Don't you understand that that is why I want you to stay away from her at all costs? I refuse to have you exposed to her malice.'

'It really doesn't matter to me,' Jazz fibbed with pride. 'It's not as if I'm going to be living here under her roof for ever, so I don't care what she thinks of me or what she says to me.'

'I care,' Vitale ground out fiercely, thinking of what he had learned about himself after he had forced out the

admission to his mother that his marriage was not to be of the permanent variety. 'I care a great deal.'

'Why are you in such a mood?' Jazz asked, running a teasing pale hand down over his bare bronzed chest, feeling him tense against her, watching his eyes flare with luminous revealing gold.

'I'm convinced you're a witch, *moglie mia*,' Vitale growled, his passionate mouth crashing down hungrily on hers.

Smiling inside herself, Jazz slid like a temptress along the long, taut and fully aroused length of him and, returning that kiss with equal heat, concluded the awkward conversation.

Three weeks later, Queen Sofia had the last laugh, after all, Jazz conceded as she watched her six bridesmaids fuss over her train and her veil, both of which demanded considerable attention due to their length and ornate decoration. Less was not more in the Queen's parlance, but Jazz had picked her favourite of the options presented to her. The pressure of starring as the leading light in a royal wedding sat heavily on her shoulders and it was several days since she had enjoyed a decent night of sleep.

It was a fairy-tale wedding gown and very sophisticated. It was composed of tulle and glitter net with a strapless dropped-waist bodice adorned with metallic embroidered lace. The neckline and waistline were richly beaded with pearls, crystals and rhinestones. Exquisite and stylish, the draped full skirt glittered with delicately beaded lace appliques. The veil was full length and fashioned of intricate handmade lace.

The bridesmaids, however, were a cruel plunge of a

knife into Jazz's still beating heart. The file of bridal candidates she had hidden in the bottom of her lingerie drawer were all fully present and correct in the bridesmaids. So, naturally, Jazz was studying them, listening to their chatter, struggling to work out which one Vitale would eventually marry for *real*. Would it be Elena, who never ever shut up? Carlotta, who out of envy could barely bring herself to look at Jazz? Or Luciana, who either didn't speak any English or who didn't want to be forced to speak to the bride? Or one of the other three young women, all bright and beautiful and perfect?

The organ music in the cathedral swelled and Jazz walked down the aisle on the arm of Vitale's uncle, Prince Eduardo. Her family were present but her mother had shrunk from such public exposure when her daughter had asked her to walk her down the aisle, so the Queen had, once again, got her wish and had co-opted her brother into the role of giving away the bride.

Jazz was troubled by having to go through a religious service when her marriage was already destined to end in divorce but nobody had asked Jazz how she felt about taking such vows in church and she suspected that nobody would be the least interested in her moral objections. There was no fakery in *her* heart, nothing false about *her* feelings, she reminded herself resolutely as she knelt down before the Cardinal in his imposing scarlet robes.

Disconcertingly, Vitale chose that same moment to cover her hand with his and she turned her head to look at his lean, darkly handsome face, her heart jumping behind her breastbone, her tummy fluttering with butterflies while she marvelled at the compelling power of that sidewise glance of his and the curling lashes darker and more lush than her own false ones. His wide sensual mouth curled into a faint smile and she thought, Why is he smiling? and only then did she remember that there were cameras on them both and quite deliberately Jazz beamed back at him, doing what was expected of her, fearful of the misery inside her showing on the outside and equally fearful of doing the wrong thing.

Once again a wedding ring slid onto her finger and once again there was no kissing of the bride, Vitale being no fan of public demonstrations of affection. They left the cathedral to a barrage of whirring, clicking cameras and the roar of the irritatingly happy crowds assembled behind the crash barriers in the square beyond. It was lovely that people were happy for them, Jazz reflected, trying to find something positive in the event, but sad that those same people would be disappointed when their marriage ended again.

She would not miss being royal, she told herself as they stepped into the waiting horse-drawn carriage and Vitale complained bitterly about how rocky and uncomfortable it was to travel in such a way. Then without any warning whatsoever he gripped her hand, almost crushing her poor fingers, and shot something at her in driven Italian. '*Cosa c'e di sbagliato?* What's wrong?'

'Nothing's wrong!' she snapped, trailing her hand back in a trice.

'That is so patently a lie that my teeth are gritting,' Vitale told her roundly.

Well, that was tough but he would just have to live with it. She had been forced into a second very public wedding with the future replacement-wife candidates trailing her down the aisle as bridesmaids. Hadn't he even recognised them? Of course, he would have looked at the ladies in that file at some stage because his mother was too pushy to have let him sidestep it. Jazz felt very married and very cross with her two wedding rings and her husband who didn't love her. Not that that meant that he kept his hands off her though, she reflected hotly. Of course, she was in a bad mood. Yes, she was doing this for her children, but deciding to do it had been considerably easier than actually living the experience.

Vitale flipped mentally through every possible sin or omission he could have committed and acknowledged that he had made more mistakes than he could count. It made him uncomfortable when Jazz went quiet because she was never naturally quiet. 'Did the doctor say something that worried you?' he asked.

'Will you stop *reminding* me that I'm pregnant?' Jazz launched at him. 'Can't I just forget about being an incubator in a wedding gown for five minutes?'

Vitale clamped his mouth firmly shut because even he could take a hint that landed with the crushing weight of a boot. Maybe it was hormones, something like that, he reasoned uneasily. Or maybe she was feeling sick again. He parted his lips to enquire and then breathed in deep to restrain the urge, relieved that the palace was already in view. *An incubator in a wedding gown?* Where had that bizarre image come from? He would have a word with his father at the reception. Charles Russell had impregnated three women. He had to know something about pregnancy. Jazz sounded really upset and she didn't get upset, at least not in his experience. He stole a covert glance at her rigid profile and watched in absolute horror as a tear slid down her cheek.

'Jazz…?' Vitale stroked a soothing forefinger down over her tightly clenched hands. 'What can I do?'

'I just wish…' she began in a wobbly voice, 'that we were already divorced. Then it would all be done and dusted and in the past and I could get *my* life back.'

Vitale froze, his shrewd banker's mind going utterly blank at that aspiration. 'I don't want to discuss that,' he finally replied flatly. 'I don't want to discuss that at all.'

'Tough,' Jazz pronounced grittily.

Vitale decided at that point that talking was sometimes a vastly overrated pursuit, particularly when it was heading towards what promised to be a multiple-car crash of a conclusion. It was definitely the wrong moment. In a few minutes, they would be the centre of attention again at a reception attended by the crowned heads of Europe. What he said to Jazz needed to be said in private. It would have to be measured, calm and sincere even though it wouldn't be what she wanted to hear, even though he would be breaking his word. That acknowledgement silenced Vitale because he was appalled at that truth.

The reception was endless. Jazz shook hands and smiled and posed for photos, feeling like a professional greeter at a very upmarket restaurant. Charles Russell warmed her by giving her a hug and saying, 'Well, when I sent Vitale in your direction I wasn't expecting a wedding but I'm delighted for you both, Jazz.'

The older man greeted her mother with equal friendliness while Vitale bored the hind legs off her aunt by telling her all about Lerovia. At least he was *trying*, she conceded, striving to be more generous in her outlook. But that she was in a bad mood was really all his fault. They had supposedly only married to give the twins legitimacy, so why was he still sharing a bed with her? Why was he draping her in his grandmother's fabulous jewellery? She had more diamonds than she knew what to do with and he kept on buying gifts for her as well.

She thought about the tiger pendant with the emerald eyes that she cherished. She thought about the ever-expanding snow globe collection she now possessed. Vitale had given her the wrong signals from the outset and it was hardly surprising that she had fallen for him hard or that she had foolishly continued having sex with him, hoping to ignite emotions that he wasn't capable of feeling. He had as much emotion as a granite pillar! Didn't she have any pride or sense of self-preservation? Lashing herself with such thoughts, Jazz held her head high and continued to smile while deciding that things were about to change…

CHAPTER TEN

'THE STORY'S ALL over the internet...' a vaguely familiar voice was saying urgently. 'And apparently the *Herald* is publishing the article tomorrow, complete with revealing photos. Your mother's request that they pull the article was refused. The whole household is in uproar and Sofia's planning to flee to her Alpine chalet. Nobody knows how to handle this.'

'Yet you *knew* and you didn't warn me,' Vitale framed with raw-edged bitterness as Jazz peered drowsily at the clock by the bed and noted that it was three in the morning.

'It wasn't any of my business. She threw me out of the palace the day before her coronation. Saw her kid brother as competition, you see, refused to accept me as family.'

'*Sì*, Eduardo,' Vitale agreed flatly. 'I'll get dressed and see what I can do.'

'There's nothing anyone can do!' Vitale's uncle proclaimed on a telling note of barely concealed satisfaction. 'Too late for any emergency cover-ups now!'

As the bedroom door closed Jazz sat up and stared in the dim light of the lamp by the door at Vitale, naked but for a pair of black boxers. He looked shattered. 'What's happened?' she asked straight away.

'Apparently my mother's been involved in an affair with her best friend, Countess Cinzia, for over thirty years and it's about to be exposed in the press. The scandal's already online,' he revealed with harsh clarity.

'A gay affair?' Jazz questioned in astonishment.

'How did I *not* know?' Vitale groaned. 'That's why my parents divorced. Apparently, my father once found my mother and Cinzia together. After I was wakened and told, I phoned Papa at his hotel because, at first... I couldn't believe it. But he confirmed that it was the truth. Yet I *still* can't believe it,' he admitted with growing anger. 'I've lost good friends, friends who left this country because of the restrictive laws that the Queen actively promoted. How could my mother oppose gay liberation when she's gay herself? What kind of hypocrite behaves like that?'

'I don't know...' It was completely inadequate but Jazz could think of nothing to say because she was equally stunned by what he was telling her.

'I'll deal with it as best I can,' Vitale said angrily. 'But we won't be helped by the number of enemies the Queen's made of influential people.'

'Is there anything I can do to help?' Jazz enquired weakly.

'Go back to sleep,' Vitale advised succinctly. 'My mother will step down from the throne. She's too proud to face this out.'

'But *that* means...' Jazz gasped and then dismay sentenced her to a silent stare of consternation at the lean, powerful male poised at the foot of the bed.

'*Sì.* Let's hope you take to being a queen better than you took to being a bride a second time,' Vitale pronounced with lashings of sarcasm while secretly wondering how he would take to the transformation of his own life. He could barely imagine a future empty of his mother's constant demands and complaints, but the prospect loomed ahead of him with a sudden brightness that disconcerted him, like the light at the end of a dark tunnel.

Jazz hunched back under the covers, too exhausted to snark back at him. She had collapsed into bed late the previous evening so exhausted that she had had all the animation of a corpse and had immediately fallen asleep. Certainly, it could not have been the second wedding night of any bridegroom's dreams. She had, however, been looking forward to escaping the palace in the morning and relaxing on the yacht Angel was loaning them for a Mediterranean cruise. Now she reckoned that any chance of a honeymoon was gone because, whatever Sofia Castiglione chose to do next, Vitale would be heavily involved in the clean-up operation and far too busy to leave the palace.

Vitale reappeared while she was having breakfast out on the terrace that overlooked the gardens. He told her that people were marching with placards outside the palace and that she was fortunate to be at the back of the building.

'How's your mother?' she asked awkwardly.

'She's already gone,' he breathed almost dazedly, as if he could not quite accept that astonishing reality. 'Cinzia and her together. She wasn't willing to talk to me and she released a statement declaring that her private life was exactly that, so no apologies either for a lifelong deception.'

'Did you really expect any?' She studied him worriedly, recognising the lines of strain and fatigue etched in his lean, strong face, and he shook his head in grim acknowledgement of that point.

The silence stretched while a member of staff brought fresh coffee to the table. Even the staff were creeping about very quietly as though there had been a bereavement rather than a massive scandal that had blown the Lerovian royal family wide open to the kind of international speculation it had never had to endure before. Jazz poured coffee for Vitale and urged him to eat. After his mother's hasty departure, he was heading straight into a meeting with government representatives.

'The Prime Minister persuaded her to abdicate,' Vitale groaned. 'Nothing to do with her being gay. Ironically, she could have come out of the closet years ago had she been willing, but she wasn't. It was her hypocrisy in opposing equality laws that are normal in the rest of Europe that brought her down. Her behaviour was indefensible.'

'Just move on from it,' Jazz muttered, feeling useless and helpless when she wanted to be the exact opposite for his sake.

'We all will,' Vitale declared more smoothly. 'But, more importantly, I've made arrangements for you, your mother and aunt to fly out to Angel's yacht this morning.'

'I can't leave you here alone!' Jazz exclaimed.

'There's nothing you can do here,' Vitale pointed out with inescapable practicality. 'We have protestors outside the palace and in the city. Lerovia is in uproar. I cannot leave right now but you and your family can.'

'But—'

'It *would* be a comfort to me to know that you are safe on Angel's yacht and protected from anything that

could distress you,' Vitale incised in his chilly take-no-
prisoners command voice that always made her tummy
sink like a stone.

Jazz's protests died there. He didn't want her to stay.
He was sending her away. It was clear that her presence was neither a consolation, nor a necessity. It was
a lesson, she conceded painfully, a rather hard lesson
and overdue. Vitale didn't *need* her. She might feel a
need for him pretty much round the clock but that bond
did not stretch both ways. She sucked in a steadying
breath and contrived a smile when she felt more like
crying, a reaction he certainly did not deserve. 'OK.
What time do I leave?' she asked quietly without a
flicker of reaction.

Relief at her assent showed openly in Vitale's stunning dark golden eyes and her heart clenched that her
leaving could so obviously be a source of respite for
him. Of course, he wasn't in love with her and he didn't
depend on her, so she was, very probably, just one more
person in his already very crowded life to worry about.

It was way past time she began accepting the limits
of their relationship, she reflected unhappily, because
here she was even now, always looking for more from
Vitale, asking for more, *hoping* for more. And those
fond wishes were unlikely to be granted. Nor, to be fair
to him, had he ever suggested that there would be more
between them than he had originally offered.

Carmela had already packed for the proposed cruise
round the Mediterranean and Jazz chatted on the phone
to her mother and her aunt, who were all agog and fascinated by the newspaper revelations but wildly overexcited at the prospect of staying on a billionaire's yacht
for at least a week.

Back to basics, Jazz told herself firmly as she climbed into the helicopter that had landed in the castle grounds with her mother and her aunt already on board. And the basic bottom line on her marriage with Vitale was that they had married solely to legitimise their unborn children. It shocked Jazz to force herself to remember that modest truth. When had she begun moving so dangerously far from that original agreement? Hadn't she known in her heart even at the beginning that she felt far more for Vitale than she should? In other words, she was suffering from a self-inflicted injury. He had not asked her to love him, had never sought that deeper bond or hinted at more lasting ties. In fact, Vitale had married her while openly talking about divorcing her, so she couldn't blame him for misleading her or lying in any way. No, she could only blame herself for not keeping better control of her emotions.

Angel's yacht, *Siren*, rejoiced in such size and splendour that Jazz's mother and aunt were completely overpowered by the luxury and quite failed to notice Jazz's unusual quietness. Separated from Vitale, she felt horribly alone and empty.

Over the next few days while the trio of women sunbathed, swam and shopped in the island towns the yacht visited, Jazz continued to avidly read online reports of the latest developments in Lerovia. Vitale had been declared King and the popular unrest had subsided almost immediately because he was expected to be a modern rather than traditional monarch as his mother had been described. He phoned Jazz every evening, polite strained calls that did nothing to raise her spirits. The coronation had been scheduled for the following month.

Vitale was free now, Jazz thought unhappily, free for the first time in his life from his mother's demands and interference. But he wasn't free in his marriage, Jazz acknowledged wretchedly, feeling like the final obstacle in his path to full liberation. After all, if she hadn't fallen pregnant he wouldn't have been married to a woman unqualified to become his Queen. But what could he possibly do about it now? He could hardly divorce her while she was still pregnant, so he was stuck with making the best of things until he was free to make a better choice.

Thinking such downbeat thoughts, Jazz studied her changing body shape in the bedroom mirror. Her stomach was developing a rounded curve while her waist was losing definition and her breasts were now overflowing her *new* bras. Shopping for maternity clothing could not be put off much longer but the very idea of such a trip made her feel unattractive.

'I've decided to go home to London with Mum and Clodagh tomorrow,' Jazz informed Vitale when he phoned that evening. 'It would get me out of your hair.'

An abrupt little silence fell on the line.

'What if I don't want you out of my hair?' Vitale demanded with sudden harshness.

'Well, you did say that you were comforted by the idea of me being away from you on this yacht, so I thought that possibly me being in London would have the same effect.'

'It *wouldn't*.' Vitale's voice was cold and clipped and very emphatic in tone.

'Oh… I expect I'm needed for things at the palace,' she muttered ruefully.

'You are,' Vitale confirmed without skipping a beat,

wondering what on earth had got into her, and from where she had picked up such strange ideas.

Only slowly and with effort did he register that avoiding talking about the kind of stuff he had always avoided talking about could be the single biggest mistake he had ever made. Silence didn't work on Jazz as it had on his mother. Jazz wasn't content to fill the silence with the sound of her own voice. She would be too busy judging everything he said and did as though it were a crime scene and reaching her own dangerous conclusions.

Vitale got off the phone very quickly after that exchange and it unnerved Jazz, who had assumed that he would encourage her to go to London. She wondered if she would ever understand the conflicting signals he gave her. First, he wanted her, next he didn't want her, then he wanted her again. She supposed the crisis was over now and possibly that was the cause of his change of attitude. Weary of speculating about a man who had always confounded her expectations but whom she would have walked over fire to protect, Jazz dined with her family and then went for a shower.

When the helicopter came in to land, she was wrapped in a towel and seated out on the private terrace off the master suite watching the sun go down in flaming splendour. Having assumed that the craft was merely delivering supplies, she sped indoors again to escape the noise and was completely taken aback when Vitale strode in only minutes later.

'What are you doing here?' Jazz gasped in disconcertion while her eyes travelled with guilt-ridden enthusiasm over his lean, powerful figure, admiring the fit of his jeans over his long, hard thighs and the breadth of his chest below his black shirt. He returned her scrutiny, attention lodging on the edge of the towel biting into the exuberant fullness of her breasts, and she reddened, horribly self-conscious at being caught undressed and without a lick of make-up on.

'I… I missed you,' Vitale declared with unexpected abruptness.

Her green eyes widened. 'You…*did*?'

'Of course, I did. I only sent you away for your benefit and I assumed you'd appreciate a private break with your family,' Vitale asserted almost accusingly. 'I had too much official business to take of at the palace and very little time to spare for you.'

Jazz stiffened at the reminder. 'I understood that.'

'No, you seem to think I wanted to get rid of you and that is not true at all. In fact it is *so* untrue, it's ridiculous!' Vitale informed her on a rising note of unconcealed annoyance. 'If you'd stayed on at the palace you wouldn't have been able to go out those first few days and I was in back-to-back meetings. It would have been selfish to keep you cooped up just for my own pleasure.'

Jazz froze. 'When you sent me away I felt like I was an annoying distraction to you, just one more burden.'

Vitale stilled by the door that led out to the terrace, his lean, darkly handsome features rigid. 'You are not and have never been a burden. In fact you are the only thing in my life that has ever given me pure pleasure…'

Jazz loved to hear nice things about herself but that was too over-the-top and from Vitale, of all people, to convince her. 'I can't believe that.'

Vitale's hands knotted into fists of frustration and he made a gesture with both arms that telegraphed his inability to explain what he had meant with that statement.

'I'm being snappy because I was hurt when you sent

me away,' Jazz admitted guiltily, badly wanting to put her arms round him and only just resisting the temptation by filling the uneasy silence for him.

'Do you think it didn't hurt me to be without you every day?' Vitale shot back at her at startling speed. 'Not even to have a few minutes I could call my own with you? But I was trying to do the right thing, only somehow it seems to have been the wrong thing...the story of my *every* dealing with you!' he completed bitterly.

'Would you like a drink?' she asked uncomfortably.

'No, thanks. I had a couple of drinks after you announced your intention of returning to London and it didn't noticeably improve my mood,' he admitted wearily.

'I thought you might welcome my departure. Clearly I misunderstood,' Jazz said for him, reading between the lines, reckoning that he had flown out to the yacht because he was panicking at the idea that she might run out on their marriage even before the coronation and cause yet another scandal. 'I wasn't threatening to leave you, Vitale.'

'*Per meraviglia*...you *weren't*?' Vitale froze to prompt in open bewilderment and disbelief.

'No, I wouldn't let you down like that. I wouldn't do that to you. As you said, we're in this together. Whatever happens, I'll stick things out at the palace until you think it's the right time for us to separate and go for a divorce,' Jazz promised him earnestly.

Vitale paled below his bronzed complexion, stunning dark golden eyes narrowing as if he was pained by that speech. 'I don't want a divorce any more. I want to stay married to you until the day I die, *amata mia*. I know we didn't start out with that understanding and that I'm ignoring the terms we agreed on but… I've changed.'

'Have you?' Jazz said doubtfully. 'Or is it that you feel us divorcing so soon after your mother's abdication will look bad?'

'You are a very difficult woman to reason with,' Vitale groaned, raking long brown fingers through his already-tousled black hair. 'When I said I changed, I meant *I* changed, nothing to do with the crown or my mother or anyone else. You and I are the only two people in this marriage and I really don't want to lose you. That's why I'm here. I also had to resign from the bank.'

'You've resigned?' Jazz was taken aback.

'Naturally. I can't be a king and a banker as well. I also need time to be a husband and father. Something had to go to give us enough space for a family life,' he pointed out. 'But if you still want a divorce, of course—'

'I didn't say that!' Jazz interrupted in haste.

'Everything you've said and done implies that, though,' Vitale condemned with curt finality, squaring his broad shoulders as if awaiting a physical blow.

'You take the worst possible meaning out of everything I say,' Jazz scolded without meaning to. 'I'm waiting for you to tell me why you decided you wanted to stay married to me…'

'I answered that,' Vitale contradicted squarely. 'You make me happy…and,' he hesitated before adding with visible discomfiture, 'I love you.'

He said it so quietly and so quickly that she wasn't quite sure she had heard him correctly.

'I mean,' Vitale began afresh with a faint air of desperation, 'I *suppose* it's love. I *hate* it when you're away from me. I miss you so much. I can't imagine being with any other woman. You're different somehow—*special*—and you know how I think—which I didn't like at first—but I'm beginning to believe I should be grateful for that. I know you're not happy at the idea of me becoming King... I *did* see your face when that reality dawned on you but I really don't think I can do it without you,' he told her awkwardly. 'If it came to a choice between the throne and you, I would choose you...'

Jazz's heart expanded like a giant warm globe inside her ribcage as she appreciated that she was listening to a genuine but rather clumsy declaration of love and in a sudden movement she moved closer and wrapped both arms round him. 'I'd never ask you to make a choice like that. I'm not thrilled at the idea of being a queen or being on show all the time, but if I have you with me I'll survive it,' she declared breathlessly, her hands sliding up over his torso and round his neck. 'Why? Because I love you too, you crazy man. How could you miss the fact that I love you?'

Vitale released his pent-up breath in an audible surge and closed both arms tightly round her, a slight shudder of reaction rocking his lean body against her. 'You do?' he pressed uncertainly. 'But why? I'm kind of boring compared to you.'

'No, you're not!' she argued feelingly, hurt that he could think that of himself.

'You're chatty and funny and lively, everything I'm not,' Vitale persisted argumentatively. 'It's like you're a magnet. You pulled me in even though I tried very hard to resist you.'

'You didn't resist for very long,' Jazz commented,

thinking about their encounter in the kitchen on the first night of her stay at his town house.

'You were more temptation than I could resist. Everything about you attracted me.'

'No, you tried to change everything about me to make me presentable,' she reminded him. 'All those lessons.'

'That was educational stuff to ensure that you could hold your own in any company. I live in a different world and I wanted you to feel as comfortable and confident in it as I do. That's past. We've moved way beyond that level now,' he pointed out.

'Yes.' Momentarily, Jazz simply rested her brow against a warm shoulder sheathed in fresh scented cotton and drank in the familiar smell of him. A silly, happy sense of peace was flooding her because Vitale was finally hers, absolutely, irretrievably hers. He had learned to love her in spite of their many differences and perhaps the most wonderful discovery of all was that, mismatched or not, together they made a very comfortable and secure whole.

'But you kept on reminding me that we were supposed to be getting a divorce,' he muttered grimly.

'Well, that is how you set up our marriage,' Jazz reminded him helplessly.

'I know,' Vitale groaned out loud. 'But every time you threw that at me, panic gripped me. I'd dug myself into this ridiculous deep dark hole and I didn't know how to get out of it again. I didn't want to let you go but I'd *promised* you that I would and I always keep my promises. I made such a mess out of everything between us. I should've told you sooner that I no longer wanted a divorce but I was afraid you'd tell me that you still wanted your freedom back and I couldn't face that. In fact I thought it was wiser to keep quiet about my plans.'

'Honesty works best with me...even if I don't want to hear it, and what you *didn't* say,' she told him for future reference, 'was what I most wanted to hear these past few weeks.'

'Why did our royal wedding upset you so much?'

Jazz withdrew her arms and stepped back from him to look at him. '*Seriously?* You're asking me that when *six* suitable wife candidates followed me down the aisle?'

His brow furrowed in bewilderment. 'Suitable wife candidates?'

'From that file of your mother's. Didn't you recognise them? I mean, you must have met at least a couple of them prior to our big day,' she reasoned.

'The bridesmaids were the women in that file?' Vitale demanded, dark colour edging his hard cheekbones as comprehension sank in and he muttered something unrepeatable in Italian. '*Madonna diavolo*... I never looked at those photographs or that file. It's called passive resistance and I refused to encourage my mother's delusions by playing along with them.'

'You never even looked?' Jazz repeated in astonishment.

'No, I refused. Even when she spread the photos on her desk in front of me, I refused to look. But that she asked them to act as your bridesmaids sickens me,' Vitale admitted with a furious shake of his proud dark head. 'It's hard to credit that even she could be that vindictive. You should've told me.'

'I assumed that you would recognise them. Anyway,' Jazz framed uncomfortably, 'reading that file was bad for my confidence. I started making these awful comparisons between me and those women and my self-esteem sank very low and that made me very touchy and more inclined to misinterpret everything you did.'

'Even though you are head and shoulders above the women in that pointless pretentious file?' Vitale demanded. 'Because you are the woman I love and the *only* woman I want as a wife!'

And he *meant* every word of that declaration, Jazz recognised with her self-esteem taking a resulting leap as she accepted that wonderful truth. He thought more of her than she thought of herself, she registered in awe.

'Even though you once said I was as flat as an ironing board?' she began teasingly.

'Not a problem we have now,' Vitale told her with a flashing smile as he unwound the towel and backed her purposefully towards the bed. 'As for the hair—I love your hair and you know I do. I've told you often enough.'

And he was always playing with her hair, she conceded thoughtfully while she allowed herself to be rearranged on the bed, a little tremor of awareness and hunger sliding through her as Vitale lowered his long, lean, powerful body down over hers. 'I love you,' he said again. 'And I haven't slept a night through since you left me. I miss the hugs.'

'Well, you have to start hugging back to get them,' Jazz informed him with dancing eyes of challenge.

And he hugged her and she giggled like a drain. 'Again!' she demanded like a child.

The happiness Jazz had brought into his life far outweighed every other concern, Vitale appreciated, and his answering smile was brilliant.

'Oh, I do love you, Vitale,' she whispered when she could breathe again, because he was a little too enthusiastic with his hugs. 'When did you realise how you felt about me?'

'I should've realised the day I almost punched Angel for flirting with you because I was jealous.'

'You *were*.' Jazz savoured that belated admission with unhidden satisfaction.

'But it took me a lot longer to realise what you'd done to me.'

'What I'd done to you?' Jazz queried.

'*Sì*...turned me upside down, inside out and head over heels and all without me having a clue about what was happening,' Vitale confided ruefully. 'And then you never missed a chance to remind me about the divorce plan. That was a real own goal on my part.'

Jazz smiled. 'Glad you recognise that.'

Vitale rubbed his jawline gently over her smooth cheek. 'I shaved... Do I have to keep on talking all night?'

Jazz laughed, feeling amazingly cheerful. 'No, you don't have to talk any more.'

'*Grazie a Dio,*' Vitale's sigh of relief was heartfelt. He realised that he was much more like his emotional father than he had ever appreciated, although he still lacked his father's ability to easily discuss his feelings. But the key to his happiness was Jazz, he acknowledged. Jazz, who had taught him how to enjoy life again. He could cope with anything as long as she was by his side.

And Jazz looked up at him with eyes that shone with love and appreciation and, eagerly drinking in that appraisal, Vitale kissed her with all the passion she inspired in him. They made love and the rest of the world was forgotten. Later, much, much later, she twitted him about the prenup agreement that had so depressed her and he kissed her again, contriving to avoid talking once more with remarkable efficiency, but then when Vitale learned anything to his advantage he was always quick to use it.

EPILOGUE

FIVE YEARS LATER Jazz lay back on her sun lounger in the shade and watched the children play in the new swimming pool. Angel was on duty as a lifeguard and, considering that a good half of the overexcited children belonged to him and Merry, that was only fair. Jazz had had to nag at Vitale to get him to agree to a pool at the Italian farmhouse because he liked their lifestyle there to be simpler and less luxurious than life in Lerovia.

'Enrico!' her husband suddenly yelled full throttle at the four-year-old trying to push his twin brother into the pool. 'Stop it!'

Enrico grinned, mischief dancing in his dark eyes, and while he wasn't looking his twin, Donato, gave him a crafty shove into the water.

'That was dangerous!' Vitale thundered.

'The men get so het up when the kids are only doing what comes naturally,' Merry marvelled from her seat beside Jazz while her own little tribe frolicked in the water, noisily jumping up and down and splashing each other.

'But then they're not as accustomed as we are to the daily shenanigans.' Jazz sighed, smoothing her light dress down over the prominent swell of her abdomen.

'Are you hoping for a girl this time around?' Merry asked with the casual curiosity of a close friend.

'I think Vitale is but I don't care as long as the baby's healthy,' Jazz confided, thinking how worried and stressed she had been when her newly born twins had had to go straight into incubators after their premature birth.

Enrico and Donato had thrived from that point on and had soon gained sufficient strength to take up residence in the colourful nursery their parents had created for them at the palace. But, still, Jazz would not have liked to go through the experience of having to leave her babies in hospital again while she went home alone. Her current pregnancy, however, had been much easier than the first. She had been less sick and she felt much more relaxed about her condition, although, if anything, Vitale fussed even more than he had the first time around.

Their lives in Lerovia had gone through a dizzying cycle of change in every sphere. First of all, they had had to move into what had previously been Vitale's mother's wing of the palace. A full-scale redecoration had been required and Jazz still sometimes suspected that she could smell wet paint. Vitale had opened up the ceremonial rooms of the palace to the public for the first time and now Jazz's mother was happily engaged in running the palace gift shop and café opened in a rear courtyard.

Peggy Dickens had made a new life in Lerovia. She had wanted to be close to her grandchildren and she now occupied a small palace apartment where her sister, Clodagh, was a regular guest. Jazz had been relieved when her mother had passed her most recent health check with flying colours and she was delighted to have her only parent living within easy reach. Vitale had been very generous agreeing to that development, she thought fondly. Not every man would have wanted his mother-in-law living on his doorstep. He had been equally generous when Peggy had told him that she wanted to get involved with the huge challenge of opening part of the palace to the public. Able to engage in meaningful work again, Peggy had gone from strength to strength and had rediscovered her vitality and interest in life.

When the twins were a few months old, Jazz had completed her degree in the History of Art at the University of Leburg and had graduated with honours. Now she was one of the directors of the Leburg Art museum and all the paintings in the palace had finally been exhaustively catalogued, which had led to the exciting discovery of an Old Master of one of Vitale's ancestors. Her life was incredibly busy but she loved it.

The tiny country of Lerovia had become her home and she was a very popular working royal. Prince Eduardo now regularly conducted public engagements on his nephew's behalf and was fully restored to the status his sister had once taken from him. Jazz had been shocked when Vitale had informed her that it had been Eduardo who had choreographed Queen Sofia's downfall by tipping off a friend in the media about her affair.

'It was payback for a lifetime of slights. Mean and cruel of him,' Vitale had conceded of his uncle's behaviour. 'But who am I to criticise? Eduardo was once a very popular member of the family and my mother cut him out of our lives and kept him criminally short of money. He didn't deserve that and her mistreatment of her brother came back to haunt her.'

Sofia Castiglione, now known as Princess Sofia, was still living in her opulent Alpine chalet with Cinzia. She phoned Vitale from time to time to reprimand him about changes she had heard he was instigating and she warned him that he would lose the respect of the people if he lessened the mystique of the monarchy by embracing a less luxurious lifestyle. She had flatly refused to ever set foot in Lerovia again, confessing that she had never liked the Lerovians, and Vitale had laughed heartily when he'd shared that particular gem with Jazz. He had visited his mother on several occasions but he did it out of duty, rather than affection. His failure to divorce Jazz had infuriated his mother and Jazz was still waiting, but not with bated breath, for an invitation to the Alpine chalet.

Charles Russell, on the other hand, was a regular visitor, particularly when the family were vacationing at the farmhouse where he too enjoyed relaxing. He was a great grandparent, always ready to put his book down to enter the world of small children and entertain them.

After dinner that evening, Jazz stepped gratefully into the candlelit bath awaiting her and smiled widely when Vitale brought her lemonade in a wine glass.

'You're not supposed to climb in until I'm here in case you fall,' Vitale censured, his lean, darkly handsome face full of concern.

'I'm not as big as I was with the twins,' Jazz murmured softly. 'I'm not going to fall.'

Vitale smoothed a coiling ringlet back from her damp brow. 'Naked in candlelight you look incredibly sexy, *bellezza mia*…'

'Don't call me beautiful like this,' Jazz scolded with

a slight grimace down at the swell of her stomach. 'Or sexy.'

'But it's the truth.' Vitale levelled stunning dark golden eyes on her and smiled again. 'You want me to lie?'

'Oh, for goodness' sake,' she muttered, passing him her empty glass and rising to leave the bath.

Vitale wrapped her in a fleecy towel and scooped her out.

'You're getting wet!' she cried crossly.

Vitale grinned wickedly down at her. 'I won't be keeping my wet clothes on for long.'

Jazz rolled her beautiful green eyes. 'Now there's confidence for you,' she teased as he carried her back into their bedroom, a big airy space with a cosy corner by the fire for their winter visits.

'Am I wrong?' Vitale husked, pressing a kiss to the pulse point at her throat, sending her body haywire with response.

'Sadly, no. I'm always a pushover,' she sighed, finding his beautiful mouth again for herself and exulting in the love he gave her so freely and the happiness they had found together against all the odds.

* * * * *

LET'S TALK
Romance

For exclusive extracts, competitions and special offers, find us online:

- **f** MillsandBoon
- **𝕏** @MillsandBoon
- **◎** @MillsandBoonUK
- **♪** @MillsandBoonUK

Get in touch on 01413 063 232

MILLS & BOON

THE HEART OF ROMANCE

A ROMANCE FOR EVERY READER

MODERN
Prepare to be swept off your feet by sophisticated, sexy and seductive heroes, in some of the world's most glamourous and romantic locations, where power and passion collide.

HISTORICAL
Escape with historical heroes from time gone by. Whether your passion is for wicked Regency Rakes, muscled Vikings or rugged Highlanders, awaken the romance of the past.

MEDICAL
Set your pulse racing with dedicated, delectable doctors in the high-pressure world of medicine, where emotions run high and passion, comfort and love are the best medicine.

True Love
Celebrate true love with tender stories of heartfelt romance, from the rush of falling in love to the joy a new baby can bring, and a focus on the emotional heart of a relationship.

Desire
Indulge in secrets and scandal, intense drama and sizzling hot action with heroes who have it all: wealth, status, good looks…everything but the right woman.

HEROES
The excitement of a gripping thriller, with intense romance at its heart. Resourceful, true-to-life women and strong, fearless men face danger and desire - a killer combination!

To see which titles are coming soon, please visit

millsandboon.co.uk/nextmonth

GET YOUR ROMANCE FIX!

Get the latest romance news, exclusive author interviews, story extracts and much more!

MILLS & BOON

MODERN

Power and Passion

Prepare to be swept off your feet by sophisticated, sexy and seductive heroes, in some of the world's most glamourous and romantic locations, where power and passion collide.

MILLS & BOON
True Love
Romance from the Heart

Celebrate true love with tender stories of heartfelt romance, from the rush of falling in love to the joy a new baby can bring, and a focus on the emotional heart of a relationship.

MILLS & BOON

Desire

Indulge in secrets and scandal, intense drama and plenty of sizzling hot action with powerful and passionate heroes who have it all: wealth, status, good looks…everything but the right woman.